RATHEN

The Rathen Series: Book 2

RATHEN

Into Bramblewood Forest

A Novel By

Grant Elliot Smith

And

Steven H. Stohler

DRAKARIUM
PUBLISHING

Rathen: Into Bramblewood Forest
© 2018 Grant Elliot Smith
www.grantelliotsmith.com

Cover Art
© 2018 Matthew Stawicki

Cover design
JD&J Design
www.jdandj.com

Formatting
Polgarus Studio
www.polgarusstudio.com

Published by DRAKARIUM PUBLISHING, LLC
333 N. Alabama Street, Suite 350, Indianapolis, Indiana 46204
contact@drakariumpublishing.com

Printed in the United States of America
First Edition

ISBN: 978-1-949271-00-3 (ebook)
ISBN: 978-1-949271-01-0 (softcover)
ISBN: 978-1-949271-02-7 (hardcover)

Dedicated to Gerry E. Smith: friend, mentor,
modern-day warrior, my father.

Acknowledgments

I would like to thank Donna Peerce and Sandra Haven for their wonderful editing services and once again a big thank you to the very talented Matthew Stawicki for his incredible cover art. I also want to thank the individuals who were willing to read and give their feedback on the many drafts of this book; Moose and Brittany Peters, Darius called Omega, the Serpentduke, Noelle West, Joe A. Unsinn IV, Jake Thompson, and Bradley Buschman.

I want to give a very special shout out to Jeffrey Skaggs and Tom Harbison for their continued support and enthusiasm for the Rathen Series. You two are fantastic! Thanks so much.

Chapter 1

A sense of disquiet descended over the three riders as they neared the ominous shadow of Ghrakus Castle. The crumbling stone walls of the ancient fortress grew ever larger as their horses crept down the overgrown, winding path. Sinister and imposing, the castle rose larger than Rathen remembered, its four twisting towers ripping into the clouds. Rathen's eyes settled on the tower to the far left—the tower of Ghrakus Temple.

Rathen rode in the lead, searching the horizon for signs of movement. Two weeks' worth of grime and sweat clung to his body as the summer sun beat down on him. The weight and insulation of his chain armor chaffed his limbs. A bead of sweat rolled from his left brow into the jagged scar that began just above his eye and split in two just above his chin.

As the castle loomed ever closer, anxiety festered in Rathen's gut, twisting his insides into a sickening knot. He slid his hand over the hilt of his sword, fingering the grooves carved into the metal.

He wiped the sweat from his brow with his forearm and

shaded his eyes to look up. The massive stone structure before him seemed to go endlessly higher in its grand design. He could see an ancient forest stretching along behind the castle, its gnarled trees warped and grotesque, hiding all manners of creatures in the darkness of the shaded branches. Closer to the castle walls, the surrounding dirt and stone grounds were devoid of all vegetation.

Rathen's attention shifted to the sound of an approaching horse, and he turned to see the second rider, Bulo, trotting up from behind on his right. Bulo's shoulder-length brown hair was drenched with sweat. He was a large man, tall and thick, with a great barrel chest and enough muscles to lift a horse. His light leather armor covered only a portion of his exposed chest and arms, the sight of which would have sent many ruffians and thieves running for easier prey. As imposing as his body was, his dark-brown eyes betrayed the fear that filled him.

Bulo ran a hand through his wet hair, brushing it out of his eyes, and flashed Rathen a nervous glance. "Are you sure we can do this?" he asked, his sweat-covered face showing his fatigue.

"Of course." Rathen smiled despite the dread filling his chest. "We must, with so many counting on us."

The large stone wall surrounding the castle and its holdings cast a shadow over the riders as they approached the gates. Riding through first, Bulo shifted in his saddle, his hand ready on his axe while his eyes scanned the surroundings. At his nod, Rathen followed, with Bandark—the third rider—farther behind.

The trio entered a run-down courtyard filled with dead trees, shattered statues, and the remnants of a marble fountain. Rusty armaments, decayed wooden shields, and long-forgotten bones lay scattered across the dirt and cracked stone of the courtyard floor, fragments of a great battle fought long ago. Before them stood the massive wooden doors of the castle.

"I smell death," Bulo said.

The musty scent of death and decay penetrated Rathen's senses as well. He turned his head. The odor was most palpable in the direction of the large stone building adjacent to the castle. "The temple," Rathen said, pointing to the shadowed structure rising high into the clouds.

The temple sat to the left of the castle, its spiraling tower taller than all the others, with high arched windows set into gray stone. Stone columns connected the walls surrounding the windows with great stone arches fifty feet above their heads. The arched doors leading into the temple stood atop long stone steps, guarded by stone dragons carved along the balustrades that ran along the base of the roof. Moldering tombstones filled the graveyard beside the temple.

Rathen's horse began to snort and pull away from the path as they moved closer. Rathen stroked the horse's neck and assured her everything would be all right, but he felt it too. A menacing shadow draped the stone structure in defiance of the sun shining overhead. It was obvious, to man or beast, that those ancient walls housed a great evil.

Bandark called out, urging his steed forward to Rathen's left. Bandark wore only long gray robes with no visible armor. He was clean shaven with a thick, kind face and a strong jawline, and his long brown hair was tied behind his head. Though he was similar in age to Rathen and Bulo and had traveled the same distance, Bandark appeared fresh.

Rathen thought it peculiar that he lacked any noticeable sweat. The gray tint to his skin was another striking difference.

"Looks to be bodies near the temple doors," Bandark said, his deep voice booming in a strong, exotic accent that shook Rathen from his thoughts.

Rathen nodded, and they increased their pace, encouraging their horses toward the temple.

Soon, all three horses stopped in place, snorting and stomping their hooves in protest. The three riders dismounted. Three bodies lay in the dirt just before the steps. Bulo handed his reins to Rathen and walked carefully to them, keeping an eye on the shadows as he did so. He knelt down to examine the remains. "They've been dead maybe… three months."

Rathen unpacked a large burlap bag from his horse and placed his reins over the saddle. He knew the horses would likely walk back to the grass away from the temple but didn't think they would be difficult to find when he, Bulo, and Bandark came back—if they came back. Rathen shook his head, attempting to clear his mind. He walked over and inspected the corpses, Bulo dragging the burlap bag behind him. The bodies wore charred black robes, and beneath the robes, their skin was pulled taut against the bones. Their limbs were rigid, their fingers were curled tightly in a dead man's grasp, and their eyes were missing, devoured by birds or insects long before Rathen's men had come upon them.

Bulo inspected one of the bodies more closely, reaching into the folds of the robe. He lifted a silver amulet into the light, studying its insignia. "We've seen this before. It's from the Guild of Ghrakus," he said, tossing the amulet back onto the corpse.

Rathen nodded. "Then the report is accurate. No doubt killed by the very creature they tried to keep locked away." Rathen hefted the bag over his shoulder. "Fitting end, I suppose."

"Let's hope we don't end up the same," Bulo muttered.

Rathen forced a weak laugh as he approached the temple doors, sidestepping the corpses.

Rathen glanced back to see Bandark silently walking behind them. He adjusted the sword at his side, exposing it from under his robes. Rathen turned back around and pushed the temple doors open.

The smell of rotting flesh choked the air inside the temple. The marble columns were mostly destroyed and the holy statues of long-dead priests had been toppled or reduced to unrecognizable rubble. A scattering of several more black-robed bodies littered the massive hall, some burned while others were strewn about in pieces. Splatters of dried blood and soot marred the floors.

Rathen took a deep breath as he thought back to his last visit to this chamber, recalling how his men had narrowly escaped their own deaths. Rathen moved the large bag he carried to his side and tread carefully through the hall to inspect the more recent damage. One corner of the room had been scorched black; ash still clung to the walls. Each wall bore several impact divots with debris piled on the floor beneath each one, but no sign of what caused the impact.

Undoubtedly, this had been a battle of magic.

There was nothing the three men could do to help the dead now. Moving to his left, Rathen led Bulo and Bandark into a dark hallway inside the stone structure where sunlight did not reach. A door stood lonely at the end of the hall. He focused on the door as he fought the dread that all but overwhelmed his senses. Rathen had faced this magic before, something he hoped to never face again. With a quick glance behind him, he pushed the door open and stepped inside.

Rathen's breathing grew heavier as his eyes fell upon a dark-robed figure standing in the middle of the room, facing the doorway. The pale light from a half globe in the ceiling flickered off a golden crown around the figure's bony head. Its black robes were old and tattered, exposing its skeletal form through holes worn through the fabric. Two fine points of crimson light glowed from inside its empty eye sockets, and long, gray clumps of hair clung to the side and chin of the figure's skinless skull.

Again, Rathen faced the lich.

The same lich Rathen had fought before, a once-powerful mage who had used the dark spells of necromancy to cast aside his mortality and magically bind his soul to his phylactery and live within a decayed body to escape death.

The lich let out a serpentine hiss as he raised his skeletal hands.

"Wait, Prince Magom. It's Rathen!" Rathen shouted, holding his hands in front of him.

"I know who you are. And this time, you shall not escape me." The lich's voice echoed cold and deep, like a damp cavern far beneath the reaches of the sun. As he spoke, a surge of energy swirled around his skeletal body like a windstorm, sending an electrical buzz through the air.

The hair on the back of Rathen's neck stood alert, yet he did not move.

Bulo crouched down into his ready stance beside Rathen, lifting his axe in a defensive posture. Bandark stood directly behind Bulo, out of the lich's view.

The lich thrust his hand forward, igniting his bony digits into bright flames that spewed onto the floor. The flames collected in front of the lich, mixing with the windstorm that surrounded him. They swirled violently, twisting and growing until they reached the stone ceiling. With a flick of his fingers, the lich sent the fiery twister speeding toward Rathen.

Rathen's eyes widened as he tensed every muscle to resist the urge to flee. The twisting flames roared forth and crashed abruptly less than a foot in front of him. As they dissipated, Rathen could just make out the lich through a shimmering blue shield that surrounded and protected the three men.

"Impossible," the lich fumed, looking from his hands to Rathen in confusion. As his gaze shifted toward Bandark just behind him. "It's you!"

Rathen turned to see Bandark with his hands stretched out in front of his chest, focusing on his protection spell.

"I know this magic you employ," the lich shouted, his bony arms up, energy building around him. In the next instant, bolts of lightning sprang from the lich's hands, crackling in the air, striking the barrier to no effect. Undeterred, the lich took a step forward and unleashed a barrage of fire, ice shards, and energy spells that crashed against the barrier, each attack just as ineffective as the last.

Rathen turned to Bandark and raised his brow. Could the mage keep fending off the attack? Bandark nodded at Rathen.

"We need your help," Rathen yelled, turning to regain the lich's attention.

The lich lowered his arms, allowing some of the energy to dissipate. "Help?"

"Our world needs you," Rathen said, taking a step forward. "Over a year ago, when last we met, we removed a book from this castle—the Book of Ziz—written by a demi-god from another world many centuries ago. It holds instructions for protection spells against an evil deity known as Gothoar, who once threatened to spread his power of death and destruction in this world and others."

The lich's energy crackled angrily. "Do not presume to explain the Book of Ziz to me, mortal! I know well the book of which you speak and have suspected its true origins. However, the majority of its spells are impossible to decipher, even with my power." The lich looked at Bandark. "Though perhaps not for him. Your companion is of the same world as the book, is he not?"

Rathen nodded. "Yes."

The lich hissed.

Rathen rushed on, "But that does us no good, seeing as a dark cleric named Vargas stole the book from us and took it back to his master, Litagus. These past months, we know Litagus had been working to decipher the book for his own power. He intends to return the book to followers of Gothoar, so the deity can gain power within this world unchecked. If Gothoar gains power here, no one will be safe."

The lich let out a hissing laugh. "Why should I bother with the woes of mortals? This Gothoar's power may be the end of your kind, but it could not harm me. Whatever devastation befalls this world, I will go on existing through all eternity."

"We can offer you something you want," Rathen said with a sly smile.

The lich laughed as he began to increase the swirling

energy around him again. "What could you possibly offer me?"

Rathen stood straight, head high to evoke an air of confidence he did not feel. "You spoke before of your desire to reverse your transformation and return to your human form. Bandark has agreed to help with your efforts, using your own research along with the spells within the Book of Ziz."

A moment passed; neither side spoke.

The energy around the lich flared briefly, dissipated, then completely faded as the lich asked, "While I long suspected that book holds the magic required to undo this… fate, how do I know that what you say is true?"

Rathen watched as Bandark lowered his hands, causing the protective shield to disappear. "I stake my life upon it. If we can retrieve the book, I will aid in your research to restore your humanity."

The lich stood motionless, like the long-dead skeleton it appeared to be. Rathen dared not move. Finally, the lich spoke: "Yes… I believe you will try, but I am not yet convinced my condition can be restored."

"I will take you back to my world for further assistance if necessary," Bandark added.

"Then what is it you want from me?" The lich's skeletal form floated closer to Rathen.

Looking into the lich's crimson eyes, Rathen fought the urge to back away. "When last we met, you claimed to be able to sense the location of the book."

"Yes… It was my father's book and in my possession for almost a hundred years. I know the feel of its unique magic well," the lich hissed.

"We are planning to infiltrate the stronghold of Litagus undetected, recover the book, and escape before we are discovered. We need you to join our group and lead us to the book. Without you, it would take days to search the fortress for a well-guarded book."

The lich stood motionless.

"Well?" The smell of decay in the room overwhelmed Rathen's senses and threatened to turn his stomach.

The lich closed the distance between them. "How did you know to find me back in my temple?"

"Boder, a friend of ours who left the Guild of Ghrakus, informed us of the Guild's destruction. We assumed you reconstituted and took your revenge on it."

The lich let out a hissing laugh as his skull looked up to the ceiling. "The fools brought about their own destruction. They removed the protective shield around this castle, assuming I was gone forever. When they discovered me, their failed attempt to kill me in my own temple was their final mistake. Do you remember Salamar?"

Rathen nodded. "Leader of the Guild."

The lich gazed intently at him and raised his skeletal hand. A shuffle could be heard from a dark corner of the room.

Rathen's hand instinctively reached for his sword.

A figure in black robes lumbered toward them. Fumes of rotting flesh swirled around them, making Rathen's nose burn and his eyes water. The figure moved into the pale light of the room. Half his face and upper body were charred, exposing rotting muscle and bone. The eye socket on the burned side of his face was empty while the other eye was dry and crusted over. The remains of Salamar.

Rathen heard Bulo behind him mumble something under his breath. Not even Rathen had words for what had been done. The rotting corpse stopped and stood motionless, the chunks of flesh hanging from its bones threatening to fall off at any moment. Although appalled by the sight, Rathen felt little sympathy for Salamar, whose ego had offended even Rathen when they last met.

"I reanimated his body after I killed him, for my... amusement," the lich said. "An ironic fate, don't you think, for the Guild leader who hoped to steal my research and live forever?"

Shaking off his disgust, Rathen faced the lich, his mouth stern. "Do we have an agreement?" They required this creature's assistance. Yet Rathen questioned if his group could endure this undead monster's presence or his past acts. Could he? In Rathen's own past, as King Delvant's captain, he'd witnessed unspeakable acts of violence and led men in noble causes against formidable foes, but this walking corpse made his skin crawl.

The lich eyed him. "I sense sincerity in you. However, if you or your friends attempt to trick me or break your promise to assist my research, I will kill you," the lich hissed. "All of you."

"So, that's a 'yes'?"

"Yes. However, I fail to see how I will be able to travel outside these walls without causing panic."

Rathen picked up the large brown bag he had carried in and sat it beside the lich.

Thack raised his axe over his head and brought it down, chopping a wooden log in half. The sweat on his gray skin glistened in the bright afternoon sun, dripping down his exposed upper torso along the various scars crisscrossing his body. There were far more scars than any young man should have in his early twenties, and combined with his muscular frame and his astonishing height, Thack looked quite frightening as he butchered the wood. However, while few would call a half-orc handsome, he had a kind of allure that emanated from the gentleness in his gray eyes. He was made even less threatening by his left side, which lacked an entire arm and most of the shoulder, but this did not seem to hinder him in his task.

Leaning the axe against the wooden stump, Thack picked up both halves one by one and tossed them into a large, freshly cut pile beside him. He picked up another log and placed it on the stump. Before picking up the axe again, he pulled a cloth from his belt and wiped the sweat from his face, taking a minute to look up at the tavern in front of him and the grassy field that stretched down to the edge of dense woods. He closed his eyes and heard the sound of water splashing off rocks in the nearby stream.

With a long sigh, Thack picked up the axe, lifted it over his head, and swung down, cutting the log before him cleanly in half. He sat the axe down again and threw each piece into the pile. *That's enough for now.* Tonight, he would be preparing a large dinner for a special group at the tavern, and he needed the ovens blazing hot and ready.

Thack toted the axe over his shoulder as he headed back up to his tavern. He stopped and soaked in the sunlight one last time, breathing in the smell of damp leaves and pine that carried on the air from the woods behind him. As he moved closer to the tavern, the pungent scent of horses that traveled along the busy streets of Tobermoar added to the mix.

He was greeted at the back entrance by a thin youth dressed in a white apron. The youth had bushy, bright red hair. Freckles dotted every inch of his face, and his smile stretched from ear to ear.

"Fala, fetch the wood I've cut," Thack said. "Make sure to get it all."

"Right away." The young man began to remove his apron. "It's going to be a special night, isn't it? Can I ask who's coming?" Fala set down his apron and looked up eagerly, his eyes wide and his body rocking back and forth.

"I'm sorry, Fala. You won't be able to join this evening," Thack said, patting the young man on the back as he towered over him. "Next time." Thack appreciated his enthusiasm. Fala had only been working at the Traveler's Rest for a few months and had retained the sincerity and willingness so telling of his youth.

Fala's eyes seem to widen even further. "Is tonight that special? Is it Duke Blackmane again?"

"Fetch the wood, Fala," Thack gently directed him. There was still too much to prepare to worry about explaining everything to an assistant.

"Yes, Master Thack. Right away." The young man shot out the doorway.

With a sigh of relief, Thack entered the tavern, placing his axe on a hook on the wall. As he neared the kitchen, he could hear the sounds of a busy lunchtime from the guests who had gathered downstairs. Servants ran orders out just as quickly as the cooks could prepare them. As one-third owner of the tavern, Thack had more important priorities to deal with, but he always lent a hand cooking when needed. With the thought of helping the cooks in mind, he headed upstairs to clean off.

Back downstairs, cleaned and dressed in a loose-fitting blue shirt with the left shoulder sewn shut, Thack helped the cooks finish up the rush. The tavern's business had prospered over the past several months; he hated to shut its doors to the public for the next few days. But this was a request from Rathen himself. Thack ordered the serving maids and barkeeps not to rent any rooms for the night and to remind those who remained that they would need to leave shortly.

Thack stepped through the swinging wooden doors and hung a notice over the "open" sign, notifying the public that the tavern would close for a few days. He read it, shook his head. Days of lost revenue annoyed him. Yet so much hung at stake.

At a voice behind him, he turned and waved in response to a greeting from one of the newer merchants across the way. Thack swept his eyes over the marketplace, nodding at the new shops and stalls for metal and leather wares opening their doors. Beyond them, hammers pounded timbers into more homes and barns. He smiled with pride.

This land had consisted of little more than the crossroads of two trade routes when he, Rathen, and Bulo had searched for a place to build a tavern just over a year ago. They'd gambled their pooled resources, reasoning that a busy tavern at a busy crossroads could sprout a village in time. And so the town of Tobermoar in the Blackmane territory had expanded into a vibrant community.

Blackmane itself had been a haven for Thack. Ruled by Pradius Blackmane, a duke who had been a well-known gladiator, it had developed into a civilized yet rugged environment. Being a half-breed, this was the first place Thack had found acceptance. People focused more on the prowess, honor, and courage of an individual rather than their appearance.

Lost in his thoughts, Thack stepped back inside the tavern. As the patrons slowly trickled out, Thack settled down at a table to relax. He expected Rathen and the rest of his band would be returning soon. He still did not understand why Rathen wanted everyone out of the tavern, including the employees, but he trusted Rathen enough to know that all would be explained upon his return.

"I've cleaned the rooms and washed the floors," a voice called out behind him.

Thack turned to see Fala standing at attention, still wearing his smile, his apron back around his waist.

Thack smiled. "No, Fala, you are done for the night. Hang up your apron and go home."

Fala stood in place, his hands clasped in front of him, his eyes shifting from side to side as his body rocked back and forth in his usual habit. "You sure there isn't an—"

"Go home, Fala," Thack said in a gentle voice.

"Yes, sir… of course, Master Thack," Fala said, backing out toward the kitchen.

A loud knock shifted Thack's attention to the front door. "Right on time," he muttered under his breath as he rose to his feet.

Thack opened the door with a welcoming smile that quickly turned to surprise when he saw two unknown men standing on his front step. By the light of the fading sun, he could see they both stood almost as tall as he, making the two figures some of the tallest men he had encountered. One was of a meatier build, with a thick body and a gruff-looking face. He was dressed in what appeared to be light scale armor, which struck Thack as a bit unusual with each scale sculpted and patterned in an intricate design. Thack could see two sword hilts just over the man's back. The other man was just a shade shorter, much thinner, and had a soft, gentle face. He wore hard leather armor and only a dagger on his hip.

"My apologies, gentlemen. We are closed for the evening. Please come back in a few days." Thack started to shut the door.

The larger man placed his hand on the wooden door, forcing it open.

"We are here to see Bandark," he rumbled in an exotic accent.

"Bandark?" Thack stared at the men blankly before suddenly realizing his mistake and opening the door to them. "Oh, yes, of course. He's not here now, but please come in. I was told you wouldn't be arriving until the morrow."

"We are early." The large man spoke loudly and slowly, his face bearing no emotion.

"That shouldn't be a problem. They should be here soon." Thack waved them in with his only hand.

The two men stepped inside, selected the farthest table from the door, and sat down with their backs to the wall, giving no second glance at the half-orc.

Following them, Thack asked, "Would you like some food or drink?"

"No," the large man replied. The other remained silent.

Thack paid no mind to their peculiar and rude mannerisms.

All manner of travelers and their eccentricities crossed his threshold, and the dust on their clothes testified that these men had been traveling for some time, no doubt too weary for pleasantries or other wasted words. However, Thack felt an obligation to keep them company since, willingly or not, they were guests to his tavern. Thack took his time sitting down across from them, giving them a chance to reject to his presence, but not even a whisper of contempt crossed their solemn faces. Without a word, the three men sat at the table for some time, the eyes of the two guests fixed on the door.

After a while, the thinner man turned his attention to Thack.

"If I may ask," he said, eyeing Thack in a silent request for permission to continue. His voice was softer than his companion's but bore the same accent.

Thack nodded, knowing the questions that would follow.

"What manner of man are you?" the thin man asked.

The large man glanced at Thack with interest.

"Will you ask such a personal question before we've been introduced?" Thack countered. The two men only stared and waited. "My name is Thack. And you are?"

"I am Garrick," the thin man said with a smile. "This is Rendrak." The large man nodded.

Thack returned the nod. "Pleased to meet you. I am half-orc and half-human."

The two men looked at each other. "If I may ask, what is an orc?" asked Garrick.

Thack raise his eyebrows, a bit surprised. "Well, they are a tribal people, often brutish. They usually have a… less sophisticated way of living and surviving."

Garrick pointed to his own jaw, asking the question with his eyes.

"Yes, orcs have tusk-like teeth, but larger than mine," Thack said, using his finger to line the tooth that extended just above his lower lip. "Their hair is as black and thick as mine and often worn down to their backs." Thack's own hair, extending just past his shoulders, was pulled back and tied with a strand of leather. "Their skin is a darker shade of gray than mine as well." Thack noted the two men's skin had its own, much lighter, tint of gray that hinted of their unique origin.

"In describing such a breed, you speak with a high level of what you call sophistication," Garrick pointed out.

"Well, my mother more than made up the difference," Thack said with a smile.

"Indeed…" Garrick replied, an almost sympathetic look on his face. "Did you lose your arm to these orcs?"

Thack laughed. "No, I lost it while fighting an ogre. An even larger and more savage beast than the orcs."

Garrick's eyes widened. He appeared about to ask about ogres as well when Rendrak snapped, "Where's Bandark?"

"Bandark is with Rathen and Bulo on an important errand. Now that I think on it, they should have returned by now." Thack glanced out the nearest window, hoping to see the small band of men riding up, but the night was still. Rendrak let out a growl of frustration.

Casually, Garrick asked, "Tell us about this Rathen. You followed him before, did you not?"

"I did," Thack said. "Almost a year and a half ago, he led our group into Ghrakus Castle, where we faced perils and adversaries that would have destroyed an army had they a less proven leader, but Rathen stood fearless against our foes. In the end, he was the only one of us who could resist the magic that had immobilized us all and was able to strike and kill our enemy, an undead mage." Thack smiled, thinking back to the battles they had fought together.

"Impressive," Garrick said with a smile.

"Before that, he was captain of the King's Legion, serving until the king's death," Thack said, proudly.

"That all may be true, but he will still need to prove—" The sound of the door opening made the three men stop and turn.

Thack grinned with relief as Rathen entered the lit tavern and quickly glanced around. Bulo followed close behind, and Bandark came after him.

"Bandark," Rendrak called out as he entered.

Bandark stepped over the threshold, another shape becoming visible behind him, and Thack's relief turned to dread as the hair on the back of his neck stood on end.

A heavily cloaked figure entered the tavern, casting a shadow over the entire room. From under the cowl, two piercing eyes of glowing crimson froze Thack to his seat.

The lich!

Garrick placed his hand on the hilt of his dagger and slowly backed away. Rendrak unsheathed the two swords he carried on his back, their onyx blades reflecting the firelight, let out a roar, and charged the cloaked figure. Before Thack could react, a loud thud echoed out from the back room.

Chapter 2

Rathen waited for the cover of nightfall to enter the town of Tobermoar. He could not afford the lich being discovered by the town's inhabitants. No amount of reasoning would persuade these people to allow such a creature among their homes. The thick robes Rathen had carried in his bag for the lich had been enchanted with powerful spells to lessen the ominous feeling that radiated from his being. However, even wrapped in the robes, the lich still emanated an eerie presence simply by his slow, unnatural movements.

On horseback, they traveled through the streets as briskly as they could without drawing undue attention. The lich's steed had flinched as the lich had mounted it, quaked in agitation throughout the entire trip, and threatened to throw its rider a few times. Rathen wanted to get through this last stretch without another incident.

A sigh of relief escaped his lips as the tavern came within view. The group dismounted in haste near the front door and secured their horses. Rathen saw the sign on the door and knew Thack had done his part, but he needed to make certain no patrons remained inside.

Opening the door, he was greeted by the light of the roaring blaze in the fireplace and the smell of ale and roasting meat. Glancing around the room, Rathen noticed Thack and two men sitting at one of the back tables. Both of them closely matched the description Bandark had given of the companions he would be expecting. Satisfied no other eyes were in the room, Rathen entered and waved for the rest to follow, anxious to get the lich off the open streets.

Rathen moved toward Thack and the two men, anticipating their repulsion upon seeing Magom. Even covered with the enchanted robes, the lich radiated an immense aura of danger. One of the men called out to Bandark, and all three quickly stood. Rathen heard a dull thud from the back room, but before he could investigate, the larger of the two men drew two swords, let out a roar, and charged the lich.

"Hold your ground!" Rathen yelled, his hands out in front of him.

The large man charged past.

"Yakud!" Bandark shouted, his deep voice rumbling across the room.

The large man stopped instantly, breathing heavily in his battle frenzy. He held one of the gleaming swords in front of him and the other by his side. Rathen noticed both swords looked to be crafted of onyx, the same material as his own. The substance was called Meriante and unique to Bandark's world.

"Mafoud grek domglid!" the big man shouted back, pointing to the lich. His face was tense and flushed.

"Here we speak their language, Rendrak," Bandark said in a calmer voice. "Now lower your swords and we shall explain."

Rendrak slowly backed away, his eyes fixed on the lich. Bandark made his way over to Rendrak and waved his hand, signaling for Garrick to approach.

As the three otherworlders gathered to talk, Rathen walked toward the lich and called him by name. "Magom, please rest over near the tables." He hoped that showing respect would help keep the lich containable.

The lich hissed in response and moved toward the back of the tavern as if he were floating.

Rathen gave Thack a nod. "Well done on the preparations. Let's get some food on the table." Rathen's stomach growled angrily, but despite his hunger, he was more anxious to wash the weeks on the road from his body.

"Right away," Thack replied.

Rathen turned to the front. "Bulo, bar that front door to be safe," he shouted.

"Already done," Bulo replied.

"Rathen," Thack called out.

Rathen shot a glance to the lich, fearing the worst. Yet the lich sat silently still in a chair with his cloak over his head. Rathen looked for Bulo and rushed toward the kitchen.

"What is it?"

"Look," Thack said, pointing to a motionless body on the floor.

Rathen studied the red hair as he knelt down beside the fallen young man. "Fala? What's he doing here?" Rathen had hired Fala just after the boy's sixteenth birthday. His aid in the care of the tavern was significant, but he sometimes seemed too eager for excitement and adventure. Rathen knew such longings to be dangerous for a young man of simple means with little skill in swordplay.

"I told him to go home for the night, but he seemed eager to stay. He thought we were entertaining some important guests again," Thack replied. Bulo's notoriety as an ex-gladiator often brought in prominent people from around the area.

Rathen placed his fingers to Fala's neck and felt it pulse with blood. "He's fine. Must've passed out."

"Ah, that explains the sound I heard when… *it* walked in." Thack smiled.

"Foolish boy saw more than he expected," Rathen said with a chuckle. "I'll take him upstairs." Rathen carefully lifted Fala. He looked through the kitchen door and saw the lich sitting still in the corner and the three otherworlders hunkered in quiet discussion. "I'll wash up a bit too before I come back down."

Thack nodded. "I'll keep an eye down here." He began carving hunks of hot roast onto platters.

Sometime later, after Rathen and his two fellow travelers had washed their faces and changed into clean clothes, all the men sat together in the tavern at a large table. Wicker baskets of dark-grained breads and bowls of steamy broth sat beside the platters of meats, all spread out for their enjoyment. Bulo, who sat to Rathen's left, ate furiously, drowning down mouthfuls with a large mug of frothy ale. Rathen too enjoyed the food, dunking the hearty bread in the hot, salty broth. Even Bandark, who rarely ate during the journey, helped himself to a large plate of meats and fruits. Magom sat next to Rathen in an eerie, motionless silence. The space next to the lich remained vacant. Beyond the empty seat, Thack and Garrick picked over their food.

Rendrak sat next to Garrick with his arms crossed. He

glared at Magom, eating nothing. Rathen flashed a look at Bandark, who nodded.

Rathen broke the silence with, "Those are impressive weapons, Rendrak. They're glass swords, if I'm not mistaken. Forged from the substance called Merianite."

Rendrak's eyes did not move from the lich.

Bulo smiled and spoke up. "Indeed, I thought as much. I'm experienced with many weapons, but those are new for me. They appear thinner than a metal blade, almost curved in their design. They remind me of the gladiator kopis we used in the arenas. I would enjoy inspecting them closer with your permission. The color resembles your blade, Rathen."

Rendrak's head whipped around. "I was told your world does not have Merianite."

"He found it at Ghrakus," Bulo responded.

"Show me," Rendrak snapped, standing.

Rathen stood, grateful the topic had pulled Rendrak from his silence. He slid the onyx blade from its sheath. It was longer and wider than Rendrak's swords, but the shiny onyx color was identical.

Rendrak looked at the blade closely and snatched it from Rathen's hands.

"How can this be?" Rendrak looked at Bandark. "This is Lord Rodimar's blade."

"Yes," Bandark said. "Rodimar had fallen outside Ghrakus Castle. I allowed the blade to pass to Rathen."

"You should have told us…" Rendrak said, handing the sword back to Rathen. Energy drained from this formidable man with each word, like a filled leather water bag punctured and depleted of its contents drop by drop. Hanging his head, he walked to Bandark. "With General

Carlack's death in the battle of Kastmont and now Lord Rodimar's disappearance explained by his death, I..." Rendrak trailed off, emptied of all but sorrow now. Rathen recognized the misery of a warrior whose leaders were lost.

Bandark stood and placed his hand on Rendrak's shoulder. "Yes, and if I'd had the time, I would have explained everything. We have lost so much already." Bandark waved his hand for Rendrak to sit again. "The battle that wages in our kingdom and the search for the Book of Ziz have consumed all my focus."

"Yes, my lord. But our kingdom in on the edge of collapse," Rendrak said, taking his place once again at the table.

Bandark leaned forward. "This is why we must retrieve the Book of Ziz," he said softly.

Rathen sheathed his sword and sat back down. "Perhaps it is time to discuss the details."

Everyone set down their food and waited for Rathen to continue.

"I'm certain you all want to know why Magom is here," Rathen began, glancing over to the lich. "We are going to retrieve the Book of Ziz from the betrayer who took it from us, the dark cleric Vargas. Magom is the son of King Mathyus, who came into possession of the book many years ago. The book was sealed within Ghrakus Castle for over a century. Magom has studied the magic and can sense the book when it is nearby, meaning we can't succeed in this quest without him. We know the structure where the Book of Ziz is being kept, but it is a large, complex, and dangerous place, and we cannot afford to spend too much time there. Now, to keep us alive in the face of the magic we will likely encounter, we will need to hire a healer. Bandark has agreed to supply the funds, and I have already made arrangements with a nearby temple."

"Why not find a temple closer to where we are going?" Bulo asked. "We could then meet the healer along the way."

"I've tried," Rathen said with a shrug. "The few temples within the area close to the forest do not offer their services to the public. From what I saw within their darkened walls, I doubt they even have healers."

Bulo nodded.

"The area that Vargas is holed up in is called Bramblewood Forest. As the name suggests, it's tough terrain to maneuver in. Since we need to get in and back out as quickly as possible, we've hired a druid to help. We are to meet him closer to the forest. This will bring the group to nine members." Rathen paused, looking around the table. Thack and Bulo nodded in agreement; Garrick, drawn and pale, appeared exhausted; Rendrak wore the same defiant look on his face as he had all evening; and Magom sat motionless, his crimson eyes burning holes in Rathen's confidence.

Rathen quelled a shiver as he turned away from the lich. What did it think about this proposed group, or think at all? And would this undead creature truly be the ally they needed in this mission?

Magom sat at the table listening to Rathen's speech. He could not actually see the man since his vison as a lich greatly differed from his once mortal eyes. No colors added definition, nor did shapes determine the objects in his vision;

his awareness involved sensations and intuition more than sight. He sensed the people sitting around him as well as the occasional passerby along the street outside as a mortal might sense heat or cold and the pressure of winds, each sensing unique to the individual. Compared to his human eyes, he considered his sight now far superior. The powers he gained after his transformation some eighty years ago had been far beyond anything he could have accomplished as a simple human. Without the fear of death, he had been able to continue his studies and increase his power without significant limitations. Thus, he struggled to understand why, with all the advantages of his current form, his soul was tormented by the idea of being human again.

That longing ached in him as he observed this dinner, seeing as he could neither eat nor drink. Part of him scoffed at the need for such things while another part longed to be as these men—relishing the textures of food, the quenching delight of beverages. These all-too-human longings had forced him to join in this mission. If he could regain the red book, the one they called the Book of Ziz, then this quest would be worth all the trouble. After speaking with Bandark at the temple in Ghrakus, he considered it possible to not only regain his humanity but to permanently extend his life, as a human, using the powers of the red book coupled with his own years of study on immortality. Unfortunately, long ago, when his father and others around him had attempted to study the book, Magom had remained satisfied with his own research and scoffed at their efforts. If only he had joined in their research, maybe… but later, too late, and on his own, he fully sensed the book's magic yet failed to learn any of its secrets. Now, he had his chance.

Magom expected this little adventure he had been pulled into would likely work out well in his favor. He looked around at the people sitting at the table and saw tools. Every one of them displayed dispensable potential for this mission; however, their true abilities had yet to be tested.

Magom had no reason to question Rathen's skills, for it had been Rathen who had entered the impenetrable shield around Ghrakus Castle and killed Magom's brother, Tyus, a being who had infused his essence with demon kind and had even defeated Magom himself. It had taken months for Magom to reconstitute himself after Rathen had severed and crushed his skull. This mere human had proved more resourceful than Magom had expected. Rathen's followers had also shown they were formidable and loyal. As the son of a king, Magom had seen those of skill and courage flock to a man with the capacity to lead. However, from their brief discussion on the road, this tavern was the only occupant of Rathen's time. Even a lich could see that Rathen's talents were squandered on an existence as simple as this. Something held him back. Perhaps a physical injury… or a psychological one.

Magom did not fear Rathen, for the man needed him, and the others might be strong of body but would be no match for a lich if trouble were to arise. The druid was of no consequence, since the powers of nature were insignificant in comparison to his own dark magic. The healer, on the other hand, would likely take great issue with Magom. Temples with the power of restoring life, as the one their healer would be coming from, were linked to a deity who granted that power to his followers—a deity dedicated to life preservation by healing the body. Such a deity would likely abhor the concept of death magic.

In life, Magom had once belonged to the temple of a deity himself, but one who favored a neutral view on the balance of life rather than an absolute line between good and evil. That deity had not been consumed with spreading their ideas or converting more followers. Though the healing powers of that deity had been limited, they had been sufficient to meet Magom's needs at the time.

After leaving the temple, the art of magic had consumed Magom's mind, as it required neither a deity nor a set ideological belief. While recreating spells from the ancient knowledge of past mages proved more difficult than he anticipated, by using the right materials, actions, and voice manipulations, Magom shot fire from his hands. The more he studied over the years, the deeper his understanding of the elements grew, and he could even create new spells with which to better control them. As his focus turned to the dark arts, Magom learned to better comprehend the fine line between life and death—for it was this death magic he had used to transform himself into a lich, the same magic shunned by the healer temples.

Bandark's deep voice caught Magom's attention, drawing him out of his musings and reminiscences. Magom paid special attention to Bandark; he wished to discover the secrets of the other world to which Bandark belonged.

"We have had eyes in the compound for a short time. Using his abilities, Garrick was able to move around undetected," Bandark said, flashing a nod to Garrick.

Garrick looked around at everyone and stood up. "By use of a cloaking spell, I remained undetected; however, I never discovered where the Book was being kept. Vargas appears to be a powerful adversary, but it is his master, the man they call Litagus, whom we need to avoid. Although I remained invisible and kept my distance, it seemed as though he could feel my presence. He looks like a man, but he may be something more. Vargas is Litagus's second in command, and a woman named Davale seemed to be the third, although I could sense some animosity between the two. There were also several guards and servants around the compound. We must avoid them all and enter undetected."

"Are your spells good enough to render us all invisible?" Bulo asked.

"No, not everyone while we are on the move. I can only hide us if we remain still."

"Then what are you expecting us to do?" Bulo pressed.

"I heard talk of a secret entrance and was able to locate it within the compound. The inside entrance is behind a wall in the kitchens, but I do not yet know where it leads outside the compound. I never had the opportunity to investigate, but if we can find the outer entrance, we can sneak in unseen."

"Then how do we find it?" Thack asked.

"I must enter the compound once more and take the secret entrance from the inside, which will lead me to the outside entrance."

"What will we do while we wait for you?" Rathen asked.

Garrick paused as if thinking. "Bramblewood Forest has a reputation for being too dangerous for the common man to explore. That is why Litagus and his men have settled there. It is unlikely that someone would stumble upon their compound, and it is easy to defend, even against a direct assault. The forest is situated between a mountain range on the east side and a treacherous river to the west. Litagus has made arrangements with the small town to the north just outside of the forest, to which he offers protection in return for their trades of food and goods. Unfortunately, we will need to avoid this town; newcomers are not welcome and simply being there would draw unwanted attention. Litagus's men would soon know of our presence. We can only enter the southern side, which we can expect to be guarded.

"Within the forest, if we stray from the trails in the heavy bush, it is rumored that there are beasts lurking in the trees that could kill you in an instant. For that reason, I never left the trails. However, if we use the trails as a group, we will be discovered by the compound's patrols traveling by horseback every so often. With their greater numbers, we cannot defeat them all. We will need to seek refuge in the forest, and there is one area to the south that the patrols do not go."

"And why is that?" Bulo asked.

Garrick slowly looked around the room. "Because no one comes back. Litagus sent men to investigate disappearances in that area. When no one returned, he sent more men who failed to report back. Since then, Litagus has considered the area restricted for his men."

Bulo smiled, leaning back in his chair. "And you expect us to seek refuge there?"

"Well, near it. I do not know what is in the area, but it has since been marked to prevent Litagus's men from accidentally stumbling upon it. If we can stay close to the marked spot and avoid what is inside, no one from the compound will come looking."

Magom could sense the tension in Garrick's voice; the

thin man's very core resonated with fear. *These weak-minded fools. These… simpletons.*

"You are leaving some details out of your story," Magom said, leaning forward. Everyone at the table shrank back at his voice, though Rathen was better at concealing his uneasiness. "If you describe this Litagus as more than a man, there is more to the reason why he avoids the area."

"What do mean?" Rathen asked.

Magom did not answer.

Garrick's eyes darted back and forth. "No, it's true. There were a few rumors in the compound, but I could never confirm anything. They referred to whatever was in the area as 'the old one' and 'the evil' within."

Rathen sighed. "Garrick, from now on, tell us everything you know. Do not spare us details that you think we do not want to hear or that you couldn't confirm. There is a bit of truth to even the strangest of rumors."

Garrick nodded. "Yes, Captain."

"And no more 'Captain.' That rank and time are both well behind me."

Garrick lowered his head.

"Rathen, Garrick means well," Bandark said. "He is weak and still recovering from his task. We have asked so much of him to spy on our enemy under the constant fear of being discovered. I am confident his efforts will aid us, but I request that he be allowed to rest."

"You're right," Rathen said, taking a deep breath and letting it out slowly. "We could all use a rest." Rathen stood, stretching his arms and shaking his shoulders. "We leave early for the temple, so rest, eat, and make yourselves ready."

The group acknowledged Rathen's words with nods and

moved upstairs to their rooms, leaving Magom sitting alone. Magom sensed them go. Neither his body nor his mind required sleep. Instead, he went back over Garrick's words for several hours. Something he said concerned Magom, but he could not yet decipher what.

Rathen woke early, dressed, and went downstairs. With such a challenging journey ahead, he had found it difficult to sleep. The sounds of movement and the smell of roasting meat from the kitchen suggested the preparation of breakfast. He turned into the dining hall to see Magom sitting in the same position he was in the night before. Since they were alone, this would be a good opportunity for a private conversation.

As Rathen approached the table, Magom did not move. He was still dressed in the thick robes and cowl that covered most of his face. The lich so resembled a corpse propped up at the table that were it not for the eyes glowing out of its expressionless skull, Rathen would assume it was truly dead. Rathen did his best to shrug off his apprehension and sat down across the table from Magom.

"Magom, how did you know Garrick wasn't being forthcoming with his information last evening?"

The lich responded with a serpentine hiss. "It was in the way he described Vargas's master, Litagus."

"Oh. How's that?"

"Garrick showed his ignorance in not knowing with what he dealt," Magom said, moving for the first time by shaking his head. "I expect Litagus is more than an average mortal, and his intelligence is likely vastly superior… so his reasoning is not unlike my own. If he sent men into this forbidden area and they did not return, there is more behind his restrictions than not wanting to lose more men—men are replaceable. I suspect he knows what this evil is, especially since the men whisper rumors of 'the old one.' Because no one returns alive, perhaps Litagus himself approached this area and survived this creature and brought back the rumors of the danger. And a man able to survive such evil and escape more or less unharmed must be very powerful indeed."

Rathen nodded.

"Since this 'old one' seems limited to a single location, it is not as great a threat to the mission as Litagus. We do not yet know how this high priest came to obtain his powers, but we can assume he will be our most formidable opponent."

"Understood. As Garrick said, we should avoid Litagus as best we can."

Magom leaned back in his chair, his white jaw bone jutting out from under his cowl. "Rathen, why are you doing this?"

"What? This quest?" Rathen asked, unprepared for the question. "Well, to help defend Bandark's world and to hopefully protect our own. That's certainly a worthy reason."

"Is that enough for you?"

"Of course it is," Rathen lied. A vision flashed through Rathen's mind of stabbing the traitor Vargas through the heart, but he kept his face composed.

"Then what will you do after we succeed in this quest?"

A sharp pang of guilt gnawed at Rathen. He considered not answering the question. It was not a topic he wanted to discuss with Magom. He was sure that finding and killing

Vargas would bring closure for the blame he felt for the deaths of his men. They had died when Vargas had thrown them into battle, coincidentally, with the lich himself. Rathen wanted to ask Magom if he would have attacked without Vargas's accusation of betrayal, but he wasn't ready for the answer. For the benefit of keeping things friendly for now, Rathen said, "I'll most likely retire from adventuring and maybe set up a second tavern."

Magom said nothing.

Rathen grew frustrated with the silence, wishing he could read the thought behind those blood-red eyes. The lich couldn't possibly know his overwhelming feelings of revenge. Rathen had played these mind games when first they met in Ghrakus Castle, but he didn't feel like playing a second time.

"What? That's not good enough?" Rathen spoke up in a slightly raised voice, shifting in his chair.

Magom raised his hand, and from under the heavy cloak, a skeletal finger pointed at Rathen. "That's what you need to decide."

Annoyed, Rathen remained silent, uncertain how to respond. When he heard footsteps from the stairway, he took the opportunity to turn his head and wait for the person to enter the room. Bulo stepped into the dining hall, looking around.

"I could smell breakfast," Bulo said.

Rathen gave a nod to Magom, politely indicating their conversation had ended, and walked over to Bulo.

"Well, a man can't starve in his own establishment," Rathen said with a smile. "I'll help dish it out. It's time the others came down to eat before we leave."

Bulo nodded as he stretched his arms and yawned widely.

Rathen entered the kitchen to see Thack wearing an apron and stirring the pots with his one well-muscled arm. Rathen smiled at the sight of the half-orc, who had proven himself a fearsome fighter on their previous quest, now looking completely domesticated.

"Good man, Thack. Because of you, we will start this mission on full stomachs."

Thack smiled.

Rathen caught a glimpse of movement from the side door that led upstairs from the kitchen. Making his way over, he discovered the red-headed Fala sitting on the bottom step.

"Is… is it safe?" Fala asked, looking up from the floor. His voice was shaky.

"It is. But stay here in the kitchen until we leave," Rathen said, helping the young man to his feet.

"Wh-what was that thing?" Fala asked.

"I'll explain when we return," Rathen said with a smile. "For now, take care of the tavern while we're away."

Fala looked at Rathen. "Yes, Master Rathen. I'll do my best."

"I'm sure you will, Fala," Rathen said, patting the young man on the back. "And nothing that you've seen here is to be spoken of to others." He waited for the boy's nod, then finished, "Now, help Thack with the cooking."

Fala nodded again and stepped up beside Thack.

As the rest of the members trickled down to eat, Rathen helped Thack dish out a hot pork stew with extra helpings of green vegetables grown just outside the tavern. Rathen enjoyed a mug of water with the hot meal and tried to preoccupy his mind with thoughts of the mission ahead, but the words of the lich still filtered through his thoughts: *Is this enough?*

Chapter 3

After a filling breakfast, Bulo and Thack prepared the horses while Rathen did his final check on the supplies they had prepared. Once the horses were packed and ready, the group set out based on Rathen's assessment of the group: Thack riding a length ahead, Rathen and Bulo riding in the lead, Magom riding in the middle, Bandark just behind, and Rendrak and Garrick bringing up the rear.

The town had just begun to awaken with a few people outside performing their morning routines. Rathen noticed that almost every person they passed looked up and watched curiously as the men rode out of town. Even with the enchanted robes, the lich still created a chilling ambience.

Just over a day and a half's ride through open country, the small town of Andar came into view. With good weather and empty roads, the group had made good time, stopping only briefly to camp for sleep.

"This is it," Rathen called out.

"Whoa, steady." Bandark's voice rose up behind Rathen, trying to calm a horse.

Rathen turned to see Magom's steed fidget yet again, snorting and flicking its tail. The horse had kept a steady enough gait once on the trail, as if forgetting the fearful creature on its back. Yet at each rest stop, as if awakening, the horse had turned its attention to its rider, snorting and stomping each time. Magom patted the horse's neck as gently as he was able, but that only frightened the horse more. It bolted out of line, lowered its head, and raised its hindquarters, trying to throw its rider. The second buck lifted the lich into the air. He shot forward a few feet and landed in a patch of weeds with a soft thud and a clatter of bones. With its rider gone, the horse galloped away from the group, stopping some yards away to graze.

Magom slowly rose from where he had landed, seeming again to float just above the ground. He let out a long hiss full of malice. Energy, like steamy air, began to swirl around the lich.

"Magom!" Rathen yelled out, unsure what the lich intended to do.

At the sound of Rathen's voice, the energy dissipated. "That... cursed animal," Magom said angrily.

"Bulo, fetch that horse," Rathen directed. "I've made arrangements for us to stay in a barn nearby while we visit the temple."

A troubled look passed over Bulo's face, his eyes darting suspiciously to the lich.

"Rathen, I don't know—" Bulo started.

"Just get the horse," Rathen said sharply.

Rathen dismounted and walked with his horse beside

Magom. Rathen's steed took in Magom with a wide-eyed glare but held steady under Rathen's firm grip to his bridle. The two proceeded on foot while the others continued up the road on horseback. Magom walked in silence and Rathen did the same, questioning just what he had gotten himself into. It was never more evident that a lich could not function outside his seclusion.

Up ahead, Thack could be seen waving them over to a large barn on the edge of a small field just outside of town. The others dismounted and entered the wooden structure, handing their horses' reins over to Thack. He had the animals tethered together next to the barn by the time Rathen and Magom finally arrived on foot.

The barn was the brown of old, rain-soaked wood, and many of the roof shingles were missing, rotten, or sticking up at awkward angles. Inside smelled of the stuffy musk of animal fur and the faint odor of manure. It was vacant except for the straw strewn across the floor. Shafts of late afternoon sunlight streamed through the rotting planks and the jagged gaps where planks were missing entirely. Aside from lacking the smell of stale ale, the barn reminded Rathen of his temporary home in the backwoods town of Khorell during his seclusion. But he could appreciate that not everyone would find it as comfortable.

"We will only be away a short time. In our absence, rest, eat, and drink," Rathen said. He noticed Rendrak wrinkling his nose, but the rest of the group appeared content.

The lich hovered over to the side of the barn and stood motionless next to the wall while Thack unpacked the refreshments.

"Am I going with you?" Bulo asked.

"Of course. You, Bandark, and myself," Rathen replied.

Bulo nodded and set his axe down in the straw.

Bandark, who had been speaking with Garrick and Rendrak, ended his conversation and approached Rathen. "Are we ready?" he asked.

Rathen looked back over to the two men Bandark had just left. Garrick sat down on the dirt floor while Rendrak continued to stand, arms crossed, a frown furrowing his forehead.

"Rendrak, we could use your help," Rathen called out. In any world, Rathen knew the importance of making a warrior feel useful.

Rendrak looked up in surprise.

"Just leave your weapons," Rathen said, unfastening his sheath and placing his own sword in the straw by the door.

Rendrak grunted in confirmation and quickly took off his two swords.

Bulo gave Rathen a curt nod; he had also felt Rendrak's tension.

Rathen and the three men walked into town, appraising their surroundings. Some homes included an expansive front porch; others sported turrets or elaborately detailed wooden spindles and shutters. Yet despite the elaborate builds, a state of disrepair—split boards, gates hanging crocked on hinges—marred the beauty of nearly all the homes. Rathen noticed that a number had even been boarded up or completely leveled. Only a few people wandered the streets or lingered near their homes. It was clear to Rathen that this town had once been much bigger.

The temple stood tall near the middle of town, next to a row of shops and a couple of empty structures. Aside from bird calls and buzzing insects, the town was quiet.

"This is a bit too peaceful," Bulo said. "What's this town called again?"

"Andar," said Rathen, noting the stillness.

"Was it like this when you visited before?" Bulo asked.

Rathen shook his head. "This is my first time here. The priest I spoke with who visited us in Tobermoar came from Andar when I arranged for the healer."

"Well, Andar has certainly seen its better days," Bulo said.

"Agreed," Rathen said, opening the temple doors.

Table candles and wall torches lit the inside of the temple with a soft, welcoming brightness. The fragrance of myrrh and the faint guttural hums of recited meditation could be heard coming from within.

Stepping inside, Rathen immediately noticed a large man standing beside the door, his back to the wall. The metal helmet he wore had a thin guard running down his nose and another around the back of his neck. Only the eyes and mouth of the man were visible, and both were cold and set. Leather armor covered a white tunic that stretched down to the man's knees. Both his hands were resting on the pommel of a large, two-handed sword that stood chin high. The exposed blade looked to be almost the full width of a man's hand, making for an interesting weapon. In the middle of the blade and extending down its length was some kind of writing that Rathen did not recognize but could guess were prayers of protection.

"We are looking for the head priest," Rathen said to the statue of a man as the others entered the temple.

Bulo also took interest in the man and his weapon by

commenting on the splendor of his sword, but his praises went ignored. The man stood as tall as Rathen and just about as thick as Bulo.

Before Rathen could question the man further, a voice rang out behind them. "Welcome to the Temple of Thandrall. I am Piltan. May I help you with something?"

Rathen turned to see a thin, younger man dressed in light gray robes. His face was boyish and smooth, his hair short and well groomed.

"We are here to see the head priest," Rathen said.

The young man smiled. "You mean the high priest."

"Yes."

"Please wait here," Piltan said, heading back to the front of the temple.

While waiting, Rathen and Bandark looked over the several intricate statues along the walls, Rendrak gazed to the vaulted ceiling, and Bulo, still enamored with the guard's massive sword, continued to study the blade.

Piltan soon returned with a much older man dressed in a long, black, extravagant robe lined in shimmers of gold and silver. His silvery hair caught the light as he approached. "I am Lazlo, high priest. How may I assist you?" His demeanor was calm and sophisticated.

"My name is Rathen. Your priest, Domar, took payment for a healer we wished to hire. We're here to collect the healer and start on our journey."

"I see," Lazlo said. "Unfortunately, Domar has moved to the city of Ryefall to serve another of our temples. Perhaps you can visit him there to obtain a healer."

"How far is that?" Rathen asked.

"A little over two days' ride to the south," Lazlo said.

Bulo sighed loudly behind him.

"We are headed west, I'm afraid, and do not have the luxury of time," Rathen said, doing his best to remain calm. All the careful planning he had done could fall apart if they did not get a healer.

"Since Domar was still a member of this temple when he collected the payment… we can return it," Lazlo said, gesturing to Piltan.

The young man hastily walked back to the front of the temple and disappeared behind a door.

Rathen felt his face flush in anger. "Listen, we paid—"

Bandark walked forward, cutting Rathen off. "Your temple has healers, yes?"

Rathen took the opportunity to step back and collect himself.

Lazlo cocked his head ever so slightly at Bandark's accent. "Yes, we do. But only one currently. The others have also moved on to Ryefall."

"Then allow us to discuss a new arrangement with you," Bandark said, pulling a leather pouch from his pocket. The pouch clinked softly, full of coins.

"Well, I'm sure you've noticed that our temple could use the funds," Lazlo said, eyeing the pouch. "This town has fallen on hard times since many of its occupants have moved to Ryefall. However, we cannot abandon those who choose to remain."

"Then let us contract for use of this healer," Bandark said, removing several gold coins from the pouch, an amount double what Rathen had already paid.

"And how long will you require the healer's services?" Lazlo asked, placing his open hand in front of Bandark and accepting the gold.

Bandark nodded at Rathen, barely suppressing a grin.

"About three weeks," Rathen spoke up.

"Well… I suppose we can make do without a healer for that long," Lazlo said. "But I should tell you that this will be the healer's first hired service."

"Can he fight?" Bulo chimed in.

Lazlo shook his head. "We are healers, not fighters. But I will send a temple protector with the healer for no extra fee."

Piltan returned with a small pouch that Rathen assumed was a refund for what he had paid Domar, but Lazlo shooed him back with his hand. "Fetch Drynwen and the healer."

Piltan held on to the pouch and ran back toward the front of the temple.

"Does this Drynwen have actual fighting experience?" Bulo asked.

"Well, no. But Drynwen has been trained by our order's best warriors," Lazlo said, offering a smile.

"He'll likely get himself killed," Bulo grumbled, turning to Rathen.

Rathen found it difficult to disagree. Without actual fighting experience, Drynwen would not be much help. He did not want to be responsible for the death of the temple's protector.

Rendrak spoke up before Rathen could. "Keep him. We would be better off without him."

"Our healer must be protected by our own." Lazlo's face was strained.

"He'll likely be unprepared for what we will face," Bulo spoke up. "Nothing against him, but the lack of experience will get him killed."

"Drynwen must be the protector," Lazlo said, raising his tone. His face flushed and his body tightened. "This is our way."

A moment of awkward silence passed. Rathen struggled to think of a solution.

"I'll serve the cause!" a deep voice boomed from behind, breaking the silence and echoing off the cavernous halls. Everyone turned to see the door guard amble forward. The tip of his long, two-handed sword scraped against the stone floor, making a screeching sound that attracted the attention of everyone inside the temple. The thick man moved his massive blade to his side and held it in one hand. He walked directly to Rathen and removed his helmet. The brown hair cut close to his head had turned mostly gray. His looks were rough, his nose crooked, and his forehead and face carried scars.

"Do *I* satisfy your requirements?" the man asked Rathen, staring him directly in the eye.

"You're in," Rathen said without hesitation. As captain of the King's First Legion in his former life, Rathen knew the look of those who had seen battle: men who had taken lives on the battlefield while knowing their own lives could end at any moment, who had felt the pain of seeing their fellow warriors fall beside them but found the courage to move forward. Regardless of the years away from battle, there remained a look in such a warrior's eyes of something cold and hard. And this man clearly had it.

"Very well," Lazlo said. "Marduke will be the healer's protector."

"Marduke," Rathen said with a nod to the big man.

Marduke returned a slight nod, his eyes still focused and hard.

Lazlo shook his head, giving Marduke a wary look. "But I doubt Drynwen will stay
behind without protest."

Caswen sat on her bed in her small stone room, reciting her meditations. The serene repetition of the words flowed through her mind, calming her. The speed and complexity of her recitations were those of someone who practiced often and with vigor. At barely twenty years old, Caswen already surpassed many of the more experienced healers of the Order.

A knock at the door rang out, interrupting her meditations.

"Yes?"

"It's Dryn. Lazlo wishes to see us right away." Her sister continued to use her name without the feminine 'wen' suffix given to all female orphans at the temple.

"I'll be right there," Caswen said, jumping to her feet at hearing her sister's voice. Caswen changed in a hurry from her simple meditation robe to the white robe that indicated her healer status within the Order. She ran a brush through her long, chestnut-colored hair and tied it up behind her, out of her eyes. Her ambition demanded that she always make a good impression, even with something as simple as her appearance.

She placed her silver amulet of Thandrall around her neck and straightened her robe. Stepping out of her room, she walked down the hallway to the Temple Hall, where Dryn awaited her, wearing a wide smile. Caswen looked at her older sister quizzically.

"What is it?" Caswen asked.

"Lazlo wants to assign you to a journeying group as their healer," Dryn said through her continuing smile.

"Really?" she asked. Caswen could hardly believe her luck. She had been waiting for two years since receiving her official white robes from the Order to be sent out into the field, much longer than most new healers. *This is my chance.*

Caswen reached past Dryn and opened the door, doing her best to conceal her excitement and smile. Her healing powers would be more than sufficient for a small group. Caswen wondered what quest called them to seek out a healer. The last group who had come to hire one of her order had been a band of miners, off to work in dangerous mines. The last of the healers to leave for Ryefall had been sent on that task. She hoped this was something a bit more exciting.

Caswen walked into the Hall, followed by Dryn. She could see Lazlo talking with a group of four men. Her pace slowed as she looked over the strangers; two were taller than an average man, with one wearing robes like a mage. The other two loomed large and wore the armor of warriors. The man closest to Lazlo appeared to be their leader, an attractive middle-aged man with brown hair falling to his shoulders and a noticeably large scar that ran down the entire left side of his face. He had a peaceful look about him, she thought.

"Ah, Healer Caswen," Lazlo said, turning to greet her.

"High Priest," she addressed him with a bow.

When she looked up, the four men's expressions had changed to wide-eyed disbelief.

"A woman?" one of them questioned.

Rage flashed through Caswen, but she kept her emotions in check. This was her first chance to prove her skill in two years, and she did not want to lose it just because these men assumed her to be weak. Caswen wasn't always fully confident in her abilities, but she did not want anyone else to doubt her. She needed this opportunity to prove to everyone, even herself, that she was capable.

She heard Dryn take a step forward, ready to defend her, but Caswen held up a hand. She looked behind the four men to see Marduke standing with his helmet off. He flashed her a wink and a nod. Left on the temple steps as babies, she and her sister had suffered a quiet, monastic childhood. Although ever grateful for the temple's kindness, it had been left to the lumbering Marduke to watch over these young charges, to fulfill to their deeper needs for affection and to lend his ear when she needed it. His show of support now gave her the calm she needed to reply.

Taking a breath to steady herself, Caswen stepped forward. "A woman I may be, but I am a skilled healer of the Order of Thandrall and am on the path to becoming a high priest." She spoke with passion to mask her fear. She looked back and saw Marduke break his stern expression with a smile.

"Caswen aims to be the first female high priest in the Order. She has both talent and ambition," Lazlo said.

The four men glanced at each other.

Caswen could hear their unspoken words but chose to ignore it. She was used to being underestimated and knew that to get what she wanted, she would have to take it, as her sister did. "When do we leave? It will only take me a moment to prepare," Caswen said, attempting to seal the agreement before the men could object.

"We shall depart as soon as we are able," the man with

the scar answered. "We just need a word with Lazlo alone."

Reassured that Marduke would not let the group leave without her, Caswen nodded. "We shall pack immediately." She walked back toward the door from which she had entered, proud of how she had handled the situation, but stopped when she heard the voice of the man with the scar.

"We?"

The two sisters looked at each other and back at the high priest.

"This is Drynwen," Lazlo said hurriedly. "Caswen's sister and one of our protectors."

"Sister?" The men all turned and stared in surprise. Caswen could understand their confusion. At first glance, Dryn looked like a young boy, just barely old enough to be called a man. She wore light leather armor over the same white woolen tunic as Marduke, her legs covered by loose leather trousers ending in lightweight boots. Her hair was shorter than the man with the scar's, cropped close to her head to keep it out of her eyes. Unlike Caswen, Dryn had no curves to speak of, any semblance of breasts being bound tightly beneath the armor she wore. The only similarities between Caswen and Dryn were their green eyes and chestnut hair.

"I'm called Dryn," Dryn insisted. "And I go where my sister goes. I'm her protector."

A few of the men smirked, and the scarred man said, "Marduke already offered his services as protector, but thanks for the offer."

Dryn's eyes narrowed. "I don't care who else is protecting her—Caswen is my responsibility."

The larger man grunted exasperatedly. "We don't have the resources to look after the safety of two young women."

"I will look after myself *and* my sister." Dryn stood tall for a woman, almost six feet, and in her fury, she seemed to tower over everyone in the room.

"I thought this had been decided. Let us pass on the services of this protector," the large armored man said.

Caswen eyed Marduke standing silently behind the men. *What had been decided?* She wondered why he did not speak up to defend Dryn. He knew her ability better than anyone.

The scarred man took a step toward Dryn. "With which weapons do you consider yourself proficient?"

"Long sword and bow," Dryn said at once.

Lazlo placed a wizened hand on Dryn's shoulder. "Dryn really is one of the finest warriors we have. She and her sister were abandoned at this temple as infants, only one year apart in age. We train all our orphans as healers, but Dryn refused to learn the art, determined to prove her skill in combat. Marduke trained her himself."

"They will be both be my charge. My responsibility," said Marduke, finally speaking up. His tone was determined.

The leader nodded. "As long as it doesn't interfere with your protection of the healer."

Marduke held a stern gaze and gave a slight nod.

"Very well." The leader turned back to Lazlo. "Now, shall we talk in private?"

Caswen waited for her sister to join her, noticing the meld of pride and simmering defiance in Dryn's determined steps. Then she made her way once again toward the doorway through which she had entered. As she stepped through, she looked back to see Lazlo walking with the leader and the tall man in the gray robes, leading them to his private rooms.

The summer being warmer than usual and her few belongings made packing a simple affair. She strapped her bag over her shoulder and walked out of her room, closing the door behind her. As she passed Lazlo's quarters, she heard loud voices and stopped to see if there was trouble.

"No… no. I will not!" Lazlo's raised voice rang out even through the thick wooden doors.

The responding voice was softer and had a thick accent. She tried to listen where she stood, but she could not make out the words. Another voice spoke, and finally Lazlo's voice replied, softer than before. The sound of footsteps from the Hall made her hurry down the passage lest she be caught eavesdropping. Up ahead, she saw Dryn making her way toward her.

"Ready to go?" Dryn asked, tilting her head.

Caswen nodded. "You really don't have to come, you know," she said, looking at the floor. "Marduke is more than capable."

"It's not a lack of trust in Marduke," said Dryn, trying to catch Caswen's eye. "If anything happened to you, I would never forgive myself for leaving you alone. This way, I can be sure I am doing all in my power to keep you safe."

As Caswen's personal protector these last two years, Dryn had never been away from Caswen for more than a night's sleep. Caswen had been looking forward to being out from under her ever-watchful eye for a bit. Plus, she had been glad at the chance to spend time with Marduke. Prior to her being appointed healer, the old soldier had acted as her protector. She knew he must have volunteered because of the kinship he felt for her.

Caswen wondered if she should tell her sister what she

had overheard in Lazlo's chambers, but thought better of it. Dryn's protectiveness would only be agitated. Even though the way Dryn hovered over her irritated Caswen, she could not deny that she felt safer with both Marduke and her sister protecting her—especially with the sound of Lazlo's fearful shouts still ringing in her ears.

Rathen and Bandark thanked Lazlo for his understanding and walked out of his room. The conversation had lasted much longer than they expected, but Lazlo still scowled as they left. Rathen had expected the priest would not take lightly the news of a lich traveling with them. Without Bandark's extended explanation of his world and theirs being at stake, he doubted Lazlo could have ever been convinced to allow his best pupil and only healer into such danger.

Returning to the Hall with Bandark, Rathen rejoined Bulo and Rendrak near where Marduke stood.

"How did it go?" Bulo asked quietly.

"It's done," Rathen said.

Lazlo returned to the Hall wearing a heavy look. "Marduke, find Dryn and come to my chambers."

"Right away," Marduke said, walking toward the front of the temple.

Rathen supposed that Lazlo wanted to explain to Marduke and Dryn the peculiar circumstances of his group. Marduke looked like an experienced warrior; he would be accustomed to sacrificing his own sense of morality for the good of the kingdom. Rathen knew he would understand. But would young Drynwen?

"It's getting late," Bulo said.

"Yes," Rathen replied. "I expected to travel at night, but maybe we should stay and leave in the early morning."

"In that barn?" Rendrak crinkled his nose as he spoke.

Rathen and Bulo laughed heartily. Bandark remained silent.

"Not all of us. You and some of the others can find the local inn and get some rest. I'll keep Magom company," Rathen said.

"I'll stay with you," Bulo piped up.

"Well then, you should follow them to the inn and pick up some ale for us. It might be a long evening," Rathen said with a smile.

Bulo returned the smile. "Yes, sir."

Before they left the temple, Rathen explained to Lazlo that because of the hour, they would return for Caswen, Drynwen, and Marduke in the morning. Though Bandark and Thack expressed their intentions of spending the night in the barn, Rathen talked them into getting a good night's rest at the local inn with Garrick and Rendrak. The lack of patrons in the area made the rates for room and food cheap, not to mention he judged they would sleep easier without a lich in their bedchambers. Rathen, on the other hand, felt an obligation to keep Magom company, and he just couldn't say no to Bulo.

As it grew dark, Rathen made sure the horses were taken care of before preparing their own sleeping areas for the night. Bulo arrived back from the inn and pulled together a large mound of straw to sleep on while Rathen made do with the dirt floor. Magom simply continued to stand near the wall of the barn.

Bulo unpacked several ales he had purchased from the

local inn and handed one to Rathen, who took it with a nod and held it up in a silent salute.

The two sat enjoying their drinks in the dark barn without much conversation. Both had served in the same kingdom's legion and lived the life of soldiers. The memories that haunted them, the strategies for days ahead, the late-night longings, and pride in past battles fought, all these passed between them without a word spoken. The only topic Rathen desired to discuss with Bulo was that of Vargas, yet it remained a conversation he did not want the lich to overhear.

After the ales were gone, they both settled down for the night.

Rathen found it difficult at first to get comfortable around the coal-red, unblinking eyes of Magom, but after a while, he drifted off to sleep.

Rathen woke to the sounds of a haunting moan. He reached for his sword lying next to him but stopped, remembering the lich. He blinked several times, trying to clear his eyes well enough to see Magom. The moonlight shining through the cracks provided enough light to see the standing lich. He had not moved.

"Magom?" Rathen asked. The moan continued to echo through the rafters, waking Bulo, who grabbed his axe.

"Magom! What is it?" Rathen asked, sitting up.

The lich turned his head to Rathen, showing his crimson eyes. Rathen shrank back at the sight. The eyes glowed brightly in the darkness.

"Lost souls," the lich said, ending in a long hiss.

"What do you mean? Stop that moaning at once," Rathen said, standing. The continuous noise scrabbled at

Rathen's nerves. Besides, it was bound to attract attention in the village.

"I assure you, it is not my doing," Magom said. "Weaker beings often seek out the powerful—someone who can lead, protect… even control them."

"I still don't understand," Rathen said.

"There are souls caught between this world and the next. They sense my presence and have sought me out."

"Ghosts?" Bulo asked.

"Among other things," Magom said. "I can feel their presence just as they feel mine."

Rathen walked over to the door, cracking it open to glance out into the night. In the direction of the moan, he saw the ghostly form of what looked like a man from the waist up, floating above the ground. The wavering image remained still under the moonlight, emitting an eerie wail. The sight sent shivers down Rathen's neck.

"Send them away," Rathen ordered Magom.

"They are not mine to control," Magom said. "They will not come closer unless I allow it, but I cannot make them leave."

"Sleeping at the tavern sounds like a good idea right about now," Bulo said.

"You can still go," Rathen suggested.

"I'm not going out there," Bulo said, lying back down and covering his head with the cloth he used to rest his head.

Magom moved for the first time since they arrived at the barn. He glided over to Rathen and stood in front of him.

"I sense even a wraith out in the trees behind the barn," Magom said. "The form I took to visit you in your dreams the first time."

"Don't remind me." Rathen still had a difficult time shaking that nightmare. It had been his first contact with the lich, directing Rathen to Castle Ghrakus. A wraith, like a deadly leech, was a ghostly undead creature that could suck the very life out of a person and cause them to become a wraith themselves.

"Do you wish to see it?" Magom asked with a hissing laugh.

Rathen paused. He was not ashamed to admit the wraith frightened him, for he did not even know how to fight such a creature. Yet a warrior needed to size up any enemy, and this was his only chance to see it without fear of being attacked.

"Alright," Rathen said, gathering his courage.

"Really?" said the lich. "Rathen, you continue to surprise me."

"How often does a man get the chance to face his fear without a risk to his life?" Rathen looked over to Bulo lying down with the cloth over his head. "Let's go outside."

"Very well." Magom moved toward the door.

They both left the barn and closed the door behind them. The horses on the other side of the building whinnied and bumped against the old wood.

Rathen's heartbeat hastened as he and the lich walked toward the trees. The moon shone full and bright, but the area seemed covered in a thick shadow. The constant moans and occasional glimpse of a ghostly specter in the distance made Rathen question his sanity in this little exercise.

Magom stopped and stood on the edge of the tree line. He lifted the thick cowl from his head, and the air became charged with the dread Rathen remembered so well. It added to the menacing feeling of knowing there was a wraith hidden within the trees. The lich's eyes blazed as he softly hissed. Slowly, a shadow emerged from the tree line and glided into the moonlight.

Rathen stood in awe at the wraith's dark figure. It emanated such an overwhelming sense of danger that his skin tingled and his nostrils flared. His hand instinctively reached to his side for his missing sword, still lying beside his pallet bed in the barn. The wraith materialized just as the one in his dreams, the image of death itself.

The moonlight shined through the wraith's incorporeal body, silhouetting what appeared to be an outline of segmented spaulders extending over its shoulders. Rathen's heart pounded, his breathing heavy. He wanted to step back, but his determination to face this creature made him hold fast.

"Is that… armor?" Rathen asked, startled but intrigued.

"This is a dread wraith. It is a shadow of its once human form," the lich said. "It senses your life force and is hungry."

Rathen grew concerned. "You can control it, right?"

The lich let out a hissing laugh. "Of course. But we should not linger. There are more souls in these trees that desire contact." The lich stepped forward and held out his bony hand. The wraith approached, reaching out its own. When their hands touched, it was as though a lightning bolt had struck in front of him. There was no light, but electricity crackled through the air, causing Rathen's hair to stand on end. The lich let out a hiss, and the wraith disappeared back into the trees.

"What happened?" Rathen asked, his heart still racing.

"I gave it what it craved. A small bit of life force," Magom said as he pulled the cowl back over his head.

"Alright, best we get back," Rathen said, anxious to leave. Even as they walked to the barn, Rathen could not help looking over his shoulder.

Back in the barn, Bulo's snoring worked well to drown out the sounds of the ghosts. Facing the wraith as he did somehow made Rathen feel more confident. He hoped the occasional wraith dreams that still plagued him would now cease. Though, he realized, seeing that bit of the immense power that Magom possessed was sure to bring about a whole new string of disturbing nightmares.

Rathen sat down on his bedding as the lich returned to where he once stood, his eyes still glowing like beacons in the dark. The danger of the wraith was gone, but he still felt his hairs standing on end. For over two decades, Rathen had led legions of men into battle for King Delvant against warring kingdoms, bandits, and sometimes savages like orcs and ogres. Some of those times he found himself in hand-to-hand combat against greater numbers, never faltering, never once backing down. But this whole magic thing was unknown territory. He didn't know how to fight against the unpredictable uses of the elements or forces of evil set on killing anything alive. Yet it was undeniable: battling these mysterious forces had pulled him out of his depression and seclusion he fell into after being discharged from his position as captain. Being hired to explore Ghrakus Castle had restored his sense of purpose.

He had defeated the evil at the source of the disruption he had been sent to uncover over a year before, yet Rathen had never felt confident in its success. And now, with this renewed charge to bring yet a greater evil to task, his confidence wavered again. This time he had a power on his side able to help fight the evil they sought to conquer. He turned to look at the lich and frowned. Even if Magom wanted to help, his frequent outbursts of violence could get them all killed. But *did* he intend to help? Maybe he didn't care what happened; maybe, being the undead creature he was, he'd lost his human nature and motives. Was Magom now more monster than man?

Rathen sighed, shaking his head. He wanted to kill Vargas and get back to a life of leisure. Tavern life wasn't so bad. Hanging up his sword and building a new tavern had been a relatively satisfying path. Perhaps this would be his last mission. That was... if he made it back from Bramblewood Forest. He knew success all hinged on his ability to control the lich.

Chapter 4

Caswen awoke in the early hours of the morning, unable to sleep in her excitement. She rose and dressed quickly, donning the white robe and silver amulet of her order, and checked the bag she had packed the day before to ensure she had not forgotten anything. Realizing she had room to bring extra healing tools, she removed the large saddlebags she kept under her bed and filled them with potions and medicinal herbs for the wounds and ailments her amulet could not heal, being sure to include a few of her favorite spellbooks. She had been annoyed yesterday when Lazlo had told her that the journey would not start until the morrow, but now she was glad for the extra time to prepare.

Once her bags were fully packed, Caswen stood and took one last look around her chambers, taking in every last detail of the only home she had ever known. A thickly woven woolen cloth covered her bare wood floor, a small desk with its quill at the ready stood to one side, and her pine board pallet bed, now neatly made, had welcomed her dreams and fostered her deep night plans of serving as healer. Now, it was her time. She was certain she would return, but she needed to be able to recall the room exactly should homesickness set in. With a sigh, Caswen closed the shutters over her window and turned to leave the room. Remembering the arduous ride ahead of her, she pulled her long chestnut hair back into a loose braid before stepping out into the hall. She would send someone up for her bags before she departed.

Caswen headed down to the dining hall to wait for breakfast. It was still an hour or so before the rest of the temple would be up and about, but the kitchen workers rose hours before everyone else to start the fires and begin cooking the morning meal.

As Caswen entered the dining hall, she noticed that Dryn was already seated at one of the benches, a flagon of warm mead steaming in front of her as she sharpened a dagger. Caswen approached and sat across from her sister. "No breakfast yet?"

"They've barely started, but there's hot mead and fresh milk if you can't wait."

Caswen shook her head.

"Couldn't sleep?" Dryn asked, her eye on her dagger.

"I was going over my chants all night. I hope I don't forget anything."

"Relax. You're a great healer. If anyone knows that, it's me. You've patched me up more times than all of the other warriors combined."

"That's because you're reckless," Caswen scolded.

"You have to take risks if you want to be the best," Dryn responded. "Something for you to remember if you ever want to be high priest."

"*When* I become high priest," said Caswen, crossing her arms, "I'll make sure to do that."

Dryn was silent for a moment as she slid the whetstone

across her dagger. "I didn't mean that I don't believe you can do it. But there's never been a woman as high priest before. You can't just be the best. You have to be better than the best. They hold us to a different standard, Cas, it's going to be more challenging for you than it is for any of the others."

"I know the challenges I face," said Caswen indignantly. "Everyone already underestimates me, even my sister." Dryn tried to protest, but Caswen spoke over her. "But I've watched you my whole life. I saw you argue for your chance to become a warrior. I saw you command Marduke to teach you. I watched as you fought day after day in training, while I practiced my healing on you every night so no one would see the extent of your wounds. For all the twenty years of my life, I've seen you struggle to be taken seriously, and I've learned from it. But we are different, Dryn. You stand before the world and demand that they respect you; I stand before the world and try to persuade them to change their minds."

"You must demand if you—"

Caswen raised her hand, stood up, and walked away from the table. She would come back for breakfast later, but for now, she needed a break from Dryn and her arrogant lectures.

Dryn watched Caswen walk away without a word, knowing it was better to let her sister cool off on her own. What could she have said to set Caswen off this time? The girl was usually so patient, but any time Dryn opened her mouth, she somehow sent Caswen storming off in the opposite direction.

Dryn had only meant to tell Caswen that she could relate

to the pressure Caswen faced. Dryn had been there, in the thick of it, fighting to be seen and heard for who she was and not for who the world wanted her to be. Dryn remembered watching the warriors train out in the yard as a young girl. She loved following their movements and envied their ability to protect themselves. Dryn had often felt helpless, unable to protect herself or her sister from the world around them.

At eleven years old, Dryn had asked Marduke about the sword he carried. She remembered asking to hold it and being told that swords were not for little ladies. She remembered her anger and confusion at those words. The next day, she had approached Lazlo with her decision to be trained as a warrior.

"But Drynwen," Lazlo had said, smiling condescendingly, "very few are meant to be warriors, even among men. It requires great strength and agility. Why not train in the art of healing instead? Your sister has already expressed an interest in joining our order for that purpose."

Dryn had known this already. She knew that as a healer, Caswen would need protection, and Dryn did not trust anyone else to protect her sister as well as she.

"I want to train as a warrior," Dryn had repeated, her jaw set.

Lazlo had laughed. "Very well. If you can convince Marduke to train you, you may train as a warrior."

Of course, Lazlo had never expected Dryn to do it.

Dryn did not have to try very hard to convince Marduke. The swordsman had been in his mid-thirties then, battle-hardened but still young. He had laughed at the idea of training a little girl in swordplay but praised her for her persistence and finally agreed just to shut her up. He told her that he fully expected her to quit after receiving her first bruise, but Dryn was much more stubborn than anyone had given her credit for.

Dryn had shortened her name early in her training. She knew that none of the boys would respect her as Drynwen, with the feminine "wen" suffix. She needed to show them she was no different than any boy. So Dryn had cut off her long hair and dressed only in the same leather tunics as the other warriors in training. Her insistence on being called Dryn was eventually honored by all in the temple, except for the occasional slip-up by Lazlo. And finally, finally, after many years of proving herself, Dryn had been acknowledged for her skills and dedication and finished her training with distinction.

Throughout her trials, Dryn had learned a lot about being a woman in a man's world. She only wished to impart some of this wisdom to her sister. Caswen was only a year younger, but she had always been more naïve, and her training, unlike Dryn's, had always been encouraged by Lazlo and the others.

Dryn realized that she could be overbearing, but she had been looking out for Caswen their whole lives. Dryn had been barely a year old, and Caswen a newborn, when they had been dropped at the steps of the temple, and Dryn had always felt very protective of Caswen. Dryn knew how capable Caswen was, but she also felt responsible for her sister's safety and happiness. If Caswen suffered any discontent, Dryn always blamed herself. Caswen was all that Dryn had in this world, and she intended to protect Caswen with her life.

As the morning sun began to rise, Caswen, Dryn, and Marduke gathered outside the temple with their belongings. Caswen's bags were carried down from her room, and the stable boys met them with their horses. Caswen's horse was a white mare reserved for traveling healers, while Marduke rode a warrior's black stallion. Dryn was given a dark brown quarter horse, usually reserved for farm work, but it was all the stables could spare.

As the stable boys and Marduke were strapping the saddlebags onto the saddles, four riders approached the temple. Caswen recognized two of the men from the day before: the tall one wearing mage's robes and the large man with heavy armor. Their leader did not appear to be with them today.

The tall man with the robes approached Marduke. "Marduke, is it? I'm Bandark. You will remember me from yesterday?" He had a very strong accent.

"Aye." Marduke nodded. "We are ready to depart as soon as our saddles are loaded. But I do not see your leader anywhere. The man with the scar?"

"Rathen. We will meet up with him and the rest of group just outside town."

"Very well," said Marduke, turning back to the straps on his saddlebag.

"Need any help?" asked one of the men Caswen did not know. He was very tall, much taller even than Bandark, and he had only one arm, but that arm was tight in its sleeve, the fabric outlining the muscles beneath. His skin was a light gray, and his features were thick and large, though he did not look much older than Caswen and Dryn. He would have been almost frightening had it not been for his kind eyes.

Caswen had never seen anyone like him. He caught her staring and gave her a shy smile. Blushing, Caswen turned away, checking that her saddlebags were secure.

Dryn spoke up. "I think we're alright, but Caswen might need some help mounting her horse."

Caswen shot Dryn a look of wide-eyed horror and began stammering out a protest. "No, no—that's alright—don't bother—I mean, no need—I—"

"It's no problem," said the gray young man, dismounting his horse and stepping over. He held out his arm to her. "May I?"

Caswen nodded weakly, and the young man knelt beside her, lifting her onto his shoulder before standing to deposit her on the horse. When Caswen was safely on her steed, she said, blushing furiously, "Thank you, sir."

"I am Thack," he replied with a smile and short bow. "At your service."

Dryn looked like she was trying not to laugh.

Once everyone was on their horses and introduced, the group made their way to the outskirts of town. Caswen rode side-by-side between Marduke and her sister, the four men riding ahead. Thack was just in front of her, giving her the perfect position to examine all the muscles in his back. With his height, strength, and unfamiliar features, Caswen wondered where Thack was from. She thought about the way he had smiled at her, and her stomach lurched the way it did before she was supposed to demonstrate a new spell for evaluation.

Dryn, beside Caswen, watched her sister watching Thack. Dryn thought her sister might have a small attraction to the young man, and from the way Marduke was scowling at him, she believed Marduke thought so too.

Dryn wondered whether she should have teased her sister in that way, encouraging such feelings, given her sister's ambition. Healers of the Order were not allowed to marry, or even live outside the temple, and the rules were stricter for a high priest than for the average healer. Even though nothing could ever come of it, Dryn decided that she wanted her sister's happiness above all else. She wanted Caswen to experience as much of life as possible before her life was no longer her own. Yet she also hesitated to allow anything to interfere with her younger sister's life-long ambition to be a healer and high priest. She could be sure of only one thing: whatever Caswen wanted to pursue, Dryn would not stand in her way.

Chapter 5

Rathen woke remarkably refreshed despite the uncomfortable dirt floor, Bulo's snoring, and the thoughts of spirits just outside. Facing the wraith as he did had freed him from his self-guilt over his fear of the wraith and his dreams.

He looked around with the light of the dawn shining in. The lich stood near the wall, and Bulo still slept with the cloth over his face. Bulo looked as if he hadn't moved all night.

Rathen collected his sword and woke Bulo, asking him to meet up with Bandark at the inn and visit the temple to collect the healer and her protectors. With a big yawn, Bulo slapped his face with his cupped hands and stretched his arms.

When Bulo left, Rathen sat back down, looking into the straw piles and trying to calculate how long it would take to reach the meeting point with the druid. With the loss of time by staying in town overnight and the likelihood of Magom being thrown from his horse a few more times, they would be lucky to reach their destination in twelve days. He had made the journey himself a month prior to map out the best paths and places of rest.

"Rathen," the lich said, standing beside him.

Rathen jumped at the sound of his voice. He had not heard Magom approach.

"I wanted to speak about last night," Magom said.

"Yes?" Rathen asked, standing.

"Those spirits approached me because of what I am—for my ability to control and protect them."

"I understand."

"You have a similar ability with humans. Do not let it go to waste."

Rathen paused. He thought back to the days in King Delvant's army and how quickly he rose to the rank of captain of the King's Legion. If not for the king's death and the noblemen squabbling over the gold-filled coffers and disbanding the army, he would still be fighting for the king. Those were good days for him. He forged a sense of pride from the trust he received from the king and his men, and from the trust he felt for them in return.

"Maybe. But those days are gone," Rathen replied. "I'm not a captain anymore. And the kingdom fell apart long ago."

"There are always other kingdoms… other men to lead."

Rathen sighed. Magom's words made sense, but he did not want to admit it. The deep-seated desire for revenge he felt toward Vargas made him question his leadership abilities. He had never felt so betrayed before and found it difficult to put it behind him.

"Why are you so interested in me?" Rathen asked, hoping to lead the conversation in a different direction.

"You may now only see me as a creature, but I once was a prince to a flourishing kingdom. My father tempted me down the path to finding immortality… even when I had other plans. In time, that path became an obsession for me. Yet I had desired to be king, and I think I would have made a great ruler."

Rathen nodded. He had heard Magom's story before but found it difficult to think of the lich as the person he was in life or of even being once human at all.

"What will you do after you become human?" Rathen asked, further steering the conversation away from himself.

Magom stood silent for a short time. "I am not convinced it can be done… but if it could, I would create a new legacy for myself. I would work to benefit mankind in the hopes of rewriting my name in the pages of history as a noble man… instead of the prince who became a monster."

Rathen nodded silently.

Magom took control of the exchange once more. "What legacy will you leave behind, Rathen? What mark will you carve into this world? For that is the only true form of immortality for man."

Rathen's thoughts went directly to his father, who had obtained the rank of captain in his legion just before he retired. His father often spoke of his hopes of Rathen making general one day since the captain rank had come at such a young age for him. In his heart, Rathen knew he could have risen through the ranks sooner, yet he'd avoided the political games that entailed, preferring to rise for his talent as a leader alone. He had thought time was on his side. However, after his legion was disbanded, and having not earned a commission as general by that time, he didn't have the courage to face his father. Instead, Rathen found a dried-up town to hide away in and kept himself drunk until he was offered the job of leading a group into Ghrakus Castle. Good men were killed on that mission because of Rathen's inability to see Vargas for what he was, and Rathen nearly lost his own life, but leading men again felt right, even comfortable. Perhaps his plans of opening a second tavern were not as fulfilling as he once thought. At the very least, he owed his father an explanation.

"You're a wise man, Magom," Rathen said, pulling himself out of his thoughts.

"Being around for over two hundred years will have that effect."

The sound of horses caught Rathen's attention. He walked to the door to see the entire group ride up. Caswen rode a white steed and Marduke a large black one. Behind Marduke rode Dryn on a simple quarter horse. With her inexperience, he hoped she lived to see her sister to safety.

The riders pulled up alongside the barn, and Bandark, Rendrak, Garrick, and Thack dismounted as Bulo hurried over to help with the horses. Bandark entered the barn first, followed by Rendrak. Garrick began adjusting his saddlebags to prepare for their departure, and Thack busied himself unloading what appeared to be ingredients for the morning's breakfast. As Marduke helped Caswen from her horse, Rathen noticed Thack sneaking furtive glances at the healer. Rathen took a deep breath, trying to find the right words to explain and introduce the lich to the new members.

Rathen turned to look at the lich, and Magom backed up to the far side of the barn, standing still as usual.

Caswen made her way to the barn door, Marduke right

behind her. Before Rathen could intercept them, Caswen stepped over the threshold, caught a glimpse of the lich, and promptly tripped backward over her own feet, her fall stifling a scream. She grabbed hold of her amulet and jumped to her feet, one arm held out defensively in front of her. Marduke, seeing her reaction, burst through the door with his large sword in hand.

"It's alright!" Rathen yelled. "He's with us." He had expected Lazlo to explain the situation to them, but perhaps he thought they would not agree to the mission and he would be expected to return the handsome price paid. Or maybe his description had been inadequate.

Marduke charged the lich ferociously as Caswen moved behind him, her hand still clutching her amulet.

"Stop!" Rathen yelled. He scanned for Bulo and Thack, but they were still outside.

Rathen could only watch as Magom began to create swirling energy, sending straw flying around the barn. A humming started to emanate from the energy around him. The lich's cowl came off his head, revealing a boney skull. The straggling long, white hair that clung to it blew in the growing wind.

Marduke swung his massive sword with both hands. The lich flung his arm over his face, and the blade crashed to a stop against it. Yet Marduke's expression and flushed face showed he was determined to strike again.

Rathen rushed to intervene as Caswen backed away.

In an instant, the lich flung Marduke to the side with a wave of his hand. Marduke hit the far side of the barn and fell.

"Stop!" Rathen yelled again, positioning himself between

the two with a hand held out to each.

Marduke sat up, shaking his head clear, and stood. Lifting his sword to his shoulder, he charged again.

"I *will* kill him," the lich said calmly to Rathen.

Rathen's mind raced. He had to pull Marduke out of his battle frenzy. He could see Thack and Bulo entering the barn but knew they could not stop Marduke in time. In desperation, Rathen faced the old warrior and held his hands out in front of him, a few feet away from the lich. Marduke did not slow down.

Thhhp! Rathen heard the unmistakable sound of an arrow as he turned from Marduke to the lich. An arrow protruded from his right eye socket, bathed in the crimson light that glowed there. Magom pulled the arrow from his eye socket and stared at it, quizzically. Everyone else turned to see Dryn standing in the doorway, her bow drawn and ready again, but hesitating, seemingly uncertain now how to stop this non-living creature.

Taking advantage of the momentary confusion, Rathen stepped fully in front of Marduke and gripped his left arm. "Please stop. He's working with us—he wants to return to his human form."

Marduke lowered his sword. "This thing seeks redemption?"

Rathen's mind flashed in comprehension. If he could link the temple beliefs into this situation, he might persuade Marduke to understand.

"Redemption, yes! To become human again, and we are going to help him," Rathen said in earnest.

Marduke looked toward the lich, his eyes scanning the length of this undead form. His lips curled. "Is this true?"

Magom allowed the energy to dissipate, settling the

swirling air and flying straw. He reached up and placed the cowl back over his head.

"It is true. I became this—" He gestured down to his skeletal body. "—at a desperate time in life. I desire to become human once more."

Marduke paused thoughtfully. "Our order teaches that everyone is entitled to redemption. I will stay my sword for now. But if this is a trick and any harm befalls Caswen, I will not hesitate to end your existence."

Magom remained silent.

Both Bulo and Thack stood on each side of Marduke with their hands out, prepared to take ahold of the man if he proved hostile.

"Let's talk outside," Rathen suggested.

Marduke nodded, and after one final look at the lich walked back toward the door. Caswen and Dryn, still standing beside the entrance of the barn, followed him out into the sunlight.

Rathen turned to Magom with a nod. His crimson eye seemed completely unaffected from the arrow the lich had since removed and dropped to the ground. Rathen knew the lich could have killed Marduke with ease, just as he had witnessed before in the temple beside Ghrakus Castle. It was a relief that Magom had kept his fury contained and allowed Rathen to stop Marduke.

Outside, Marduke set a large hand on Caswen's shoulder. She smiled appreciatively, placing her own hand on his arm. Rathen noted the closeness of the two. Rathen noticed Dryn retreat to her horse upon seeing Marduke and Caswen.

Rathen strode over to Dryn. "That was a risky move back there."

Dryn shrugged. "Marduke is fearless. He never backs down."

Rathen nodded, remembering that Marduke had trained her. "You have some skill with a bow, and our group does not have an archer."

"Lucky for you I'm coming along then, isn't it?" said Dryn, raising an eyebrow.

Caswen did her best to stop her body from shaking. She would not show her fear here before all these strangers. Even as she brushed away Marduke's fatherly concern, repeating over and over that she was completely unscathed, she found it difficult to erase the image of those red eyes. Before they left the temple, Lazlo had explained in detail that this group traveled with a monster. But nothing had prepared her for the immense feeling of evil and the ominous stare that came from the lich.

For once, Dryn was not hovering over her, demanding to be told of any injuries, which Caswen appreciated. It was embarrassing enough to have fallen over at the sight of the lich without her sister treating her like a child.

Caswen did not mind the treatment so much from Marduke though. He did not worry for her because he thought her incapable. Besides, Caswen never could hide her true feelings from Marduke. As she looked back longingly toward the safety of the temple, the old man caught her eye. "Don't go getting cold feet now, Cassy," he said.

"I'm not," she said, crossing her arms.

"Good," said Marduke, "because you need to do this. This first test from Thandrall is the beginning of your journey to the position of high priest."

"I know the way ahead, Marduke," said Caswen. She noted the kindness in his eyes and gave him a sheepish grin. "I will not let a little fear stop me from my chosen path."

Marduke beamed with pride. "There's nothing to fear, Caswen. I vow that this creature will not harm you. Besides, you heard it. It seeks redemption for its past evils. Perhaps part of Thandrall's test is for us to help it."

Caswen started to protest such a notion, but remembered the temple's teachings and knew that Marduke was right. "I distrust the creature, but I will find strength in my faith," Caswen said, taking hold of her amulet. She never expected her first service to be such a monumental task.

"I have no doubt," Marduke said, bowing slightly.

Caswen felt more confident in her strength as she climbed back onto her horse. If this monster truly sought redemption through Thandrall, then she was determined to help. However, as the lich slithered out of the barn, an uncontrollable urge to run flowed through her. Even her horse grew skittish. The lich gave off an aura of terror and death that affected all humans; even Marduke, a veteran warrior who had witnessed unspeakable miseries, shuddered involuntarily at its presence. The other men had had some time to grow accustomed to the feeling, but she noticed that even they followed the lich with their eyes.

Caswen would not let them see her fear. She forced herself to look at it; the thick robes it wore hid its body, but the way it moved seemed so strange and waves of foreboding flowed from it. She wrestled with her instincts. To gather her strength, she closed her eyes and began to repeat her meditations, calming her mind.

"You alright?" a voice interrupted her thoughts.

Caswen opened her eyes to see Thack. He had pulled his horse up alongside hers, his one arm holding the reins in a fist, and was staring at her questioningly. "I'm fine. Just meditating. It helps to relax my thoughts."

"I'm sorry. I didn't mean to interrupt."

"That's alright, I'm sure we're about to leave anyway." Caswen looked down at her horse's mane, examining the white hairs.

"May I ride beside you on the journey?" asked Thack. Caswen looked up into his face abruptly, trying to read his intentions. There was no trace of entitlement in his voice, and no threat of violence in his body language should she refuse him. Still, she hesitated, her previous experience with men telling her that either answer came with its own dangers.

Sensing her, Thack turned his horse with a smile.

"You're welcome to ride beside me if you wish," she said, but he had already ridden away.

Caswen was not used to men putting the power of pursuit in her hands. Confused by their interaction, she rode her horse beside Dryn for the familiarity of her sister's presence. At the same time, the scarred man, Rathen, rode to the head of the group, and everyone fell silent.

"Let's ride out. Tonight, I will explain the quest in detail and answer questions you might have," said Rathen.

Caswen felt some relief at Rathen's words. His ability to command was evident, and he clearly inspired loyalty and courage in his men. She did not understand why a dreadful creature like the lich was necessary for this mission, but she immediately trusted Rathen and his word to explain everything.

Rathen began divvying up responsibilities to the riders and ordering their placement in the line of horses to the best advantage. Caswen was to ride between Dryn and Marduke just behind Rathen and Bulo, while Thack, Caswen noticed, was sent ahead to scout for dangers, relieving her of the question of whether to ride beside him or not. Before he rode off, Thack caught her eye and sent her an apologetic shrug.

The group began to move with the lich far behind. Regardless of her fears, it felt great to be out of the temple and in the world. The smell of the dew-kissed pines, the cool morning wind in her hair, and the sun's brightly promised warmth on her face made her smile. Her studies consumed so much of her time that she rarely left her quarters. Today began a new stage in her life, for today she was Healer Caswen in service to a band of adventurers.

Rathen had sent Thack scouting the road ahead. He had chosen these paths because they were not as widely traveled, but trouble traveled many roads. The fewer unwanted eyes, the better. Rathen had placed Magom back behind Bandark and the others to keep distance between the lich and the healer.

Not many people had passed them, and the ones who did were merchants in wagons who paid them no mind. The ride was peaceful for a long stretch of road until Bandark's voice broke the silence.

"Whoa," Bandark said, trying to calm Magom's horse again.

Rathen turned his steed around, gesturing for Caswen, Dryn, and Marduke to ride past. Magom's steed once again tried to buck its rider, its eyes wide and wild, craning its neck back at its skeletal rider. The lich did the best he could to stay on but finally fell, his bones rattling, as the horse bolted away. Rathen rode toward the fallen Magom. As the lich rose up, he raised his hands, conjuring a swirl of energy. Before Rathen could speak out, a flash—a bolt of electricity—shot from the lich, striking his steed. The horse let out an agonized shriek of pain before falling over. The commotion turned the heads of all in the group, though they were too far to see the extent of the grotesque scene that played out for Rathen.

The horse lay dead, legs rigid. Rathen gritted his teeth. He was happy to let Magom walk to suffer for his violent outburst, but it would only slow them down.

With an angry gesture, Rathen motioned for Bulo to lead the group out and hoped the others would follow. Caswen had shifted in her saddle to see what happened, but her horse stayed the course. Rathen breathed a sigh of relief when Caswen turned away.

With the group moving ahead, Rathen rode to Magom, who knelt beside the horse. A blackened hole smoldered in the animal's side.

"Well done," Rathen said, sarcasm dripping. "That was a fine tantrum."

The lich remained silent next to the body. He took off his hood and looked over the horse.

"What do you plan to do now? We don't have time to let you walk the rest of the way," Rathen said, dreading the idea of the lich riding with him. By the way his steed stamped and flared its nostrils, he doubted it would allow the lich on its back.

The lich started to chant, raising his skeletal hands and placing them on the dead animal. The area around them darkened as the words Magom repeated grew louder. Rathen shivered at the ominous feeling; it rose like a thick mist, covering the area in a blanket of fear that would have sent a lesser man running. Soon, the horse's body began to twitch, its legs moving to right itself. Rathen's own horse jittered and backed away.

Magom's horse stood back up, its eyes half shut and the wound still smoldering.

"There," Magom said, mounting his dead steed.

Speechless, Rathen stared. He knew this would not go over well with the three from the temple. Raising the dead— even a dead horse—spoke of the dark forces that the temple considered the vilest of evils. But at least there was no longer a fear of Magom being thrown again.

"Just… ride behind the group," Rathen said. "With the heat, let's hope we arrive before the smell of that thing becomes unbearable."

Surprisingly, Magom rode his dead horse at a quicker pace than when it was alive. Assured Magom could catch up, Rathen trotted back to the front with Bulo, avoiding eye contact with Caswen.

"Everything alright?" Bulo asked.

"Don't ask."

The remainder of the ride was uneventful, and as the sun went down, the air grew cool and comfortable. Rathen knew the road would lead them to a resting point he had scouted out on his last journey, but it would become difficult to find at night. Just as the remaining sunlight faded, the resting site came into view: five large stones shaped in blocks and spread out in a circle. Thack stood beside them, holding the reins to his horse.

"This is it," Rathen said, pulling up his horse's reins. "Bulo, get a fire going in the stone circle."

Bulo nodded and dismounted.

Rathen rode to Thack and handed him his reins. He needed to prevent Magom from bringing his dead steed into the area.

"Let's get some food started," Rathen said to Thack.

"Right away," Thack said, leading the two horses away.

Rathen walked past the others riding up. Bandark flashed him a look.

"No sign of trouble, but let's scout around to be sure," Rathen said to Rendrak. Rathen was certain Rendrak heard his order, but it went ignored. He turned instead to Bandark.

"Bandark, let's secure this area just to be safe," Rathen said loudly in Rendrak's direction. Bandark nodded and asked Rendrak to scout the area on foot, which he did immediately.

Not far behind, Magom rode up on his steed. Rathen rushed over to him. "Find a place to secure that thing. I can't have you bringing it around the others."

Magom replied with a hiss. He dismounted, and the dead steed turned to walk away.

"Where's it going?" Rathen asked.

"Away," said Magom. "*I* control it now."

Magom stood along the tree line, watching the group as they ate next to a roaring fire. He did not feel hunger as a lich, but he yearned for the ability to taste. Not for the bland meat and bread the group ate, but for the feasts he enjoyed back at Castle Ghrakus: the creamy and pungent cured cheese, the yeasty hard rolls, the platters of fowl stuffed with savory fruit and nuts, sheep and boar raised for the sole purpose of being served to the king's family, and the endless barrels of wines made from the sweetest grapes.

Being undead for so long left him with the desire to feel what it was like to be human again. The words he spoke to Marduke in the barn were not lies, but neither were they all true. Magom did want to be human again, but he did not feel that any form of redemption was necessary. Returning to his human form and resuming his studies in immortality to become more than just a man, rather than this lich form, was his true plan. Bandark, or even this Litagus whose fortress they sought to infiltrate, might be useful in showing him how to achieve this goal.

Magom noticed Rendrak return and inform Bandark that he had not found any immediate threats.

After the meal, Rathen explained the mission of retrieving the Book of Ziz to Caswen, Marduke, and Dryn. After they had absorbed the information, Rathen asked if they had any questions.

"What is the name of this evil deity who is trying to gain power?" Caswen asked.

"Gothoar," Rathen replied.

"Hmph," Marduke huffed. "You speak of dead gods."

"I assure you, Gothoar is not dead, and his followers grow across my home world," Bandark said. "If his powers increase in your world, so will his control over it. Even now, his priests and followers wage war on our kingdom, fighting for control of the lands."

"You speak of your world and our world. How many worlds are there? I am astonished to learn there is more than one," Dryn said, sitting next to Marduke.

Bandark stood up. "There are eleven worlds of which my people know." He used the end of his sword's wooden sheath to draw circles in the dirt near the fire.

Magom could not see the drawings but listened carefully to Bandark's words, for this was information even he did not know.

"Between these worlds are gaps where travel is sometimes possible with the assistance of powerful spells," Bandark said, connecting the circles with lines.

"Then where is this Gothoar now?" Marduke asked.

"Each world has higher beings that can influence their own worlds and sometimes others, depending on their power. Gothoar is an evil deity known as the Insane One from yet another world. Wherever he is, through his followers, he has gained power within my world and is attempting to gain power within all the known worlds to dominate the universe," Bandark explained.

"Thandrall will not allow that to happen," Caswen said. "He will protect us."

Magom noted the young healer's naïveté and desired to tell her so, but he remained silent.

"In our experience, these deities either cannot act against each other or choose not to," Bandark explained. "Their work is done through their followers."

"What of the creator of the Book of Ziz?" Magom asked. He could sense Caswen jump at the sound of his voice.

"Ziz was a demigod from our world. He wrote the Book to protect us from Gothoar's influence and minions," Bandark explained.

"How is a demigod different from a deity?" Magom asked, his interest piqued. Perhaps there were other ways to obtain the in-flesh immortality he sought, something beyond even human.

"To answer that, I must explain the origins of each. It is our belief that these worlds were here long before the deities," Bandark began. Caswen made a skeptical face but did not speak.

Bandark ignored her and continued. "The deities all began life as humans, first gaining power as demigods. Demigods are beings with great powers who are not yet deities, existing as something in between a human and a god. Over thousands of years, some humans who became demigods became deities. All worlds have deities that only affect the world from which they came. It is uncommon for deities to gain power over other worlds, since they are relatively unknown. But deities such as Gothoar have often sent out followers and minions, during times when the gaps are open, to preach of their gods to others in an attempt to gain power. With his lack of power here, Gothoar may seem dead to you now, but as his followers grow, you will feel his influence upon your world once again."

"Wait. If the deities have so much power, why must they be known across a world to influence it?" Rathen asked.

"From belief comes power. The deities gain their power from all who believe in and worship them and, in return, often grant their followers powers of their own, such as healing powers," Bandark added, flashing a look to Caswen. "However, the powers Gothoar grants his followers are tied to destruction."

Magom could sense frustration from the healer, and her

crossed arms and rounded shoulders indicated how uncomfortable she felt with the conversation. But Magom wanted to know more.

"How did Ziz become a demigod?" Magom asked.

"Ziz was a brilliant mastermind in the ways of spells and the manipulation of energies," Bandark explained. "In protecting us and improving our lives with his knowledge, he became a hero not only to our people but to the people of our world. Ziz's teachings and ideas were beyond our own imaginations and even led one of our world's most skilled blacksmiths, Cronis Merian, to create the Merianite glass with which our weapons are crafted. Ziz's supporters turned into his loyal followers and eventually became his worshippers. Certainly, an extremely rare occurrence nowadays, but this gave Ziz limited powers in the world as a demigod. Once he died, however, even with an extended life, his powers grew into that of a deity."

"Impossible!" Caswen said. "Gods are not people, and they never were. Are we just supposed to accept your word as absolute truth?"

Magom welcomed the healer's outburst, the stimulation of ideas exchanged, and the new concepts to grasp from those from other worlds. Having been alone for so long, he appreciated the conversation. He looked at the young healer. If she were not careful, if she allowed herself to truly listen, she may actually learn something.

Bandark glanced at Caswen and then to Rathen, who gestured for him to stop. "Perhaps we could use a break," Rathen said.

Bandark nodded. "I'll explain more tomorrow," he said, using his boot to cover over the drawings he made.

Magom remained sitting, sorry the exchange had

stopped, as most of the group got up and walked toward their pallets laid out in the clearing. Soon, only Caswen, Marduke, and Thack remained. Magom could sense she was still troubled by what she had heard.

"You could learn from that man, healer," Magom said. He intended to open her eyes, not to provoke her. But if pushing her was what it took, he was willing.

Caswen glared at him. Then she smiled impishly. "I'd rather learn from you, since you clearly know all. Tell me, lich, what's it like being dead?" she asked, her lip curled. She was obviously still upset, but her courage rose in defiance.

Magom pondered her question. "It is… undeath. Another level of existence," he said, aware of her increased tension.

Caswen scoffed. "A higher level, you mean? You are no better than I. A walking corpse is no substitute for the vivacity of life. You look down your nose at me because I am young and a woman, but you are nothing more than a soulless bag of bones."

Magom remained silent, contemplating a response. He had not expected this level of hostility from one so young when he had sent older, experienced men fleeing in terror. But how could a woman he guessed to be barely in her twenties understand what he had seen and accomplished in the past two hundred years? How could he begin to explain what it meant to be deathless?

"My body—this shell—withers with the passing of time, but I still retain my human soul," Magom said. "Further explanation would no doubt be incomprehensible to you."

Caswen rolled her eyes, snapping her head away from his gaze. Both Marduke and Thack sat a few feet away from her but did not intervene.

"I meant no offense," Magom said. "Such an existence is incomprehensible to anyone who has not experienced it." Alone for years, his conversational skills were rusty. He would have to learn to take care with his words.

Caswen turned back to face him, her expression softer. "That may be so, but as a priest of Thandrall, I have been taught that undeath is an abomination of nature, corrupting and twisting the balance of the natural order. The deities bless us with—"

"Huh!" Magom interrupted. "As you heard, it is likely these gods were once human. Why should they govern us?"

Caswen's eyes narrowed. "You want to become a deity." There was no hint of a question in her tone.

"Do not be ludicrous. This balance of which you speak is an idea, not a rule. The line between life and death is not absolute, and we have power to influence it. Man's desire to extend his life is more powerful that you can even begin to comprehend. As you see the years go by and your time on this world dwindles, there is nothing you would not do to extend your life, even by a few days. Nothing makes you appreciate life more than the approach of death."

Caswen lifted her head. "I have faith that Thandrall will allow me to fulfill my purpose in this life. With my purpose fulfilled, my death does not frighten me."

Magom fought back the urge to lash out with harsh words. Finally calming himself, he said, "Find power within yourself."

"Faith gives me my power," Caswen replied without hesitation.

"We both heard Bandark speak. He is from another world that seems more knowledgeable than our own. Are you saying he is a liar?"

"I have no doubt he believes his own words, but I will not question my faith, the very foundation of my life, on the basis of a campfire story. You think me naïve for my faith, but you must be far more gullible than I to believe the words of a stranger without proof." Caswen stood with finality and walked away. Marduke started to follow but sat back down upon seeing Thack's pursuit of the determined young healer.

Such a closed mind at such a young age, Magom thought to himself. He did not doubt her potential or her ambition, but she would never achieve her desires of she did not expand her limited thinking.

Caswen stalked off through the trees, stopping when she reached a small creek about three feet wide. She picked up a large rock from the mud and hurled it into the water. It landed with a loud splash as she took deep breaths to control her irritation.

Branches snapped loudly behind her. "Caswen," she heard Thack say, "you shouldn't run off alone like that. There are plenty of unseen dangers in these woods."

"I can take care of myself," Caswen barked. She could feel Thack shrink from her tone.

"I didn't mean to imply…" he began. "No one should be out here alone, not even me. At least let me send for Dryn, if my presence offends you."

Caswen sighed sadly and turned to face him. "No, I'm sorry, Thack. I shouldn't have taken my frustration out on you. You were just being thoughtful." Caswen turned back around and sat on a fallen log beside the water's edge.

"May I join you?" At Caswen's nod, Thack sat down

beside her. He was silent, waiting for her to speak. After a few minutes, Caswen sighed again.

"I shouldn't have gotten so upset," said Caswen. "I behaved like a child."

"Not at all," said Thack. "I thought you sounded like a woman who sticks to her convictions."

Caswen shrugged.

"No, I mean it," said Thack. "It's really admirable how dedicated you are to your faith and your order, especially with the lich trying to rile you up like that."

"The lich thinks I'm a mindless sheep, blindly following my order without an original thought in my head." Caswen laughed. "But I won't pretend I've never questioned things. I've had my share of doubts—we all have—but maybe I like living in a world with a natural order. The deities protect us, and in return, we do their work on their behalf. If that's not true, then the world is just… chaos."

"Would that really be so bad?" asked Thack.

"I guess I just like knowing that there's a reason for everything that's happened to me," said Caswen. "Dryn and I were abandoned at the Temple of Thandrall as infants, and growing up, that caused me a lot of sorrow. I wondered why our parents didn't want us. But as I grew older and began my studies in the Order, I realized that everything happens for a reason. If my parents hadn't abandoned us, I may have never become a healer. How many lives may have been lost had I not learned this craft?"

"That's a fair point," said Thack. "Though, to be honest with you, I still have a lot of doubts about the deities. I admire your faith because it is so difficult for me to find." Thack paused, and Caswen waited for him to find his words.

"As I'm sure you've noticed, I look a little… different from everyone else. That's because I am half orc. My mother was raped by an orc during an attack on our town, and… well, here I am." Hearing the pain in Thack's voice, Caswen laid a hand over his, which was clenched in a fist on his lap. The warmth of his gray flesh surprised—and pleased—her. Thack's hand relaxed under her touch. "She knew the hostility and ridicule that would follow if she birthed me. But she did it anyway, and her life became very difficult. We lived together secluded from others, and she never married."

Caswen lowered her head.

"It's alright," he continued. "I've accepted it. And I knew nothing but love from my mother, who had every reason to resent me. She shielded me from a lot of harsh words when I was a child, but I always knew how cruel the world could be from the way we were treated. After she died, and I left home, I was met with even more unkindness, fear, and intolerance. I lost my arm. I questioned why this was happening to me, why my life was the way it was. And I still don't have the answers. But ever since I found Rathen, things have been good. Rathen was kind enough to give me a chance when we came across each other on the road, even when all the members in his group didn't approve. Sure, we've had our difficulties, my little adopted family and I, but we've stuck together through it all, and I don't see that changing. But even though my luck has changed for the better, I've never been able to find my faith in it all."

"You have faith in Rathen," Caswen said, her hand still over his.

"Well, that's true," Thack said, offering a smile.

"Let me ask you something, Thack," said Caswen. "If

you could change any of the bad things that have happened to you in your life, would you?"

Thack thought for a few moments, then looked over into her eyes. "No, I don't think I would. Almost everything that's happened to me has made me who I am. It's led me to Rathen, and… to this log."

Caswen squeezed the side of his hand, her fingertips pressing into his palm. "I wouldn't change anything either."

Chapter 6

In the dark hours of the morning, Rathen and his group prepared to leave. They were soon back on the road with several days ahead of them to reach the meeting point with the druid. From there, it was a half day's travel to Bramblewood Forest. It was vital to the success of the mission they keep to the schedule.

Rathen instructed Bulo to lead the group, with Thack scouting ahead, while Rathen rode close to Magom a few yards behind the rest of the group. The lich's horse already smelled of decay, and it looked as if wild animals had chewed pieces of flesh off its body during the night. The sight of the dead horse staggering along the road and the cloaked lich riding atop made for an ominous sight—one that Rathen did not want unknown eyes to witness.

Bulo lead the group on the predetermined path, bypassing all towns and well-traveled roads. After a long ride, they found the second resting spot in a clearing off the road before dark and again prepared for camp. Still several days from the forest, Rathen felt the need to set up night sentry duty for caution. The scar on his face carried a reminder of the dangers of letting his guard down. Never would he allow such a tragedy to happen again.

As light of the day faded, the group ate their evening meal gathered around the fire.

Bulo bit off a large chunk of salty jerky and filled whatever space was left over with bread from his other hand. Rathen saw him stop chewing and sniff the jerky. He went to smell the bread and then the air around him. "What's that smell?" Bulo asked, nose wrinkled.

When the wind blew across them again Rathen could smell the stench of rotting flesh.

"Magom, move that thing farther downwind," Rathen said.

The lich hissed but remained still. "Done," he replied. "Now, tell us again of your knowledge of deities," he said, looking toward Bandark.

Bandark nodded, setting his remaining food aside.

"You said the worlds were here before the gods. Do you have knowledge of who was the first deity? What occurred that made him a god?" Magom asked.

"We have stories of a warrior named Boc thousands of years ago. He was a skilled warrior of extraordinary ability who saved his people from a giant rytelkud—or 'dragon' in your language—and became a hero. He united people from around his world, and they sought out his teachings and started to worship him. Boc's powers grew from the worship, allowing him to further help his people. When he died a few hundred years later, he ascended to godhood. Warriors even to this day continue to pray to Boc for his favor in battle, although his power is not as great as it once was," Bandark said. Every eye around the fire was on him, rapt with attention.

Bandark continued, "Our lore goes on to tell of the second god that came into existence, a being named Kollormog, who lived in a world of nonhumans. He, much like Boc, saved his people from a great threat and became worshipped."

"I have heard this name," Thack said with a look of surprise. "Kollormog is one of the gods my orc brothers worship. He is known as a fierce fighter and an extraordinary hunter. The orcs consider him to be one of their own. I have seen statues standing in his honor... a warrior's god."

Bandark smiled. "Our lore does not state what kind of being he was, so it is possible Kollormog was once an orc."

Rathen could sense that Thack found comfort in Bandark's words. It also heartened Rathen, for the link between Bandark's story and Thack's experience told Rathen there was some truth to these stories.

"How did this Boc ascend into godhood? Was his body lost in the process?" Magom asked.

Bandark shook his head. "No one knows exactly how one ascends, but certainly godhood is a higher plane of existence."

"How many of these worshipers does one need to become a demigod?" Magom asked.

Caswen, who had been silent the entire time, sighed loudly at Magom's words.

"Many thousands," Bandark explained. "Right now, in my world, our kingdom fights the forces of Gothoar. Their numbers grow quickly as ours dwindle away."

Rendrak jumped in. "Before I arrived here, we fought a three-day battle against Gothoar's forces in Kastmont. We lost our general and a large number of our warriors when the city fell. Our kingdom currently forbids the worship of Gothoar, but that will be overturned if we fall. If they are allowed to gain control, evil will quickly take over."

Rathen nodded toward Rendrak. "I know it's difficult to leave the battlefield after such a defeat. What will be your next move?"

"We will work to fortify our two remaining cities so that when we are attacked, we will be better prepared. Ziz's book will help us in doing so," Rendrak said, taking a deep breath. "However, in the Kastmont battle there were rumors of demon men among the forces. This… raises the stakes."

"Demon men?" Rathen asked. This was new information.

"Demon-like men would be a better translation," Bandark explained. "Minions of Gothoar from his original world, where many nonhumans reside. They are said to wear black armor and have elongated red heads topped with horns. They possess unnatural strength and just as impressive combat skills. Their presence is confirmation that Gothoar's will is being carried out."

"Indeed, powerful opponents," Rendrak said. "We need the book and as many reinforcements as possible to defeat them all."

"We will find the book and get it back to your world in time," Rathen assured Rendrak. Rathen noted the flickers of remorse and resolve in Rendrak's eyes as the man gazed into the campfire. Yet Rathen knew Rendrak saw no flames but the fields of the dead, the maimed, and the lost he'd left behind. Rathen too had witnessed such scenes and felt a silent kinship with this warrior from another world.

"Let us hope so for all of our sakes," Rendrak said.

Changing the subject, Rathen announced, "Well, tonight starts night sentry duty. Bandark and I will take the first watch. Bulo, you and Garrick take second."

"I do not require sleep and can handle guarding you alone through the night," Magom said.

Rathen nodded in gratitude. "Thank you, Magom, but sentry duty helps us all focus on the possible dangers. You can take your turn near morning."

"As you command," Magom said.

Rathen could not tell if Magom was being condescending or attempting to show respect. But from the looks of the rest of the group, it appeared as if Rathen had control over the lich. Rathen suspected another of Magom's games but decided to trust the creature for now.

After dinner, Caswen picked out a spot to roll out her pallet and began preparing for bed. As she brushed her hair, Dryn walked up beside her and began laying her bed roll out next to Caswen's.

"I have third watch tonight with Thack," Dryn said, smoothing out her pallet.

Caswen blushed at hearing the young man's name, but said nothing.

"So I should probably get some sleep while I can."

"Probably should," Caswen remarked, tying her hair in a loose braid so it would not tangle as she slept.

Dryn lay down on her bedding, staring up at the stars. "Interesting conversation tonight."

Caswen huffed loudly. "The only thing interesting about it was how so many grown men can believe such nonsense."

"I don't know," said Dryn. "It made a lot of sense to me."

Caswen turned to stare at her sister. "How can you say that? After the way we were raised?"

"It's *because* of the way we were raised that I can say that," Dryn said. "I saw a lot of people do and say things in the name of Thandrall that weren't right, Caswen. Why would Thandrall still give them his power if they were bad people?"

"Maybe he hoped to redeem them," Caswen said, lying down onto her pallet. "That is his main tenet."

"You didn't seem to care much about redemption when you were yelling at the lich the other night," Dryn retorted. "I heard you all the way from my bedding, calling him gullible and a bag of bones."

"He called me naïve!" Caswen said indignantly.

"Caswen, you are naïve if you think you have the entire world and all of its mysteries figured out just because some powerful being you can't see lends you his power from time to time as long as you say the exact right chants in the exact right order," said Dryn. "If the deities were really all powerful, why would they even need to lend us their power? They could just stop all bad things from ever even happening. It makes much more sense to me that these beings were once humans like us—imperfect, fallible, messy humans. It'd be a lot easier for me to forgive all the bad in this world if I knew that."

"Hmph," Caswen said, turning away from her sister.

Dryn sighed. "Just think about it from the lich's point of view. Something awful must have happened to him to make him want to become... that. And if something awful happened to him, that means there wasn't a deity around to protect him. It's easy to have faith in a deity when your life has been mostly happy, but you can't expect those who have suffered to put their trust in something that has always let them down."

Caswen did not respond, and Dryn sighed again but said nothing. Caswen fumed silently for a while, listening to Dryn fall asleep. She could not believe the nerve of her. After all the order had done for her. After all that Thandrall had provided for them! What an ungrateful, spoiled brat, thought Caswen. But as her anger began to cool, her sister's words started repeating over and over in her head, and Caswen finally fell asleep wondering if perhaps she had been too hasty to dismiss the lich and his beliefs.

Magom stood outside of camp, away from the sleeping group, while Thack and Dryn watched over them on sentry duty. Thack stood within the shadows, his axe in hand, leaning it against his shoulder as Dryn paced back and forth in front of the fire holding her bow. Magom could sense the half-orc's experience even at his young age. Dryn, on the other hand, clearly visible in the firelight, was making herself a perfect target for any would-be attackers. The lich did not expect the young woman to make it through this journey alive.

Magom recalled Bandark's words in his mind over and over. He tried to plan how he could become a demigod. If it were based on the number of followers one had, he could just whip up an army of the undead. However, all the stories Bandark told them involved performing grand deeds and being worshipped out of free will. Certainly, that scenario would not be possible as a lich, but if he could become human again and create that following, he might have a chance. Whether he needed his body restored or not still remained a question. If one ascended only by one's soul essence or being, then Magom did not need to completely restore himself. But how could he perform great deeds within a withered body for others to worship?

The dilemma and ideas swirled around in his mind, igniting new desires. Desires stronger than his previous intent of just becoming human once again. Desires stronger than his hopes to yet find immortality as a human. And desires stronger than any loyalty to assisting this mismatched band in their mission—or to protecting them from harm in the process. Only Bandark mattered to him—he could take Magom to his world to learn more about his new desire: transformation into a god.

As the hours went by and the sentries changed to Rendrak and Marduke, Magom thought it would be entertaining if he and Caswen were to take the final sentry duty. He knew she hated him for what he was and would only view him as a repulsive undead. That fact did not make him dislike her. He actually found her passion for life refreshing. She reminded him of a woman from his past, so many years ago.

He could sense where Caswen slept but could not see the color of her eyes, the length of her hair, or how fair her skin was. Magom thought back to a time where he felt happiness and the day he made his fateful decision. He could still see Arina's face, her long dark hair and crystal blue eyes. So long had it been since her last touch, but he remembered it like it was yesterday.

"My love, will today be the day you tell your father?" Arina asked, the wind blowing her shining strands of hair in her face as she lay on the blanket in the grass.

"Soon, my dear," Magom said, lying beside her. He looked up to the sky and then over to Ghrakus Castle in the distance.

"You always say that," she scolded. "But if you don't really tell him soon, the wedding can't take place next month." Arina sat up, straightened her yellow sun dress, and then bent her slender legs and her graceful form as she cupped her knees.

Magom looked at her apologetically. "These days, my father is too busy to even grant me an audience. It seems he's spending all of his time on a new project."

"Is it because of your mother's death?" she asked, her voice sincere.

Magom frowned. "I do not know. Maybe. In the months following her death, he has been researching old tomes and scrolls."

"Then do it today, for me," Arina said, looking him in the eyes.

He hesitated. Looking into her blue eyes, he could see the love in their depths, and her face held a sincere beauty he could never refuse. Yes, he thought to himself. *This is the woman I will marry.*

"Very well… For a price," Magom said with a mischievous grin.

Arina giggled. "Oh? What's that?"

"A kiss," Magom said with a smile.

"Of course, my love." Arina leaned over. Magom sat up, sweeping his arms around his beloved as they embraced into the sweetness of that summer's kiss.

Later that day, Magom went to visit his father. His father's steward stood next to the doors to his chambers.

"I wish to speak with my father," Magom said, reaching for the door.

"The king does not wish to be disturbed," the steward replied, blocking him.

"You don't understand. I need to tell him something," Magom pleaded, raising his voice so his father might hear.

"Let him in," the king commanded through the door.

The steward glared at the prince, but opened the door, and Magom walked in. "Father, I need to talk with you."

The king sat at his desk, upon which were strewn various books lying open and numerous piles stacked several books high. His broad shoulders hunched over his desk, his graying brown hair messed and unkempt. "What is it?" the king asked impatiently.

Magom gathered his courage. "I wish to marry Arina."

His father looked up, closing the book he held in his hand. His jaw tightened, and his eyes narrowed. "Arina? The common-born girl you've been spending so much time with?"

"Yes, Father," Magom said, ignoring the insult.

"No," his father said, opening the book and resuming his reading.

"Do not dismiss me so easily," Magom said, growing angry. "Mother would have wanted this."

The king stood abruptly, throwing the book across the room. "Your mother is dead!" he yelled. "Taken from us by a simple illness."

Magom lowered his head. "I know, Father. I apologize."

"You are barely out of your twenties. What do you know of

love and marriage?" The king continued to rant, flailing his arms.

Undeterred, Magom continued, "It's my decision and my right as prince of this kingdom."

The king slowly turned back toward him. His eyes narrowed; his lips tightened. "Then make your choice, boy. Marry and be cast from this castle to live like your commoner girl. Or assist my research with your brother to find life-preserving magic so we will not suffer the pain of loss again. And no more of these distractions with young girls."

Magom sighed in frustration at this dismissal.

The king's face reddened, and his body tightened as if he might charge to strike him. "Make your choice, here and now."

Magom looked at his father in surprise. Truly, did he mean such a choice? Be cast from the castle, a prince no more, to marry Arina? Or remain the rightful heir to the kingdom but dismiss Arina to spend his days locked away poring through musty books? As heartbroken as Magom felt, he dared not challenge his father. He would lose everything he had come to expect in life: money, prestige, and power. His desire to be king one day would also never be fulfilled and would ultimately be passed to his brother, Tyus. "I will stay with you, Father," Magom said.

The king smiled widely as his body relaxed. "Good. Then your duties in this castle will change as of right now. Fetch your brother, retrieve your magic books, and help me!" the king demanded, desperation hanging on every word. "Together we will find a way to live forever."

"Yes, Father. Right away." Magom left the room, slamming the door behind him.

Magom recalled the look on his father's face when he had spoken of immortality. At the time, Magom had respected it as a show of powerful resolve, but after all these years, he knew it was the look of a man who had completely lost his mind.

Magom was forbidden from seeing Arina again, and with no way to get word to her without his father knowing, Magom was never able to tell her how much she meant to him. How heartbroken she must have been when he never returned. As a commoner, she would not have been allowed to enter the castle without permission, which the king would never have granted her. Did she curse his name to the wind for the rest of her life, or did she find love again? Magom wished he knew. It was Magom's own selfishness that had denied their love… his greed.

Magom raised his skeletal finger to his eye sockets as if he were wiping his tears, a response triggered by the human emotions still living within him. That day had been over one hundred and fifty years ago, but he still held Arina's memory close. He glanced toward Caswen, the same age as Arina was then. He could not help but feel a certain softness for her. He considered how different his life would have turned out if he had left the castle and his father behind.

Magom had lived a long life as a human and had existed as a lich for even longer, every day obsessed with gaining another month, another year, another decade. But to what end? Was success in life only measured by the days he had survived or the amount of gold he held in his pocket? And at what loss?

Chapter 7

Deep inside Bramblewood Forest, Vargas stood outside a large stone compound situated within a wide clearing. The massive two-story structure extended to a large stone spire at the far end. Statues of various animals standing on two legs had been carved into the walls as if supporting the roof with their claws and hooves. Dark green vines sprawled out over the entire building, encasing it like a spun cocoon.

He paced back and forth on the dirt pathway with his hands clasped behind him, his eyes frequently flashing over to the closed front doors.

Finally, he stood still, adjusted his red robes and the black sash around his waist, and looked up into the bright, clear sky. He took a deep breath, trying to calm his nerves. Closing his eyes, he felt the early afternoon sun on his face and listened to the wind blowing through the surrounding trees. He needed to get his nerves under control quickly since Litagus, his master and high priest of Gothoar, had requested his assistance.

The sound of the front doors opening jostled him from his concentration. He opened his eyes, unclasped his hands, and stepped toward the door. A tall, thin figure dressed in black robes and a cowl that covered his face marched out and down the steps. He wore the same black amulet of Gothoar around his neck and held a large package under his arm, wrapped in dark leather.

"I am ready," Vargas said, standing at attention.

The thin man looked at Vargas from under his cowl. His cold, dark eyes seemed to pierce Vargas's mind, causing him to look away. Without speaking, Litagus walked around to the side of the compound and into the trees.

Vargas followed until they were fully enclosed in a small clearing, obscured from view. Litagus scanned the area and, satisfied that they were alone, carefully unwrapped the leather from a large red tome. Vargas knew the book well, for it was the same he had taken from a man named Rathen and the group he had led to Ghrakus Castle. When he saw the opportunity, he had thrown the group into a deadly fight with a lich so he could take the book and make his escape.

Recovering the book at his master's command had placed him in a favored position that could ensure him power and authority within Litagus's following. Vargas's only competition for Litagus's favor was a young woman named Davale, whose purpose in the compound still remained unclear to him. During Vargas's six-month absence from the temple while searching for the book, Davale had gained a high level of favor that almost rivaled Vargas's own. He could see the ambition in her eyes and sense the jealousy she held for him when they were around each other. Vargas did not feel threatened by the woman but knew he had to watch his back, for she was known to be short-tempered and violent. He could only speculate what favors this woman had been doing for the high priest these past several months.

Vargas watched as Litagus held the tome in one hand and pulled the cowl from his head with the other. His hair, short and dark, spiked like tufts of wire. His face looked thinner and paler since the last time Vargas had seen him just a few months ago. Litagus opened the book and looked over the pages carefully. Finally, he looked up and waved Vargas over. *This is it.*

Litagus had informed him the day before of his desire to practice a certain spell away from prying eyes—a spell Litagus had been working on since he had retrieved the tome almost a year and a half ago. As far as Vargas knew, only he was allowed to assist his master with anything related to the red book, but even to him, Litagus did not divulge any of its secrets.

Litagus sat the volume on the ground and held his arms out high. He began to chant strange words, throwing a fine silvery dust in the air around him. A shimmering, transparent, yellow wall materialized in front of him, extending to a height just above his head.

As he had been previously instructed, Vargas took hold of the black amulet he wore around his neck, bearing a circle crossed with a horizontal line, the symbol of his temple. He took a deep breath and started chanting his own spell, Desolation, a power granted to him from his deity, Gothoar. The spell could kill man and beast alike and required much of the caster's strength. Litagus had requested Vargas cast this powerful spell to test the strength of his conjured shield. Vargas knew that if his spell succeeded, it could mean the death of Litagus. The repercussions to himself would be disastrous. Yet if he failed to deliver the spell as required, it could mean his own death by Litagus's hand.

At a nod from Litagus, Vargas held his amulet high and began casting the spell toward his master. A black mass of humming energy shot from his hand, his strength draining from him like water swirling down a deep hole. He watched as it hit the yellow shield and passed through without resistance. To his horror, the spell hit Litagus in the chest, sending him tumbling to the ground. Concerned for Litagus's life, Vargas rushed toward him despite his own weakened state. To his surprise, his master jumped up and dusted himself off.

"Are you alright?" Vargas asked through labored breath.

Litagus turned toward him with anger glinting in his eyes, the veins above his pale forehead throbbing.

Vargas backed up a few steps, uncertain of what he should do.

"No! I am not alright. This spell continues to elude me," Litagus thundered, his complexion even more drawn now beneath the mottled red of his rage.

Vargas felt relieved that Litagus had not been injured. He wondered if the shield had protected Litagus from the full force of the spell or if his master was so powerful that it did not affect him. Either way, he felt the burden of his master's wrath and wished to divert it.

"During our mission to Ghrakus Castle, I saw a mage cast a protective barrier to stop spells and physical attacks alike. Although the color was blue," Vargas offered.

Litagus's eyes shot over to him. "The tall mage you mentioned in your briefing?"

"Yes, that's the one."

Litagus held his hand up to his chin, staring at the

ground. "You said the shield around the castle was green?" Litagus asked.

"Yes. Perhaps if I assisted you in your research, I could—"

"I must reconsider my approach," Litagus interrupted, wrapping and placing the red book under his arm.

"Yes, High Priest," Vargas said. "Are we to further postpone presenting the book to the Order?"

Litagus turned and approached Vargas with a stoic face.

"I have decided the book shall remain with us," Litagus replied sternly.

Vargas knew well not to challenge his master but feared the Order would not approve. The purpose of Vargas finding and retrieving the book was for Litagus to present it to the Order to gain favor. Litagus had made that promise over three years ago, but it had taken them that long to trace the book down to Ghrakus Castle. The shield that had covered Ghrakus for over a hundred years had hidden the book from the world. However, now that it was out of the dome shielding, there were some who might be able to trace its unique magic, revealing that Litagus already possessed it and that the Order had not been informed.

"You disapprove of my decision?" Litagus asked gruffly when Vargas did not reply.

"No, of course not. But if the book is not returned, some in the Order may come looking for it."

"Then let them come." Litagus abruptly walked away, his thin form hunched.

Vargas watched as Litagus sauntered back into the trees. He could not help feeling concerned for his master since his health appeared to be deteriorating from his constant studies. By keeping the book, his master was likely to incur the wrath of the Order of Gothoar. The book had such an important meaning to them that even Vargas did not fully understand it. He did, however, understand that if it was determined that he had been complicit in hiding the book from them, their wrath could fall on him as well.

Vargas sat down in the grass, taking some time to regain his strength. He dared not show his fatigue to Litagus, but now that he had left, Vargas could relax. The more powerful the spell one channeled through the body, the more energy it usually required.

Vargas thought it would be another few months before he saw his master again. In the interim, he needed to make certain everything was as it should be.

After a short break, he walked back to the compound and over to a small shack just outside the doors. The shack had no walls, allowing him to see the man sitting inside.

"Captain Unsinn," Vargas called out.

"Yes, Master Vargas." A man with a slim physique and short brown hair with graying sides stood at attention. He wore hardened leather armor and a sword at his side. He had been the captain of the guards for the three years since Litagus moved his base to Bramblewood Forest.

"Anything to report?"

"Nothing, sir. All is quiet," the captain reported. "The only scheduled event for the day is receiving a food shipment from Deepbriar."

Vargas eyed the surrounding area, looking at several guard posts nearby and noticing some vacant. "Speaking of Deepbriar, where are your men, Captain?"

Captain Unsinn looked at Vargas and, with a sigh, said, "In Deepbriar, sir. I'll pull them back immediately."

"Do not allow your defenses to weaken despite the lack

of threats," Vargas said sternly. "See to it your men remain at their posts and do not go sneaking off to town to fill their guts with ale."

"Yes. Yes, of course," the captain said, breaking his gaze with Vargas.

The compound guards numbered around thirty men, and Vargas knew they often visited the small town to the north for drinks and fun. Aside from subduing the local tribesmen when they had first arrived and fighting off a few wild animals, there had not been any attacks on the compound, giving everyone a false sense of safety. Vargas knew better.

"Double the patrols through the forest for now. Give the men something to do," Vargas said.

"Do you anticipate trouble?"

Vargas considered anything to be possible. The group he had traveled to Ghrakus Castle with was likely killed by the lich or remained locked inside the protective dome. While no one in the group seemed to know about the secret of the red book, he knew that if any survived, they might seek revenge for what he did. He considered a more likely threat would be spies from the Gothoar order who might come looking for the book.

"Just do not let your defenses down. Now issue the orders," Vargas said.

"Right away," Captain Unsinn replied as he walked toward the guard posts.

Vargas watched as the captain issued his orders to the surrounding guards. He scanned the tree line, searching for movement, but found nothing.

Day turned to evening as Davale rode into the small town of Deepbriar. She jumped off her horse and handed the reins to the stable master, who stood just outside the door. Without a word, she turned and headed to the tavern for a meal. She had been riding the entire day and was anxious to settle in for some rest before reporting back.

She strode through the streets and eyed the people around her. Most were common folk going about their business within the small farming community. A number of small houses lined the western side, while fields and pens for farm animals covered the majority. The tavern sat in the middle of the town, surrounded by a few shops that sold leather and metal goods. However, the blacksmith and leather workers had their operations set up on the far end of town near the stables.

Among the various townspeople, she also saw a few guards from the compound standing in the street, boisterous and apparently drunk. *Undisciplined fools.* She gave a disgusted growl as she walked past them.

She opened the door and stepped into the small tavern, which wasn't much more than a log cabin. Inside were six tables in the back, a stairway to the left leading up to a few rentable rooms, and a roaring fire to the right with slabs of sizzling meat hanging over it. All six tables were occupied with a mixture of young farmhands, older merchants, and a group of four compound guards.

The smell of the roasting meat made her stomach rumble in anticipation, and the dust from the trails had readied her throat for some ale. She made her way toward the innkeeper and caught the eyes of a few men as she walked by. She looked down and dusted off her tight leather tunic, shorts, and black, knee-high leather boots. She caught the glances and slid her hand down and over the handle of the dagger she wore on her side.

"Ale and boar," she called out to the innkeeper.

The innkeeper was a stout middle-aged man with a jolly smile sitting in a chair near the fire and watching over the cooking meat. His large, round head was topped with a thick patch of dark curly hair. A freshly healed cut could be seen just above his right eye. As he turned his attention to Davale, his carefree demeanor quickly changed to apprehension.

"R-right away," he said, scurrying up and avoiding eye contact with her.

Davale sat down in the innkeeper's chair with a sigh of relief. Her last mission had taken her farther than usual, but she felt as though she had completed it as ordered. She hoped she could rest for a while before she was sent out again. She leaned back and stretched her arms, untying her hair behind her and combing her fingers through it. Her long black hair had days of road dust mixed in it. She looked forward to enjoying a hot bath when she got back to her room. She tied her hair behind her again and looked deeply into the fire.

"No, please... no." His final pleas drifted back into her mind. She recalled the fear on his face and the desperation in his voice.

"I'll give you whatever you want..." he had pleaded from the floor while she held her dagger to his throat. She had severed the tendons just above his ankles, making it impossible for him to escape.

She smiled as she recalled how she had placed her lips gently next to his ear and whispered, "What I want... is your life," before slowly slicing through his skin.

Her orders were to make his death look like an accident, so she burned down the building to hide his injuries. Job complete.

Her eyes focused on the fire pit as she recalled watching the building blaze. She couldn't help taking pride in her work.

"Here you are," the innkeeper said, handing her a mug of ale and a plate of meat.

She looked up and dug into her pocket for some coin.

"No cost," the inn keeper said and hurried away.

He's so well-mannered today. He must have remembered their last meeting. The cut above his eye had healed nicely.

The flavor of the meat was almost perfect. A bit overcooked for her taste, but the sweet, full-bodied and fruity ale helped make up for it.

As she ate, she looked over at the guards from the compound and wondered if their captain knew they were here. All four wore their leather armor and appeared drunk, but she didn't recognize any of their faces. One of the drunken men noticed her looking at them. He settled into what he must have felt was a flirtatious look, a cocked eyebrow and crooked grin, and started to walk toward her. Two of the other three quickly pulled him back down into his chair, one whispering something in his ear. His face paled and sobered as he shrank back into his seat, avoiding any further eye contact with her.

Davale turned away, uninterested. She had already been warned several times about killing guards and lectured on how expensive they were to replace. Pity. Besides, she needed to finish her meal and report back to Litagus before night's end.

Davale finished her meal and decided to walk the trail back to the compound. Riding horseback with the animal stumbling in the dark was a slow, tedious process. Anyway, she had plenty of time left, and the walk would help with her saddle-sore body.

The forest was pitch black, and the rustle and chirps and scratching of animals surrounded her. The darkness engulfed her, and she felt well within her element. Her eyes quickly adjusted to the dark, and her tight-fitting clothes allowed her quicker movement and less material for someone to grab onto in a fight. She did not fear attack since the savages that inhabited the forest had an agreement with Litagus and his men. Litagus protected the area and shared his food and supplies with them, and in return, the savages kept unwanted guests out of the forest. The only real threat was from wild animals, but unfortunately, that happened rarely anymore, giving her little opportunity to hone her skills. She walked the trail with her hand on her dagger simply out of habit.

As she reached the compound, a guard rushed from his post to confront her, his sword at the ready. Once he recognized her, he saluted and returned to his post. The guards were not usually so attentive, especially at this time of night. In the past, it wasn't uncommon for her to approach the compound completely undetected. She wondered why they were on such high alert. Had something happened? Had she missed something fun and potentially bloody?

She wasted no time in getting to Litagus's study. She didn't see his assistant anywhere, so she knocked on the door.

"Go away," Litagus's voice commanded from within.

"It's Davale," she replied through the door.

"Come," Litagus said, his harsh tone softening.

Davale opened the door into a large room. Three long tables were spread out across it, each containing large piles of books. The stale air carried a number of odors emanating from the components lying open on the tables and around the room. Among them she saw incense, various plants, mushrooms, jars of blood, several gemstones, and what appeared to be the internal organs of large animals. She did not know much about spellcasting and its rules, but she knew enough to know these components were for mage spells and had nothing to do with the powers of the temple.

Litagus looked up from a smaller table where he was scribbling across a piece of parchment.

"Well, is it done?" he asked her.

"He breathes no more."

Satisfaction flashed over Litagus's pale and tightly drawn face. "Well done. Rest now," he said to her before resuming his writing.

"Did something happen in my absence?" she asked.

"No," Litagus said without looking up from his writing.

"The guards seemed to be on alert,"

"Pay them no attention."

"Is there anything else you need?" She hoped Litagus would allow her a break from the incessant missions.

Litagus looked up. "In two months, I need you to visit Dark Hills. Until that time, I only have a few missions for you, obtaining some unique materials I need. However, for the next few days, you should rest. You have served me well."

"Thank you, High Priest," Davale said, walking back out of the room.

She closed her eyes and took a deep breath, smiling. *Ah, to be free to enjoy the next few days.*

Vargas awoke to the sound of knocking on his door. Early morning light barely crept through the window covering, and he bristled that someone would interrupt his sleep while he was still recovering from channeling the spell the day before.

"What is it?" Vargas snapped.

"It's Bucomus. The high priest would like to see you right away," Litagus's assistant said on the other side of the door.

"Yes. I will be right there," Vargas replied. He dressed quickly and rushed upstairs to his master's chambers.

The door stood open with Bucomus standing beside it. He was a short man, with short dark hair streaked with gray, and wearing simple gray robes.

Vargas walked inside. "High Priest, what can I do for you?" He noticed there were more jars of matter and piles of dried vegetation spread around the room than in his previous visit.

Litagus stood at one of the tables, straightening the books into separate stacks.

"I have just received news that the high priest in Blackridge has passed away."

"That's unfortunate. What happened?"

"I heard it was an accident."

"That makes the sixth high priest to die in the past seven

months," Vargas pondered. "Are you concerned for your own safety?"

"I need you to visit the Blackridge temple and spread the word of my name and our work here, just as you have done before. Explain they will be considered under my protection there in Blackridge," Litagus said, leaving Vargas's questioned unanswered.

"Yes, High Priest. Shall I leave right away?"

Litagus paused briefly. "In two days. We do not want to appear insensitive to the previous high priest's death. Allow them the opportunity to mourn. However, prepare now and turn your duties over to Davale before you depart."

"I will do so," Vargas said with a bow.

"One more thing. Speak to the Blackridge temple of a great gathering in the Dark Hills temple two months from now, on the eve of the full moon. Tell them it is Gothoar's will for everyone to attend. Revisit the other temples and tell them the same."

"Yes, High Priest. What of the high priest of the Dark Hills temple? Shall we send word for him to secure himself?"

Litagus looked up from a pile of books. His eyes narrowed. "Rest assured that I shall see to that myself."

"You and he are the only remaining high priests of our order. Should I reinforce our men for your safety?"

"It wouldn't hurt to bolster our defenses," Litagus said half-heartedly, waving Vargas away with his hand.

Vargas shut the door and returned to his room. He found it telling that Davale had returned to the compound at the same time that news of the death of Blackridge's high priest had arrived. Vargas had suspected Litagus had been killing the other high priests, and now he deduced that Davale had been his tool. The reasoning was not yet clear, but he dared not question Litagus out of fear for his own safety. He recalled just the day before how his Desolation spell had little effect on the high priest. It would be safer to assume that all his spells would be useless against him.

With an order-wide meeting planned in just two months at the Dark Hills temple, Vargas could assume the last surviving high priest aside from Litagus did not have long to live. He only had two months to answer his burning question: what was the connection between the red book and Litagus being the only high priest of the Order of Gothoar?

Chapter 8

The next morning, Rathen had the group back on the road with just a quick meal. Thack continued scouting while Bulo rode in the lead. Rathen fell in line with his horse as Magom rode up. Rathen noticed something out of place.

"Magom, stop your steed," Rathen shouted.

The lich stopped as Rathen dismounted. Pulling his sword, Rathen cut a large string of intestine that snaked from the horse's underbelly and dragged behind for a long stretch of road. The beast was in a sad state of decay; several chunks of rotting meat had dropped to the ground, while the exposed ribs held most of the internal organs in place. Insects buzzed around the carcass in dark little clouds.

Rathen wiped his blade clean and climbed back on his steed.

"We need to do something about your horse," Rathen told the lich, covering his nose.

Magom remained silent.

As the day passed, a dull ache crept up Rathen's backside from the constant jostling of his saddle. The heat of the sun on the open road once again added to his discomfort. He saw trees in the distance that would offer a much-welcomed relief from the hot afternoon.

Soon the group entered a dense forest. The trees stood tall and covered the sky with their thick green canopy. The air grew cool, and the trail darkened until only a few brilliant rays of sunshine broke through the distant canopy above. The sound of birds, the smell of dampness, and the scent of the wildflowers eased Rathen's nerves. Nothing felt out of place, although the lush density cut their visibility.

The trail had started wide from the forest's entrance but soon grew narrow, forcing them to ride in single file. Rathen recalled from his scouting trip that these trees stretched on for almost three days. The first campsite he had planned was just off the trail, within the remnants of an old building. The remaining foundation had kept the ground mostly clear from the undergrowth. The challenge would be finding it before nightfall.

As Rathen and the lich rode deeper into the forest, the sounds of the birds ceased as if they sensed something unnatural approaching. Rathen glanced behind him. The cold, dead eyes of Magom's steed caught his glance. He looked up to Magom's robed figure.

"Something… troubles you?" Magom asked without moving.

"No, it's nothing," Rathen said. "Just uneasy not being able to see around us well. Do you sense any threats out in those trees?"

"Only birds, deer, and a few boars resting within the undergrowth."

"It might be a good idea to do some hunting tonight.

Fresh meat would do us all some good," Rathen said, giving notice to the rumble of his stomach.

Magom sat silently.

Rathen smiled at himself, having momentarily forgotten Magom would not find satisfaction in a good meal before sleep. The lich was so far from being human Rathen found it difficult to relate to him. Perhaps riding in silence wasn't so bad after all.

Thack soon rode back to them, carefully passing each rider in the narrow trail. His half-orc face bore a look of confusion.

"What is it?" Rathen asked.

"I think we already arrived." Thack's eyes glanced nervously at the dead horse and its state of continued deterioration.

"That can't be right. There's still plenty of travel time before nightfall," Rathen said.

Thack shrugged. "It is just how you described it. An old stone foundation roughly ten steps off the path creating a small clearing."

Rathen smiled and nodded. "Well then, well done. This is my mistake."

Thack struggled to turn his horse on the narrow path in front of Rathen. "Perhaps some rest and a good night's sleep will do us all good," he said.

"Tell the others. Prepare the camp."

Thack hesitated; his eyes shifted to the lich and his steed.

"We'll hide this… beast somewhere out of smell range," Rathen said.

Thack nodded and rode back up front.

When the rest of the group stopped up ahead, Rathen

searched for a suitable place for Magom to hide the dead horse—hidden from the path and upwind from the camp.

Walking into the campsite, Rathen saw the other members had unpacked and were setting up their bedding. Rathen surveyed the area carefully, looking at the clearing and the stone foundation underneath. The western side of the foundation had the ruins of an old building, forgotten and allowed to decay. The walls would be welcome shelter for camp, but the scattered stones and debris on its floor would not provide suitable comfort.

No mistake about it, this was the site Rathen had selected. Without being able to see the sky overhead, he had trouble determining the time of day, but he guessed that even if they took time to catch food, cook it, and eat it, it would only just be getting dark. Hopefully, today's shorter ride wouldn't hurt their timing to meet the druid.

As usual, Caswen and Dryn prepared their bedding close to each other with Marduke not far away. Bandark, Garrick, and Rendrak took the other corner, clearing off rubble to lay their bedding in a circle. Bulo and Thack prepared their bedding closest to the path, creating a barrier of protection for the rest of the group.

"Bulo, why don't you take a bow and hunt for us?" Rathen asked loud enough to be heard by everyone.

"I'll help him track," Thack said.

Bulo smiled. "I'll do what I can. But we might be eating the slowest animal out there. My aim isn't what it once was."

Before Rathen could reply, Dryn spoke up. "I'll go," she said, grabbing her bow. "I think Thack and I will do just fine together." Dryn flashed a look back at her sister, who protested with her eyes.

"Alright. Get to it. But be careful out there," Rathen said. "We'll build a fire so it will be easier to find your way back."

Dryn smiled at Caswen as she turned to leave with Thack. Caswen's look of disapproval almost made Dryn laugh out loud. She knew the last thing her sister would want her to do would be to talk to Thack about her. But Dryn knew this was a great opportunity to learn more about the man her sister was so keen on.

Dryn kept her smile as she inspected her arrows. This hunt should be enjoyable. She held confidence in her ability with the bow, but the dense trees would be a challenge. Her training had only been in an open field, but she remained determined to prove her worth to the group, and more importantly, to Marduke.

They headed out. Dryn eyed Thack as he walked in front of her. He used his axe to cut a small path as he went. "You're not clearing that path for me because I'm a woman, are you?" Dryn asked.

Thack glanced back at her nervously.

"I'm not my sister. I can make it through on my own."

"Right," Thack responded with a nod. He stopped cutting and began maneuvering gracefully over the fallen trees and through the underbrush.

Impressed by how such a large man could be so nimble, Dryn soon found herself struggling to keep up with him. But she was determined not to fall behind.

Thack led her farther away from camp than she thought necessary. But as she traveled deeper into the trees, animals could be heard again. It occurred to her around the camp had been strangely silent, as if something spooked them. It didn't take her long to connect the undead creature that traveled with the group and the reaction of the wildlife around them.

Thack stopped ahead in the trees and raised his axe. His eyes narrowed at something through the dense vegetation. Dryn slowly approached his location, peering through the trees. A large buck grazed off in the distance. The large antlers told her this was a full-grown male. The meat this animal would provide for the group would make up for taking its life.

Thack pointed at her and then at the buck.

She silently drew an arrow and notched it. Slowly, she pulled back on the string. Just like Marduke had taught her, she took two breaths to calm herself and then held the third in her chest. She aimed for a point between the buck's shoulder blades. As the buck raised its head, she loosed her arrow. It felt solid. But before the arrow reached the buck, it passed under a tree, hitting a small branch and glancing off. A complete miss. The buck ran off, hearing the arrow hit the nearby brush.

Dryn took a deep breath and slowly let it out. Obviously, she needed more training in such confined areas.

"It's alright. These are dense trees, and there're bound to be more game out here," Thack said, offering a smile.

Dryn smiled back, noting his kindness. Marduke was a stern teacher and would always make her study her mistakes. She would spend hours answering his questions on why she made the choices she did. A waste of her time. Better to simply try again, as Thack now suggested.

Dryn watched as Thack tracked deeper into the dense

trees until he found a small animal trail. The air grew cooler, and the forest floor became covered in moss. Dryn had to concentrate on her steps for threat of slipping.

Again, Thack stopped and looked intently into the trees. He scanned the area carefully and looked down both directions of the trail. It even appeared to Dryn that the half-orc was smelling the air.

Thack turned and smiled as he started down the western trail. Soon, the sound of movement had Thack still again. He motioned for her to stay as he silently walked into the brush. He soon returned, shook his head, and continued down the trail.

Dryn grew anxious for a kill. She wanted to get back to camp and to her sister. She felt compelled to see the animal Thack had refused to kill. As she moved into the brush he had entered, she ignored his look of disapproval.

Moving the brush from her view, Dryn saw a full-grown male boar digging in the dirt not far from her. The large animal was almost waist-high, with large tusks and a dark brown hide.

Dryn pulled herself back out of the brush and looked back up at Thack. She smiled. Harvesting this boar would be the end of a great hunt. She drew an arrow and looked back at Thack.

Thack shook his head, gesturing with his hand urging her to move farther down the path.

What's the problem? She would just kill this boar and take it back to camp. They had been gone too long already. Leaving Thack standing in the trail, Dryn slipped quietly into the brush. She raised her bow and pulled the arrow back as far as she could. The animal's hide looked thick enough to require a strong pull. The boar continued to dig and snort, oblivious to her presence. She calmed her breathing despite her heart beating almost out of her chest. She loosed her arrow when the animal turned, exposing its neck.

The arrow hit its mark, but the boar's hide proved thicker than she had thought. The animal squealed, now wounded and more dangerous than ever. It tossed its head, grunted loudly, spied her, and charged.

Dryn panicked. She prepared another arrow even as she backed out of the brush trying to gain distance. As she passed the trail, she slipped on the mossy ground, falling on her back. Just as the boar broke through the brush, she got off another shot. The arrow glanced off the boar's head. Dryn frantically reached for the dagger on her belt and held it out in front of her. She prepared for the animal's impact and just hoped her dagger could pierce its hide.

Just before its tusks impaled her, Thack's axe flew through the air and collided into the animal's side. The boar toppled over. It laid there squealing in pain as blood gushed from a massive wound.

Dryn gripped her dagger and stared at the boar until it went silent. She took several long breaths and held the last, slowly letting it out.

Thack walked up. Placing his foot on the boar, he pried his axe from its body.

"Thanks… for that," Dryn said, sheathing her dagger.

Thack nodded but kept his eyes on the boar. Dryn stood up, dusting herself off. She hoped Thack wouldn't mention this to the others. Both Marduke and Caswen already thought of her as too impetuous.

Thack bent down next to the boar and unpacked several

bandages from his belt. He began to wrap them around the animal's wound.

"It's dead. You're not going to save it now," Dryn sneered.

Thack remained silent until the boar was bound and the bleeding contained.

Dryn sighed. "What are you doing?"

Thack stood and handed her his axe. "I cannot carry both."

Dryn took the axe in both hands. It proved surprisingly heavy.

Thack bent down and used his one arm to pull the boar onto his shoulder. "The bandages will stop me from tracking the blood all the way back to camp. If not, we will have all sorts of predators following us."

Dryn nodded. That made a lot of sense. Thack was proving more resourceful that she had given him credit for.

As Thack started the walk back to camp with the large animal over his shoulders, Dryn just had to ask, "Why didn't you want to kill the boar at first? You were more than capable."

Thack stopped and turned. "It is an Altarian boar. Arrows have little effect on its thick hide."

"I see," Dryn said, and she waited for Thack to start walking again. But he kept his gaze on her.

"Also, the ground is poor for stable footing, and the surrounding brush greatly cut visibility. The kill was a greater risk than it needed to be." Thack turned and continued walking.

Dryn sighed again. She still had a lot to learn about being outside the temple.

"A warrior must take everything into consideration in preparation for battle," Thack said as they walked.

"I understand," Dryn replied in the same tone she had used the many times Marduke had scolded her for her mistakes.

Dryn had no difficulty following Thack back to camp now. The weight of the boar on his shoulders slowed him considerably. As the sounds of the animals started to fade Dryn knew they were close to camp. The undead monster seemed to make everything as uneasy as it made her feel. Rightly so; it was a creature straight out of her nightmares.

Shifting her thoughts back on her sister, Dryn knew she only had a short time to ask Thack some questions. "Did you know my sister is striving to be high priest?"

"I... know," Thack answered without slowing. However, the pause between his words showed his exhaustion.

The boar weighed so much that Dryn knew she couldn't even start to carry it over her shoulders, even with her two arms. "Then you understand she doesn't need any unnecessary distractions."

Thack stopped momentarily and then continued walking. "I understand. But isn't that her choice?"

"Listen, I'm her sister. I've looked after her my whole life," Dryn spoke with the passion she felt in her heart.

Thack nodded. "This is because of what I am...?"

"Of course, it is," Dryn replied. *How could this man be so thick?*

Thack stopped and turned toward her. She read the fatigue on his face, but his eyes were full of sorrow. "I know I am not worthy of someone like her. But there's nothing I can do about my heritage."

"What? It has nothing to do about your heritage."

Thack cocked his head. "It doesn't?"

"No man is worthy of my sister. You're a man, and men are often short-sighted in their ambitions with relationships."

Thack's face slowly broke into a smile. He turned back and continued walking. "I assure you, my intentions are just." Thack glanced back behind him. "You both are special women."

Dryn nodded. She remained skeptical of his true motives, but his words about her and her sister being special caught her by surprise. While in the temple, Marduke never failed to show his support for her and Caswen, Dryn always felt as if she were a burden on the temple. She thought Caswen felt the same.

Up ahead, through the shade of the forest, she could see the light of the campfire. She had finished her conversation just in time.

Rathen let out a sigh of disbelief when he saw Thack emerging from the trees with a large Altarian boar over his shoulders. Had Thack overdone it this time?

"Now that's a meal," Bulo said as both Thack and Dryn walked into camp.

"Don't you think that's a bit much?" Rathen asked.

Dryn started to speak, but Thack interrupted. "Sorry... not my best choice." He tossed the boar from his shoulder next to the small fire. "I wanted to provide a great meal tonight."

Rathen saw Dryn flash Thack a look of surprise that turned to guilt. Thack must be covering for her. Rathen decided to let it go. "Bulo, better make a bigger fire." Rathen looked around the camp. Rendrak and Garrick remained sitting with Bandark, carrying on a discussion between them in what must be their home language. Caswen and Marduke continued looking over the ruins. Magom stood on the far edge of camp near the trees, not moving, not speaking. Rathen knew no one else was going to offer to help prepare dinner, so he helped Bulo widen the fire and prepare the boar. He smiled when he saw Dryn assisting by taking the wrappings off it.

"Dryn, come look at this," Caswen shouted from within the ruins on the west side of camp.

Dryn stood up from the boar and nodded at Rathen as if uncertain of leaving her chores. "What is it?"

Rathen had inspected the ruins in his previous trip and hadn't found anything worth noting. But something in Caswen's voice sounded dire. He nodded to Dryn and followed her, curious if whatever piqued Caswen's interest posed a risk. Had he missed something?

"Look at this statue," Caswen said, running her fingers down the side of a moss-covered stone figure that had broken into several pieces.

Behind her, Marduke held a torch he'd made from the branches burning in the campfire. He had tied some type of cloth to the end, making it more luminous.

"What is it?" Dryn asked, bending down to join her sister.

"We've been looking around these ruins while you were gone and discovered it was once a temple."

"And..." Dryn coaxed, inching closer to Caswen.

"Look at the shape of the statue, the face. The symbol carved in the base in mostly missing, but look here." Caswen traced an outline of one large circle and then a faint impression of a circle connecting. "Here, there are two circles. And here. In the middle, you can just make out the third."

Dryn shot up from her kneeling position. "The Order of Horandir?"

At the mention of the name, Marduke let out a deep grumble.

"How? Why?" Dryn asked.

Rathen stood in confusion but waited to hear the conversation.

Caswen stood up and looked over the ruins. "They must have built a small temple here for some reason."

"Not so small," Marduke spoke. "These two foundations were one building. Their temples had a different shape than ours."

Rathen looked over the entire area, attempting to see how large the building would have been. He started to speak but sensed the hush that had fallen over the three, as if they were reliving a past time in unison. He wanted to give them time.

Dryn stood and then helped her sister. Caswen carefully wiped the dirt from her white robes. They walked back over to the camp in silence. Marduke threw the torch in the now much larger campfire. Bulo and Thack had the boar strung up on a large branch over the fire. The smell of the meat was already making Rathen's stomach growl in anticipation.

Rathen, Dryn, Caswen, and Marduke sat by the fire and watched Bulo and Thack periodically rotate the boar. The flesh seared as the juices ran down, dripping into the eager flames with a sizzle. Rathen enjoyed the anticipation so much he considered placing such a pit within the tavern back in Tobermoar for the patrons. No guest would fail to order a meal with their ale with such aromas filling the air. Better yet, maybe he would build a new tavern and center a pit in the meal area. That is, if he returned to the innkeeper life. His mind hadn't been made up yet, and the lich didn't make it any easier with his urgings for Rathen to be a leader of warriors.

Rathen glanced back over to Bandark and his friends, still engrossed in their discussion. Perhaps they planned what to do with the book when they returned to their world. Or maybe they plotted the battles that would take place to save their kingdom. Rathen shook his head. He had to admit the thought of battles and war made his blood burn again. To once again taste victory on the battlefield would put life back into him. But… perhaps his time was over. Many years had passed since then, and such battles were better left to the young.

"Rathen, let's dish it out," Bulo said, cutting into the boar with his knife. The outer portions were cooked sufficiently and carved off easily, ready to enjoy. Bulo left the inner layers to roast as they ate.

Rathen nodded with a smile. "Bandark, let's eat," he called out to the three. Rathen glanced over to where Magom stood; only his eyes could be seen in the darkness. Even if the lich wasn't interested in food, Rathen hoped something would bring him into the group.

The group ate generous portions of the succulent meat, dark-grained bread, and fruit they brought with them. Rathen enjoyed ale with the meal but limited himself to remain sharp for his night sentry duty. Bulo showed no such concern, drinking his way into a blissful evening as if they were back at the tavern. Rathen turned to Bandark, expecting him to continue his conversation about the different worlds and the deities. Soon other members did the same, but the look on the tall man's face suggested his somber mood.

"Bandark, tell us more of your tales," Bulo said, raising his ale.

Rathen read the hesitation on Bandark's face. Something important was on his mind, and his face showed he preferred not to talk. "Bandark has spoken for the past two evenings. Perhaps he's due for a break."

"Fair enough," Bulo said, nodding his head. "We can find something else to talk about." Bulo's smiling face looked around, but no one spoke up. "Alright, we can all guess what this place used to be," Bulo said, looking over the foundation.

"It was a temple," Dryn said.

"That's cheating," Bulo said with a laugh. "How do you know?"

"It was a temple of Horandir. We found their symbol within the ruins. Their order once sought to control these lands."

"Now that sounds like a tale," Bulo said, looking over to Rathen.

Rathen shook his head, knowing the subject was sensitive even if Dryn was willing to talk about it.

"The followers of Horandir besieged our order for five years, killing our members and destroying our temples," Dryn continued. "They felt no remorse in the blood they shed."

Thack frowned. "What would make temples war on each other? Were they dark clerics?"

"Greed," Dryn spoke up. "They tried to expand and

convert other followers. When they came into our territory, we welcomed them as brothers and sisters. But they returned our kindness by raising weapons against us."

"So their beliefs differed from your own then?" Bulo asked.

Caswen shook her head. A hint of sorrow stirred within her eyes. "They were much like our order, with their own healers and protectors. However, the high priests in their order believed strongly that Horandir was the superior deity… the only deity worthy of worship. Their primary mission was to convert others… or kill them as enemies of the temple."

Rathen shook his head. "Doesn't sound anything like your order. It stinks of arrogance and an evil sense of entitlement." Rathen knew too well what men in power were capable of. The land and gold they took in the name of what was right, only to fill their own pockets with the riches from their dark deeds. King Delvant's reign fell to the same weaknesses of men.

"I take it they didn't last in this area?" Bulo asked.

Caswen looked up to Marduke. He nodded, and Caswen continued, "Our order fought the followers of Horandir in a five-year battle that left so many dead. We defeated their forces, and they finally withdrew. Marduke in his youth fought for many of those years." Caswen bowed her head. "It was our darkest period, and we still live with the pain of taking the lives of so many people we could have considered an extension of our family. Thandrall teaches us that everyone can find their way back to a better path through redemption. One must set aside their material obsessions and thirst for power, for we all originate from the same beginning and breathe the same air. Life is precious, just as every single one of us are. We could not understand why they were so murderous."

As Caswen continued to talk, Rathen noticed the tension in Marduke and knew the pain he must still carry of that time. "Does this temple continue to pose a threat?"

Caswen shook her head. "No. And any evidence remaining of their presence here has been destroyed. This place must have never been discovered. Dryn, see that we mention this to Lazlo upon our return."

"What were the wars like, Marduke?" Bulo asked.

Rathen grew worried Bulo's careless words might offend the old temple warrior. "Bulo, perhaps that's a conversation for back at the tavern."

Marduke remained silent.

Bulo continued to push. "Come, talk. We old warriors surely have plenty of tales to tell around the fire amongst friends."

"Marduke carries a heavy burden from that time," Caswen spoke. "We all do."

"I understand." Bulo spoke in good spirits. "I feel the same from back in my gladiator days. You can speak freely."

Marduke didn't speak, but everyone but Bulo could feel the tension building like a volcano ready to explode.

After an uncomfortable silence, Bulo started to speak, but Marduke cut him off.

"Enough! I do not glorify death." Marduke stood, tossing his remaining food on the ground. He picked up his sword and stormed off into the trees, growling as he went.

Again, the group hushed. Bulo looked up, confused. "I didn't mean…" he started.

"Please do not mind Marduke," Caswen said. "He meant no offense to anyone."

Rathen stood. "It's we who should apologize. A warrior's past is his own. He need not share it with anyone." Rathen flashed Bulo a nod. Bulo returned it.

Rathen let everyone know when their sentry duty would be and encouraged them all to sleep early. As Thack carved and packed the rest of the boar, Caswen sat next to him and they talked quietly.

Rathen settled into his bedding and glanced around but didn't see Marduke. He must be out in the trees somewhere cooling off. Rathen only hoped he would return to carry out his sentry duty near morning. If not, Bandark would wake Rathen for a second watch.

Rathen didn't need to look toward Magom. He felt the lich's presence like a chilled pocket of air that swirled silently just outside their group. He could grasp, though not justify, the greed that drove Magom to his state of unhumanity. Now Rathen wondered how those motives could drive priests and healers and protectors to war on each other in the name of their gods. He fell asleep wondering what other forces of mankind's deeply selfish nature posed yet further dangers to his small band.

Chapter 9

Bulo sat on a rock on the edge of camp as the group slept. Over half his night sentry still remained, but the ale he drank during his meal made him sleepy. His eyes fluttered and his head dropped forward suddenly, jolting him awake. He sat up, shaking the sleepiness from his head, and repositioned himself on the rock away from the slippery moss that threatened to send him sliding off. The weight of his axe on his legs made them numb. Bulo placed the axe head on the ground and leaned the handle against the stone. The moisture in the night air made all his joints ache. His thoughts drifted back to his inn back in Tobermoar, and he imagined how great it would be to rest within its warmth and comfort.

The sound of brush moving in the distance forced Bulo to focus his vision into the darkness. Mist rose from the ground, obscuring his comrades' sleeping forms, and beyond the light of the campfire, nothing could be seen. Bulo stood up, ignoring the ache in his legs, and squinted. He picked up his axe and held it ready. It might have just been an animal, but he'd better be prepared. Yet he couldn't recall seeing or hearing any animal within camp range, no doubt due to the presence of Magom or that decaying carcass he rode.

The sound came again, and soon a large silhouette came into the light. Bulo raised his axe and started to yell out to his sleeping companions when a voice called out, "It's Marduke."

Bulo held his stance until Marduke's face came into view, then lowered his weapon. "You shouldn't sneak up on a man like that," Bulo said, letting out a sigh.

Marduke approached Bulo and stood. Bulo noticed he carried his sword at his side.

"Can we talk?" Marduke asked, his voice gentle.

"Of course," Bulo replied, waving his hand to the rock behind him. He wasn't certain what Marduke wanted to talk about, but he wasn't in the mood for a temple lecture about life and death.

"I wanted to apologize for earlier." Marduke bowed his head.

"It's fine," Bulo said, relieved.

"No. I shouldn't have lost my temper," Marduke started as he sat down on the rock next to Bulo. "It's just that seeing the symbol of the temple of Horandir… it ripped open scars from long ago."

Bulo turned to Marduke with a smile. From his years as an innkeeper, he recognized the sound of a man who needed to talk. If only he had an ale to serve Marduke, he would feel right at home. "I can understand. I meant no ill toward you either. I only wanted to share stories."

Marduke nodded. He leaned his sword against the rock and cupped his hands on his lap. "My younger years were a constant struggle." Marduke's gaze remained on the ground in front of him.

"I can relate," Bulo started. "I never chose to fight, but neither could I refuse."

Marduke nodded again. "When the fighting ended, the nightmares never ceased. My fifty-two years in this world have been a continuous battle… in more ways than one."

"What age were you pulled into battle?"

Marduke paused, but his gaze never shifted. "I was very young. Our village was small and poor. We shared our food with those in need and never fought to increase our land. But we never stopped fighting to keep it, from either dominating warlords or pillaging bandits. We vowed to keep the lands our forefathers had tended many years before. When I was eight years old, my father accompanied the men in the village for a preemptive attack on a group of bandits in the area. The bandits had been gathering in the hills not far from us, and we knew a fight would be unavoidable." Marduke paused and looked up into the dark canopy of the forest.

"What happened? Did he make it back?"

"He did. But the bandits revealed their larger plan to conquer the lands within the valley, and that included our village."

"Motherless scum, the lot of them," Bulo growled. He had had his own run-in with the sort. With men bent on death and destruction, the stories never ended well.

"My father and our best fighters left for their distant base to either wipe them out or to put the fear of our strength into them so they would not invade. However, a year passed and only a few men returned."

"Your father?"

Marduke shook his head. He picked up his sword and

held it out. "Only his sword came home… He was lost."

Bulo recalled Marduke's silence when he had asked about the sword back at the Andar temple. "I'm sorry… I didn't know."

"I learned how to fight and defended our village from the age of twelve. We had lost many to the bandit base attack, not just my father. Our young and even our women had to learn to use a sword and bow."

"Like Dryn," Bulo said.

Marduke nodded. "I knew she would make a strong fighter, but the temple had rules. Makes no difference to me if she's a man or woman. We all must learn to fight to protect ourselves and others."

"Indeed." Bulo licked his lips, eager for an ale. "So, what made you join the temple?"

"My death…" Marduke said.

"What?" Bulo said loudly. "That can't be. You're here now."

"I grew as a village warrior and defended it from many threats. We had a score of wild wolves attack one time when the area grew dry and prey became harder to find. We quelled them. But when I turned twenty, a neighboring kingdom invited us to join their domain."

"That offered protection?" Bulo asked, attempting to bring out more of the story.

"We declined since we wanted neither their protection nor their taxes, knowing once within their rule, those taxes could increase unfettered. Our refusal brought a month-long battle. With their superior numbers and gear, our village was destroyed. Men, women, and children were all slaughtered." Marduke slumped forward on the rock.

"But you survived."

Marduke shook his head. "I fought with all the fury I had that day. With this very sword. I couldn't count how many lives I took. My wife stood by my side, her blade just as bloodied as mine."

"You were married?"

Marduke nodded. "Quille was her name. My love. And the mother of my daughter who was also taken from this world that day. Her name was Fallonbrade." Marduke's voice began to break.

Bulo lowered his head and remained silent.

"Even after my wife and daughter were slain... I continued. But my strength couldn't outlast their numbers. I wanted to make them pay for destroying our village... my family. Defeated and dying, I lay on the battlefield bleeding from many wounds. I couldn't move my body other than turn my head to see the bodies and destruction. I stared up at the sky and through the blood in my eyes... I watched the ravens circling above as they descended lower and lower to feast on the dead. I cursed my defeat and mourned my losses: my family, my past, and my future. My life had been taken from me at just twenty years."

"That's not the ending. I mean... you're here," Bulo said, leaning forward.

"As I lay on the ground, my body grew numb. I felt life draining from me. I was powerless to stop my end. I saw a young priest dressed in white robes walking the battle site. In my youth, I thought the white-robed figure was a taker of souls, here to claim the dying. As he passed, our eyes met and he stopped. He knelt down and asked if I wanted to be saved. I used the last of my strength to shake my head. I didn't want to live in a world where my wife and daughter no longer were. I wanted to be with them… with my people. I wanted to die. To fade away from this life and shed my fear and anger." Marduke bowed his head deeply. "I wanted to give up."

Bulo shifted but didn't speak.

"The priest smiled at me warmly. He began to tell me about his temple and the Order of Thandrall. He spoke softly, and his eyes shined with a kindness that I'd never seen. This young man took his time to talk to a dying man, yet showed so much compassion. I was captivated. He went on to explain the tenants of Thandrall and how a man could find redemption and acceptance. The warm feeling of hope coursed through my cold body. From that day, I decided to be a force of good… It was also a way I could bring honor to the memory of my family as well as redeem myself for all the blood I had shed and the lives I had taken. He healed my wounds and took me back to his temple, where I stayed and learned their ways. I devoted my life to the temple and took my place as a protector."

Bulo smiled. "You endured so much, yet your tragedy led you to fulfillment."

Marduke turned toward Bulo. "Until the Order of Horandir came."

Bulo nodded, urging him to continue.

"Horandir entered the area where Thandrall's followers had settled and attempted to convert us. We refused, ignoring their threats of bloodshed. How could the followers of such a holy deity bring themselves to take life so cherished? Well, that's what we thought. We stayed true to Thandrall and refused Horandir, but the decision was met with a five-year battle. It became known to the local kingdoms and people as the Battle of the Holies. We were mocked for fighting between ourselves, but we didn't have a choice. I fought alongside our warriors and priests to protect ourselves from Horandir. I felt as if I had betrayed myself… for taking lives again after my rebirth on the battlefield in my village."

"I can understand," Bulo said. "My life is not so much different. Violence is often a road that must be followed, willingly or not."

Marduke nodded. "I hated myself for taking the lives of their priests and protectors. They were no different than me."

"But you never gave up."

"No," Marduke said. "But when the fighting was over, I once again questioned my purpose. I couldn't just be a tool of death. I needed to contribute to the goodness I saw around me. When Caswen and Dryn were placed on our temple steps… I felt a connection to them. Maybe it was just the timing, but I needed to give them something… to provide them something. Perhaps, in my selfish mind, they helped soothe the devastating pain I continued to feel from losing my own daughter so long ago."

"You've done a fine job of raising the two," Bulo said, offering a smile. "Something to be very proud of."

Marduke nodded, wiping his eyes with his forearm. "I had Horandir in my thoughts, and when you spoke at camp about hearing the stories, my mind filled with the memories of that time… and the rage."

"I only wanted to talk," Bulo said. "I should have known my place. By the way you attacked Magom back at the barn,

I could tell you were a formidable warrior."

Marduke shifted his position on the rock. "Yes, well… my anger and fear clouded my mind then too. During my years at the temple, we fought many necromancers and the undead armies they created. I was told by the high priest a necromancer traveled with your group, but I had not expected to see a lich."

"Anyone would feel the same," Bulo said, nodding. "Sometimes I think we are crazy to bring him with us. But Rathen knows best, and he has my complete support."

"Rathen seems like a noble man, and perhaps this lich can find the redemption he seeks. But tell me of you. I feel we are close in years."

Bulo smiled, appreciating Marduke's interest. "I am forty-nine this year, so yes, we are close. When I was fourteen, I was thrown into the gladiator arena as a slave, tasked with hauling off the bloodied remains of the defeated. Overcome with fear, I thought I would soon die."

"Those arenas are barbaric."

"Indeed they were. We were not much more than caged animals. I had my first fight at age seventeen and nearly died. I became plagued with nightmares of my head being severed from my body. I knew it was just a matter of time before a more experienced gladiator killed me. The night before my second fight, I couldn't sleep from the nightmares. Over and over, my head was cut from my body. But just hours before the fight, I decided to use those nightmares to my advantage. If they were capable of stealing my sleep and nerves, then I could do the same to others. I studied the opponent's moves in my next dream to copy them, steeling myself to act the same.

"The next day, I won the fight and then cut off the head of my opponent and held it up high for the crowd to see. The blood dripped down, covering my head and upper body. I become known to the spectators and to the other gladiators as 'Bulo the Beheader.' I was often told that before facing me, other gladiators suffered nightmares of their heads being severed by me. It worked… I guess."

Marduke nodded and smiled the first smile Bulo saw from the old warrior.

"I know it was barbaric, and I can't help but look back on those days in shame. But the fame and prestige that came with the performance allowed me to secure my freedom from the arena. My owner grew rich on my success, and before his death, he let me fight for my freedom. When I won, I entered the service of a nearby kingdom as a soldier. Since fighting is what I knew best, it just made sense. Rathen served there as captain, but it wasn't until we both ended up in a small town in the middle of nowhere that we become friends."

"It is true. We old warriors have similar stories," Marduke said. "But what of your childhood? What of your parents?"

Bulo took a deep breath. This wasn't a story he cared to share. He'd never told anyone, not even Rathen. Running home as a child to see his farmhouse in flames, screaming for his parents, seeing his older brother's body trampled by the horses of the men who had killed them all—the memory had seared his brain. A powerful landowner squabbling with the owner of Bulo's family's fields had targeted his family as expendable pawns in their land grab. It became a story he carried like a locked, heavy box chained to his soul. But how could he stay silent after Marduke had shared his early misfortunes?

Bulo swallowed and said simply, "I too lost my family, but as a child. Alone and too young for use by the landowner where my family had farmed, I was sold, first as a mine slave and then to the arena." He shrugged. "My bulk and strength became my only salvation."

"I can relate to your loss. And you yourself have become something greater for enduring difficult times."

Bulo nodded. He didn't have anything else to say. The memories of his family were ones he continued to drink away. "Well, you have Caswen and Dryn to look after, so that must be nice to witness."

"It is," Marduke said. "But tell me, what good are we warriors when we are too old to fight?"

"I don't see it that way," Bulo said, raising his voice. "We have been through so much and have carved paths in this life from blood and bone. Now, in our later years, we are due a little peace. A life of leisure where we aren't looking over our shoulders."

Marduke smiled and raised his head to the air, closing his eyes. "Perhaps you're right. But as for leisure..." He shook his head. "Maybe this old warrior still has something to contribute to this world. Well, your night sentry is almost up. I should let you sleep."

Both men stood, but Bulo took a noticeably longer time doing so.

They clasped hands. "It was good to talk," Marduke said.

"It was. Rest well." Bulo walked back to his bedding, but the image of him clutching his older brother's lifeless body to his chest clung to his mind.

Caswen woke in the morning stiff and sore. The constant travel and makeshift bedding had taken its toll on her body. She remained excited about her mission but yearned for her comfortable room and bed back at the temple. She sat up and rubbed her legs to increase the flow of blood. Looking over, she saw Thack missing from his bedding and Dryn still sound asleep. She saw Bandark and his two men quietly talking around the campfire that Bulo had used to start breakfast. Rathen was nowhere to be seen, but Marduke sat on the ground next to his packed bedding. The gloomy look on his face worried Caswen. She quietly combed her hair and straightened her robes before approaching him.

"Marduke," Caswen called out as she approached. She knew better than to startle the old warrior.

When Marduke looked up, she saw the sorrow in his swollen eyes. "What is it?" she asked, running to him.

Marduke held out his hand. "Nothing. It's nothing."

Caswen sat down in front of him. "It's *not* nothing. Tell me."

Marduke smiled. "I never could keep anything from you, Cassy."

Caswen smiled and took hold of his hands.

"It's just my past. It comes to haunt me from time to time. That's all."

"You are the strongest man I have ever known. In both body and in spirit. Your past has nothing to do with all the good you continue to spread."

Marduke nodded. "I'm alright."

Caswen offered a smile and squeezed his hand. This wasn't the first time she had consoled Marduke when his past caused him pain.

"Just promise me you will continue to do your best. Be the healer you always wanted to be."

"Of course. What happened?"

"There some things I would like to tell you," Marduke started. "About my past."

"Alright," Caswen replied, unsure of what he wanted to say. He had never spoken much about his past, and she never asked; the scars were too deep.

"You better… wake up Dryn."

Marduke sat with Caswen and Dryn as she wiped the sleep from her eyes. Both Caswen and Dryn listened intently as Marduke went on to tell them his entire past and about the family he had lost.

The group's travel for the next several days settled into an uneventful pattern. Each time they camped, there was less and less conversation around the evening fire. Instead of interacting, most of the group slept directly after eating their meals and completed their sentry duty, though Rathen did notice Thack and Caswen seeking out each other's company more and more, sitting beside each other for meals and volunteering for the same night watches. Despite Thack and Caswen's budding friendship, Rathen could see his group's fatigue. They were not used to riding for days on end, but he couldn't slow now.

The closer they rode to their destination, the more desolate the environment became. In the final days, there were no other signs of life or open trails to follow.

Just after nightfall on the last day, Rathen spotted the clearing he had been looking for. This was the final camping spot before meeting the druid on the morrow.

Rathen trotted his horse up to Bulo, who had already seen Thack within the clearing.

"We rest here," Rathen called out.

"Thank Thandrall, my legs are killing me," Caswen could be heard saying.

"We meet the druid tomorrow, and then go on to Bramblewood Forest from there. Best be on our guard," Rathen said.

Dinner was prepared by Thack and Bulo and eaten in silence. Even Rathen felt tired from the road and wanted a good night's sleep on an actual bed. After dinner, everyone was finally able to settle down for the night, burrowing into their bedding.

"Bulo, you and I will take first watch," Rathen said.

"Alright," the big man said, standing and stretching.

Bulo collected his axe and positioned himself on the other side of camp. Rathen sat down on the edge of the group, not far from where Magom stood. The evening was quiet, and the moon provided enough light to see the surrounding area.

Not long into his watch, he saw movement within the group as Caswen walked toward him. Rathen contemplated what she might want to speak about. To his surprise, she walked toward Magom. Curious, Rathen watched.

"May I approach?" she asked the lich.

"Yes," Magom responded.

Caswen sat down on a rock outcropping, and Rathen could see how nervous she felt; she looked away from Magom even as she sat across from him. However, she did not appear to have the same hostility she once held toward him.

"Is it true you seek redemption?" she asked, her face turned from his.

"It is true. I seek to be human once more," Magom said slowly and calmly.

Rathen continued to watch straining to listen, curious how this would turn out.

Caswen seemed to struggle to turn to face him but couldn't fully commit.

"Redemption is a core belief within our order. Thandrall teaches that to find redemption, we must understand what we have done wrong. Only then can we fully accept responsibility for our transgressions and find the strength to correct our ways." Caswen spoke the words as if she had practiced them a hundred times. "Is this something you are prepared to do?" She looked at the lich for a short time before turning away.

Rathen held his breath and anxiously waited to hear how Magom would respond.

"Yes, I believe so. If I had known what this existence was like, I doubt I would have sought it so eagerly," Magom said. "I certainly would not do it again."

Caswen nodded as she inched herself closer to Magom. "Then join with me in a prayer to Thandrall, and let us find the redemption you seek."

Magom remained still. Caswen brow wrinkled, but her gaze never wavered. "Tell me about your decision to transform yourself," Caswen said softly. "What was it like for you?"

Magom nodded. "Many years ago, I reached my one hundred and fiftieth year. I had been locked in an impregnable shell that surrounded the castle. Trapped, I felt myself dying. You see, the magic we found to prolong life only lasted a while. My father died at one hundred and thirty-seven, and with all my research, I could only extend my life by another decade or so." Magom paused.

"Then what happened?" Caswen prompted.

"I grew desperate. I did not want to die."

"Because you were alone?"

"No. I just wanted more time to live."

"For what purpose?" Caswen asked calmly. "What made you fight death so desperately?"

"For power. The power to defeat my brother, whom I constantly fought after our father's death. The power to take the kingdom that should have been mine. Power to… live the way I wanted."

Caswen took a deep breath before she spoke. "In your search for the power to live, you became a creature that could not possibly obtain that goal."

Magom paused again for a while. "Yes," he finally said.

"Then take my hands, and let's pray to Thandrall together." Caswen knelt in front of him with her hands out, facing him.

Rathen started to feel uncomfortable, as though he were intruding on a private moment. Perhaps they were best left alone. Rathen saw Magom place his skeletal hands on hers before walking away. He did not know whether Caswen's offer was one of naïve foolishness or the wisdom of a woman with the power to change even a lich. As Rathen walked toward Bulo to change sentries, he caught sight of Marduke as he stood silently watching over Caswen and the lich.

"She's come a long way," Rathen said to him as he passed.

Marduke nodded, but the stern expression on his face showed his continued concern.

Chapter 10

The morning brought cooling weather, dark skies, and the threat of rain. Rathen led the group on their way to the meeting point with the druid. Never having met a druid, Rathen was not entirely sure what to expect. It was well known that druids preferred to keep to themselves, living simple lives close to nature and practicing their spells. Druids had an affinity for nature magic and were protectors of plants and animals. Rathen had heard rumors that the druids could commune with trees, if such a thing were even possible, and that some could even take on the forms of various animals. Whether or not the rumors were to be believed, Rathen could only hope that this druid would be a valuable asset to the team as they trudged through Bramblewood Forest.

They traveled until midday under the continually darkening sky, the land less barren now, the trees and underbrush growing thicker.

Thack rode back to speak with Rathen, riding close to Magom. "Rathen, the druid waits in the clearing up the road."

"Right. Ride ahead with the group, and we'll catch up. We need to secure Magom's horse away from the others."

"Right away," Thack turned about and rode ahead.

"Magom," Rathen started, turning back to the lich. "Can't we just burn the rotting meat from that horse of yours?"

The lich remained silent.

"I mean, it can't hurt it, can it? Or does it need that flesh? It would stop the smell if we…" Rathen dropped his question when Magom continued to ignore him. Perhaps the request was offensive? Rathen gave up the idea.

Soon Rathen spotted a small clearing nearby, some yards behind the last rider of their company. It was a sufficient distance for hiding the lich's steed until Rathen could better explain the circumstances to the druid. Leading Magom toward the clearing, Rathen noticed Caswen up ahead, looking back in their direction. When Rathen caught her eye, she quickly turned her head back around, her long hair twisting in the breeze. The fear that had been so palpable from her only a few days ago had been replaced by a hesitant curiosity.

"The healer seems to be more accepting of you," Rathen said to Magom.

"Yes," Magom said after a brief hesitation, his speech softer. "Tell me, Rathen. What color is her hair?"

Rathen had to think about it. "A reddish shade of brown, I'd say."

"What of her eyes?"

"Green," Rathen said. "What is it you want?" Rathen smirked, stealing the lich's words from earlier.

"My mind has been consumed with finding power for

such a long time that I have forgotten what the simple joys in life are like."

"Well, after this mission, you will have your chance to be human again. For now, let's put your horse over there, and we'll walk." Rathen did not intend to be blunt, but his focus was on concealing the smell of the dead horse.

Magom rode his steed to the little clearing surrounded by a few trees and rocks and dismounted. Rathen also dismounted, walking his horse the rest of the distance as Magom walked behind him.

Up ahead, Rathen could see the group talking with two unknown men. *Two men? I thought we had only hired one.*

The men wore rough-spun green robes, their hair long and wild. One man was past middle age, with lines of gray running through his dark hair. The other was much younger, just barely a man, his hair dark and curled. Both men had heavily tanned skin as tough as leather from long days spent beneath the sun.

Rathen motioned for Magom to stay a distance away and handed his horse's reins to Thack. His companions made way for him as he approached the druids and inclined his head toward them.

"I'm Rathen, leader of this company."

The older of the two spoke. "I am Apaca, your guide. This is Remric; he will take care of your horses while we are away."

"Well met," Rathen said. "I appreciate your foresight. The care of the horses had not crossed my mind."

"The common man does not usually regard animals as we do," Remric said haughtily.

"Remric," Apaca warned. "Do not speak so rudely to our employer."

Rathen laughed. "It's alright. The boy has a point. We are surely not as in tune with our horses as druids are. I thank you for making up what we lack."

Remric let slip a sheepish grin.

"Come, we have a camp set up a half a day's walk from the forest, where you can clean up and rest," Apaca said.

"Right, let's mount up and follow," Rathen ordered the group. He nodded to Thack and Bulo to take lead as he retrieved his horse from Thack and walked back to Magom. Once the rest of their company had started down the trail toward the camp, Rathen allowed Magom to call his dead horse, and the two followed a short distance behind the others.

The druids led them down thin trails late into the evening until they finally reached a well-established camp. Rathen noticed right away the straw beds that were raised just off the ground. He breathed a sigh of relief. He should be able to sleep well tonight.

After instructing Magom to keep his horse far away, Rathen walked into camp to see Caswen already taking advantage of the clean water in large barrels, where she washed her face furiously. A great fire roared in the center with a few torches erected around the perimeter. The size and sophistication of the camp was impressive.

Remric, the younger druid, prepared meat on the fire and uncased baskets filled with fruits and breads. The smells made Rathen realize just how hungry he was.

After the group cleaned up and refreshed, they ate the feast sitting in a circle. Crisp red apples that burst with juice brought smiles to his group as they bit into them. Braided breads laced with dried berries and aromatic herbs were broken off in hunks and slathered with soft cheeses. The roasted hares dripped with hot fat when, with each bite, the fire-roasted skins crackled.

Magom walked to the edge of camp and stayed within the shadows just out of the torchlight. Apaca viewed Magom for the first time as he walked through the camp. To Rathen's surprise, the druid showed no fear at seeing the lich and only gazed at Magom watchfully.

Famished, Rathen tore into the meat and sampled the fruits. The druids provided water and juices to drink.

"Bandark, how much are you paying for all this?" Rathen asked.

Bandark smiled and gestured for him to take more of the meat.

Rathen's curiosity at the origins of Bandark's fortune was quickly overtaken by more immediate interests. "Apaca," Rathen said, turning to the druid, "what can you tell us of Bramblewood Forest?"

The old druid looked up and smiled. "Gaining entrance and staying hidden will be no easy task. As the name suggests, Bramblewood bushes weave through the underbrush of the entire wood, some waiting to trip you at the ankles and others as high as your chest, creating a veritable wall. Each bush is covered in thick, barbed thorns that will hook into the skin if anyone attempts to pass through."

"But you can get us through it, right?" Rathen asked as he continued to eat.

"Of course," Apaca replied, keeping his smile. But then his weathered face became more serious. "Our people have sensed that the area of Bramblewood Forest is enchanted by some form of nature magic, making the vegetation within more alive, but we can still influence it."

"More alive?" Rathen asked.

"Oh, yes. Cut brush grows back at an incredible rate, and the vegetation itself seems to expand in a way that creates barriers, like it's protecting the area," Apaca said, his eyes wide and wild. "Our people never enter."

"What other dangers can we expect?" Rathen asked.

"There are rumors of wolf-men that live within the trees. Wolves that stand like men but fight like animals," Apaca said, his face tense.

Rathen listened intently, setting aside his remaining food. This was an unexpected development. The group needed to be prepared to face whatever was in that forest, but Rathen had not anticipated that any dangerous creatures would be able to live surrounded by the thorns of the bramblewood bushes. And he had certainly never heard of wolf-men.

"Rumors? So you haven't seen one yourself, then," Bulo said from beside Rathen.

"No," Apaca said, shaking his head. "But many tell the same stories of people being taken by these wolf-men when they enter. I have heard of groups who left with as many as twenty men returning with as few as three and raving about the wolf-like savages who ambushed and devastated their company."

"Well, tomorrow we will know for certain," Rathen said. "We shall not linger in the forest any longer than we must, but everyone should be prepared for the worst."

Bulo nodded. "We'll have our weapons sharpened and ready." There were mumbles of agreement across the camp.

"Yes, but we must also be well fed and well rested to

prepare for the dangers of the forest." Apaca raised his cup and said loudly, "Now, eat and enjoy!"

"Where's the ale?" Bulo asked.

"No ale," Apaca replied. "Ale weakens the mind and dulls the senses. We have brought many fine fruit juices instead to focus your mind and energize your spirit for what lies ahead."

Rathen heard Bulo grumble something about spiritual nonsense before taking a reluctant sip of the juice. Rathen had to stifle a laugh at the look of disgust on his face.

Looking around at all the members of the group, Rathen saw that everyone seemed to be enjoying themselves as they ate and laughed with each other. Rathen glanced back into the darkness but could not see Magom. Assuring himself that the lich was likely content on his own, he turned back to his plate and companions.

As the night grew later, everyone settled down in their selected makeshift beds with sighs of pleasure at the welcoming cushions of hay. Rathen volunteered to take first watch of night sentry duty. Settling on a stump near the head of the camp, Rathen noticed Apaca sitting away from the group on a large rock. When the druid did not move for a time, Rathen stood and walked toward him. Apaca heard his approach and turned.

"Apaca, are you helping keep watch? I've already agreed to the first watch, so you should get some rest," Rathen said just under his breath.

The old druid's face looked worried, even frightened. He shook his head, holding up a knife and a small wooden carving. "Just doing some whittling. Helps me think."

Rathen sat on the other side of the rock. "Oh? What is it you're carving?"

Apaca held the piece of wood up for Rathen to see. He could just make out a rounded head and a small beak in the darkness, tiny feathers etched along the side. "It's an owl," said Apaca. "Remric's favorite. He's always been good with animals."

Rathen chuckled. "I can see why you brought him along for the horses then."

Apaca smiled but did not reply, running the blade of his dagger along the wood and chipping away at the owl.

After a while, Rathen broke the silence. "May I inquire after your thoughts?"

Apaca sighed and looked back down at his carving, shaving strips of wood from it with his dagger. "Would you think me a coward if I admitted my fear to you?"

"Of course not. Is it the lich? If so, he isn't hostile toward us."

Apaca looked up, staring out into the night. "No, I've seen my share of necromancers and the dead they've brought back. It's not that."

"Then what is it?"

The old druid seemed to be wrestling with his thoughts, his eyes glancing all around. "The forest. I'd be lying if I said I wasn't afraid."

Rathen cocked his head. "Then why take us?"

Apaca leaned back with a sigh. "I'm an old man. I've fulfilled my purpose in this life. I have a fine son." He gestured toward Remric sleeping soundly on his straw bed. "But he is young yet. I do not want to leave my family destitute when I am gone. The money from this work will set up my wife and child for a while. It's the best I can do for him."

Rathen again wondered how much Bandark was paying for their services. "We have a strong group. If we can maintain our formation, our success is certain regardless of the dangers," Rathen said with confidence.

Apaca looked down. "Yes, you're a tough-looking bunch, I'll give you that."

Rathen nodded.

"Alright," Apaca said, sitting up straight. "I'll get us in and through those brambles, and you kill whatever comes at us." He held out his hand.

"Done." Rathen took his hand and smiled. "But I feel I need to tell you there is also an undead horse just outside of camp behind a thicket. You might want to make Remric aware for his own knowledge."

Apaca grimaced. "A human doing that to himself is one thing, but to an animal is… abominable."

"I'm sorry. It wasn't within my power to prevent it."

Apaca nodded. "I'll inform Remric."

Rathen smiled. "Now get some rest."

Apaca nodded and went to rest near his son.

The remainder of Rathen's watch passed quietly, though his mind wondered at the druid leading them into a forest that none of his kind ever entered and at the dangers the man had never witnessed himself. Confidence could win in the face of inexperience, yet this druid lacked even that.

The group awoke at daybreak, all agreeing that they had had the best night's sleep since starting their journey. Apaca brushed away everyone's gratitude with a wave of his arm, telling them to think nothing of it, but Remric could not hide a smile. The group then settled down to breakfast as Remric tended the horses. After finishing their meal, everyone began gathering their weapons and possessions, as the rest of the journey would be on foot.

"Only bring the essentials," Rathen shouted across the camp. "We must be light on our feet through these woods."

A grumble of agreement swept through the camp. Rathen carried only his weapons and a small bag of rations and gold coins, just in case. Surveying the rest of the group, he saw that all the others seemed to be packing similar items—except Caswen.

Caswen knelt in the dirt beside her pallet bed, struggling to close her backpack. Beside her were her saddlebags, previously carried by her horse, and they were nearly empty.

"That's too full, young lady," said Bulo, walking up to her. He had only his axe strapped over his shoulder. "You'll need only the clothes on your back, so leave behind any extra garments."

"It's full of potions and medicinal herbs," Caswen said, clearly annoyed. "Or would you rather I left those behind?"

Bulo smiled as Caswen finally closed her bag. She stood and tried to heave the strap over her shoulder, but the bag barely moved. She struggled for a few moments, despite the snickers of the larger men nearby. Then Thack approached, his shadow completely enveloping her.

"I can take that," he said with a smile.

Caswen tried to protest, but Thack lifted the bag in one swift motion and swung it over his shoulder.

"Being half orc comes with its perks," Thack said with a wink. "Namely, freakish strength."

Caswen looked at her toes and pulled at a loose thread

on the end of her sleeve. "Thank you," she said, blushing.

The rest of the group began to gather at the edge of the clearing, prepared for the long walk to Bramblewood Forest and beyond. Apaca, strapping a large dagger onto his belt, approached his son, who was brushing one of the horses.

"Stay off the road, Remric," Apaca said. "And keep yourself hidden. This many horses is bound to attract attention if you aren't diligent in your duties."

"Yes, Father," said Remric, setting down his brush and lowering his head in respect.

Apaca placed his hand over the back of Remric's neck and pulled the boy forward, pressing their foreheads together. "We'll be back in four or five days' time. Be safe."

"You too, Father," Remric said, placing a hand on Apaca's shoulder.

Breaking their embrace, Apaca straightened his dagger and walked to the front of the group, leading them at a brisk pace away from the camp. Remric waved, shouting his well wishes after them.

The company traveled well into the afternoon in an area with no trails, shrouded by tall grass and bushes. After hours of travel, Rathen finally saw the impossibly tall trees in the distance that could only be Bramblewood Forest. As they approached, Rathen was amazed to see that the forest underbrush, standing almost to his shoulders, appeared impassable.

With the overcast late afternoon sky, Rathen could not see beyond the thick vegetation inside the forest, but the smell of pine trees dominated the air. Numerous calls from birds and the buzzing of insects could be heard from within.

"Garrick, as soon as we get in, gain your bearings and

guide us to the forbidden area we discussed," Rathen directed.

Garrick nodded. "I will need to find some trails."

Rathen turned to the healer. "Caswen, stay within the group's center. Everyone else be on your guard. If you see anything at all, whistle like this." Rathen demonstrated the whistle he had used during his days as a captain in the army, and everyone practiced repeating the sound. "Very good. It is imperative that our presence here remain a secret, even from the birds. Do not speak without due cause, and step lightly."

Rathen turned to Dryn. "Dryn, prepare your bow and keep to the back of the group. An arrow will be the quickest and quietest way to dispatch any enemies." Dryn nodded, pulling an arrow from her quiver.

When Rathen gave the word, Apaca began chanting in a low tone in front of the underbrush. With a wave of his hand, the vegetation slowly moved to the side, opening a narrow path. Rathen relaxed.

He nodded to Bulo, who had his axe in hand.

Apaca slowly walked into the forest on the narrow path. A wolf howled deep within the trees.

"Wolf-men?" Rathen whispered, following Apaca. A few brambles from the bushes already tore at his exposed skin.

Apaca shrugged before opening more trail ahead. "Unlikely that average wolves live here."

Rathen nodded. The howls could not confirm or deny the presence of wolf-men, but it meant there could be truth to the rumors.

As they traveled deeper into the darkening trees, Rathen grew concerned. He looked back to see the group walking the trail in single file, the enchanted opening too narrow for a better formation. Thack stood directly behind Rathen, followed by Bulo

"Thack, do you sense anything?" Rathen asked, looking to his talented scout.

"Densest woods I've ever seen. Birds and animal sounds all around, but which are friend or foe?" Thack whispered back, looking up into the trees.

Rathen looked back to find Magom but could not see him. Rathen wanted to ask if the lich sensed anything around them. *I don't like this. Walking single-file without sight of the other members leaves too much at risk. If someone disappeared from the back, we might not even know until too late*

"Apaca, make this trail wider. We're too spread apart," Rathen said.

The druid looked back. "It's not easy opening the trail as much as I have."

Rathen said, "Then open a small clearing up ahead so we can figure this out."

Wolves howled close by. A spark of panic began to rise in Rathen's throat.

"Thack, how many wolves?" Rathen asked.

"I hear six, but there's likely more."

The spark of panic grew into a flame of imminent danger as Rathen's skin tingled and his breath caught. He flashed a look behind to Bulo, who gripped his axe with both hands and looked around. Bulo felt it too.

"Apaca, wait," Rathen said.

The druid turned toward Rathen just as an arrow buzzed by Rathen's head, inches from his face.

"We're under attack!" Rathen shouted, pulling his sword. "Bandark, Magom, to the front!"

Rathen raised his shield as Bulo and Thack ducked their heads, looking for movement within the trees as two more arrows flew over.

"There," Thack said, pointing off to the right.

Rathen turned and focused his eyes. Behind the brush, he could see the head of a wolf as tall as if it were standing on its hind legs. Rathen heard movement behind them and turned to see three wolves closing in, running on two legs and as tall as men. The underbrush did not appear to hinder their movements at all; the brambles slid off their black fur and broke apart with a single swipe of their long, thick claws. They growled menacingly, their yellow eyes narrowed to slits above their long snouts, fangs glinting in the light. One wolf-man continued toward Rathen as the other two broke off, heading for other sections of the group.

"To the left!" Rathen called out, raising his shield and preparing his onyx sword.

The wolf reached Rathen and clawed at his shield. Rathen swung his sword, but the wolf-man blocked with its claws, making a metallic clink sound as though the claws were made of metal. Rathen bashed his shield against its upper body and swung again, cutting into the wolf's side. The wolf yelped and backed away into the brush. Rathen turned to see that Thack used his padded shoulder to knock the second wolf to the ground. Thack's axe flew up and quickly came down onto the wolf's body, cleaving it open as the wolf howled in pain. A final swing of the axe abruptly ended the howl.

A scream pierced the air. Rathen and Thack looked up

from the dead wolf-man at their feet, turning toward the back of the line. "Caswen," Thack said, his face pale.

"Apaca, give us more room to fight!" Rathen called out to the druid behind him.

Turning, Rathen saw Apaca slowly picking himself up off the forest floor, an arrow in his shoulder. Apaca raised his dagger. "I'll do what I can," the druid said.

Rathen turned back around to see Bulo swinging his axe, attempting to hit a wolf that danced around a few steps ahead.

"Thack, help Bulo. I'll get to the back," Rathen said as he fought through the brambles to get to Caswen.

As Rathen moved further, he saw Rendrak and Garrick fighting two wolves. Rendrak swung his two swords in circular strikes with smooth precision, while Garrick defended himself with a clear glass dagger. Beyond them, Marduke swung his large two-handed sword at four or five wolves, cutting the bramble bushes in front of him. An arrow protruded from his back. Caswen cowered down behind him, uninjured. Dryn, beside Marduke, fired off arrow after arrow, but none seemed to pierce through the wolves' thick hide. Magom had built a small dark haze of energy around him but stood motionless.

More wolves began to encircle the group; Rathen could not see them, but he could smell their musty fur and hear their growls and knew they could attack any moment.

"Magom, assist us!" Rathen shouted, knowing his group was only moments from death.

The lich raised his hands, causing the swilling energy around him to spill out. A series of lightning streams shot from his fingers. Wolves yelped through the trees all around them. Marduke slew one of the wolves attacking him and backed away from Magom, pulling Caswen with him.

The lich's energy grew as he shot out electricity. Then, as his chanting changed tones, shards of ice shot forth from his hands.

Rathen looked around to see the immediate threat gone. He worried about the archers that could still be in the trees, but all the wolves had been slain or forced to run.

But Magom's fury did not end. After the ice shards, flames erupted from his hands and into the trees, igniting the brambles.

"Magom, stop!" Rathen called out.

Magom continued his assault toward the trees where the archers were last seen. Rathen backed away as he grew concerned for his safety, the rest of the group following suit. As the burning bush crept closer to Garrick and Rendrak, Bandark summoned his protective shield to block the flames.

Rathen rushed the lich and grabbed hold of his arm.

The lich looked up and cast Rathen into the air, flinging him backwards just as it had done to Marduke in the barn in Andar.

Rathen braced himself as he was flung through the brush, the brambles ripping at his skin and clothes. His back slammed into a tree. Rathen lay still and fought to regain the air that had been knocked from his lungs.

"Stop!" Bulo yelled somewhere.

Then, silence.

Rathen lay in the thick grass under the tree for a while until he heard approaching footsteps in the brush.

"Rathen?" Bulo called out.

"Here." Rathen struggled to speak.

Bulo walked over, clearing the brush with his axe. He took ahold of Rathen, lifting him up and helping him back to a small clearing Apaca had created just off the path they had made.

"There," Bulo said, gently lowering Rathen onto his back.

"I… apologize for my outburst," Magom said, approaching Rathen.

"Put out the fires," Rathen said, pain shooting from various places in his back. His concerns were immediate. He would talk to Magom later about the incident.

"They are out," Magom said, walking away.

"Caswen?" Rathen asked, unable to see anyone from the ground. He could tell several of his ribs were broken.

"I'm here," Caswen said, kneeling down beside him. She placed one hand on his chest and softly chanted, holding her amulet in front of her. Immediately, Rathen started to feel better, and the pain in his back soon disappeared.

"Thank you. Are you alright? I heard you scream," he said, standing up gingerly. He stretched, gently turning his torso side to side. No pain from where the brambles had etched themselves into his skin, no searing pain from broken ribs. He took a relieved breath. Caswen's healing skills were nothing short of remarkable.

"I shouted out when I saw the arrow hit Marduke," she said.

"Apaca was hit too," Rathen said, remembering. "Is anyone else injured?"

"I'll see to everyone now, to be sure," Caswen said.

Rathen nodded. "Thack, see about securing the area as

best you can. Just don't go walking into the trees too deeply."

"Rathen," Bandark called out. "You need to see this."

Rathen walked briskly to Bandark, who knelt down beside the body of a wolf. Garrick and Rendrak stood beside him.

Rathen knelt down next to Bandark. "What is it?" he asked.

Bandark took hold of the wolf's snout, prying it back to reveal a man's face. The wolf mask was intricate and well designed so as to be indistinguishable from an actual wolf's head.

"There're just men?" Rathen asked, examining the mask. The fur was definitely real, but the yellow eyes were made of glass, and the teeth were some kind of pottery painted white. A flap of black netting covering the back of the throat allowed the wearer to look out through the mouth.

Setting the mask aside, Rathen picked up the wolf's hand, inspecting the claws. They were fur-covered gloves with three metal hook-like blades positioned like claws.

"I thought they felt like metal," Rathen said, showing the weapons to Bandark.

Examining the rest of the costume, Rathen found it to be made of a very hard and durable leather covered in fur. "It's no wonder they were able to maneuver through the bushes so well," he said. "Very little could pierce through this hardened leather."

Rathen looked around for Apaca, who had just had his arrow wound healed by Caswen.

"Apaca," Rathen called out.

As Apaca approached, Rathen showed him the wolf disguise.

"By the Great Oak… There're not wolves at all," Apaca said, leaning over to peer down at the body.

"Why do you think they dressed like this?" Rendrak asked.

"Well," Apaca said, straightening back up. "The mystery around these wolf-men has kept my people out of this forest for years. Man or beast, they have still killed many."

"True enough," Rathen said, glancing over Apaca's shoulder to inspect where the arrow had been. Not a mark could be seen. "Caswen really has mastered her craft."

"Indeed," Apaca said. "With her skills, we just might make it back out alive."

"What do we do now?" Bulo asked, bringing Rathen's attention back to the mission at hand.

"We need to find a trail so Garrick can get us to the forbidden area," Rathen said.

"We're likely to encounter more of these savages," said Rendrak.

Rathen stood. "I'm not certain they are connected to Vargas and the compound. It's likely they're just protecting their territory," he said, hesitating.

"Orders?" Bulo asked, his eyes continuing to scan the area.

"Kill what attacks us. We find a trail and get to the forbidden area as quickly as we can," Rathen said, his eyes still on the savage's body.

"Right. Garrick, lead behind the druid," Rendrak said.

Garrick looked around cautiously, taking lead with his hand on the hilt of his dagger.

Rathen turned to Thack, who stood behind him. "What do you make of these men?"

"Their attack is not unlike the tactics orcs would use, having archers draw your attention to one side while the real attack happens on the other," Thack said.

"Stay focused. If you see or even sense anything, let me know."

Thack nodded, looking back into the trees.

As the group slowly made their way down Apaca's narrow trail, Rathen scanned the area. The sounds and movements from the birds and small animals in the trees made it difficult to look for danger. He understood how wanderers could be taken by these savages without notice.

"Trail up ahead," Garrick whispered to Rathen.

"Good. See if you can gain your sense of direction from it."

"I'll use my spells to cover myself and explore this trail quickly," Garrick said.

The group stopped just before the trail, allowing Garrick to inspect the way. As he stepped into the trail, he muttered something under his breath, and his body blended into the color of the bushes, disappearing from sight. Only a shimmering outline of his body could be seen.

Apaca opened a small clearing so the group could be closer together. Everyone settled onto a patch of earth, waiting for Garrick's return. As Rathen and Magom stood watch, everyone else sat with their backs to the center of the small space, away from the overgrowth of the perimeter and its dangers. They leaned back against tree stumps or laid on the ground, trying to rest after their recent battle. Dryn took stock of her arrows and began assembling more, pulling supplies from her bag. Thack and Caswen huddled together over a book Caswen had brought with her. Apaca took his dagger and owl carving, now nearly finished, and began adding some small details to it.

Rathen pondered the mystery of the wolf-men and looked at Magom, curious of his thoughts regarding their battle, but said nothing.

As time passed without Garrick's return, Rathen grew worried, and by the looks on some of the faces, so did the rest of the group.

"Magom, do you sense others nearby?" Rathen asked.

The lich hissed from under his cowl. "There is so much life within this forest I am unable to discern plant from animal. It is as if the vegetation has a life force of its own."

Another mystery of this forest.

The group waited in silence as they kept watch around them. Marduke stood next to Caswen, who was sitting on the ground next to the druid. Dryn stood on her other side, an arrow notched at the ready. As more time went by, Bandark grew more and more concerned. He stepped away and tried to peer down the path, but dared not enter.

Rathen knew that if they lost Garrick, the mission would be over, for he was the only one who knew the location of the compound and the secret entrance. Fearing the worst, Rathen attempted to conceive a new plan should Garrick fail to return, but nothing else seemed practical.

Just as Rathen really began to panic, the brush moved to the side and a foggy form gathered within it and then Garrick reappeared, stumbling into their small clearing. He was breathing heavily and had a few cuts on his face from the brambles.

Rathen breathed a sigh of relief.

"The trail extends north. And then northwest. The

forbidden area is just beyond," Garrick said, straightening himself.

"Good man," Rathen said, clapping a hand on Garrick's shoulder. "How far away?"

"It's not close," Garrick replied. "And I had to avoid two patrols on the road from the compound. They are more active than last time."

Rathen looked over the group. "Moving this slowly in the brush isn't working well. So, our options are to either rush down the trail and be susceptible to attacks or be on our guard, take up more time, and likely encounter patrols."

Everyone remained silent.

"Can everyone move quickly?" Rathen asked.

There were a few nods and some nervous mumbling, but no one voiced any strong opposition.

"Then we run. Apaca in front, next to Garrick to guide us. Bandark, Rendrak, and Dryn behind them, Caswen and Marduke in the middle. Bulo, Thack, Magom, and I will bring up the rear where an attack is likely. Move swiftly but quietly. Call out threats when you see them."

There was a collective rustling as everyone stood and drew their weapons. Moving into the formation Rathen had devised, the group stood together, wary but ready. From the back, Rathen's orders carried across the company: "Stay together, and… run!"

Chapter 11

Litagus sat at his table writing down all the calculations he had worked out and combining them with the ones he had done the day before. Discovering the secrets and deciphering the spell calibrations of the Book of Ziz had proven to be quite a challenge, even for Litagus's superior intellect. Decoding the spell components alone had been a time-consuming process. As a priest of his order and not a mage, using spell components was not something in which Litagus was well versed. He had been forced to postpone his studies on several spells due to his inability to even understand which basic components were necessary. He speculated that many of the components were not even native to this world, and finding adequate substitutes would be difficult.

"You wanted to see me?" Davale's voice interrupted his thoughts.

Litagus looked up to see her standing in the doorway, wearing her usual leather boots and shorts. In place of her leather tunic, she wore a cream-colored shirt that was almost as light as her pale skin. Her black hair had been tied tightly behind her head.

"Yes," Litagus said, standing up. He walked over to a large table where he kept his notes on the spell components he had yet to acquire. "I need you to find a few things," he said, handing her a piece of parchment covered in his scribblings.

Davale took the list and read it over. Her eyes paused, and she looked up. "What is a stylout?" she asked.

"A small sea beast with an ivory horn in the center of its head. I have written down the name of the beach where they are rumored to be," Litagus said. "It's not far. Just be sure to follow the instructions on the list to the letter."

"Yes, High Priest," Davale said with a bow. "I'll study it carefully and leave in the morning."

Litagus took a small pouch from his robes. "Take this. Just in case," he said, handing it to her.

Davale took the pouch and opened it. She counted a handful of gold coins and a small, well-cut emerald gemstone roughly half the size of her thumb. The gem itself was worth several bags of gold.

"Hire a wagon if the spell components are too heavy to carry."

Davale bowed without speaking and walked out the door. Litagus could see the hidden smile she wore as she left. He expected she would likely spend some of the gold on herself but knew it would keep her motivated to complete the mission. Besides, the emerald wasn't of use as a spell component because of its inferior weight. However, the two bowls of rubies and diamonds next to his chair would later be ground to dust by his assistant, Bucomus. He sat back down at his writing table, but his thoughts remained on Davale.

He had been more than satisfied with her performance in obtaining materials and the more sensitive work of taking lives. She had proven her loyalty time and time again. He had watched her from childhood as her abilities had grown to match the overconfidence she had always possessed. She was the prize of all his warriors. All the pride Litagus felt for Davale was marred by a single secret he had kept from her for almost twenty years and his fear that she would someday learn the truth. It was a truth he needed to keep from her at all costs for fear she would leave him in search of answers to the question it would raise.

Before Litagus had become a high priest of the Order, he had been tasked with recruiting members. Just under twenty years ago, he had been sent to a colony of sub-humans, referred to by outsiders as the Shadow People. They referred to themselves, however, as the Disciples of Vizilan. Litagus's order had hoped to recruit the Shadow People into the worship of Gothoar since their ways were known to be dark and violent. But the Shadow People's devotion to their demon god, Vizilan, proved an inseverable bond. Litagus had noticed that their appearance was altered from decades of seclusion and worship to the demon god. Their skin was a sickly pale, near white, while their hair and eyes were darker than pitch. The priests of the order were granted demon-like features for their devotion, the whites of their eyes turning to a shiny black and their teeth growing pointed with jagged edges. Their cannibalistic customs, sacrificial rituals, and vicious tendencies made the Shadow People despised and even hunted by the rest of the world.

The Shadow People had allowed Litagus to enter their underground village under the pretense of trade, but their hospitality was quickly rescinded when he tried to speak of the Order of Gothoar. Outraged, the Shadow People had accused Litagus of dishonoring their devotion to Vizilan by trying to sway them into worshipping another deity. Litagus was certain they would have attacked had he not been as powerful as he was even then. Instead, they had asked him to leave, the threat of what would happen to him if he stayed barely masked in their voices. As powerful as Litagus was, he knew when he was outnumbered.

As he had made his way out of the village, Litagus passed through the market, noticing all the strange goods and oddities being sold in the darkened stalls: various meats, animals, and even slaves. Litagus had no interest in the slaves but was surprised to see a young girl for sale who couldn't have been more than eight years old. Intrigued, Litagus had asked the woman selling the child why one so young was unwanted. The woman explained that the girl was stubborn and hard-headed. Abandoned as a child, she had been sold numerous times, but was generally considered untrainable and wild. She refused to obey orders and had even tried to kill one of her master's children in her last household. If she did not sell before much longer, she would likely be used for a sacrificial ritual. The woman went on to explain that the child had been fathered by a priest of the Shadow People but born from a human slave woman—a despised half-blood, fit only for the work of a slave if even allowed to live.

Litagus shuddered to think what Davale would say if she ever learned that he had purchased her on the open market for a mere fraction of the gold that he had just given her for her mission. Or that she had been cast aside by her people and condemned to die for being a half-breed. Or that he had erased all the memories of her past life.

Even back then, Litagus could foresee the usefulness of raising such a child born of the mix between human and Shadow—someone who could move in the shadows as her priestly father could and thrive in the dark, yet look human enough to function beyond the secluded caves.

Litagus had taken the girl back to his temple and fed, clothed, and raised her, using his powers to make her believe she had been dropped on the temple steps as an orphan. He had given her the name Davale, meaning *devoted one*, in the hope that she would live up to it.

Even from a young age, Davale's appearance strongly reflected that of the Shadow People: white skin, large dark eyes, and deep black hair. Unlike the other young children being raised at the temple, she never showed fear of the dark and rarely socialized. And as Litagus had anticipated, she proved to be cunning, powerful, and even violent, but none of these traits had revealed her dark heritage to any of Litagus's followers, not even to Davale herself.

Now, nearing her twenty-eighth birthday, Davale was his most loyal disciple. Litagus favored her over the other followers, and as he rose to power and became a high priest, she had also gained privilege and prestige. He had not allowed her to pursue the priesthood because he had wanted her to be a warrior, for which she had a natural talent. She had participated in weapons training and instruction in hand-to-hand combat, proving to be superior at a young age to even the more advanced soldiers.

As Davale's skills had grown, so had her ruthlessness. She trained day and night and never refused him when he demanded that she learn a new fighting style or weapon.

When other women longed to settle down and start families, Davale longed only to fight and train. She lived for the next mission, the next challenge, never stopping to rest. Her devotion to Litagus had caused many followers in their order to question the nature of their relationship. Rumors of a love affair had plagued them since Davale had grown into a woman, but neither party paid them much mind. Litagus saw Davale almost as a daughter.

When Litagus had brought Davale into seclusion with him three years ago, he had expanded her duties and made her his right-hand woman, knowing how hard she had worked to prove herself to him over the years.

Litagus was aware of the petty rivalry between Vargas and Davale that developed soon after they first met when they arrived in Bramblewood, but felt it was nothing more than two children fighting over their father's attention. Vargas had also been raised by one of their temples even before Davale arrived and, through his own efforts, had climbed the ranks and become a highly capable priest at the age of thirty-five. Litagus had high expectations of Vargas becoming a high priest himself one day. Both Vargas and Davale were essential to the fulfillment of Litagus's goals, but they served very different purposes.

Litagus was pulled abruptly from his thoughts as Bucomus ran into the room. "There's a commotion outside," he said, bowing before Litagus and trying to catch his breath.

"Explain," Litagus replied, standing up and leaning over the table, his palms flat against the parchment scattered across the surface.

"The wolf tribes say they've been attacked by outsiders

within the forest," Bucomus said, his face flushed.

Litagus's thoughts immediately jumped to the Book of Ziz and who might be coming to steal it from him. It was obvious from the look on Bucomus's face that he was thinking the same. Bucomus was a servant and nothing more, but he did possess a sharp mind and good insight. In order to keep the young man from becoming a threat, Litagus had ensured that Bucomus had never been trained as a fighter or a cleric, grooming him instead to be Litagus's personal steward. Bucomus had Litagus's complete trust.

"Call upon Vargas and Davale, and then return to my room," Litagus said, walking to the door.

"Right away, High Priest."

Litagus walked up and out unto the balcony, overlooking the entrance of the temple. He could see Captain Unsinn under the cloudy afternoon sky and just over twenty of his guards gathered around two members of the wolf tribe. Litagus noticed the tribesmen were wounded, both holding their sides. As they spoke with the guards, they frequently turned to look behind them into the trees. Litagus knew whatever was out there had terrified these tribesmen, a disturbing thought considering the fierceness of the wolf tribe.

Even so, Litagus felt certain Bramblewood Forest provided an easily defendable position. It rested between mountains to the east and the river to the west. He had trusted informants stationed in the only town to the north where the valley ended. The marsh to the south near the middle of the forest also prevented any large groups from attacking. Often, men who ventured inside never came out. With all of these obstacles, Litagus felt assured this invasion could only involve a small number, and that this situation would be over quickly, allowing him to resume his studies.

Litagus was watching the road leading to his compound when he saw movement from the trees to the left. Three men burst from the tree line wearing black armor and wielding black swords. Their skin and elongated faces were red, and what appeared to be horns grew from the tops of their large bald heads.

"Gothoar…" Litagus muttered under his breath. Behind the three came more of these men, until their numbers totaled ten.

The two wolf-men scrambled past Captain Unsinn's men, who were running off in the other direction. The guards backed up, visibly shaken at the sudden appearance of such strange enemies.

"Fall in line!" the captain commanded his men.

The guards stopped moving back and raised their shields. They created a squad of eight men in three rows. The guards held their position as the ten armor-clad warriors let out a shrieking battle cry and charged.

The two forces came together with the sound of clashing metal.

"To the sides!" the captain ordered.

The guards in the last row and those standing on the sides began to close in and surround the ten attackers.

"Seize their flanks!" the captain shouted and drew his sword.

Litagus watched intently as guard after guard fell to the black blades. As one of the ten demonic men moved toward the compound's doors, the captain rushed in front of him, blocking his way. They exchanged blows and appeared evenly matched in skill until the black blade cut the captain down.

Litagus ground his teeth as guard after guard fell to the black swords. His eyes scanned the area, but he could not find Vargas or Davale. If they did not show, he would have to enter the battle himself.

"Vargas! We're under attack," Bucomus yelled at the door to Vargas's room.

Vargas stood. "By whom?" he asked, but Bucomus had already left to warn someone else. An image of Rathen's face flashed across his mind as Vargas picked up a mace from a rack of weapons on the wall. *Well, if it is Rathen, I shall put an end to this blood feud once and for all.*

Racing down stone staircases and long hallways, Vargas burst through the front doors of the temple just in time to see Captain Unsinn fall to a black-armored man wearing what looked like a red demon mask. Vargas could see other masked men behind this one, slashing their way through the guards holding a tight formation around them.

Vargas held his black amulet in one hand and mace in the other. As the masked man approached, swinging his weapon, Vargas blocked with the mace. He began to softly chant, channeling a spell through his amulet. The spell evoked the opposite of a healing spell, acting to drain the life from the person it contacted; Vargas just needed to get his amulet past the armor. He blocked with his mace again and reached out his other hand, the one holding the amulet, to take hold of the underarm of the man in black armor. As he suspected, he found a gap in the armor and sent his spell through. The masked man let out a cry of pain but kept fighting.

Vargas saw another masked man approach from the side as he deflected a strike from his current attacker. Vargas lifted up his amulet and channeled a blindness spell at the oncoming man, causing him to stop and hold a hand to his eyes.

Vargas stepped quickly to the side to survey the damage. Only he and the few guards still standing blocked the rest of the masked men as they approached the front doors. Each spell drained Vargas by degrees, and he needed to maintain his strength as long as he could.

He concentrated on the weakened opponent still before him and found the opportunity to strike, his mace sending the masked man to the ground, injured. Another invader approached, and Vargas channeled his Desolation spell and sent a black mass toward him. As it hit, the masked man instantly crumbled to the ground, the spell in full power, more potent than even the strongest armor.

Vargas heard movement behind him and swung around to see Davale run out the door, a dagger in each hand. She ran toward the man Vargas had blinded and sunk both daggers into his neck, spraying a fine red mist into the air.

Vargas channeled another Desolation spell, killing a masked man as he rushed forward. The remaining attackers focused on Davale as she spun and danced around their swings, slashing her daggers indiscriminately. Vargas took the opportunity to crush the skull of a masked man before him with his mace.

The few remaining guards rallied to attack as Davale cut down another two enemies, her white shirt soaked in blood.

The remaining four masked men backed away, holding their weapons defensively. Vargas gathered what little of his strength remained for one more spell. He channeled the necessary energy in a tight swirling ball within him but held his spell ready, waiting to see what the attackers would do. Davale and the guards held their weapons at the ready.

"Kill them all!" a command roared from the balcony above.

Vargas looked up to see Litagus pointing his finger toward the remaining masked men.

Vargas sent his spell in a black mass toward one of the four attackers. The spell sent the man to the ground, crying out in pain, but did not kill him as it had the earlier man. Vargas stumbled back, weakened from his efforts. Instantly, the guards charged and attacked, impaling the wounded man as the other three masked men turned and ran into the tree line. Davale started to run after them.

"Stop!" Litagus commanded. "There may be more. Secure the grounds and heal the wounded."

Davale stopped her chase and looked over the scene.

Satisfied the threat was gone, Vargas sank to the ground. He sat breathing heavily and placed his amulet back around his neck. He knew a few spells of healing but could not channel them before regaining some of his energy. He would have to rely on the other priests.

Vargas watched as the remaining guards and Davale checked over the wounded. A few priests from the compound began to file out through the doors and help the injured.

Vargas gathered some strength and went over to one of the dead attackers. He reached down, pulling on the face to remove the mask, but it would not budge. Upon further inspection, he found that the red demon faces were not masks at all. They were the real faces of the demon men, their skin still hot to the touch.

He could hear fearful comments from the guards around him as they too began to realize what Vargas had, muttering that the creatures were not men at all.

Davale cut them off before panic set in. "They die like any other man."

But Vargas knew that the beasts had fought with much greater strength than any man, with more strength than any one of the defenders... except Davale. He turned his attention to the woman whose eyes gleamed as she poked a boot at a fallen demon man. Seeing Davale fight for the first time, he respected her ability. Yet suspicion rose that there was more to her than the eye could see.

Litagus watched from the balcony as his priests healed the injured. To his relief, the captain and eleven injured guards were saved. The others were beyond help. Three of the minions of Gothoar had managed to escape, but it was better than sending his forces into the forest without knowing how many were out there. He would send Davale to hunt for the remaining three.

Litagus walked back into his chambers, where he found Bucomus waiting for orders.

"Summon all of our guards from patrols, bring back anyone remaining in Deepbriar, and hire more if you can. Place them around the compound on watch," Litagus ordered.

"Yes, High Priest," Bucomus replied. "Do we know where the attackers came from?"

Litagus frowned. "It seems I have had the book for too long. The servants of Gothoar have come seeking it out."

"Then… they've found us. Are we even still safe here?"

"No," Litagus said. "We must move up our plans to meet in the Dark Hills temple, perhaps even moving our base there."

"Yes, High Priest. I'll make the arrangements. Is there anything else you need?"

"Send Davale to me."

Bucomus bowed and left the room.

Litagus walked over to the table in the center of the room. He ran his hand down the front of the large red book, his fingers caressing the tooled cryptic symbols on the timeworn leather. *I just need a little more time.*

Davale carried the bodies of the fallen to a pile in the clearing just off the main road. They were stripped of armor and anything else reusable and burned. There was no time for a burial. She looked down at the face of the second body she carried, recognizing it as one of the four drunk guards she had encountered at the Deepbriar inn a few nights before. *If you had trained more instead of drinking, you might have survived.*

Davale heard the swish of footsteps in the dried grass behind her. She turned to see Bucomus approaching. "Litagus wishes to see you," the steward said.

"Good," Davale replied, laying the body of the young man down in the pile. She was happy to escape clean-up duty.

As she approached the front doors, she gave Vargas a nod. The cleric stood overseeing the healing and the inspection of the dead attackers.

Vargas flashed her back a nod. Davale knew that the two of them were responsible for killing the majority of the attackers. Vargas had proven a formable caster, killing one of his opponents with a single spell. She admired his skill, but that didn't lessen her dislike of him.

Davale walked into the compound and up the stairs, entering Litagus's study.

Litagus stood in his room, ready for her. "Well done."

"Thanks," she replied with a smile.

"You can postpone your search for the spell components. I need you to find the remaining three attackers in the forest and kill them. You can take a few guards if you wish."

Davale bowed. "Right away, High Priest, but I'll be faster on my own. I was able to cut two of the three who escaped, so I should be able to follow their blood trail."

Litagus nodded. "Very well. Once you have killed them, return to me. We have one final high priest to dispose of in the Dark Hills temple."

"Understood." She preferred hunting dangerous prey in the woods than killing another old man in some dusty isolated temple. It would be even more fun to prolong this hunt. "But it's a big forest. It may take a few days," she said, concealing her enthusiasm.

"Find them and kill them. But if your hunt goes beyond the two days, leave them and return to me."

"I will," she said with a quick bow.

Davale left Litagus's chambers and made her way downstairs to her own room. She peeled off her ruined shirt, the dried blood sticking to her skin. Wiping the blood from her skin as best she could with a damp rag, Davale put on a fresh leather tunic and sat down before a large wooden box in the corner. She unfastened the two daggers she wore at her hip and set them down on the table beside the box. There was no time to thoroughly clean them now.

Davale looked over her collection of daggers lying neatly in the box, ten blades lined in a row, trying to select the right ones for her hunting trip. She decided on two long, thin blades with dark leather wrapped around the handle. The long blades would give her more reach in hand-to-hand combat but would still work well for slicing someone's neck from behind. She placed one in her boot and one on her hip.

With a smile, she left the compound and set off into the forest, ready for the hunt.

She immediately took to scouting the forest paths in search of the fleeing attackers. A trail of blood extended for several steps to a spot where it had pooled. After that, the trail completely disappeared, indicating the wounded had either been healed or bandaged before moving on.

With gray clouds shielding the forest canopy from the early evening sunlight, the trails grew dark and cold. Davale placed her hand on her dagger, walking stealthily down the trail beside the bramble bushes. Her uncanny ability to blend into the shadows made it difficult for anyone to see her until she was right upon them.

Her eyes constantly scanned the path ahead for signs of movement. She knew she needed to be careful; these attackers had proven to be dangerous. She could use the element of surprise as her first offensive line before resorting to a face-to-face fight. Given more time, she would enjoy toying with her prey, but Litagus made clear her time was limited—and she intended to return with three more kills to her growing credits.

Davale silently made her way deeper into the forest, her eyes scanning the trees, her senses on full alert. Catching an unfamiliar scent on the wind, she licked her lips.

The hunt was on.

Chapter 12

Rathen and his group hurried down the Bramblewood Forest trail as quickly as they could. The hard dirt allowed for a rapid pace, but the rattling of metal armor and weapons gave away their presence to anyone within earshot. Rathen, concerned by the noise they were making, glanced behind himself several times, ensuring that nothing was following them.

Rathen noticed that Magom floated quickly beside him and wondered if the lich's skeletal legs moved at all under his robes. Looking ahead, he could see the two youngest and most inexperienced of the group—Caswen, running beside Marduke, and Dryn, just ahead of her—slowing with exhaustion.

"Rathen," Magom called out. "I sense movement ahead."

Rathen nodded, nudging Bulo in front of him, who then nudged Marduke and Rendrak. They turned and got the attention of Garrick and the druid in the lead. The group stopped and stood silently, each member carefully scanning the area through their heavy breaths. The snorting of horses could be heard up ahead where the trail started to curve to the left.

The druid stepped to the side of the trail and started to clear bramble bushes as Garrick pulled a spellbook out of his bag. The group slipped past the bushes into the cleared area Apaca created. Everyone crouched down behind the vegetation, securing their gear as Garrick cast a spell in the area with a hushed chant.

"Remain still and they will not see us," Garrick whispered.

Rathen did not see a barrier around them or feel any difference, but he trusted Garrick's word. He lowered himself between Bulo and Thack but rested his hand on the hilt of his sword just in case. Only Dryn's heavy breathing broke the group's silence.

"Get it under control, Dryn," Marduke whispered from between Caswen and Rendrak.

Dryn took a few deep breaths, and the group fell silent.

In the silence, they could all hear the hooves of the patrolmen's horses growing closer and closer. As the patrol began to pass their hiding place, the horses whinnied and stamped their feet in distress.

"What is it?" a male voice asked from the other side of the brambles.

Through the heavy bushes, Rathen could not make out how many riders filled the path. Even if only one saw them and ran, it would be impossible to catch the rider on horseback while Rathen's band was on foot.

"Something's spooking the horses," a second male voice said.

Rathen's mind immediately flashed to the lich. The heavy enchanted robe helped conceal his aura from human eyes, but animals were more sensitive. He looked over his group as they readied their weapons.

Rathen carefully moved to glimpse out from the bushes. He could only see one rider, a young man wearing dark leather armor that bore metal studding on the front and back. From the side, Rathen could not make out what weapons he carried.

"Should we investigate?" the first voice asked.

"We don't have time. We'll just report it to the captain," the second voice replied.

Rathen let out a silent sigh of relief as he heard the riders coax their steeds forward and away.

They waited until they could no longer hear the riders before returning to the trail. The break seemed to give Caswen and Dryn a chance to catch their breath. The group climbed back out onto the road and continued their sprint in Rathen's ordered formation.

Another long distance went by before Magom again got Rathen's attention.

"Movement within the trees," he said evenly.

Before Rathen could signal the others, wolves howled from both sides of the path.

"Run until they attack," Rathen called out. He considered their cover lost, but he hoped to reach the forbidden area before the wolf-men overwhelmed them on the trail.

The howls continued as the group came to a stop. Rathen peered over the heads of those in front of him to see why they'd quit running and saw Garrick studying an area in the brambles. The trees past the bushes were marked: a circle with a horizontal line through it had been magically cut into the bark.

"This is it," Garrick called out.

Rathen recalled his conversation with Garrick a few days

ago about a marked, forbidden section of the forest that supposedly housed "the old one." Shivering, Rathen gathered the group close and turned toward the howling, placing the edge of the forbidden area behind them. They waited for an attack, but nothing showed itself.

"It's like they're trying to push us into this area," Thack said.

"Yes, well, if we make it out, we can likely expect them to be waiting for us," Rathen said. "Apaca, clear the path where the trees are marked, and let's see what the mystery is."

Apaca nodded and worked to create a narrow trail into the marked area. Everyone filed in, and they trekked deep within the vegetation. Soon, the howling grew muffled through the dense undergrowth and then ceased altogether.

The deeper they ventured into the area, the more the air grew foul and humid, creating the taste of mold on the tongue and the slick of slime on the face. Up ahead, the trees finally gave way to a large clearing. Inside the clearing was a marsh, small patches of muddy ground separated by murky pools of still water. They had no way of knowing how deep the pools were. Yards away, in the middle of the marsh, Rathen could just make out the shape of a small shack covered with moss and vines. The group stopped at the edge of the marsh and turned to Rathen for instructions.

"I suppose this is it. Something living in that little shack is considered 'the old one'—a creature so powerful that not even Litagus will enter this part of the forest." He paused, letting the weight of his words sink in. "I expect each one of you to remain alert and ready to handle whatever comes at us."

Everyone nodded, eyes scanning the scene warily.

Rathen looked up at the early evening sky shrouded in dark clouds. He gathered his courage before stepping into the watery ground and leading his group into unknown dangers. As fear coursed through his veins, he reminded himself that every step was one step closer to Vargas, the Book of Ziz, and saving Bandark's world.

Holding their weapons above their heads, the group trudged through the marsh, the muddy water reaching up to their waists in certain places. The water was cold, thick with putrid swirls, and smelled foul, which kept the group moving at a very slow pace. Every once in a while, someone would stop to pull their leg free from the suction of the dense mud below. Rathen tried not to think about what could be swimming around.

Turning to check on the group, Rathen saw that Magom seemed to be walking on top of the mud, the hem of his robes dragging behind him, weighed down with water. He then noticed Caswen, perched atop Thack's shoulder, her white robe pulled up to her knees. Rathen gave Thack a disapproving glance; the half-orc needed to keep his arm free in case of attack. But Thack just grinned in response and held up his axe in his hand, showing that he was prepared to defend himself and her.

Behind Thack and Caswen, Rathen caught Marduke also shooting the two a disapproving glance. Dryn walked beside Marduke, holding her bow above her head. As protective as she was of her sister, Dryn did not seem as bothered by Caswen's friendship with Thack as Marduke was. Shaking his head, Rathen turned back to face the front.

Something in the mud up ahead caught Rathen's

attention. He paused to inspect it and found the decomposing corpse of a wolf-man, the mask of his costume still over his face. The smell emanating from the body threatened to overpower his senses, and he pulled up the crook of his arm up to cover his nose. He wondered how long it had been rotting away in the marsh.

"Rathen!" Thack shouted from behind him.

Rathen turned to see ripples in the water as if something swam underneath.

"The water is shallow. It can't be that big," Rathen said, trying to alleviate his friend's concern while knowing full well that deadly dangers could come in small packages.

As they walked knee-deep toward the shack in the distance, several more bodies were seen lying in the muck. Some were of the wolf tribe, a few looked like they wore the same armor as the scouts on the road, and others were just skeletons, their garments long since rotted away. The danger was growing closer.

"On your guard!" Rathen called out, his eyes focused on the shack.

Soon, the ripples swished past them again. This time they circled the group, growing to an unnatural speed. Rathen held his hand up, and everyone stopped in place. Thack carefully removed Caswen from his shoulder, and she gasped sharply as the cold water hit her legs.

The ripples increased to small waves as if something very large moved underground.

"Stay together," Rathen said. Whatever sort of creature it was, it moved with great speed. Certainly nothing like anything he had ever encountered before.

The flowing mud moved toward him, plowing the muck

and water aside. Rathen pulled his sword and readied his shield as he heard weapons being drawn behind him. The soggy ground would put them at a huge disadvantage to a creature that made this environment its home.

The movement stopped directly in front of Rathen. He planted his feet firmly in the mud and steadied himself. The ground started to rise, and the mud began to amass in front of him, taking shape as it rose up to his height. Rathen looked at it in amazement, still uncertain if it were hostile. The mud took a humanoid shape but lacked a face or any other distinct features.

"I am Arg'grimorem," a voice rang out loudly in Rathen's mind.

The voice startled him. This thing, whatever it was, spoke to him in his mid. He turned to see the faces of the others, confirming that they had heard it too.

"You have been sent to me in sacrifice," the voice said slowly.

"No… no, we haven't," Rathen said loudly. "We've come seeking the old one." He could only hope this being could hear him.

"Defeat the elements, or rest eternally within my waters," the voice said. Slowly, the mud figure sank back beneath the murky surface.

"We come in peace. We wish to talk with you," Rathen said, trying to reason with a being he no longer saw. There came no answer.

He turned to the group.

"Elements?" he asked. "Apaca, what is this thing?"

The druid glanced over, a troubled expression on his face. His eyes were wide, his mouth almost quivering. "I… I do not know," he said in a shaky voice.

Everyone else in the group shared the same blank look. In the distance, where the forest met the water, a flat stone shot up from the ground, then another beside it and all around them, a circle of solid stones. In an instant, a stone wall trapped them within the marsh.

Rathen grew nervous. What did they have to overcome within these walls to survive? What were they about to fight?

Everyone could sense the severity of the situation. Apaca's head turned frantically from side to side, his eyes wide and frantic like those of a caged animal.

Magom removed the cowl from his head, and for the first time, he removed the dampening robe and dropped it into the mud. He stood there in his tattered black robes, his bone-white skeletal form near naked. The immense feeling of dread mixed with Rathen's panic almost caused him to turn heel and run. Yet run where? He braced his mind and stood his ground, determined to pass this test and find Vargas.

Bulo and Thack moved forward to flank Rathen on either side, holding their weapons at the ready and looking around for signs of danger. Marduke stood on the other side of Thack, with Caswen just behind them. Dryn stood to Caswen's left, an arrow notched and ready. Garrick was in the middle on the other side of Caswen, with Rendrak and Bandark just behind him. Magom brought up the rear. Apaca slowly backed away.

Rathen noticed the druid's apprehension and wondered if the lich's dread pushed him too far. "Apaca, stay together!" he called out.

A large mass of water and mud started to swirl in the

distance in front of them. It slowly picked up speed, and a massive indeterminate form rose up from the muck.

"Cassy, stay behind me!" Marduke shouted, holding his massive sword in front of him.

The healer put a hand on her protector's back, assuring him that she was there, her other hand gripping her amulet. The druid backed farther away from the group.

"Thack, Bulo, stay on your sides. Everyone else, keep close," Rathen shouted, looking them over.

Magom held out his boney hands, his jaw agape. His eyes glowed brightly as his chanting flowed over them. The eerie sound made Rendrak and Bandark step away from him. The area around the lich grew darker. Soon, the dead bodies and skeletons that littered the area started to pull themselves from the mud. Rathen could hear the mud sucking as if the ground were attempting to restrain the bones from rising. Soon the decayed carcasses rose, stood, and sloshed through the water to stand in front of the group. It was an eerie sight, but these undead minions, numbering around twenty-five, stood as their first line of defense against whatever monstrosity was coming for them. Even Caswen gave no protest.

The massive figure took on shape: hands of jagged rock, legs and body of rock and muck, and a huge boulder for a head. It stood over twenty feet tall, towering over Rathen and his group.

Rathen's mouth fell open. A few shouts of panic erupted. Apaca started to run for the rock wall to their right, no doubt hoping to scale it, and Dryn turned to follow, grabbing Caswen's arm to pull her away.

"Dryn, hold fast!" Marduke shouted, his sword at his side. "You're a protector! Stand and fight."

Dryn stopped, took a deep breath, and turned back around, but Apaca continued his flight.

Rathen readied his sword, flashed a look to Bulo and Thack, and quickly glanced back at Bandark. "Do what you can!"

Bandark nodded, already preparing his bag of spell components.

The massive figure moved toward them at a much quicker pace than Rathen would have expected. This thing seemed to glide through the muck while the terrain hindered his group's mobility. It let out a roar that sounded like massive rocks being ground together.

The massive stone and mud figure turned toward the druid running toward the right edge of the wall. It hopped across the water, leaping into the air. As Apaca continued to run, the monstrosity landed and flattened the druid into the mud, out of sight. The tremors of the figure's impact threw water and mud into the air almost as high as it was tall. No sound came from Apaca, and Rathen knew such an attack would be impossible to survive. The creature lifted its stone foot and turned back toward the group.

Rathen needed to be careful or they were all likely to share the same fate. "No one run. Stand firm!" he shouted, taking a step forward in the mud.

Magom shifted his undead minions to the right side, where the rock monster now approached.

The massive figure moved back toward them. As Magom's skeletons and other undead lurched toward it, it used his rock hands to bat them away like shooing away pesky flies.

"Magom, use your ice spells on this thing to slow it

down!" Rathen called out, recalling the spells the lich used in the previous battle. He was uncertain what other attacks might affect this creature.

The massive figure crushed the remaining undead and came toward the four fighters who gathered in front of the group: Rathen, Thack, Bulo, and Marduke. It took a swipe at Thack, who moved out of the way just in time, swinging the hammer side of his axe at the stone hand as it crossed before him. The hit sounded with a thud, yet the massive figure did not react.

A spray of ice came from Magom's hands, striking the creature's feet and freezing the water around it. The four men backed away until the lich completed his spell. The ice froze the figure's feet in place momentarily. Taking his chance, Rathen struck at the stone leg with his onyx sword. It hit the stone and muck with little effect but reverberated against his grip. Bulo, Thack, and even Marduke all struck the legs before the creature broke free of the ice. A few cracks in the stone were noticeable, but they needed something more substantial.

The creature raised a foot and attempted to stomp Bulo, but to Rathen's relief the old gladiator was able to move out of the way.

An incredibly strong gust of wind flew from Bandark's hands, striking the top portion of the creature and tearing away mud and dirt, leaving only the rock underneath. Magom froze its feet again as a massive hand came crashing down next to Rathen. Anticipating the strike, Rathen dove to the side, out of the way and into the mud.

With the immediate threat of the strike out of the way, Rathen turned to the group. "Bandark, blast the legs with your wind! Magom, freeze the rock, and then burn it! We have to crack the stone!"

Both Bandark and Magom, standing farther back with the others, readied their spells. Dryn stood with her bow drawn, eyes wide. Garrick stood in place with his glass dagger in hand. Caswen's face reflected her terror, but she held her amulet in her hand and started casting a spell as well. The four fighters at the figure's feet readied their attack once the creature was frozen in place.

The massive hand rose again in the middle of the group, aiming to strike Dryn and Garrick. Caswen shouted words of Thandrall's protection, and a golden shield of light appeared above the two. The massive fist crashed down, hit the shield, and stopped. Both Dryn and Garrick scurried out from under it before the golden shield gave way. The creature's fist hit the mud, sending up a spray of muck.

Another blast of wind from Bandark ripped the dirt, mud, and muck from the creature's legs. The wind gust knocked over Marduke and Thack, who could not move out of the way in time. The two men stood up covered in mud.

Magom froze the stone legs and called out, "Fire," causing Rathen and the fighters to scurry aside. An intense wave of flame shot from the lich, engulfing the creature's frozen legs. The four fighters rushed back in, striking at the legs and making greater progress with the now weakened rock. The creature used both of its hands to swing at the warriors at its feet, but they were blocked by Caswen's golden shield.

Another gust from Bandark took the remaining mud from the creature's midsection, leaving only rock on its entire body.

The creature broke a now cracked stone leg free and

raised its foot to stomp at Thack and Rendrak. Thack nimbly jumped off to the side, but Rendrak seemed stuck. Rathen rushed to him, dropping his sword and shield in the process. He grabbed ahold of Rendrak, pushing him out of range as the hand came down. Rathen had no time to move himself to safety and waited for the strike that would no doubt end his life, but it didn't come. He looked up to see Bandark's light blue shield over his head and the hand of the creature on top of it. Rathen leaped from under it and into the mud beside Rendrak.

Rathen turned to call out for Magom to throw more ice. He saw Dryn lower her bow and rush to the other side of the group.

"Stay together!" Rathen yelled. "Magom, concentrate more ice on the feet." With his weapon lost in the mud, he backed away, surveying the battle and calling out orders.

The three warriors at the creature's feet backed away for the ice spell. Marduke watched Dryn working her way to the other side of the creature, her bow drawn and aimed at the creature's head. "Dryn, no!" he yelled.

Ignoring Marduke, Dryn loosed three arrows in rapid succession, drawing the creature's attention to her and away from Magom and others. As Dryn notched another arrow, Marduke ran to Dryn through the mud, shedding his helmet and dropping his sword in his haste to reach her.

Magom shot ice at its feet again until the rocks were well frozen. Turning its attention away from Dryn, the creature struggled to move and lashed out toward Magom. It slammed both hands down toward the lich. Magom moved quickly, but Caswen's golden light shield again stopped the attack.

Bulo and Thack backed away from the creature as Magom cast fire at its frozen feet. When the lich was done, the two warriors struck vigorously at the legs, creating even larger cracks and chipping away massive chunks of the pitted and weakened stone.

Dryn shot a few more arrows at the creature, once more gaining its attention. "Dryn, stop! You'll get yourself killed!" Marduke yelled, running for her.

Dryn's face was set as she fired more arrows, completely ignoring Marduke's commands. Rathen knew she was being reckless, and if she did not heed orders and stay within the group, she would probably end up like the druid. Rathen wanted to help, but he had to focus on saving the whole group, not just one person.

"Bandark, shield Bulo and Thack while they work on the legs!" Rathen yelled.

The creature's full attention was on Dryn now as arrow after arrow struck its head and torso. It ignored the warriors at its feet, and with one enormous step, it closed the distance to Dryn. Clearly startled by its quick movements, Dryn turned to run, but her feet sunk into the mud and she could not move. She screamed in frustration.

"No, Dryn!" Caswen yelled. She held her amulet, creating a shield barrier between the creature and her sister.

Dryn swung her bow over her back so she could pull on her leg with both hands. The creature pounded on Caswen's shield, attempting to get to her. Caswen kept up her spell, but Rathen could see the strain on her face.

Marduke finally reached Dryn and leaned over her in the mud. Taking hold under her arms, he pulled her free and threw her to the side just as Caswen fell to her knees, exhausted, her shield giving way. The creature's massive fists came crashing down where Dryn had been stuck. The creature barely missed her, falling instead on Marduke and pounding him into the mud.

"No!" Caswen screamed, still on her knees. "Marduke!"

The healer stood, tears in her eyes. She held her amulet in the air, chanting for Thandrall's Judgment in a loud voice, a strange glow emanating from her skin. Instead of a shield, a large golden hammer of light formed before the creature, striking it in the chest. The impact pushed the creature back and sent a massive crack down its chest.

Once again, Caswen fell to her knees, the glow fading. Thack rushed to her side, catching her just as she fell backward into the water.

"There!" Rathen yelled. "Magom, hit that crack with everything you have!"

The lich chanted, a whirlwind of humming energy swirling around him. Bulo backed away from its legs, moving to stand beside Thack and Caswen as Bandark kept the shield barrier up, deflecting the creature's attacks.

Ice shards shot from Magom's bony hands, freezing the creature's chest and encasing it in ice. Next, he sent a barrage of large fireballs that exploded on the creature's chest. The crack widened with each strike, sending chunks of stone falling into the mud below, splashing muck across the group. The creature paused and focused on the lich.

Finally, Magom summoned a mass of energy and sent a large bolt of lightning into the cracked chest. The bolt hit with a thundering crash and shattered the stone. The chest split into three pieces and fell from the creature's body. The creature's head and arms followed, leaving only the waist and cracked legs standing motionless. A beat passed as everyone waited to be sure it was dead. When it did not move, Rathen and Caswen ran toward Marduke.

Rathen arrived before Caswen, but Dryn was already there, cradling Marduke's head in her lap where he had fallen. Silent tears dripped off her nose onto his face.

Rathen stopped in his tracks, looking down at Marduke's broken form, trying to assess the damage. Seeing Marduke's crushed body, he grimaced. Blood ran from the old warrior's nose and mouth.

Caswen ran passed Rathen and knelt beside Marduke's body in the mud. "Marduke," she cried, her face full of tears.

Marduke opened his eyes. "Cassy?"

"I'm here! I'll heal you. You'll be fine," she said, reaching for her amulet. She barely had enough strength to hold herself up.

"Oh, Cassy. Not even Lazlo himself could heal me now," Marduke said, trying to move his arms. Rathen could see they were both broken.

"No. I am stronger than that," she cried, wiping the tears from her face. She tried to lift her arms up over Marduke but collapsed on his chest. Caswen cried out in frustration.

"Cassy, listen to me. You are stronger. I saw you summon Thandrall's Hammer of Judgment. Not even Lazlo has the ability to do that," Marduke said, his voice becoming weaker.

"But it wasn't enough to save you," Caswen said into his chest, her head close to his.

"My little Cassy, this old warrior finally gets to rest."

"No!" Caswen pleaded.

"It's your time, Cassy. Your faith and your power rival even the high priest himself," Marduke said, his voice soft. "I'm so proud of you."

Caswen sobbed, too weak to move.

"Marduke, I'm sorry," Dryn said, her voice cracking.

Marduke seemed to only just notice Dryn's face hovering above his own. "Dryn," he said, his voice barely a whisper now, "You always were reckless." He chuckled, his laughter turning into a horrible cough.

"This is all my fault," said Dryn, barely holding herself together.

Marduke looked into her eyes, trying to make her understand. "No, Dryn. I knew what I was doing. I'm glad it's me, instead of you. You're very… brave, Dryn. Keep… making me proud. You two… take care… of each other," he gasped between his words.

Marduke closed his eyes, a smile etched on his lips.

The only sound was of Caswen sobbing as Marduke took his last breath.

Rathen looked around at the others. Magom stood motionless where he had cast his spell, his robes still off and the energy around him dissipated. Garrick stood next to Bandark, close to Rathen. Thack and Rendrak pulled themselves through the mud over to where Marduke's body lay. Thack knelt beside Caswen, carefully lifting her off of Marduke. She started to protest but collapsed into his arm as soon as she saw Thack's face, sobbing into his shoulder. Thack held her with his one arm, stroking her hair. Dryn's eyes did not move from Marduke's still face, apparently in shock. Behind them, the creature's legs, still standing, started to sink into the mud.

Bulo came up next to Rathen. "Here," he said, handing Rathen his shield and sword.

Rathen nodded with a smile.

Rathen and Bulo stood together surveying the battlefield, a familiar feeling for the two. Rathen had to rethink his plans. Now, with no druid and missing a skilled fighter, they had lost much of their edge. He looked over to Bulo, who showed the same concern, but neither of them spoke. This was a time of grief.

The mud stirred again.

"On your guard!" Rathen called out, shooting a look to Bulo and Thack. Caswen pulled herself away from Thack and onto her knees, holding out her amulet. The others prepared for another attack.

Chapter 13

The stirring mud again took the shape, this time of a man-sized figure. Rathen wanted to slice the figure with his sword, but stayed his hand.

"You have defeated the elements and are free to go," the voice who called himself Arg'grimorem said.

"Why? What was this for?" Caswen yelled from where she knelt next to Marduke's body.

There came no reply.

Caswen strained to stand, declining Thack's outstretched arm, and pulled herself through the mud to reach the man-sized mud figure. Rathen noticed the amulet around her neck had begun to glow, the light spreading across her body, radiating her holy power even in her weakened state.

"What was this battle for? Your amusement? What are you? A demon?" Rage dripped from her voice as she shouted.

"I am… Arg'grimorem. The bringer of life."

"You are death!" Caswen screamed.

Rathen prepared to intervene in case the mud figure attacked, but made no attempt to stop Caswen.

"I am worshiped as an element of nature. Not death," the voice said.

"By whom? The dead that lay within your waters?" Caswen shouted.

"No. Once, I was whole. My essence was contained there," the voice said in their minds as it created an arm from the mud and indicated toward the shack in the marsh.

"Your essence? Of what foul creature?" Caswen asked.

"My previous self," the voice said. The mud figure turned toward the shack and slowly glided over the mud toward it. Caswen plodded after it, not ready to give it leave. Rathen and the group followed.

As they approached, they noticed the heavy vegetation on the building was a rich green, with flowers and sprouts of various kinds lining the sides in vibrant color. The shack was only large enough for two men to stand in and was built like an oval. The walls were thin planks spread every so often, making for an exposed wall.

"What is this?" Bulo asked.

The mud figure stopped in front of the shack.

"From here, I came. Once, my trees spread far, and my forest provided home to many."

Thack looked up at the planks that ran into the mud and used his hand to move the vegetation. "These are bones!" he said running his hand along one of the plank's surface. "Hard as stone and ancient." Thack looked over the entire area with amazement.

Rathen assessed the size and shape of the oval shack. It had the appearance of a giant ribcage. He tried to imagine how large this creature must have been to have such a large chest. He guessed it would have been about the same size as the earth creature they had just fought, if not larger.

"You died here?" Caswen asked, her tone turning soft. Her glow continued.

"I have not died. I am one with nature. I reside here and protect this forest."

Rathen made the connection: this being must be creating the enchantments that made the bramble bushes grow to protect itself within the forest.

"Were there more of your race?" Magom asked.

"I am a singularity, coming into existence the same time as this world."

"What were you? A demigod?" Magom pressed.

"I came before any others. My temple lay to the north, and my green realm extended far. I had many followers even before the days of man. Animals and beasts and so many other creatures that have long since passed from this world all sought to live within my protection. When my physical body came to rest here and I become one with nature, most of my followers abandoned me. Over time, my powers have grown weaker as my remaining followers chose to leave this place. Now, only this small forest stands to honor me. And even it shrinks with each passing cycle."

"You called us sacrifices. Why?" Rathen said to the mud man. "You've killed two good men."

"My followers, the children of the wolf, still pay me tribute. They are descendants of the ancient wolf tribe that once protected the forest and my followers. They continue to honor me by bringing a sacrifice each cycle. If not outsiders as yourself, then one of their own."

"Then you are death!" Caswen shouted. The glow around her slowly pulsated with power.

"I am Arg'grimorem, the bringer of life."

"You may have been once, but you are not any longer," Caswen decreed. "You reward your followers by taking a life from their numbers? That is not tribute. It is fear!"

Arg'grimorem offered no response.

"Share in their lives, bring them happiness. Use your powers to give life or help protect it," Caswen prodded. "You still have followers, and that might be what keeps you here. But if you continue killing them, eventually they will either all die out or be too afraid to worship you. Without them, you might fade completely."

"They are mine!" the voice shouted. "Life is mine to give and mine to take."

"Their lives are their own. Your greed to possess life has made you a monster," Caswen pressed. "Arg'grimorem, the giver of death!"

"I am Arg'grimorem, the bringer of life!" the voice shouted in Rathen's head forcefully, almost painfully.

"Then live up to that title!" Caswen lashed back just as strongly, her voice strained with emotion. The glow around her intensified, illuminating the area in its golden light. Rathen noticed the lich, who had already been standing away from Caswen, back away even farther from the glow.

The man-shaped mud did not respond or budge. Rathen and the others stood waiting in silence for a while, but no one dared to move.

"Perhaps you are right," Arg'grimorem's voice finally replied, its tone hushed. "I can sense goodness within you— something I lost many cycles ago. I had almost forgotten…"

"You can still redeem yourself," said Caswen. "It's not too late."

"I did not want them to leave me," said the voice. "I did not want to be alone, so I kept them with me." The broken corpses rustled slightly in the water.

Caswen's voice filled with compassion. "You were afraid they would leave you if you did not keep them here any way you could. But death does not keep anyone here—it only sends them farther away."

"I... do not want to bring death, only life," said Arg'grimorem.

Caswen nodded in satisfaction. "Then you are on the path to redemption." The glow about her dimmed until it completely disappeared.

The gloom of the marsh lifted as sunlight broke through the clouds. The grimy water rippled, then started to seep into the ground.

"This wetland will be cleansed, and each life that was taken here shall be honored. Inform the wolf tribes that I welcome them back and will no longer receive their sacrifices," Arg'grimorem said.

"I don't think we speak the same language," Rathen said, knowing that getting anything through to the tribes would not be easy.

"Then take this rock and hold it up in their presence. I will speak to them through it." The mud figure held out its hand, and a fist-sized blue stone rose up from the mud to rest in its palm.

Rathen reached out to take the stone as the mud figure melted back into the ground. In the distance, the rock barrier sunk back into the earth, revealing the forest outside. The ground began to shift beneath their feet, and the water drained away, revealing the mud underneath. As the mud dried, small grass sprouts poked up and grew with exceptional speed, turning the entire marsh into a rich green plateau. The damp and rotten smell of the water faded, giving way to the fragrance of flowers and fresh vegetation.

Rathen looked around to see that where piles of bones had lain, rocks were shooting up from the ground in human shapes. The speed of the transformation from a swampy death pool to a grassy retreat of granite statuary amazed him.

Caswen, rushed over to where Marduke's body had lain, her brown, mud-stained robe trailing her. Everyone followed.

His body was no longer there, and in its place stood a gray marble statue. The details in the stone closely resembled Marduke down to the stern expression on its face. His armor looked exactly as it had just before his injury and death. Caswen placed her hand on the statue's chest and bowed her head in prayer. Dryn stepped forward and, taking her sister's hand, bowed her head as well.

Rathen watched with intrigue as Bulo retrieved Marduke's sword and handed it to Dryn. "This was his father's sword, and I know he would want you to have it."

Dryn looked up through her tears and took hold of the blade. Rathen wondered how Bulo knew what he did and if Dryn would even be able to use the large sword. But for now, the blade had been passed to the next generation.

Turning away, Rathen walked toward the area where Apaca had died. To his surprise, Rendrak accompanied him. As they passed other statues, Rathen could see that many were of the wolf tribe and others resembled simple druids. He saw at least four that resembled the scouts connected to Vargas's compound.

"Rathen," Rendrak said as they walked together.

Rathen turned to look at him.

"Thank you… for what you did during the fight," Rendrak said, offering Rathen the first friendly smile.

Rathen nodded, knowing it wasn't necessary to say anything else.

Soon, they came upon the image of their fallen druid, Apaca. His statue stood straighter and appeared more serious than he had in life.

"Find peace, my friend," Rathen said, reaching out and placing his hand on the statue's shoulder.

Something at the base of the statue caught Rathen's eye. He leaned over to pick up Apaca's finished owl carving. Turning it over in his hand, he saw that Apaca had carved *Remy* into the base of the figure, and he knew that Apaca had intended to give the owl to his son. Pocketing the trinket, he vowed to himself to return the carving to Remric at any cost.

Walking back toward the middle of the plain, Rathen could see the vine-covered ribcage sink into the ground. In its place, a large stone statue of a man wearing robes rose up from the ground. It stood nearly as tall as the mud creature that had attacked them, now with its arms held out, palms turned up as if it were welcoming the world to its green plateau. Its gentle face and wide smile revealed what appeared to be canine-like teeth. Its nose and jaw protruded in a small snout. Surmising that the statue was the likeness of Arg'grimorem in life, Rathen looked in awe at the image, understanding why so many would follow such an inspiring being.

The group gathered beneath the statue, and Rathen saw Bandark and Garrick in a deep discussion. Bandark turned to Rathen as he approached.

"Rathen, Garrick is ready to venture into the compound to discover the hidden entrance."

Garrick nodded.

"Tonight? It will be evening soon, and we're all exhausted from the fight. Why not relax and take some food?"

"Nighttime is better for sneaking about. The workers are gone or asleep, giving us more freedom to search inside," Garrick said.

Rathen nodded. "Very well. I'll have Thack provide some food before you go. It may give you time to dust the dried mud from your clothes."

Garrick agreed and cleaned his clothing and armor while Thack prepared something to eat.

Rathen approached Bulo, who was sitting next to the others in the grass beside the giant statue of Arg'grimorem. "We should make a fire tonight. This area is still considered off limits to the rest of the forest for now. We should be safe, but we'll keep watch on all sides."

"I'll see to it," Bulo said, picking up his axe and moving toward the trees.

"Find dead branches if you can," Rathen said, taking note of the strong connection to the living vegetation and the being called Arg'grimorem.

Bulo nodded as he walked toward the forest.

Rathen turned to see Caswen and Dryn sitting in the grass, talking about Marduke. They held each other's hands as tears rolled down their cheeks. He knew it must be difficult for them. Marduke had a strong warrior's spirit and gave his life to save another. He would not forget the old warrior's courage, or his sacrifice. Caswen and Dryn turned as Rathen approached.

"Marduke was a great warrior. Fearless and strong," Rathen said.

Caswen looked up, her face stained with tears. Dryn wiped her eyes.

"I was too rash," Dryn said, resting her other hand on Marduke's sword beside her. "Too arrogant. He died because of me."

Rathen knelt down next to them. "Marduke gave his life for yours, to enable you to become the warrior he knew you could be." Dryn nodded. "He's given you a second chance, and you must seize it to learn from your mistakes and be the woman you are supposed to be."

"I will… I promise," Dryn said, lowering her head.

Caswen squeezed her sister's hand.

Rathen stood and walked over to Magom. The lich remained still and silent in his black, ragged robe, overlooking the green field where Arg'grimorem had appeared in mud form.

"Magom," Rathen said, attracting his attention. "Great work on those spells."

The lich did not move, ignoring Rathen's praise. "Such an amazing being to change the nature of the landscape so quickly," Magom said. "Such an immense power over the elements."

"Indeed."

"I have always considered druidic power to be a weaker discipline, but it is obvious that I was mistaken."

"This being was a druid?"

"No," Magom said, still looking off into the distance. "But he wielded the same power. This being is where druids may have likely obtained their abilities."

"And Caswen had the ability to reason with it?" Rathen

glanced toward the young woman, uncertainty in his voice.

The lich hissed. "Not exactly. Perhaps the young healer is stronger than she realizes. She greatly emanates her deity's power of goodness. Perhaps you cannot feel it, but it is strong enough to even affect me… at times."

Rathen thought back to when Caswen had spoken with the lich during the evening and how the lich had seemed to be charmed. "I think I understand."

"As she spoke with Arg'grimorem, I could sense the presence of the deity her temple worships."

"The glow," Rathen said, trying to make sense of the situation.

Magom nodded. "Her deity bestowed his powers to the young healer, allowing her to further influence Arg'grimorem, helping him to find redemption."

"Marduke spoke of redemption," Rathen said, making the connection. "It seemed to stop his attack on you back in Andar."

"Yes… This redemption seems paramount for their temple," the lich said.

"Why would her temple's deity give Arg'grimorem so much attention?" Rathen asked. His knowledge of temples and deities was limited at best, but for one to actually get involved was something he had never witnessed.

"The deities usually act with purpose, although their intents are rarely known. Perhaps the act of redeeming this ancient nature deity, who had been corrupted by time, was worthy of his attention."

Rathen nodded and sighed in relief. He looked around the new landscape with a sense of ease as he breathed in the fresh air.

"What does it look like? Describe it to me," Magom said.

"Describe what?"

"I can only sense that the land has changed and the water has dried up, but I cannot see its beauty."

Rathen nodded. "The land is as green as after a rainfall in spring. Yellow, blue, and purple flowers are scattered about. The smell of the air is fresh and clean and breathes of life," he said, attempting to give the beauty justice.

The lich stood there, letting out a soft hiss.

Rathen had heard the hiss many times from the lich. It had even haunted his dreams once. "Magom, if I may ask, why do you hiss?" Rathen hoped Magom's mood would allow for some honest talk.

Without moving or changing his focus, Magom said, "I have no need to breathe since my internal organs no longer function. However, out of habit, I take in air, and the hiss you hear is that air escaping from my ragged form."

"I see," Rathen replied, amazed at such a simple explanation for such an ominous sound. "May I ask something else?"

"Yes," Magom said, unmoving.

Seizing the chance, he asked the question that had been burning through him for months. "Back in your temple when we first met," Rathen started.

The lich turned slowly, his crimson eyes set on Rathen.

"When Vargas stole the Book of Ziz and claimed I had planned to take it from you, it caused you to attack." Rathen paused, observing the lich, who remained silent. "If it were not for Vargas, would you have attacked us?"

The long-dead flesh on the bottom of the lich's rotten chin formed what looked like the shadow of a smile. "Is this what it comes down to?"

"What?" Rathen asked, confused.

Magom stepped closer. "The reason you have become an innkeeper and squandered away your life is because you feel regret for the loss of friends in that fight? Or is it because of an unquenchable thirst for revenge on the man that threw you into that battle?"

"Neither," Rathen lied.

"You have shielded yourself from responsibilities, attempting to shake your anger."

"No."

"Ah, yes... now, it is clear."

Rathen immediately regretted asking. "Then answer the question," he said with a smile, attempting to keep the conversation lighthearted.

"No. I would not have attacked you."

Rathen nodded. His anger boiled, and his desire for revenge burned even stronger. He wanted nothing more than to run his sword through Vargas's gut and watch the life fade from his eyes. He was responsible for the men who had died in that battle, not Magom. Even Rathen had narrowly escaped his own demise.

"Does this greater fuel your fire for vengeance?" Magom asked.

Rathen remained silent. He did not feel the need to lie again, and the truth was better left unspoken.

"I have learned many things in my time. Especially from fighting my brother," Magom said. "One is not to take on your enemy's traits. You are an honest man compared to that dark cleric."

Rathen nodded. The lich's words rang true but didn't remove his desire to kill Vargas.

"The second is that a man's actions will come back to him when he does not expect it."

Rathen smiled. "I always appreciate your wisdom."

"Give it some thought and remember what we have discussed of you finding your legacy," the lich said, walking away.

Rathen took in a deep breath and slowly let it out. Finally, he knew the answer to the question that had kept him awake countless nights. Vargas was, in fact, behind the deaths of his men. While the answer did not please him, finally knowing gave him a sense of satisfaction.

Rathen walked back toward the giant statue where Bulo had a fire crackling. Thack stirred a pot of what limited provisions they had brought. Garrick ate quickly and left to find the secret door into the compound. The others gathered around the fire for a mournful but relaxing dinner, the absence of Apaca and Marduke sorely felt by everyone.

Rathen noticed Magom turn away toward the darkness. "Magom, what is it?" Rathen asked. "Something out there?"

"Just a restless spirit lurking out in the darkness," the lich said, turning back toward the group.

"Please, no more spirits," Rathen said with a smile. "See that it keeps its distance."

"Yes," Magom replied, standing and moving toward the statue of Arg'grimorem. There he stood, looking out into the darkness, himself statue-like in appearance.

Rathen turned his attention to Thack and Bulo, who were discussing plans to approach the compound the next day, after Garrick returned with information on how to enter. No longer able to clear the brambles without the druid, they decided to take the trail and dispose of any guards they met along the way. They expected to be free from attacks by the wolf tribe now that they carried the blue stone from Arg'grimorem. Their only concern was how to defeat Vargas and his master once they encountered them.

"You know I want to kill him," Rathen said to Bulo and Thack. The three sat far removed from the rest of the group for privacy.

"We all want to kill him," Bulo said.

Thack nodded. "But how do we defeat a dark cleric? He proved powerful before when he escaped from us."

"Well, an axe to the head should do the trick," Bulo said with a laugh.

Rathen smiled but allowed his expression to become serious. He looked around the group to see everyone relaxing near the fire. He spoke softly, attempting to keep the conversation secret. "I need your word on something."

"Of course. Anything," Bulo said.

"Indeed, anything," Thack agreed.

"If we encounter Vargas and I am to fall…"

"That's n—" Bulo began, but Rathen cut him off.

"If I am to fall, I want Vargas dead," Rathen finished.

Both Bulo's and Thack's expressions hardened. They nodded in agreement.

"As long as one of us still lives, Vargas's head will roll," Bulo pronounced.

Rathen's seriousness turned back into a smile. He knew the two warriors would do their best. "Right, Bulo. Let's take first watch tonight."

Bulo nodded.

As they prepared to settle down for the evening, Caswen and Dryn expressed their interest in sleeping near the statue of Marduke. The distance between the camp and Marduke's statue was too great to secure with only two people on guard duty. But Rathen did not want to refuse their request. The forbidden area was likely safe from attack, but the scar on his face remained a constant reminder of the unexpected and prevented him from lowering his guard. Rathen asked Thack to be a third guard near Caswen and Dryn, to which he quickly agreed.

The three young people walked out toward Marduke's statue, Thack's arm around Caswen's shoulder. When they reached the statue, Thack called out Rathen's name, showing he was within voice range if anything happened. Rathen waved back.

Rathen took a position between the giant statue and the edge of the forest, while Bulo sat on the opposite side as everyone else settled down to what Rathen hoped was a very peaceful sleep.

Caswen sat staring at the figure of Marduke, studying every line and curve she could make out in the darkness. To her left, Dryn slept soundly, exhausted from fatigue and grief. Thack sat to her right, facing away from the statue to keep watch over the sisters.

"You were brilliant today, Caswen," Thack said suddenly, breaking the silence.

Caswen shrugged.

"I mean it. The way you conjured the shields… and that hammer? It was amazing."

"It wasn't enough to save Marduke," said Caswen, never taking her eyes off the statue.

"You did everything you could. Marduke knew that. He thought you were even more powerful than the high priest!"

"How can I become high priest if I can't even protect those closest to me?" Caswen said angrily, her eyes welling with tears.

"You protected all of us, Caswen," Thack said quietly. "We would all be dead if it weren't for you."

Caswen was silent for a moment. "I summoned Thandrall's Hammer of Judgment," she said finally, surprise in her voice. "I've only ever heard of a handful of high priests in the past who were able to perform such a feat. In any other circumstances, I would be celebrating." She looked back up at Marduke's statue. "But it feels wrong to be happy when Marduke isn't here to share in it."

Thack reached over and grabbed her hand. "I felt exactly the same way after my mother died. As though somehow, by being happy, I was dishonoring her memory. I didn't want to know that I could still feel happiness without her."

Caswen nodded, squeezing his hand.

"But then I realized that my mother wouldn't have wanted me to be unhappy. Instead of trying to make myself numb, I began allowing myself to feel joy again—and sadness and anger and all the other emotions I had been suppressing." Thack paused. "You don't have to feel happy right now, but you are allowed to feel more than one emotion at a time. You can feel proud of your accomplishment while still mourning Marduke."

"Thank you," Caswen said, looking Thack in the eye. She turned back to the statue, and they sat in silence for a while before Caswen said, "Marduke was like a father to me, and I never really had the chance to tell him."

"I'm sorry," said Thack, rubbing the back of Caswen's hand with his thumb. Her hand felt so small in his.

A determined look settled over her face. "I don't want to make that mistake twice." She looked up at Thack, his gray eyes so warm and comforting. "Thack, I..." She blushed, looked down at her hands clasped together, and looked back up. His kindness and understanding were so much more than she ever expected to find in another person. But how to tell him?

He waited patiently for her to finish, never taking his eyes off her. Caswen thought back to the first time she had seen him, how she had thought that she had never seen anyone like him before. She still felt that, but it was different somehow. She searched for the words to explain, but the more she looked into Thack's eyes, the fuzzier her thoughts became, until only one solution presented itself.

In one swift motion, Caswen squeezed his hand and tugged it toward her, pulling Thack into a kiss. A noise of surprise escaped his lips before he settled into it, letting go of her hand to place his palm on her jaw. Caswen's heart leapt into her stomach and stayed there even after they broke apart.

They smiled at each other for a bit, Thack's hand still on her cheek. He began to laugh softly. Caswen blushed.

"Was it that bad?"

"No, no, of course not. Just really took me by surprise." Thack grinned.

"It was the only way I could think to tell you how I feel," said Caswen, matching his grin. "Though I'm sure you had already guessed."

Thack shook his head. "Not at all. I'm still a little in shock to be honest."

"But we've been spending so much time together," said Caswen. "And you've been… teasing me! We were just holding hands before."

Thack started to laugh again, louder than before.

"Shh!" said Caswen. "You'll wake Dryn!"

"Sorry," Thack said between chuckles. "It's just, I really liked you, but I never thought you would have feelings for me. I had told myself from the beginning that a friendship with you would be more than enough for me. Everything I said and did was just trying to be friendly and supportive."

"Well, why wouldn't I have feelings for you?" Caswen said defensively.

"There's a million reasons. Namely, I'm a half-orc innkeeper with one arm, and women don't exactly swoon at the sight of me."

"You're worried about your looks?" Caswen asked, incredulous.

"When people turn away rather than look at you and whisper 'monster' as you pass by, you start to feel a little self-conscious."

Caswen put a hand on his face. "When I look at you, I see a man with kind eyes who has seen his share of hardships but never let them drag him down. Who has a good head for business and wants to take care of people. Who listens— really listens—and respects my thoughts and opinions. One thing I definitely don't see is a monster."

Thack smiled at her, pushing her heart right back into her stomach. Putting his one arm around her, he pulled her to him, her head resting against his chest. Caswen heard his heart beating quickly, in time with her own.

They sat like that for some time, enjoying each other's

company, before Thack asked, "So, what now?"

"What do you mean?"

"You live in Andar; I live in Tobermoar. You are on track to become a high priest; I run a tavern. Our lives are very separate."

Caswen was quiet for a moment. "I don't know," she said. "I should tell you that high priests… high priests are not allowed to marry while they remain within the Order."

"Oh," Thack said quietly.

"To marry, I would have to surrender my amulet and leave the Order of Thandrall."

"No," Thack said sternly. "I won't ask you to do that. I mean, yes, I wish we could marry, but… you deserve to be a high priest, and the world deserves to benefit from your gifts."

"Thank you. I've worked very hard to get where I am," said Caswen. "But I don't want to say goodbye to you. Yet even to be around each other, you'd have to move closer to Andar, and I couldn't ask you to give up your livelihood."

"I know."

They sat quietly for a moment, a cloud of sadness threatening them when Thack turned his face to hers and smiled. "But tonight. We still have tonight. We can't let our happiness tonight be tainted by thoughts of the past or worry of the future. We can enjoy the time we have and figure something out once we're safely out of these woods."

Caswen nodded, smiling a little at his wisdom. She knew it was futile, but she pushed those thoughts from her minds, glad for the moment in his arms.

"I'm feeling tired," Caswen said, suddenly noticing her fatigue.

"You should get some rest. It's been a long day."

"Yes," Caswen said, nestling into Thack's chest. "It certainly has."

Closing her eyes, she drifted off to sleep.

Chapter 14

Davale stalked her prey deep into the forest as evening descended. The trails grew dark, but her unique vision allowed her to see well. All was quiet; not even the tribal wolf calls could be heard. Before her lay the marsh area Litagus had decreed off limits, although she had adventured there a time or two. She knew better than to go too far inside its muddy terrain. She didn't expect anyone else, even Gothoar's demon men, would want to either. As she started to turn left, she glimpsed movement out of the corner of her eye. She stopped and pulled her dagger from its sheath, careful not to make a sound. She glanced around, peering through the trees, trying to find the source of what she had seen. Suddenly, the movement came again from farther up the trail where she had been standing a few moments ago. Had it passed her without her seeing it?

Davale turned carefully on her heel and crept forward, her eyes peeled for any trace of motion. One patch of the bramble bushes appeared blurred, its edges wavering in the darkness. The blur moved in front of the bushes. One branch tugged slightly as it snagged at the figure, though she could not see what it was hooked on. The signs of cloaking were unmistakable.

Davale's breath caught with excitement. This would make for an exceptional hunt.

The cloaked figure was moving down the trail in the direction from which she had come, its frame hunched slightly for easier walking beneath the bramble branches. Perhaps this figure was one of the attackers returning to assess the damage to the compound. At the figure's pace, Davale did not think it was aware of her pursuit. The cover of darkness and her expert ability to blend into the shadows kept her well hidden.

Davale followed at a distance, watching for any weak points. When the trail started to curve, she closed the gap between herself and the figure, using the bushes to conceal her approach. Her heartbeat quickened, and her senses sharpened as she closed in on her prey.

When she could not contain her bloodlust any longer, she reached out to what she deduced was the figure's head, grabbing what felt like hair. With her full force, she tugged the head back and ran her dagger along her victim's throat, slicing a deep, vicious cut.

The figure fell to the dirt trail and went limp, letting out a desperate gurgle. A human male began to materialize as the cloaking spell wore off. He was not one of the demon men after all. The man lay on the ground, face up, as blood flowed from the deep gash in his throat. His eyes were wild with fear as he looked up at her, choking for air. Oddities about the man puzzled her. Middle-aged, he wore dark leather armor, and he was covered in dirt from head to toe. His skin was gray-tinted, not losing its color as the blood leaked from his body, and his face was broad with bold features. Davale did not know from where he had come, but she was certain he was a stranger to these lands. He certainly was not connected to the compound or the town to the north.

She crouched down beside the man, watching the life drain out of him. He continued to look at her with strained eyes, silently pleading with her. Davale had seen the same expression of sadness and regret many times before.

"Shh… It'll be over soon," she said.

Before long, his eyes shut and he breathed no more.

With a sigh of satisfaction, she rifled through his pockets, finding only a few pieces of gold and silver. She noticed the man wore a dagger at his side and pulled it from its sheath, letting out an audible gasp of wonder as she saw the clear blade. She had collected many daggers over the years, but never had she seen such a metal. She felt the edge with her finger and knew it was a better blade than her own. Taking the sheath from the man's belt, she tucked her new dagger down into her leather boot.

Davale stood up and looked over the body one more time. She doubted this man was with the attackers and thought he might be part of another group planning to assault the compound. By the direction of his movement, he must have come from the restricted marsh, explaining the dirt that covered his person. Litagus would need to be informed of this development as soon as possible, but if she could take out the entire group and eliminate the threat altogether, she was sure her master would reward her well. She still had two days to search for the remaining three attackers—plenty of time to take a small detour. She certainly wasn't ready for this hunt to end.

Davale moved the body into the bushes, making certain it could not be seen from the path. She wanted to recount the entire story to Litagus herself once she had taken out the dead man's group, and she did not want a simple patrol guard to take that privilege away from her.

With a smile stretched across her face, she continued back down the path and into the marsh in search of more of these invaders. It was more difficult to track in these woods, as any damaged vegetation—unless damaged with magic— grew back within a few hours, leaving no evidence that the area had been traveled.

She looked up to see the markings Litagus had magically cut into the trees, warning everyone that the area was off limits. With extraordinary agility, she passed through the brambles, scanning the area for any unusual sights or sounds. As she came to the end of the green belt of trees that enclosed the edge of the marsh, she stopped. She knew better than to adventure inside. Even if Litagus had not forbidden entry into the marsh, Davale would have been wary of its waters. She had always felt something out there below the surface, something ancient and powerful.

She paused, confused why her acute sense of smell had not yet picked up the unavoidable stench of the marsh. Carefully, she peered beyond the trees to find that the marsh wasn't there at all, having been replaced by a grassy plateau, a large fire roaring in the distance. For a moment, she wondered if she had gotten lost. She had clearly walked past the warning markers, but perhaps she had gotten turned around.

Faint voices drew her attention as she scanned the plateau

for any sign of familiarity. She focused her eyes in the direction of the voices and made out a giant humanoid figure towering over thirty man-sized shapes spread across the plateau, all standing still. *What is going on here?* She had a mind to turn around and run back to the compound, but her curiosity got the better of her. She knew she couldn't fight them all, but she had to see what they were, if only to have something to report back to Litagus. If these were more of the demon men that had attacked earlier, the compound was in imminent danger.

Carefully, she stepped out of the trees and onto the grass, keeping herself low. She pulled her new glass dagger from her boot as she approached the closest lone figure. Within striking distance of the figure's back, she could not sense him move or even hear him breathe. She slowly reached out and poked the figure with the tip of her dagger. The flesh of the figure did not give way to the dagger, instead making a light clinking sound. Davale reached out with her free hand, placing it firmly on the figure's back. It was made of stone.

Moving around to the front of the statue, Davale saw that it was a perfect sculpture of a druid dressed in robes. His mouth was open and his face strained, stuck in a silent battle cry.

She could reasonably assume that the other standing figures were also statues, but she would not let her guard down around them until she could prove it. She hoped more than anything that the giant figure in the distance was also just a statue.

Her focus turned to the fire beside the giant and the faint voices she heard there. Now she could make out several people sitting around the fire, eating and talking. Taking advantage of the statues, she hid behind them one by one, creeping closer.

As she neared the group, a feeling of dread washed over her, chilling her to the bone. It was such an unfamiliar sense to her that she smiled, excited by the challenge. She paused her advance to assess the situation. From where she stood, she could make out nine figures, one of which stood apart from the others. That figure was hooded in rags, though the little of its body she could see was sickeningly thin. Deep within the hood over its head were two burning red lights shining out into the darkness—a horror like none she had ever seen. She immediately tried to devise a plan to attack it. She assumed an assault from the back would be all she needed to tear the skull from its neck. If she were patient enough and the opportunity presented itself, she could whittle the group down one by one until there were few enough to attack openly. But she needed to understand their strengths.

Silently, she crept forward, hiding behind another statue. She could hear the voice of a woman dressed in a brown robe as she talked with the group. At least four looked like capable warriors, and the others appeared to be spellcasters. Davale took a step closer, and as she did, the skeletal figure turned in her direction. She froze, one foot still raised above the ground. She saw the burning red eyes and knew it must have sensed her. Moving her still hovering foot behind her, she slowly backed away. The skeletal figure rose and moved, seemingly floated, over to the giant statue, surveying the area like an undead guardian. She knew she could get no closer.

Davale stood in the distance and watched the group begin to settle down for the night. The woman in the brown robes moved off from the group with a slim, short-haired woman and a tall warrior with only one arm. Meanwhile, the group by the giant statue prepared for sleep, laying out cloaks and pallets over the cold ground. As she expected, two of the warriors walked on each side of the camp, taking guard. Perfect. It would be easy for her to kill each guard in silence, then slit the throats of the others as they slept. She readied herself for her moment to strike, her blood pumping as her heart pounded against her ribcage.

Suddenly, from where the two women and the one-armed man had walked off to, Davale heard the tall man call out, "Rathen!" The guard closest to her waved in response.

Davale froze, the pounding in her chest rising. Could this be the same Rathen that Vargas had encountered on his mission to retrieve the Book of Ziz? Davale didn't think Rathen to be a common name. This must be the same one. *Has he come looking for Vargas?* She tried to recall what Vargas had told Litagus upon his return with the red book. She had been beside Litagus as Vargas presented him with it and told the story of its retrieval.

"I joined a group led by a man named Rathen," Vargas had said. At the time, Davale thought she detected a hint of fear in his voice when he spoke the name. "They led me straight to the Book of Ziz, guarded by an ancient lich. I thought Rathen would give me some trouble when I tried to take the book, so I provoked a battle between his men and the lich and used the distraction to escape. Rathen and the others are almost certainly dead."

"Almost certainly?" Litagus had asked. "You don't know for sure?"

"Very little can face a lich and survive," Vargas had

replied. "And none in that group had the power to destroy one, to my knowledge."

Litagus had accepted Vargas's reasoning, and to her knowledge they had not spoken of it since. But it appeared that Vargas was to eat his words as she watched the man called Rathen circle the camp, walking past the hooded being with the crimson eyes. Wait! Davale thought, finally recognizing the creature. That skeletal form and red eyes… *That's the lich!*

Davale grinned, amazed by the situation. How wrong Vargas had been to underestimate this man. She could not wait to taunt him with his own stupidity and arrogance. Litagus would certainly be displeased to know that Vargas had not cleaned up any of his messes. She wondered whether the lich and Rathen had joined together to defeat Vargas. What powers did this Rathen have that allowed him to control the undead?

She took a step back and placed the dagger back into her boot. The man she had killed earlier had to be with Rathen's group. Perhaps he had been sneaking to the compound to check the defenses. Were the demon men just a coincidence then? There was no evidence to suggest the groups were together. But with the power to control a lich, this man may be capable of anything.

As she stood there in the darkness, she felt more and more determined to learn about this man who struck fear into the heart of a senior priest in Litagus's temple, who could control the undead and had somehow turned the dead marsh into a grassy field full of lifelike statues. He was a mystery she wanted to unravel.

Davale moved away, creeping toward the nearest tree line

to devise her plan while she waited for everyone to settle down. She had to wait especially long for the brown-robed woman and the one-armed man, sitting so far away from the others, to quiet down. They seemed to be sharing a private moment, but Davale was too preoccupied with her plan of action to eavesdrop.

When they finally appeared to be sleeping, Davale set her plan in motion. Making sure the glass dagger was well hidden in her boot, she walked along the edge of the forest, moving into the trees closest to where Rathen sat in the grass. She took the dagger resting on her hip and secured it under her leather tunic, watching the man as he patrolled the camp, scanning the darkness. She knew that startling him was not likely to go well, especially if he raised an alarm. She pulled the leather strap that held her long hair tight to her head, shaking out her black locks. She unbuttoned the top three ivory buttons of her tunic. In the trees just behind him, she deliberately stepped on a twig, snapping it in half. She knew she was taking a chance that he might shout to the other guard for assistance, but she hoped he would come closer to investigate.

Rathen jumped up and pulled his sword, setting his feet in a defensive stance. His eyes focused somewhere near Davale, and he walked quickly toward the forest, his blade at the ready. Just before he reached the tree line, Davale ran out, falling to the ground at his feet.

"Halt!" Rathen said, the tip of his sword inches from her face.

Davale stared at the sword pointed squarely at her nose. It was unusual in shape and color, very similar to the dagger she had lifted off her earlier kill. She tore her eyes from it to look into the eyes of the man who stood before her, giving him her best terrified expression. She hurled herself back away from the blade, throwing her hands up in front of her.

"Please!" she shrieked. "Please, don't kill me."

Rathen watched her with narrowed eyes, his sword in hand. Reading the look in his eye and the tension in his muscles, Davale could see this man was ready and willing to attack. She had to show to him that she wasn't a threat. "Who are you?" he asked.

Davale began to cry. "Please, let me go," she begged. "I'm lost in the woods."

"Lost?" he asked. Davale could hear the suspicion in his voice. "Where did you come from?"

"I…" Davale paused, unsure how to proceed. The compound was the only settlement within miles. She couldn't have come from anywhere else, and no one other than those who lived at the compound dared to travel into Bramblewood Forest.

Rathen seemed to read her thoughts. "Are you from Litagus's compound?" he asked, raising his sword a few inches.

Davale knew better than to lie to him. She nodded. "I work in the kitchens."

Rathen lowered his sword slightly, relaxing his defensive stance. "What are you doing all the way out here? Didn't Litagus forbid his people to enter this area?"

Davale feigned surprise. "Am I in the forbidden area?" She glanced around. "But this isn't the marsh."

Rathen sighed. "That's a long story. Still, you're awfully far from the compound."

"I didn't really look where I was going. I just ran," said Davale, she gave a fearful look behind her.

"From what?"

Davale's eyes brimmed with fake tears. "The compound was attacked," she choked between sobs. "They were cutting down guards left and right, so I ran as far as I could."

Rathen completely lowered his sword, his face softening. How quick men were to dismiss a woman.

"Are you hurt?" Rathen asked.

Davale shook her head, quivering in fear. "I should really return to help those who are injured. I shouldn't have run like that." She hung her head in shame. "I was just so scared. I… I didn't know what to do."

"Wait," said Rathen. "Perhaps we could help you. And you help us in return."

"Us?" Davale asked.

"Me and the group I'm traveling with." Rathen held out a hand to her. She took it, and he pulled her to her feet.

Pretending to trip, she fell forward against his chest. "Sorry," she breathed with a small smile. Rathen coughed and put his free hand on her shoulder to steady her. She noticed his gaze linger on her breasts and realized just how easy this would be.

"What do you and your group need help with?" Davale asked, drawing his attention back to her eyes.

Rathen cleared his throat. "We could use any information you can tell us about the compound and its people."

Davale took a step back. "You weren't the ones who attacked us, were you?" she asked, lacing her tone with suspicion.

"No, absolutely not," Rathen said quickly, sheathing his sword. "We have no intention of attacking the compound. We just want to get in and out as quickly as possible, without shedding any blood if we can avoid it."

"So… you want to steal something," said Davale. It wasn't a question.

Rathen avoided her gaze. "Well, it's complicated." He paused, searching for the words. "Something was stolen from us. We just want it back."

Davale acted as though she were deciding whether or not to trust him. Finally, she nodded. "Very well," she said. "I'll help you if you can help me return safely. And as long as no innocent lives are harmed."

"You have a deal," Rathen said, holding out his hand for her to shake.

Taking it, she said, "I don't even know who you are."

"Rathen," he replied with a grin, letting go of her hand. She let her fingertips graze his as their hands pulled apart.

"Evah," Davale said without thinking. She wondered at how easily the name had slipped from her lips but put the thought aside, knowing that Rathen was watching her. She could pull the dagger from just under her tunic and kill this man where he stood. He was all alone, away from his group, and wouldn't even have time to react. Instead, she returned his smile.

Rathen looked over her carefully. "You work in the kitchens?" he asked. She knew he had noticed her form-fitting outfit and leather boots.

"I help bring supplies to the kitchens from Deepbriar by wagon. We had just returned with a haul of salted meats and vegetables when the compound was attacked. I abandoned the wagon when I ran."

"Deepbriar…" said Rathen thoughtfully. "Is that the town to the north?"

"That's right."

"Do you know who attacked you?" Rathen asked. She could see how interested he was in this story.

"I don't know," she said sadly. "We had just started unloading the wagon when they charged out of the trees. The guards tried to repel them, but I saw six or seven fall before I ran. I'm not even sure anyone survived." She wiped her sleeve across her eyes and shivered.

"Here, you must be cold," said Rathen. "Come and sit by the fire." Placing a hand on her back, he led her into the camp.

As they walked, she scanned the sleeping figures lying around the fire, trying to assess their strengths. Her eyes fell on the lich standing before the large statue, its lifeless skull impossible to read. It turned its head, focusing its red eyes on her, and she shivered once more.

Mistaking her chill to be from the cold, Rathen sat her on a log close to the fire. "Sit, relax," he said. He handed her a waterskin. "You must be thirsty after running all that way."

She took the waterskin and drank deeply from it. Out of the corner of her eye, she saw Rathen give a hand signal to someone she could not see. A moment later, a large man wielding a battle axe approached, and Davale recognized him as the second guard posted on the opposite side of the camp. He looked at Davale suspiciously and flashed Rathen a questioning look. Rathen said nothing, instead pointing his finger up and a making a circle. The big man nodded and walked off toward the lich. Davale watched from her peripheral vision as the big man motioned to the lich, and they both walked off together into the darkness. It was obvious that Rathen didn't fully trust her and was having the area searched.

On her various missions for Litagus, Davale had easily gained the trust of highly ranked and powerful men just by her looks and charm alone. While Rathen was certainly not immune to her charms, perhaps this wasn't going to be as easy as she had originally thought.

"Now, tell me about the compound," Rathen said, sitting across from her.

She could see his face clearer in the firelight. The scar that ran down from his left eye was the first thing to catch her interest. It must have been a nasty wound, and it had healed back jaggedly, running into his short beard. Surrounding the scar was the face of a middle-aged man. She thought he was handsome in a rugged sort of way. She had certainly had better, but there was something in the shape of his eyes and the curve of his jaw that drew her.

"What do you want to know?" she asked timidly.

"How many men are there? How many guards?"

Davale paused. She had to be careful not to divulge too much information. She couldn't care less about Vargas's safety, but she would protect Litagus with her life if need be. She knew they were no match for Litagus's power, but she would not place the high priest in undue danger.

"I've only seen a handful of guards outside, and a guard or two inside the kitchen. There are cooks, servants, and farmers who visit from Deepbriar from time to time. Really, that's all I know," she said, widening her eyes in fear. She had interrogated enough people under her knife to know the look well.

Seeing her reaction, Rathen backed off, calming his tension. "Alright," he said. "Just relax. You're safe here."

Despite his reassuring words, his gaze did not let up,

forcing her to keep up her act. Davale drank some more water and rubbed her legs through her boots as though they were sore.

Before long, the big man had returned, shaking his head at Rathen before retaking his post. Davale couldn't see where the lich stood or if it had moved. Not knowing where it was made her feel apprehensive.

After a long silence, she forced a yawn.

"Sleep if you need," Rathen said, shifting some bedding over to her. "We will talk again in the morning."

She took it with thanks and lay down, pretending to fall asleep. She listened as Rathen stood and walked a few paces away. Peeking one eye open, Davale saw the night sentries switch out for duty. This group was being extremely cautious.

Davale heard Rathen gathering up his bedding to lie down to sleep opposite her. Once he fell asleep, she could slip away. She doubted he would ever trust her enough to let down his guard, and she still had a hunt to complete.

She waited awhile, giving Rathen plenty of time to doze off. As dawn approached, Davale slowly opened her eyes and rolled over to make sure she wasn't being watched. Her eyes met Rathen's instantly, wide awake and staring at her from where he lay, his hand resting on his sword beside him.

Davale closed her eyes sharply and rolled back over, delaying her plans of escape. She wondered if this man was even human at all.

Rathen lay by the fire, watching over the mysterious woman who had walked into their camp. There was something about her—something alluring—but he knew he couldn't trust her. He had Bulo and Magom scout the area to make certain she was alone. He had invited her into camp to keep a better eye on her, and that was exactly what he intended to do. He would not take one eye off her while the rest of the camp slept, until he could be sure she wasn't dangerous. He wasn't certain of her allegiance; it seemed too convenient that she should stumble upon them in this forbidden area. However, if she really was from the compound, she might have vital information that could save the lives of his comrades and assist in completing their mission. It was a chance he had to take.

As the sun came up, brightening the area through the clouds, the woman stirred awake. She rolled over and looked at him, quickly turning back over when he met her gaze. Rathen smiled, trying to figure her out. If she really was forced from the compound and chased into the woods, then perhaps she had awoken uncertain of her location, or maybe she just wanted to slip away unnoticed. If she had lied about how she came to be in the woods and he let her go, she could alert the compound's defenses. He had to think.

He stood up and went to wake Thack, finding him asleep beside Caswen, their fingers inches apart. Thack's eyes flickered open as Rathen's shadow fell over him, and he sat up quickly, assuring Rathen that he would begin breakfast at once. Thack stood and made his way back to the main camp, kneeling to rifle through the bag of provisions.

Rathen, following Thack back to the fire, looked around at the group. Bulo was still asleep, but Rendrak, Dryn, and Magom were on guard around the camp.

"Who's the woman?" Thack asked, still assessing his ingredients.

"I'm not sure yet," Rathen replied. "Says she's from the compound—it was apparently attacked last night, and she got lost in the woods as she ran from the fight."

Thack looked up at Rathen with lowered eyebrows and pursed lips.

"I know, I know," said Rathen, putting a hand up. "I'm concerned as well. I'm going to keep a strict watch on her."

Thack shrugged. "I trust your judgment, Rathen. I'll make some extra for her." He counted out additional rations. "When is Garrick returning?"

"I hope he'll return later today. We need to find out more about this attack on the compound and who was behind it. I'm anxious to get there and get the book before anyone else does."

Thack nodded and took a bag of grains, ground acorns, dried berries, and pine nuts over to the fire to make a hearty gruel.

As the group started to wake, everyone took an interest in the mysterious woman sitting in camp. The group gathered with their food and sat around the fire. Rathen explained to everyone how Evah had walked into the area during his night watch. Magom stood away from the group near the giant statue, seemingly uninterested.

"Your name is Evah?" Caswen asked the stranger.

Evah nodded timidly, peering around at everyone through her raven hair.

"Where are you from?" Caswen asked.

"Tonillias, a region to the east, but I was raised in a temple," Evah said, picking at the contents of the plate she held in her lap.

"Me too," Caswen responded, her face lighting up. She

patted a hand on Dryn beside her. "My sister and I were raised in a temple of Thandrall, and I was trained in the ways of a healer. What art did your order teach?"

"I wasn't allowed to train with the priests," Evah said quietly. "I was put to work as a maid, doing odds and ends." She set her empty plate aside.

"So you are no longer with your temple?" Caswen asked.

"Not at all."

"That's too bad," said Caswen.

Rendrak cut forcefully into their conversation. "What of the compound? Who attacked you? What did they look like?"

Evah turned to him, surprised at the outburst. "M-men," she stammered. "I suppose there were about... ten? They seemed well armed and well trained to me. But I know little about such things," she added.

"Why did they attack? What did they want?" Rendrak pressed, leaning toward her.

Rathen waited to see Evah's reactions to the questions before asking Rendrak to take it easy.

"They didn't say anything," Evah said nervously. "They ran out of the trees and started killing our guards and workers. It was terrible."

Bandark spoke up next. "Do you know of Vargas or his master, Litagus?"

"Well, they live in the compound, but I've only ever seen them briefly. I'm not allowed out the kitchens unless I'm fetching supplies from town." Evah flashed her eyes over to Rathen.

Rathen recognized the look as a plea for rescue. "Let's go easy on the questions," he said. "The lady has had a harrowing night." He hoped he could convince her to stay with them until they left for the compound. He did not want to be forced to restrain her, but he could not risk letting her go.

"Evah, what can you tell us about the compound?" Rathen asked softly.

Evah told them about her day-to-day life, keeping stock of the kitchens and supplies against an inventory and facilitating deliveries from the town of Deepbriar when food, supplies, and equipment were low. She explained what she knew of the guards and claimed not to know anything about the inside of the compound aside from the kitchens and servant quarters.

Rathen watched her as she told her story, his eyes drifting over her pale complexion and dark black hair and lingering on her dark eyes. Her features were very striking. The leather boots and tunic she wore seemed well kept, and he did not notice any weapons on her. Rathen felt that she was more than just an average servant. There was something about her that did not sit right with him, yet at the same time he was drawn to her, her black eyes pulling him into their depths.

Bandark's deep voice shook Rathen from his thoughts. "Do you know of a man who may have traveled to the compound last night? Did you see anyone on your way here?" Bandark was clearly concerned for Garrick. If attackers had invaded the compound, they could have come across Garrick.

"It was dark, and I was running so fast... I didn't see anyone."

"What of the wolf tribes?" Thack spoke up. "Do they leave your people alone?"

"Yes," Evah said, nodding.

Rathen rubbed his chin, thinking about their next move. "Then we wait for Garrick's return. Until then, we will scout the edges of this area to ensure our safety."

Everyone nodded in agreement.

"Caswen, please make Evah comfortable," Rathen said and flashed her a nod. Later, he intended to talk with Evah privately and discuss the issue of entering the compound.

As the day turned to evening, they waited for Garrick's return, growing more and more concerned for their lost man. Rathen hoped no harm had befallen him; without Garrick, getting into the compound to steal the book would likely be impossible.

Chapter 15

Davale felt confident in her positioning within Rathen's group. As the day passed, she had skillfully lied her way through most of the questions without revealing any vital information. She had spoken briefly with everyone except for the lich. Both Thack and Bulo had very little to say, and their eyes showed their apprehension of her being there. They both appeared to be capable warriors, and a direct fight with either of the two would be a challenge. Conversations with Bandark and Rendrak were centered on questions regarding whether she had seen the man she had killed. These two also appeared formidable. They both spoke with heavy accents and had the same unique appearance and gray complexion as the dead man, so she assumed they were together. Caswen seemed to admire her, while Dryn eyed her with suspicion. Davale was sure she could win the archer over. The way Dryn looked at her when she didn't think Davale noticed hinted at something more than admiration. If needed, she could use that to her advantage.

She felt secure in her assessments of the strengths and weakness of each person but still wanted to talk to the lich.

Of course, she needed to speak with Rathen again too before sneaking away during the night to return to the compound.

As the darkness of evening approached, Davale looked at the group spread around the area. She noticed the lich still standing at the base of the giant statue. He hadn't moved much since she'd arrived. As she walked in his direction, his red eyes peered over to her. The immense feeling of dread hit her again; however, instead of making her want to cower in fear, it triggered her fighting instinct. Her muscles tightened, and her fingers twitched as they instinctively reached for her hidden blade. She took a deep breath, restraining herself.

"Can you talk?" Davale asked the skeletal form standing in front of her.

"Of course," he responded. The only movement from him was his torn robes slightly blowing in the breeze.

Davale smile broadly. "Amazing." She walked closer, the desire to attack fading, curiosity lessening the dread. She looked him over, trying to comprehend how such a creature could even be possible. Some areas of his body were empty gaps while his chest held deflated organs pressed against his ribs. "Are you the lich?"

"I am Magom. And yes, my current state is that of a lich," Magom responded without moving.

"This is the first time I've seen one of your kind. How's it possible to cheat death in such a way?"

"You are not afraid of my form?" Magom asked, letting out a hiss.

"No, I'm… amazed," she replied, continuing to look him over. She stuck her hand out as if to physically confirm the decayed form that her eyes continued to deny as fact. The lich did not react to her curiosity. Slowly, she inserted her hand into a cavity between a gap in the ribs. She felt nothing but air. She shook her head in disbelief.

"That seems quite strange for an orphaned wagon girl from Tonillias."

"Yes, well…" Davale hesitated, wondering how to explain the persona she'd tried to portray to the group yet so dismissed by the lich. She pulled her hand back but continued to look over the lich's figure.

"Your secret is safe with me," the lich said.

She looked up sharply, her fingers ready for her blade, but where to strike such a creature?

The lich continued, "I know it was you I sensed out in the darkness, watching us from afar. I told the group I sensed a spirit, but it was you. You had watched us for some time before you rushed into our camp."

Davale breathed a sigh of relief. "Yes, I feared running from one danger into yet another. Alone, I had to be careful, you understand. And as I watched you, I became curious. Do you mind telling me how you came to be a lich?"

"I once had a brother named Tyus," the lich explained. "We fought over the crown when our father died. We both wanted to be king and rule over the other. In order for us to live longer inside our confinements, I worked with the art of necromancy while my brother bound his soul with demonkind."

Davale listened, enraptured. "That's incredible."

"Tell me, young one. What do you know of demonkind?"

"About as much as I know of necromancy. Almost nothing."

Magom closed the distance between them. She felt as if his burning eyes peered through her soul. Davale held her ground and wondered if he'd attack.

"There is a part of you that reminds me of my brother. You said you were orphaned as a child?"

"Yes." Davale tilted her head. "Are you suggesting I'm linked to demonkind?"

His eyes glowed, and she felt as if his gaze penetrated beyond tunic and skin, studying something deep within her. "That call to darkness that no doubt lives within your soul… is not human," Magom said. "I am certain that if you wanted to discover more, all you would have to do is listen to that darkness."

Davale tried to make sense of his words. She couldn't deny that an unexplained wickedness lived in her subconscious. But having it confirmed felt disconcerting. She needed to think about what it meant, though her questions would be better answered by her temple or even Litagus.

"For now," Magom said, breaking her thoughts, "I will keep your secret from the others, but I ask you not to hurt anyone. Or we will be at odds, you and I."

"Of course," she said, understanding the strengths of this undead creature. He had sensed not just her in the woods studying the group, but her intentions or at least her inclinations as well. He had abilities that no ordinary being would, in perception and no doubt in power. "What happened to your brother?" she asked, changing the subject. "His link to demonkind sounds like it would make him powerful."

"Oh, it did indeed. But his link was severed, and he was destroyed."

"You killed him?" Davale smiled as if she already knew the answer.

"No. Rathen did."

That answer had not been what she had expected. "Really?"

"Indeed. Truth be told, he killed me too. It took me months to reconstitute myself."

Davale looked back over to where Rathen was talking to the others. "Are you telling me that man killed you and your demon brother?"

"Yes," Magom said, ending the word in a hiss.

"Impressive," Davale said out loud to herself. The mysteries of the man kept expanding. "Thank you for the information," she said with a nod.

The lich fixed her with his crimson gaze. "Remember our talk, young one. Harm no one."

"Of course," she said, walking over to Rathen. She wanted to find out more about this man.

Rathen stood speaking with the tall mage they called Bandark. Davale listened to their conversation as she approached.

"It's been a full day, and Garrick has not returned," Bandark said.

"What other options do we have?" Rathen asked.

"I am not certain, but with the attack on the compound, I fear for Garrick's safety," Bandark said, taking notice as Davale moved closer.

"Evah, tell me again. How many attackers? Were any of them killed before you ran?" Bandark asked, his eyes flashing desperation.

"I saw a few of the demon men killed before I ran into the trees," she said, deciding that honesty here would not be revealing too much.

"Demon men?" Bandark said loudly.

Rendrak shot up from his sitting position and rushed over to them.

Davale silently fumed at herself. The identity of the attackers had been information she wanted to keep from them. Her growing comfort had caused her to lower her guard. She needed to fix this situation.

"The men wore masks to frighten us just like the tribal savages in the forest," she said, trying to cover up the omission of this information from her previous story.

"Describe these masks," Rendrak commanded. Both he and the tall mage seemed alarmed.

"They were blood red, elongated faces with black horns upon bare heads," she said, shivering in fright.

"Did they have armor and weapons of black?" Rendrak asked.

"Yes… yes, I think they did. That's all I know," Davale said, trying to end the conversation.

"Minions of Gothoar," Bandark said to Rathen. "You are lucky to have escaped at all." Bandark turned to Davale. "This changes everything. We cannot wait for Garrick's return, for I fear the minions may have already killed him. If we wait any longer, the book may fall into their hands." Bandark nodded to Rendrak.

The book! Davale finally knew what Rathen and his group were doing in Bramblewood Forest. They must be after the red book Vargas had stolen from them for Litagus. She forced down the smile that threatened to light up her entire face.

"Why didn't you speak of this sooner?" Rendrak asked her in a threatening tone.

"I… I thought they were just men in masks," Davale said, slowly backing away, acting intimidated.

"Leave her alone," Caswen interrupted from the side of the group. "We cannot expect her to know everything important to us."

Davale smiled at Caswen and bowed her head. Even in such a situation, the healer was kind enough to stand up for her.

"Well…" Rendrak said, backing away.

"We must go to the compound upon first light," Bandark said, flashing Rathen a look.

Rathen and Bandark walked away from the camp while Rendrak stood there, still looking at Davale with hostility. Caswen put her arm around Davale and walked her over to the fire.

"Relax. They do not mean any harm," she said with a warm smile.

Davale smiled back. The touch of this woman felt oddly warm and friendly. Not soft and weak as the few women Davale had encountered in her life. True, she hadn't had many female friends since her interests were in weapons training in the field with the men. Yet something about Caswen was different, inviting, almost motherly. Looking her over, Davale guessed Caswen was only a few years younger than herself.

"It's alright. I understand their concern for their friend," Davale said softly.

"Let me take your mind off your ordeal," Caswen said with a smile.

Davale nodded.

"What deity did your temple honor?"

Davale thought for a moment and could not come up with a name that would sound believable. She knew better than to tell her the truth. "I… I don't remember."

Caswen's face went blank. "You don't?"

"I was only there while I was very young, and I wasn't treated well. I ran away as soon as I could," Davale lied.

"Well," Caswen began with a wide smile. "Let me tell you about our Order of Thandrall."

Davale fought her desire to scream out loud and instead faked interest in the girl's blathering. She listened to her stories about all the good performed by her order and how one day she hoped to be a high priest. As Caswen spoke, Davale sensed a power and something else hard to define, yet welcoming. Soon her mind floated in the young woman's joyful tones and presence as the girl's enthusiasm enveloped her.

Davale admired this woman's ambition and respected just how strongly her devotion showed. Davale could relate; however, in her world, if she wanted something badly enough, she would just take it. Strength and power and cunning achieved her goals. She wondered how being soft and kind like Caswen appeared could possibly bring useful results. To Davale, they usually spelled weakness and a trust that could easily be manipulated. Yet this woman exuded a strength through her softness that both perplexed and somehow comforted her.

"Right now, our temple is small… and not well funded, but we know Thandrall will provide," Caswen said with a look of determination.

"I wish you success," Davale said, offering a smile.

Davale heard footsteps and looked up to see Rathen standing next to her.

"Evah, may we speak in private?"

"Yes," Davale said, perhaps a little too quickly. "Thank you for the conversation, Caswen."

"Anytime," Caswen said with a wide smile.

Rathen led Davale away from the group.

"Sit. I need to ask you a few things."

"Of course." Davale sat in the grass.

Rathen sat down beside her. She wondered what insights or advantages this conversation might bring her. She was intrigued by the apparent abilities of this man and knew that only by knowing him better could she find the chink in his armor.

"Listen, I want to be honest here… and hope the same in return," Rathen said, looking her in the eyes.

"Of course."

"We need your help to get into the compound."

"What? I thought you just wanted information. And I've told you all I know." She feigned surprise and shifted her position as if uncomfortable. She'd expected this, of course, almost wondering why it had taken him so long to ask.

"I know," Rathen said, his face sincere. "I am not asking you to endanger your friends. We just need to get in and find a book. Then we'll leave and never bother you again."

"I… I don't know," she said, encouraging Rathen to persuade her.

"Listen, the world is at stake here. The dark cleric who took the book and his master are attempting to bring back an evil deity. We cannot allow that to happen."

Davale turned away from him as a look of confusion crossed her face. He viewed Litagus's efforts so differently than she did. For her, bringing Gothoar's dominance to this world would be empowering and thrilling. But she knew that healers like Caswen would certainly be hunted down and killed by Gothoar's order. Thoughts of Caswen's kindness wavered before her, an image both comforting and disturbing.

Rathen reached out his hand, placing it on her cheek and slowly turning her face toward his. She shivered at his touch, but not from fear.

"I wouldn't ask this of you if we had another way," he said softly, his hand lingering on her jawline.

Her eyes wandered about his face. She could not deny her attraction to him. It was not very often she met a man equal to her in both strength and looks. The jagged scar running down his face especially appealed to her, a sign of his experience as a warrior.

"Then, do me a favor in return," she said, her voice soft.

"What?" Rathen lowered his hand.

"Tell me about you. Where are you from? Where did you get this?" she asked, running her finger down the scar on his face. When the scar split into two near his jaw, she used a second finger to trace both sides. A tingle of unbidden desire prickled from her fingers to her neck, spreading warmth to her face.

"My scar?" he asked, surprised.

Davale nodded, her fingers still tracing the scar.

Rathen moved from her touch, uncomfortable. "We were attacked by a demon. It came during our group's journey to Ghrakus Castle."

"A demon?" she asked. She recalled the lich's words about his brother. "And you defeated it?"

"Our group defeated it. And I almost met my death that day."

"But you survived. And became stronger for it," she said. "You went on to defeat Tyus… and the lich?"

Rathen looked surprised. "You have been talking with Magom, I take it."

She nodded.

"The lich was an unnecessary battle that cost two of my men. It only happened because of the betrayal by the dark cleric Vargas."

Davale noticed Rathen's eyes change at the mention of Vargas. They were full of vengeance, an emotion she knew all too well. By seeing the fire in his eyes she knew his anger must be unbearable. "You seek revenge," she said with a smile that she just couldn't hide.

Rathen paused and said, "No."

Davale, highly skilled in the arts of deception, recognized it in others. But anyone could look at this man's face and know he was lying. "Then you probably don't care to learn about his weakness."

Rathen eyes widened. "What weakness?"

Davale began to piece this puzzle together. She knew there'd been a reason why she had encountered Rathen and his group. This man would be her tool to finally rid herself of Vargas. She could reveal just enough to him to cause Vargas's death and then kill Rathen herself. Her hands would be relatively clean of her rival's death, and she would become the one and only favored of Litagus. With Rathen and his group dead, no one would ever know she had helped them.

"So, you seek his weakness for your revenge?" she said, daring him to admit it.

Rathen paused. "Yes, I want to kill him," Rathen finally

confessed, seemingly coming to terms with himself.

Davale nodded, stood up, and went over to Caswen. Rathen followed.

"Caswen, may I use you in a demonstration?" Davale asked.

Caswen looked up, confused. She glanced at Rathen, who nodded at her. "Alright," she said.

"For you to invoke the powers of your temple, you always require your amulet, correct?" Davale asked the healer.

"Yes," she replied, still looking confused.

Davale took hold of Rathen's arm and extended it. With lightning speed, she pulled the dagger from under her tunic, cut across his forearm, and dropped the dagger.

Caswen's mouth dropped opened. Bulo, Thack, and Rendrak jumped to their feet, their eyes darting from the wound to the discarded weapon.

"Heal that without your amulet," Davale said, still holding Rathen's arm as blood trickled from the wound. She knew this demonstration could unmask her cover as a helpless kitchen aid, but she trusted that Rathen's gratitude over the information would be sufficient to quell his suspicions.

Rathen's face showed his surprise. "It's alright," he said to the three warriors.

The three sat back down like snakes coiled to strike.

Caswen took her amulet from around her neck but refused to place it in the grass.

Davale reached out, taking hold of the amulet with her other hand.

Caswen looked over the superficial wound and began chanting. As the chant went on, nothing happened. She chanted stronger and louder but still nothing. "It cannot be done," she said at last.

Davale handed back her amulet.

Caswen held the amulet near the wound and chanted. Immediately, the wound bound together, leaving no mark.

Rathen's face grew serious, then stretched into a broad smile.

"What's this about?" Rendrak asked.

"It's alright. I'll explain later," he said. He nodded to Caswen and turned to Davale. "I need time to think on this."

Davale smiled, knowing she had just changed his entire plan. And that hers had just been set in motion.

Rathen sat out in the dark, not far from the giant statue. He thought back to all the battles he had fought beside Vargas and other healers. He could not recall a time they had not used an amulet to channel their powers. This had to be it, the key to Vargas's weakness. If Caswen could not heal without her amulet, then Vargas could not harm without his. Rathen imagined his battle with Vargas the next day. He could cut the amulet from Vargas's neck or even from his hand if he held it. The challenge would be getting close enough to do so, a huge risk when fighting a spellcaster. In case he was killed, Rathen needed to share this information with Bulo and Thack to help ensure their success. This was the information he had been missing. It still did not help quell his anxiety before tomorrow's battle, for he knew he might not survive. Even if Vargas had a weakness, Rathen did not think his master shared it.

"May I sit?" Evah's voice asked him.

Rathen did not want to speak with her until his mind became clearer, but neither could he turn her away. She had been the one to shed light on how to destroy the darkness Vargas had cast on him. He nodded.

"You still want my help?" Evah asked.

"Of course I do."

"Then tell me more about yourself."

"Well," Rathen began, looking at Evah's intent face, "I came from a family that had limited means. My father served in the king's guard while my mother did what she could to help support us by working in the fields."

"Are your parents still living?"

Rathen paused. "I'm not certain. It's been over ten years since I saw them last."

"Were you their only child?"

"I was. When I turned sixteen, I joined the king's forces to help pay my way."

"What was the name of your hometown?"

Rathen paused. "Why such an interest in me? I think from what I have seen today, you have a much more interesting story than I."

Evah laughed. "Alright, but you first."

Rathen smiled. This woman was unlike anyone he had ever met. "My hometown is a small village close to King Delvant's dominion called Hullbeck. It's a farming village."

"So for you, it was either becoming a warrior or a farmer."

Rathen laughed. "I didn't care much for the smell of the livestock, but little did I know that living among such a large group of men didn't smell any better."

"You have no family? No children?"

"No. I almost settled down with a wife once, but things didn't turn out well."

"Tell me about it," she said with a smile, resting her chin on her cupped knees.

"Not much to tell. Her name was Sanna. We met while I served the king and had often talked of marriage and children. My legion had been sent to clear out a group of bandits nearby who were building in force and harassing the local merchants. The campaign lasted the entire summer, and upon my return, Sanna had moved in with a farmer friend of mine and was soon married," Rathen ended with a smile.

Evah laughed. "Well, I guess she didn't think you'd be coming back."

"I guess not. What of your parents? Were you really orphaned to the temple?"

Evah smiled. "Yes. I don't know anything about my mother, but I do have images of my father."

Rathen looked at her, puzzled. "What do you mean?"

"Sometimes, when I sleep, I see his image," Evah explained. "Well, it's only a shadow."

"Then how do you know it is your father?"

"He calls me 'my child' and offers up his hands for an embrace. I run toward him, but I always wake up before I can reach him. He calls me Evah."

Rathen pondered these dreams thoughtfully, knowing firsthand how dreams were often used to communicate across great distances. "If he lives, perhaps one day you can seek him out. Do you know where you are from?"

Evah shook her head.

"What about his name?"

Evah smiled. "Perhaps one day I will find him. His name is whispered in my dreams. Vizilan."

Rathen slowly shook his head. "Not familiar to me."

Evah shifted uncomfortably. "I don't know why I'm telling you this… No one else knows my secret. Something about the dreams stir me. They make me feel like a child again, longing for her parent's embrace."

Rathen smiled. For the first time, he could see the sincerity in her eyes. "What is your real story, Evah? For I see the warrior in you."

Evah smiled widely. "I knew I wouldn't be able to fool you for long. Let's just say I am also anxious to see Vargas's death. But for my own reasons."

Rathen smiled widely. With her desire to see Vargas killed, he finally made the connection. He recalled Garrick's story back in Tobermoar regarding the power hierarchy within the compound. Litagus ruled, but the second in charge was Vargas followed by a woman, with a certain amount of animosity brewing between the two. Rathen could play on this internal fight for power and use it to get what he wanted: Vargas.

Evah smiled. "What is it?"

"Vargas, you say?" Rathen smirked. "Then you are willing to help us… Davale?"

Davale smiled broadly and laughed. "I underestimated you, Rathen. You are just full of surprises."

Rathen laughed. "So, is Davale your real name, or is it Evah?"

Davale peered deeply into Rathen's eyes. "Davale is my temple-given name. The image of my father calls me Evah, so I think that is my birth name."

"You know I can't trust you now, being who you are," Rathen said, his tone grew serious.

Davale kept her smile. "You can trust me to give you what you want. Vargas."

"But your loyalty is with the compound."

Davale shook her head. "My loyalty is with Litagus, the high priest. Not to the entire compound and certainly not to Vargas."

Rathen sat silently and looked at Davale who was staring back at him. What could he do? If the rest of the group knew this woman was Davale, they would never trust her even with leading them to the compound. But if he could use her to get close to Vargas, Rathen could finally obtain his revenge.

"Well, I can't let you go now," Rathen said.

Davale smiled impishly. "You want to tie me up?" She held her hands together in front of her and pursed her lips.

"Of course not. Just don't go trying to leave or it will… complicate things."

"Then we have an agreement. I won't sneak away and will take you to the compound. And in return, you kill Vargas."

Rathen considered this agreement. He would need to inform Thack and Bulo of Davale's identity to help keep watch. However, telling the others would not go well. He needed to keep it secret. "Alright then. Just get me to Vargas and the book. I will handle the rest."

Davale slowly shook her head. "I'll help you get into the compound and to Vargas. But from there, my willingness ends. I cannot compromise my loyalties regarding the book."

"Litagus," Rathen said bluntly. "I hope to avoid him anyway." Rathen paused, contemplating his sanity. With her connection to Litagus he couldn't afford to trust her. She's the enemy. However, unless Garrick returned before morning, he didn't have much other choice. If she proved dangerous, he would take actions to keep the group safe. "Alright, do you know of the secret passage somewhere inside the kitchens?"

Davale laughed loudly, raising her face to the sky. "Was that your plan?"

Rathen looked at her confused.

"That passage is much too small for men of your size. It is often guarded with more men than even the front doors."

Rathen looked at her in disbelief.

"I'll get you in. For this, you can trust me," she said with a smile.

Rathen had no choice but to trust her. There were no other options, and according to her, their previous plan to use the secret passage would have likely failed. Garrick had admitted to not knowing much about the passage, and maybe he never heard about how big it was.

"Alright." Being someone with authority within the compound made their agreement dangerous, but he wanted to believe every word she said. He gazed deep in her eyes, trying to comprehend this complex woman. She stared back at him. Slowly, she moved her face toward his. Just before their lips met, Rathen stopped her.

"No. We go into battle tomorrow."

She once again closed the distance. "Then we should live tonight like it will be our last."

"No. Sorry, but… no," Rathen said, standing. "Be ready

to fulfill your promise in the morning." He walked away, leaving her sitting in the grass. With her charm and beauty, it took all his strength not to be tempted into her arms.

Rathen drew the attention of Bulo and Thack who followed him to the other side of camp. He whispered the true identity of Evah and about the agreement they had reached. Both men shook their heads trying to understand the situation.

"She will lead us to the book and to Vargas," Rathen whispered. "But while in our camp I need you both to watch her and stop any attempts of her escaping."

"Why would *Davale* come all this way alone?" Thack asked.

"I understand. We don't have all the information, and in normal circumstance I wouldn't agree to this plan. But if Garrick fails to return, we won't have much of a chance getting into the compound without her."

"I trust you, Rathen. We'll watch her carefully." Bulo nodded and placed his arm on Thack's shoulder.

Thack nodded, but his face expressed his concern.

"Tomorrow this will all be settled. One way or the other," Rathen said. He turned and walked toward the rest of the group and made the schedule for night sentry duty.

Rathen served on the first night duty with Rendrak on the other side of camp. Sitting in the darkness, his mind drifted back to Sanna and thoughts of how different his life would have been if they were married. He had given up on the idea of marriage and children long ago. But the concept of having a son or daughter to pass his legacy onto—much in the same way his father had tried to do for him—was something he thought still worth considering. His reluctance to visit his family started to fade in comparison to his concern for their well-being. He knew he should visit them soon.

He watched over the group and could not help looking over at Davale's sleeping form near the fire from time to time. He recalled their talks and feelings and shook his head at his desire for her. Tomorrow would see the end of the ordeal and then he would leave this area and her far behind.

Bulo relieved him of his sentry duty informing him everything was alright. But instead of sleeping close to the campfire where the others lay, Rathen moved his bedding far enough away to be alone, out of the light of the fire. He laid down to sleep, looking up at the clouds as Davale's words repeated in his mind: *Live tonight like it will be our last.* His eyes closed, and he slept.

Movement woke Rathen from his sleep. Opening his eyes, he reached for the sword next to him. Without a word, Davale's slender body slipped into his bedding. Whether it was his sleepiness or the suppressed desire in his heart, he gave in to her charm.

Chapter 16

Litagus walked into the small town of Deepbriar with two guards at this side. He had left his assistant, Bucomus, and Vargas guarding the book for the short time he was to be away. The attack on Deepbriar by the escaped minions of Gothoar was unfortunate—he needed the town for his supplies and food. Appeasing these ignorant villagers was a delicate matter he dared not leave to his assistants this time. He needed to make amends and resecure the food-and-supply trade or his compound would be in trouble.

The surrounding fields were charred, a few still smoldering. Thick, black smoke rose from the ashes of what remained of most of the buildings. A line of bodies lay next to the road in preparation for burial while several men dug graves. The smell of the casualties and the smoke in the air assaulted Litagus's senses. Crackling embers could be heard around him, and soon, voices mixed in.

As he turned and neared the center, he saw a group of townspeople, about thirty in number, gathered in front of the burned frame of what had been the tavern. Their pale complexions and drawn features showed the shock that still filled them from the tragedy. The people moved away from Litagus as he passed, either out of fear or respect.

"Lord Litagus," Lomak, the town leader, addressed him. He was a thick man, well into his later years. A ring of white hair lined his bald head, and his modest clothing was covered in dust and debris. His heavily wrinkled face bore the sorrow of losing his people.

"Master Lomak, I am pleased to see you are safe," Litagus said stoically.

"I was one of the fortunate, though many of us didn't make it," Lomak said, lowering his eyes and looking toward the crowd.

Murmurs rippled through the crowd, but no one dared speak up. Anger mixed with remorse and uncertainty filled their bloodshot eyes.

"You said you'd protect us," Lomak said. "You said you'd keep us safe."

"The attack happened too quickly for us to arrive in time. Our compound was also attacked, and we suffered our own losses."

"You pulled your men out of our town and left us defenseless," Lomak said.

"We did not expect them to attack your town."

"And you got a lot of us killed," Lomak said, grinding his teeth.

"The men who escaped from us are now being hunted. They will be found and killed."

"They weren't men!" a young male voice called out.

"That's right! Them were demons," said an elderly woman in front, hunched over and leaning on a cane.

"They killed my pa and brother in seconds. I ran from

them monsters," a young man spoke out.

"Killed my family too," a young woman wearing a mud-spattered dress shouted.

"I shot one with my bow but couldn't hurt it," a tall man from the back shouted out.

The crowd's murmuring increased.

"Our town was destroyed and *your* men weren't here to help protect us," spoke a man in front still wearing his sleeping clothes.

"That's right!" shouted several town's people.

Lomak held his hand out to the crowd and the crowd stopped their chattering. He looked Litagus in the eyes for the first time. "What kind of monsters were they, and why did they come? There were only three of them, but they couldn't be stopped."

Litagus had to be careful with his words. "They are monsters who prey on anyone in their path. They will all be destroyed for attacking your town and killing your people. Even if I have to scour the forest to find these wretched beasts myself."

A few short-lived cheers quickly died out to the murmuring again. He heard whispers doubting whether he would even protect them if the demon men returned, let alone if he could kill them. Litagus doubted he could win them over after such a loss.

"Can we count on your continued food and supplies?" he asked bluntly, dropping all forms of diplomacy.

"What food?" Lomak scoffed. "It's all gone. Not enough to even keep our survivors fed for the remainder of the summer." He allowed his tense shoulders to loosen. "You were supposed to protect us in exchange for a portion of our provisions. So the way I see it, we don't owe you nothing anymore."

The townspeople began chanting, "Get out," as the crowd moved forward, surrounding Litagus and his guards.

Litagus's temper started to boil. He'd had enough of these trivial fools.

"Enough," he said as the town's people continued to press forward.

Litagus took hold of his amulet and raised his other hand. As he chanted, he lowered his hand quickly, sending a blast of energy out in a radius around him that sent the townspeople and his guards as well falling to the ground.

"I said enough!" Litagus demanded, towering over everyone on the ground.

The guards picked themselves up while the stunned town's folk remained on the ground.

Litagus turned toward Lomak, who was still trying to lift his aged body enough to face him. "I will return with the heads of your attackers. Then we will resume our discussions on supplies."

Lomak nodded without speaking, his expression a stoic mask but the veins in his temples throbbed visibly under the skin.

Litagus turned and walked away. He needed to solve this matter as quickly as he could, or he might as well move out of Bramblewood now without the necessary food and supplies. His two guards rushed to his side, and the three of them climbed into the wagon and left Deepbriar behind.

Litagus expected Davale's return the next day, hopefully with the heads of these minions. If not, he would take some men through the forest and kill them himself. Apparently, they were smarter than they appeared since they had plotted a way to cripple his supply line. Or had they attacked the town for another reason?

His dark mood made for a somber ride back to the compound. As the wagon rolled down the trail, Litagus continued to stare into the trees, searching for any signs of the minions. It would be easier if they just attacked so he could end them then and there. He grew anxious to return and ensure the safety of the book. He considered that he should have placed a protection spell around it, just in case, before leaving it with Bucomus and Vargas.

Relief washed over him as the compound came into view with nothing seeming out of place. Vargas stood outside the front doors to greet him.

"How fares Deepbriar?" Vargas asked.

Litagus jumped down from the wagon and started to walk to the front doors. "A complete loss," he said. "We will need to relocate soon."

Vargas's face tensed.

"What is it?" Litagus asked, running out of patience.

"High Priest, if we leave and take the book… we will be open targets on the road for them to attack."

"We will kill them soon enough!"

"And if more come?"

Litagus stopped and turned toward Vargas, whose face held only concern. He realized Vargas was not disputing him but worried for his high priest's safety. "You are right," he said more calmly. "When Davale returns tomorrow, we will decide when and the best way to move out."

Vargas nodded.

"Until that time, we must protect the book and find

these three minions in the forest. They will not stop until they have it back. They undoubtedly know a direct assault with their few numbers will not work, so they will likely try to draw us out."

Vargas nodded. "I understand. Shall I scout the forest myself?"

"No. Davale is out there now, and I need you here. Perhaps it is time to explain my plans to you. Come to my quarters after you make your rounds with the guards. We shall talk."

Vargas's face lit up. "Right away, High Priest," he said, walking off toward Captain Unsinn's shack.

Litagus stepped up to the door, but before he entered, he carefully scanned the tree line for any signs of intruders. Seeing nothing, he stepped inside, shut the doors behind him, and walked up to his study.

Inside the room, Bucomus stood over to the Book of Ziz.

"Any problems?" Litagus asked.

"None, High Priest. How did your meeting in Deepbriar go?"

Litagus shook his head without speaking.

"Yes, well, that relationship had been strained from the beginning," Bucomus said, walking toward the door. "Will there be anything else?"

"Prepare to move. We will take up residence at the Dark Hills temple."

Bucomus stopped and turned around. "What of the high priest there?"

Litagus took ahold of the book and carefully placed it on a table in the corner. "He will meet an unfortunate accident just before we arrive," he said without looking at his assistant.

"Very well. I will prepare." Bucomus walked out of the room, closing the door behind him.

Litagus searched through the components stacked around the room. He picked up a handful of fine iron powder mixed with silver dust from a pot on the table and took a small pinch of diamond dust from a small ceramic bowl. He mixed the three elements together with his finger in the palm of one hand, knowing the silver and diamond dust would assist with the conduction of energies. He then walked to where the Book of Ziz rested on a small table in the corner.

Litagus recalled the words from the book and recited them loudly. He threw the mix of elements into the air near the table, and a shimmering green shield appeared, completely encasing the book and table.

Litagus stepped back and smiled, admiring his work. The spells were coming quicker to him now since his practice the other day.

"Is now a good time?" Vargas called from the door.

Litagus moved to the center of his study. "Yes. Enter."

Vargas walked in and stared at the small green glow of the shield, amazed. "That's just like what I saw at Ghrakus Castle, except on a smaller scale."

Litagus smiled upon hearing his words. It had taken him well over a year to get to this point, but now, with a better grasp on the concept behind the magic, he felt confident. Perhaps only six more months would be all he needed to perfect his defensive spells for his big plans.

"Sit. Let's talk," Litagus said, motioning to the chairs near the middle of the room.

Vargas sat quickly, looking intently at his high priest.

"As you know, I have big plans for us. You have served me well, and I would like to bestow upon you the title of high priest and grant you your own temple very soon."

Vargas eyes widened as he smiled.

"However, before that time, I will take over the Order of Gothoar. We will hold a large gathering for the followers at the Dark Hills temple on the next full moon. There, I will convince our disciples that Gothoar has lost his power and that I hold the power to lead them into a better future."

Vargas opened his mouth as if to speak, but no sound came out. He closed his mouth and tried again. "You will defy Gothoar?"

"Yes," Litagus said with confidence. "The Book of Ziz was written to protect worlds from Gothoar's reach. I will use it against him. Utilizing its power, he will be unable to affect me, and I will shut him off from this world."

"Then we would be a temple without a deity. How could we possibly survive?" Vargas asked, shaking his head.

Litagus took a deep breath. "The many followers we have will soon see me as more powerful than Gothoar. I will tell them he has betrayed them and inspire them to follow me. They will start to worship me, and I will have statues raised around the world in my likeness and many new temples built. We will slowly take over parts of the world, spreading our own order and its ways. I will gain the powers of a demigod in that way, sharing those powers with my followers, before finally becoming a deity myself," Litagus ended with an ominous grin.

Vargas sat speechless.

Litagus sensed his apprehension. "It can be done. The powers within that book are endless," he said, pointing to the Book of Ziz in the corner. "If for some reason my power is not as strong as I anticipate, we can align ourselves with another deity if necessary. Bargains can always be made."

"How did you learn this? Where—" Vargas began to ask, but Litagus cut him off.

"Among the elite council of the Order, the Book of Ziz is well known for being a weapon against Gothoar, which is why I vowed to recover it. Delivering the book to them would have given me great influence among their ranks. However, when I studied the book for myself, I found it contained much more than protection. I could not simply turn it over. Its pages contained the story of the deity Ziz himself and described in detail how he ascended to that status. It can be done, just as I described, just as it has been before, and you will be the first high priest of my new order."

Vargas's look of disbelief soon gave way to a broad smile. "I will give my life to assist you."

Litagus nodded. "The time is near. Following the death of the Dark Hills priest, we will relocate our base and prepare for our takeover of the Order."

"What of Gothoar's minions?"

"If more come before we depart from Bramblewood, we can throw the tribal savages at them to slow them down. At Dark Hills, we will increase our numbers and prepare our defenses to prevent them from interfering. Gothoar's influence in this world is still greatly limited, and we have the upper hand." He nodded toward the leather-bound book in the corner.

Vargas sat across from Litagus, his mind racing. Was such a thing possible? Could the high priest overthrow the deity

Gothoar himself? His powers from the Book of Ziz had grown, as evidenced by the green shield covering the table and book in the corner.

Suddenly, Vargas needed air to clear his thoughts. He looked up at Litagus and saw the fire and determination in the high priest's eyes. "I will prepare," Vargas said.

"Yes. Upon Davale's return, we shall all meet again," Litagus said with a grin.

Vargas stood and glanced at the shield one last time before leaving the room. He walked down the stone staircase and into his own chambers, where he picked up a mace from his weapon rack. Then he walked out the compound doors. Even though Litagus had requested he let Davale handle the minions, he thought a walk in the forest would clear his mind. Running into the demon men would just be an added bonus.

Opening the door and stepping out, Vargas saw that Captain Unsinn stood beside the entrance. The captain flashed him a salute as he walked by. The late afternoon overcast sky could be seen from the clearing. Vargas eyed the guards on duty and smiled. *Nothing can get through our current defenses.* He breathed a sigh of relief as he stepped into the shadowed forest trail. Now, he had time to think.

Vargas knew Litagus had more power than he showed, but would it be enough to take over the Order? To defy the elite council? If he did, then Vargas would become a high priest. Achieving such a position had been his goal ever since he began his studies at the temple as a child. But... was there more to be had?

Vargas recalled Litagus's explanation of what the Book of Ziz contained, instructions on how to become a deity—an immortal. Yet now it seemed the high priest already knew how this could come about—assuming one was powerful enough to achieve it. So the Book of Ziz must somehow increase one's powers enough to achieve the degree of acclamation that led to immortality. Vargas laughed to himself as he walked. It seemed ironic that the secret of immortality had been hidden inside the protective shell of Ghrakus Castle with a group of mages all looking for that very thing. He remembered their talk with the prince brother Tyus, who had explained that his father, the king, would pay small fortunes for people claiming to have the secrets of immortality. If they had acquired the Book of Ziz and knew how to unlock its secrets, they may well have achieved their goal.

The question that kept coming back to him was this: if Litagus had been able to learn such spells as the green shield, would Vargas be able to as well? Maybe or maybe not. Yet the purpose of such powers would be to develop many thousands of worshipping followers who would give their adoration to one's visage. Vargas thought back to Litagus's words about building temples and erecting statues in his honor as necessary to the process of becoming a demigod. The followers would worship the likeness of such statues, few ever seeing Litagus in person.

Vargas smiled. Litagus's high priest would oversee such an important task. What if when he oversaw the statues' construction, he had them covered until they were all complete? What if, on the day of the final reveal, all the statues resembled himself instead of Litagus? Would that immediate worship gift him with powers? And would those powers be enough to fight off Litagus's wrath? He would no longer be just a high priest; he would become a demigod himself.

Vargas's eyes scanned the trees as he considered the many possibilities this new information presented. His ambitions of becoming a high priest no longer satisfied him.

Chapter 17

Davale stood in a large stone room brightly lit by a roaring fire in the middle. The flames stretched high above her head, flickering wildly. She looked down to see she was dressed in a long black robe. Out of instinct, she scanned the area for threats. Her hands reached for her daggers but found them both missing. She continued to search the room for signs of movement and something she might use as a weapon. The sounds of the crackling fire caught her attention, and she peered deeply into the bright flames. A dark figure soon took shape, casting a shadow within the fire itself. It grew to almost seven feet high and stepped from the blaze.

"Father!" Davale rushed forward, attempting this time to reach him before she woke up. Instead of waking, like she had done so many times before, she threw her arms around the cloaked figure and pushed her head into his chest. His fiery form burned as if it were the fire itself, but she dared not let go.

"My child, it is time. Vizilan calls…" the figure's voice rumbled, his eyes of fire looking down on her.

"I won't let you go," Davale said, holding on tightly, the

heat of his body threatening to scorch her. She desperately ached to stay close to him. After night upon night of him disappearing, finally she clung to him. She opened her eyes to peer at her father. Immediately, she noticed the room was filled with people, all with the same pale white skin and black hair as her, and all dressed in the same robes, standing silently.

A bright flash and a sharp pain in her head forced her to let go. In that second, all her memories as a small child flooded back to her. Overwhelmed, she fell to her knees. Visions of her life within the Disciples of Vizilan assaulted her, the bitter taste of her life as child slave always fighting to be free souring her mouth. Realization shook her—Vizilan was not her father, as she had thought. He was a demon whose disciples considered him a god, and her true father was one of his dark priests, an evil and twisted image she remembered from her childhood nightmares with sharp jagged teeth and black eyes. She never knew her mother. Vizilan himself was something far worse. She shivered at the thought of having such a strong connection with, and a deep yearning for, such a dark being.

The raucous sounds of a marketplace from years before invaded her mind. Litagus's face loomed before her child form, his hand extended behind him to pay mere coins to the slave merchant. More memories washed over her in waves: Litagus's hand pulling her back to the temple, his incantations to alter her memories.

Davale woke from her dream gasping for air. She looked up: the night sky sparkled with stars, and the dank odor of cold campfire ashes pulled her to the present. She turned to see Rathen lying next to her, felt the warmth of his masculine form. She took a deep breath and calmed her nerves.

As Rathen slept, she silently slipped out of his bed. She walked back to her bedding, ignoring the lich's gaze fixated on her naked form. She dressed and sat on her bedding, recalling her memories. Her mind scanned the blackness inside her that threatened to envelope her soul. The lich had been right. Something infiltrated the darkness. Something so menacing it frightened even her.

She cupped her knees and fought to repress her feelings of fear and distress from so long ago. She belonged to a group that until now she had forgotten, and now she fought against the pain of a scar ripped open. All her memories reminded her of how much she had hated the Disciples of Vizilan for how they treated the small and vulnerable child she had been. Her body began to shake. She closed her eyes and demanded her body to calm.

Even at such a young age, she knew she didn't fit in with the dark cult. Nothing about that had changed even after all these years, yet this desire to cling to a follower of Vizilan felt too strong to dismiss. Why now?

No! She was her own person and would make her own decisions. Litagus saved her life, removing her from that terrible place. He did her a favor by making her forget her horrible past. Her allegiance would always lay with him. There was no reason for her to return to such a black-hearted cult. She nodded to herself, determined to blaze her own path in life… to turn away from the call to the darkness.

Despite her decision, the urge to discuss this with Litagus pulled her to her feet—if for no other reason than just to thank him, for she knew her life would have been cut short if he had not freed her from that miserable childhood. If

Vizilan thought he was bringing her closer by giving back her memories, he was wrong. They only served to reinforce her connection to Litagus. And it was time she headed back to him.

No one stirred from their slumber as Davale strapped on her gear. She was already working on a story to give Litagus, explaining why she was not able to find and kill the demon men. However, if they were not dead already, Rathen's attack on the compound would likely push all thoughts of the demon men from Litagus's mind anyway. Her plan was to help Rathen's people into the compound as carefully as she could before slipping away. Once the guards were alerted to their presence and the fighting had begun, Davale would act as though she had just arrived back from her hunt, completely surprised to see the ragtag bunch as they were crushed under Litagus's power. With the secret to destroying Vargas in Rathen's vengeful mind, she only needed to conceal herself until Vargas was dead. Then she would jump into the fray, even assist in killing the remaining survivors to help sell her story. The only challenge would be first sneaking into the compound without guards seeing her with them. If she had to kill a few guards to get rid of her rival, so be it. She could always blame the deaths on Rathen's group if any suspicions were raised.

As dawn approached and the group started to wake, she looked over the members, examining them. She had enjoyed their conversations and learning more about them, especially Rathen. Regardless of her attraction for him and the pleasurable memory of their night together, his death today wouldn't bring her any remorse. She had also felt an unusual connection with Caswen during their talks and admired the strength she showed, even if it was misguided.

She watched each tending to their morning rituals. Amusement edged into her mind; none of them knew this would be the last morning they would ever see. Their last sunrise… their last meal. The somber look on each of their faces during breakfast showed their anxiety for today's battle. Davale, however, did her best to conceal a smile as she fantasized about the death of a certain cleric. Today, finally, she would be rid of Vargas.

Rathen took a few minutes during breakfast to explain to everyone about Vargas's inability to cast spells without his amulet and that destroying it should be their first order of business. They all nodded in agreement. Bandark and Rendrak looked especially eager to leave as they hurried to finish their meal. After eating, the company packed up together.

Rathen looked over the camp and saw everyone ready to move out. Davale stood by his side, prepared to lead them to the compound. He noticed that she wore a dagger on her hip, a dagger he hadn't noticed the past couple of days.

His curiosity about the dagger was forgotten as he looked at her, remembering her feminine shape and the feel of her supple skin. Her face was solemn, but a sort of electric energy radiated off of her, and he wondered if she was also remembering their night together. Despite his thoughts, Rathen treated Davale no differently than the day before, preferring not to arouse suspicions about the nature of their relationship. The only person who seemed to know about the events of last night was Bulo, who had flashed Rathen a suggestive smile during breakfast.

Shaking his head to expel the distracting thoughts, Rathen looked past Davale at the rest of his troops. The others looked well rested and anxious to move out. Rathen pulled the blue stone he had received from Arg'grimorem and held it in his hand, wanting to keep it close in case the wolf-men attacked. He did not doubt that the wolf tribe skulked somewhere among the trees.

Without a word, he led the group out of the green field and back into the forest. The brambles made for very slow travel as Rathen hacked the vegetation from their path. As they finally found the trail, wolf calls began to echo all around them. Rathen looked back at Thack, his eyebrows raised in an unspoken question.

"Many in number and very close," said Thack, peering around through the branches.

Rathen nodded. He guessed that the wolf-men had been waiting for them ever since they entered Arg'grimorem's territory, increasing their numbers in case a few of his band had escaped. He prayed this little blue rock he held in his hand would save them from a long and dangerous battle.

Rathen maintained his course down the trail, his eyes searching for scouts and the wolf tribe.

"To the left!" Thack called out behind him.

"Bandark!" Rathen shouted.

Everyone stood still as several wolf tribesmen appeared through the trees with arrows strung. Davale crouched down and raised her arms defensively, prepared to avoid any loosed arrows.

Bandark's blue shield appeared like a wall in front of the group just before the arrows flew. Davale smiled when she saw the shield and stood beside Rathen again just as a volley of arrows struck the shield and fell to the ground.

"Be ready on the right!" Rathen warned, remembering the manner in which they had attacked before.

Bandark held his shield up, allowing the group to focus on the right side. Before long, ten tribesmen in wolf furs could be seen rushing toward the group. This time, Rathen made out three to four real wolves running beside them. Davale pulled her dagger while the others remained still.

Rathen reached out to Davale, indicating for her to sheath the dagger. She flashed him a confused look and held her dagger at the ready. He held out his hand and unclenched his fist, revealing the blue stone. The stone started to spin in his hand, heating slowly. He held it until it began to burn his palm. Wincing, he wrenched his hand away. The stone continued to spin, suspended in the air.

Before the tribesmen could attack, Rathen heard the voice in his mind once more.

"I am Arg'grimorem, the bringer of life. Keeper of this green kingdom."

The tribesmen stopped in place, looking around in confusion. Even the wolves whimpered and lay down. Rathen noticed Davale turning around frantically, searching for the voice's origin.

A tribesman in the front stepped forward, his metal claws at the ready. He shouted unintelligible words.

"They mean you no harm. They have freed me from my darkness, and they have my protection," Arg'grimorem's voice said.

The tribesman lowered his claws and took a few steps back.

Bandark lowered his magic shield.

"The time has come again, my children of the wolf. Arg'grimorem has risen! The sacrifices you have made to me over many cycles have been honored and will no longer be accepted. We return to a time of peace. Summon your brothers, summon your sisters, and once again celebrate life within my forest."

The tribesmen bowed their heads, whispering excitedly, and the wolves stood, howling. The main tribesman in front spoke again, but Rathen could not understand.

"Then we will take back our temple and cast the intruders from our trees," Arg'grimorem answered.

Rathen tried to make sense of the question and its answer. Were they referring to the compound and Litagus?

"Arg'grimorem, life bringer," Rathen said, addressing the blue stone that spun in midair. "Are you referring to your temple in the north and the dark clerics who inhabit it?"

The tribesmen look around at each other, not able to comprehend Rathen's words.

"Yes, that is my temple of long ago. But the children of the wolf will ask them to leave peacefully."

"And if they don't?"

"They *will* leave."

Rathen clearly understood the message, and with such a large number of tribesmen, the people in the compound would quickly understand too. Several tribesmen started to howl as if calling others.

"Take my stone, children of the wolf, and place it within the halls of my temple."

The tribesman in front stepped forward and took hold of the blue stone with his clawed paw. He bowed slightly to Rathen and turned back to his people. He raised the stone high in the air and let out a loud howl that was returned by the entire group. The sound of comradery gave Rathen a chill. He could understand just how important this day was for their entire tribe.

The main tribesman led his men down the trail toward the compound. Rathen and his group followed a few feet behind them, blending in with the stragglers. As they walked, more and more tribesmen joined, running up beside them and dropping down from the trees. Rathen knew the wolf-men would not fight Vargas and his men, but their presence was the perfect diversion for his group to gain entrance to the compound. Rathen looked over to Davale, who grinned at him.

They walked behind the wolf tribe for a good distance, until up ahead Rathen could see two compound scouts approaching on horses. Rathen ducked his head behind the tribesmen, crouching low, and gave a signal for his group to do the same.

The riders backed their horses against the oncoming horde of tribesmen and wolves. "Return to the trees!" one of the riders commanded.

The tribesmen continued their march. The scouts glanced at each other and then turned and rode back toward the compound. Rathen knew they would inform their superiors immediately, but maybe he could use that to their advantage.

In the distance, Rathen saw the trees thin and part into a clearing. Davale grabbed his shoulder and pointed away from the trail. He nodded for her to take the lead, and the group left the massive march, cutting their way around the clearing. Although he could not see the compound through the bushes, Rathen began to hear shouts calling the guards to arms.

Davale continued to lead them around the clearing, then suddenly motioned for them to stop. "Wait here," she whispered to Rathen, and she stepped into clearing before he could stop her.

Rathen could not see where she went. Soon Davale returned, a toothy smile playing on her lips.

"It's clear," she said. "Come."

Rathen followed her out of the clearing and saw the large stone compound for the first time. Various animal statues were carved into the sides, and vines sprawled out over the entire building, hiding its more intricate details. A large stone spire stood in front of them. By the commotion on the other side of the building, Rathen guessed they were on the far back side of the compound, opposite the wolf-men.

Davale rushed to the wall, her feet nimble and silent, and beckoned for him to follow. Rathen walked past an alcove, noticing the body of a guard sprawled on his back, his throat cut and fresh blood spilling into the ground. She was serious… and now he knew just how dangerous she could be.

"Now, we go up," Davale whispered, looking up the side of the stone wall before them.

"You mean climb?"

"Yes, quickly. This is how I sneak in." Davale gestured for them to hurry as she stepped onto a small stone ledge at the base of the wall. Choosing a large vine, she pulled on it, testing its strength. Satisfied it would hold her, she began to climb, using the statues and ledges carved into the stone for her footing. Reaching a balcony on the second floor, she swung herself over the ledge, disappearing from sight. Her head popped out over the side of the balcony, and she gestured to everyone below to get moving.

"Bulo, you next," said Rathen. "Then Thack, Bandark, and Rendrak. Dryn, you help Caswen. Magom and I will go last." Everyone nodded and lined up, Bulo taking hold of the vine.

"Be on your guard when you get up there," Rathen said to him.

Bulo nodded and started the climb. Surprisingly, the thick vine held his weight without much give. Thack was next, and with his one arm, he relied more on the footing than lifting his weight. The half-orc scaled the wall with ease.

One by one, they all climbed up, Dryn practically sprinting up the wall before helping to pull her sister over the ledge. Lastly, Rathen stood near the vine, waiting for Magom.

"I cannot make it," the lich said.

"What?" Rathen asked, looking around for guards.

Davale's face appeared over the ledge with a look urging them to hurry.

"I cannot climb," Magom said.

"Can't you fly or something?"

Magom remained silent.

"Fine, get on my back," Rathen said desperately, turning around.

"I will not—"

"Quickly," Rathen insisted, crouching down.

Magom pressed himself against Rathen's back and threw his skeletal arms around his shoulders.

Crinkled patches of the lich's withered skin brushed against his neck, and Rathen forced himself not to cringe. If they stayed visible too long, a guard would surely spot them.

Wrapping Magom's bony arms closer around his neck, Rathen started to climb. The lich's dried and bony form weighed little, but the lich lacked structure, and Rathen struggled to balance himself for a swift climb with a bag of loose and shifting bones on his back.

Halfway up, Rathen started to waver, and he felt the lich's body shifting too far to one side. Rathen stopped and shifted the lich toward the center of his back with a sound of clacking bones.

"I want you to know I am not enjoying this," Magom hissed, his skull next to Rathen's ear.

"The feeling… is mutual," Rathen said between breaths as he struggled to pull himself up, using the head of a giant owl statue for balance. He looked up and saw Bulo and Thack with hands lowered over the side of the balcony. Rathen fought to climb up to them and offered his hand. Bulo took hold and pulled him up. Thack helped the lich.

"It's about time," Davale said, glaring. "You're lucky the guards were drawn to the front or you would both be riddled with arrows."

Rathen looked around to see a stone balcony covered in moss and vines. The only door leading into the compound had been bricked up long ago, but he noticed a stone staircase at the end of the balcony that spiraled up into a tower.

Davale led them up the stairs, skipping over steps that had crumbled away with age, running her fingers along the tower walls for balance. At the top of the tower, a doorway led onto the roof of the compound. The stone spire stood in the center.

Davale walked to the stone spire and bent down. She

cleared the vines to the side and slid a thin stone door open.

"In here," she said.

Rathen walked over and peered through the trapdoor at the small, dark attic beneath. He could see light shining up into it from a hole in the floor. A rope tied to a wooden beam in the attic trailed through the hole. Davale lowered herself inside and, gripping the rope, dropped down into the gap. Again, Rathen ushered his group ahead as he kept watch. Each dropped into the tiny attic and climbed down the rope through the hole. Seeing that Magom was able to lower himself down the rope, Rathen sighed with relief and quickly followed.

As Rathen climbed down the rope, he looked around at the cavernous chamber below him. The rope was positioned right behind a gigantic statue that hid the hole in the ceiling from view. Rathen could not tell who the statue depicted from behind, but once he reached the ground and walked around to the front, he immediately recognized the face of Arg'grimorem, just as he had appeared on the grassy plateau. Narrow openings in the wall allowed the outside light to brighten the room. The walls were lined with man-sized animal statues, all holding their paws up to Arg'grimorem, who towered over them on a stone altar. Stone benches had been carved before the statue for followers to sit and pray. Rathen recognized the common layout of a temple dedicated to a particular deity, though this temple had none of the offerings and burning candles that filled most temples.

"It looks just like our temple," Caswen remarked to Dryn. "Except the statues are different." Dryn nodded.

"This area isn't used," said Davale. "We can enter from here."

Rathen turned to the lich. "Can you sense the book?"

Magom stood still for a moment. "No."

"Right, let's get closer," Rathen gestured for Davale to lead on.

Davale moved around the side of the room and into a wide hall. The group followed, looking around at the statues and detailed architecture. A thick layer of dust covered every surface.

"Here. Let me go first," Davale said as she opened a thin stone door on a back wall. She slipped in and disappeared.

Rathen looked around at the group members, their nerves clearly readable on their faces. No one knew what they were about to encounter inside. Even Rathen's anxiety began to build as he thought about finally facing Vargas.

Davale's face reappeared in the darkened doorway. "Come," she said.

This time, Rathen went in the lead, followed by Bulo and Thack.

"Vargas's room is this way," Davale said, almost sprinting through the stone hallway.

Rathen gripped the handle of his sword hanging from his belt and rushed to follow.

Davale stopped in front of a large wooden door. "Here," she said with a smile.

Rathen flashed a look to Bulo and the rest of the group. He cracked the door open, peering in. Unable to see anything in the darkness, Rathen stood back and gave the door a strong kick. It flung open, revealing a dimly lit room sparsely decorated with crude furniture, an empty weapon rack, and a few books. Rathen's heart pounded wildly as he rushed inside, determined to strike Vargas first.

The rest of the group entered behind him, their eyes scanning every corner for Vargas, but the room was empty. "Where is he?" Rathen asked.

Davale slammed her fist on a nearby table in frustration. "He must be out front."

Magom hissed, and Rathen turned to see the lich looking up at the ceiling. "I can sense the book, but it is faint," he said.

Davale followed the lich's eyes up to the ceiling. "No, that's Litagus's room. We *need* to kill Vargas first," she said, her tone turning dark.

Rathen struggled between his desire for revenge and his need for the book. He took a deep breath.

"I'm sorry," Rathen said to her. "The book is our priority."

Davale's face flushed. "Then I can no longer help you," she spat, running from the room.

Bulo made to follow her, but Rathen stayed him with his hand. "Leave her. The book is all that matters now." He turned to Magom. "Lead us to it."

Magom floated from the room, followed by Rathen and the rest. They found a stone staircase and went up. At the top, Magom turned down a long hallway and stopped in front of a door at the end. "The sense is weak, but it is in here."

Rathen stood next to the door and motioned for Bulo to stand beside him, then addressed them all. "This Litagus is supposed to be a superior spellcaster," he whispered. "If he is inside, give it everything you have on the initial attack."

The group nodded.

Rathen opened the door slightly and kicked it in as he

had done before. A short man in gray robes stood behind three large tables in the center of a large chamber. Rathen rushed the man. Bulo burst forward and, with a loud grunt, threw his battle axe across the room. Rendrak and Thack pushed in, weapons drawn, while Bandark stood back, preparing a spell.

Bulo's axe struck the little man in the chest. He slumped to the ground, crying out in pain. Rathen stabbed his sword directly into the man's heart, finishing him off before he had a chance to utter a spell.

As the group filed into the room, Magom called out, "It is here."

Rathen turned from the body before him, focusing on the lich in the corner. His eyes widened as he noticed a small, circular green shield encasing a table, the red book visible within. "Just like Ghrakus," he said. "Bandark, get that open. Thack, shut the door."

Magom looked around at the reagents on the tables. "The shield weakened my ability to sense the book," he said, almost to himself.

Thack shut the door as quietly as he could, and Bandark rushed to the corner. The rest of the group gathered around the tables to look at the green globe.

Rathen set his shield against the wall and bent down to inspect the dead man. He did not see an amulet, nor did this man appear to be a mage. Rathen doubted that the body before him belonged to High Priest Litagus. His lack of weapons suggested a servant. Pulling the axe free, Rathen walked it back over to Bulo and handed it to him with a nod.

"I will need time to take down the shield," Bandark said.

"Just do it as quickly as you can." Rathen looked around

the room, examining the piles of books and containers of spell components.

Bandark began to murmur his spells, but before he managed to open the shield, Magom turned toward the door.

"A group approaches," the lich said.

Not quick enough. Had they been discovered, or had Davale alerted the compound to their presence? "Everyone except Bandark to the back of the room. We'll fight in this open space. Bandark, we will cover you as long as we can. Disable that shield."

Bandark nodded, looking over the tables and containers for anything he could use to speed up the process. Dryn, Caswen, and Magom moved in front of the tables and prepared themselves for battle. Rathen, Bulo, Thack, and Rendrak stood before the others, drew their weapons, and waited.

Footsteps could be heard at the door. Slowly, it opened.

Vargas stepped inside dressed in red robes, a mace in his hands, looking just the way Rathen remembered him. Vargas looked around the room, brow furrowed, taking in the group primed to attack. His eyes fell on Rathen, and his nostrils flared, his eyes widening.

"Rathen," he growled, lifting his mace.

Chapter 18

"Vargas," Rathen muttered under his breath, raising his sword. His anger propelled him toward the dark cleric. His desire for vengeance burned hot, almost blinding him.

"Rathen," Bandark's voice rumbled.

Rathen stopped in his tracks a few yards from Vargas, regaining his composure.

Vargas glanced around the room and raised his black amulet as he began to chant. Behind him, several guards rushed in. Vargas's eyes focused on Rathen, but he repeatedly glanced over to the lich as if he couldn't believe what he saw.

Rathen's group waited on the far side of the room. Vargas smiled as he shot black energy toward Rathen. Bandark conjured his transparent blue shield, stretching it across the room; the mass hit it and dissipated. Vargas looked at the group behind the blue wall, the frustration clear on his face. Six guards stood in front of it, searching for a weakness. One of the guards hit the shield with his weapon, but it held firm.

Vargas glanced over at the Book of Ziz still resting within its green shield. He turned to leave.

"Bandark, drop the shield and focus on the book! Thack, Bulo, Rendrak, keep the guards away from me. I need to get Vargas," Rathen said, bent in a stance and ready to run.

Magom raised his arms as he built energy around him, Dryn raised her bow, and Caswen stepped forward with her own amulet in hand.

As the blue barrier dropped, Rathen ran toward the door. A guard struck out with his sword as he passed, but Rathen deflected the blade with his own. Rathen had left his shield lying against the wall and relied on his sword for both attack and defense.

Bulo and Thack rushed to the side, engaging the guards and giving Rathen the space he needed.

Behind him, Rathen heard clashing weapons, spells cast, and arrows whizzing through the air, but his vision never strayed from the path down which Vargas had escaped. He couldn't allow him to warn Litagus. If he did, their escape would be much more difficult. Besides, Rathen trusted the others well enough to handle the guards.

Rathen raced down a stone hall, following the sound of Vargas's footsteps. As he turned the corner, he could see the dark cleric in the distance.

"Vargas," Rathen shouted.

The dark cleric turned slowly, his eyes narrowed and filled with fury. "Rathen…" he said, facing him, his mace in hand.

Rathen slowed his approach but kept his eyes on the amulet around Vargas's neck. If he reached for it, Rathen was prepared to strike.

"You've come all this way to find me?" Vargas asked with a smug smile, his body tense and his weapon at the ready.

"We've just come for the book."

"No chance. You may have somehow survived the lich and convinced him to help you, but none of you will escape here alive."

Rathen flushed with anger and wanted nothing more than to satisfy his revenge that very moment. Slowly, he brought the tip of his sword up, pointed directly at Vargas. He waited for the dark cleric to enter his striking range. Seconds passed and neither moved. When Rathen couldn't wait any longer, he lunged forward.

Vargas blocked the strike with his mace and smiled, springing at Rathen with his own attack. Without his shield, Rathen used his sword to deflect the oncoming attacks as best he could. Vargas tossed the mace to his left hand and swung it down toward Rathen's head. Rathen moved to easily block the strike, questioning the technique. As Rathen's sword deflected the mace, his eyes flashed white, and he felt a hard punch to his jaw. Rathen backed up, his hand to his mouth, realizing he had just been tricked.

Vargas smirked. He placed the mace back into his right hand and attacked viciously. Rathen took the defense, still trying to assess the cleric's skill with his weapon. He had underestimated Vargas, and he couldn't afford to let it happen again.

After a short barrage of attacks, Rathen grasped Vargas's abilities and methods. They were shrewd but predictable. Rathen exploited the pattern, plunging forward, pushing Vargas back. He countered a spinning attack and struck Vargas's leg, slicing through the robes. The cut, while superficial, proved Vargas's vulnerability given the right timing. Vargas paused his attack and looked down at his leg, before fending off Rathen's next attack. His eyes bright with fury, he reached for the amulet around his neck.

Rathen leaped toward Vargas as he held up the amulet, knowing it could mean his death. Vargas chanted under his breath as he deflected and danced around Rathen's attack. At Rathen's next lunge, Vargas shot out the hand that held the amulet, taking hold of the edge of Rathen's armor near his armpit. It made Vargas a stationary target, and Rathen swung his blade toward his head, but Vargas raised his mace and deflected it. The blade slid past the mace, down through his robes, leaving a clean cut across the dark cleric's side. Vargas didn't flinch as blood seeped through his robes. He tightened his grip on his amulet and Rathen's armor.

Rathen tried to cut the hand holding the amulet and his armor, but Vargas defended with his mace. Out of instinct, Rathen reached his free hand up and took hold of Vargas's arm, planning to wrench it away from the amulet. As Rathen's fingers touched Vargas's skin, his body convulsed from a severe jolt of pain, and he collapsed on the floor. Rathen shook his head, his senses spinning. He blinked to clear his fuzzy vision, all sound muffled as if he were underwater. He raised his weapon as Vargas stepped forward, his mace overhead. Rathen's strength faltered as the mace slammed into his sword and onto his left shoulder. The sharp flash of pain told Rathen his shoulder has been shattered, and his left arm radiated with incapacitating pain. His mind raced; this could be the end of him, and he prayed that either Bulo or Thack would be able to finish Vargas.

Vargas reared back for another strike. Rathen held his sword above him with what little strength remained to protect his head. As the mace came down, a golden shield appeared over him. The mace recoiled and shook when it struck the shield. Rathen turned to see Caswen in the distance, her amulet in hand.

Vargas let out a grunt and chanted, his eyes focused on the healer. Rathen took advantage of the interruption, inhaled, forced his senses to clear. Vargas shot a black churning mass toward Caswen; it hummed through the air as it closed the distance. Caswen reacted quickly, creating a light shield for herself. But not quickly enough. The shield blocked most of the black mass, but a few black beads passed through it, hitting her in the chest. She fell to the floor with a gasp of pain, and the light shield quickly faded. She lay there, motionless.

Vargas laughed in triumph.

Seeing Caswen fall filled Rathen with rage. As long as he was still alive, he would not let any more harm befall his group. As Vargas turned back toward him, Rathen gathered his remaining strength and swung his sword at Vargas's amulet hand. His glass blade hit its mark and severed Vargas's hand at the wrist, sending it and the dark amulet to the floor.

Vargas cried out in pain as he stared at his missing hand and the blood spraying out from the stump.

His pain seemed to ease Rathen's own as he pulled himself from the floor and stood, holding his shoulder. Vargas watched Rathen rise, and his eyes searched the floor for his amulet. Rathen stepped forward between the dark cleric and the amulet, kicking it behind him. He raised his sword, ready to strike again. Without the amulet, Vargas could not attack or heal himself.

Vargas's eyes focused on Rathen's face. "You've won," he

said, dropping his mace and falling to his knees. He pulled the sleeve of his robes down over his stump, trying to staunch the flow of blood.

Rathen raised his sword. This was what he had been waiting for so long now: to kill the man who had betrayed him and avenge the men who had died as a result. All his feelings of regret and anger boiled to the surface, ready to be released with a single strike of his sword. Yet he paused.

Vargas's strained face looked at him in confusion. "Get on with it," he snarled.

Rathen held the sword high, ready, yet Magom's words burned in his mind: "I have learned many things in my time. Especially from fighting my brother. One is not to take on your enemy's traits. You are an honest man compared to that dark cleric. The second is that a man's actions will come back to him when he does not expect it."

As Rathen stared down at Vargas, crippled and in pain, he realized that only someone with no honor, someone like Vargas, would strike down an unarmed, wounded man. Severely injured and without his amulet, Vargas was no longer a threat to him or his band. He had been defeated, and that was all that mattered. Whether he lived or died now would not make a difference as long as they escaped with the book. Rathen's anger dissipated, his mind calmed, and true clarity for the first time in months opened his eyes. He lowered his sword.

"I'm not going to kill you, Vargas," Rathen said. "I want you to live with the shame of knowing I bested you." He leaned over Vargas. "Every time you look at that useless stump, I want you to remember that you are nothing more than a spineless coward who couldn't even get a lich to do his dirty work." Rathen straightened back up and glanced over at Caswen, still lying on the floor. "We're leaving here with the Book."

A wave of relief washed over Vargas's face. "Take it," he said, lowering his head.

Rathen glared at Vargas. "I have spared you this time, but if you follow us or try to stop us, I will not hesitate to kill you."

Turning away, he rushed to Caswen, but before he could reach her, he heard a shout of pain behind him. He turned back around to see Vargas staring, wide-eyed and open-mouthed on his knees, just before he fell face-forward onto the floor. Davale stood over him, a bloody dagger in her hand and a smile that chilled Rathen to the bone.

He knew he didn't have the strength to fight Davale in his condition if she turned on him... not with her skill. Vargas's spell had stolen all his energy. Yet he stood tall and squared his throbbing shoulder as if ready to fight.

Davale stood there, her eyes on Vargas's body motionless on the ground. One last rasping breath escaped his lips, and she smiled. Her lips moved in a silent last comment to the dark cleric that Rathen could read, *he breathes no more*. She looked up at Rathen intently, as if considering her next move, but her deadly smile never faltered.

Rathen scanned her face. He glanced at the weapon in her hand, hoping to anticipate her movements before she struck. Instead, his eyes widened in disbelief as he recognized the glass blade. He looked back up into Davale's eyes, and she flashed him her most devious smile, confirming his suspicions. She'd killed Garrick! He felt sick as images of their night together sped through his mind, how he had welcomed her embrace, how she had whispered his name in his ear.

"Rathen!" a shout rang out behind.

"Here," he said weakly as Bulo rushed to his side. When he looked back up, Davale was gone.

Bulo put an arm around him as he wiped the sweat from his face with his sleeve, checking for any sign of Davale.

"You alright?" Bulo asked.

Rathen nodded. "Just help me over to Caswen." Bulo put his arm under Rathen's and helped him limp to the fallen healer, setting him carefully on the ground nearby. Dryn and Thack entered and knelt beside Caswen, whose face was pale.

Bulo glanced back at Vargas's body. "Vargas?"

"Dead."

Bulo nodded.

"What happened?" Dryn asked firmly, holding Caswen's hand. Rathen was relieved to see the healer still alive.

"She saved my life," said Rathen. "Vargas was about to strike a killing blow, but Caswen sent up a shield just in time. Vargas turned on her and hit her with some kind of spell. I was too weak to stop it."

Thack looked positively murderous. Rathen suspected that if Vargas had not already been dead, Thack would have gladly dispatched an axe into the dark cleric's skull.

Caswen groaned and opened her eyes.

"Cas?" Dryn said, putting a hand on her sister's face. "Can you hear me?"

Caswen groaned again, too weak to move. Thack grabbed her free hand with his own. "Don't be afraid. We're here."

Rathen looked up at Bulo. "The book?"

"Bandark is still working on it. The guards are dead."

"Let's regroup there."

Thack started to lift Caswen, but Bulo stepped in, better able to cradle the unconscious healer in his two arms. He nodded for Thack to assist Rathen to get back to the room. When they arrived, Rathen saw Bandark still standing over the green shield, chanting furiously. The guards' bodies had been dragged to one side of the room. Tables had been moved, and many of the spell components were scattered on the floor.

Dryn cleared one of the tables, knocking the pots and materials to the floor, and Bulo laid Caswen down.

Who could heal the healer? Rathen noticed Magom standing near Bandark, watching as he performed his spells. "Magom, can you help her?"

The lich turned and glided to the table. "I can find something to help her regain her strength from the negative energy spell. But I cannot heal her."

"Do what you can," Rathen said, slumping into a chair.

Magom picked up a few of the components from the floor and tables and combined them with some of his own. He moved beside Caswen, looking her over. The lich began to chant.

Rathen tried to move his left arm, but the pain in his shoulder blurred his vision and forced him to stop. They needed to get the book and get out before anyone else came looking for them.

Magom looked over the young healer's body after he cast his spell. Unfortunately, without the right healing potions, there wasn't anything else he could do for her.

Dryn knelt down next to the table with her hand on Caswen's head, whispering, "It's going to be alright," over and over. Thack stared at Caswen's face, his expression unreadable.

"She will regain her strength," Magom said as he walked back over to Bandark. He had hoped to watch every spell the tall mage used to open the protective shield. To his disappointment, he found that Bandark had already opened a part of the shield and was enlarging the hole wide enough for the book. Any further attempts by the mage to widen the hole wouldn't provide Magom with the knowledge he wanted.

Magom's attention shifted back to the young healer on the table, then to the components strewn across the floor. Her life force was weakening, but maybe if he could find some quick silver and enough gem dust within the mess, he could give her enough temporary strength to walk out of here. Magom's eyes fell on a white ceramic bowl on the floor partially hidden within a pile of books and papers. Inside were three large rubies. He picked them up and inspected each one's size and weight. He preferred to use diamonds, but these would be enough. He searched for quick silver or even a piece of cinnabar from which he might be able to extract some of its essence. He frantically turned over spilled pots of metal dust, dirt, and plant matter, but his search continued in vain. He glanced over to Rathen, who was slumped over in his chair. He could tell that Rathen had suffered from the same negative energy attack and had very little strength left. His time to find the last ingredient was growing short.

"I've got the book!" Bandark shouted as he pulled it from the green shield.

"Then let's get going," Rathen said, struggling to stand.

"Caswen isn't better yet," Dryn said angrily.

"Carry her. We don't have time to wait," Rathen said weakly.

"It's alright," Caswen said, her voice just barely a whisper. Dryn broke out into a smile that did not conceal the worry in her eyes. Just behind Dryn, relief washed over Thack's face, and he wiped the back of his hand over his eyes, sniffling slightly.

Magom held out the three rubies, about to discard them onto the floor, but stopped himself. These gems may not have been used to heal Caswen, but maybe they could provide her with life. For all she had done for him, the memories of his sweet Arina and the other human emotions she helped him remember, he could only offer this small gift. Magom approached the healer on the table and slipped the three gems into the flap of her pack while the others kept their attention on her.

"Give me... a brief moment," Caswen said, still lying on the table. She smiled at Dryn and Thack beside her, held up her amulet, and then closed her eyes. "Thandrall, give me the power to see this mission through. Grace me with your healing and your protection." Her amulet lit up, and the holy energy from it forced Magom to take a few steps back. The holy power wasn't something he wanted to get close to.

As the energy around her faded, Caswen slowly sat up and edged herself off the table. Rathen walked over and placed a hand on her shoulder.

"Thank you," he said warmly. She returned his thanks

with a small smile. Turning back to the others, Rathen said, "Time to go."

As the group left the room, Magom noticed that Rathen had neglected to take his shield. He hadn't moved his left arm since his fight with the dark cleric.

"How do we get out?" Thack asked.

Magom knew that Rathen and Caswen were too weak to climb back up the rope they had used to get into the temple, and Rathen seemed to realize it too.

"We fight out the front door and try to make it to the trees," Rathen said. He stumbled and almost fell. Bulo stood beside him, offering his shoulder to lean on.

"Understood," Thack said, leading the way.

Magom looked over to Caswen, who seemed to have gained some of her strength and energy back.

They passed the hallway and the body of Vargas on the floor. It appeared to Magom that Rathen had obtained the revenge he sought. Perhaps now, Rathen could move forward with his life.

As they neared the front of the compound, several voices could be heard from outside the doors, only one of which was open. Rathen held up his right hand. They stopped in front of the closed door and peered around it. Magom could sense even through the walls that a large group of tribesmen were still gathered in the front. But there was one being in the mass that stood out from the others, almost lich-like in its essence. Magom assumed it was the high priest, Litagus.

Rathen gave the go-ahead to follow as he passed through the doors to the compound. The group began to hurry along the side of the building, toward the tree line. When Magom made it outside, he traced the location of the high priest to be in the middle of about thirty to forty tribesmen on the each of the clearing. A few guards like the ones they had fought before were scattered among the mass. They were far enough away from them to attempt a stealthy escape. With some kind of heated negotiation still going on, the troop crept by unnoticed until a voice rang out from the high priest. "Don't let them escape!"

Magom could hear Rathen yell, "Take the book and run into the forest."

Bandark passed the book to Rendrak and cast his blue wall in front of the group.

Magom saw Rendrak run off toward the tree line with the book in hand, keeping Bandark's shield between him and the mass.

Black bolts of negative energy hit the shield as the tribesmen scattered into the trees for their own safety. A tall man dressed in black robes stood casting the bolts as four guards rushed the barrier. As the guards tried to circle the protected area, Bandark brought in the ends of the shield, sealing the group in a hemisphere. One of the guards ran off toward the trees, following Rendrak.

"Throw everything you have at that priest," Rathen said, looking at Magom. "Dryn, use that bow. Bulo, Thack, be ready for those guards."

Magom turned his attention to the high priest as Litagus began spreading a fine dust into the air. As he did so, Bandark's protective shield slowly started to open from the top. Magom looked around to see that all the wolf tribesmen had gone.

"No... I do not know how he has done it, but he is lowering my shield," Bandark said. "We do not have long, and I cannot keep his spells off us."

"Then we fight," Rathen said.

"He's too much to fight!" Bandark called out. "We need to ensure the book gets to safety."

"Go," Caswen said. "I'll hold him off as long as I can."

"No, you're not strong enough," said Dryn.

"We need you," Rathen said.

"It's the only chance we have. Just go," Caswen insisted. Her face was determined as she clutched her amulet to her chest.

Magom found himself moved by the young healer's words. He would never have thought she would be willing to sacrifice herself for the group despite the high ambitions she had set for herself. When they had first met her, she was such a naïve, simple-minded child, but now she was a true warrior, a woman, and a protector in her own right.

"I'll stay too," Magom said, looking at Caswen. He could not allow one so young to sacrifice herself. He would do his part and protect her the best he could.

"Me too!" said Dryn and Thack, their weapons at the ready.

Rathen nodded to them. "Meet you at the horses," he said before Bulo grabbed him, ready to run as the shield continued to come down.

When the shield fell just over their heads, the three guards on the other side anxiously raised their weapons.

Magom prepared himself, pulling from the most ancient spells he knew. He raised his arms and created a reservoir of energy around him. He formed a wind shield around himself and prepared his spells.

When Bandark's blue shield fell to their waists, Bulo jumped over with Rathen and rushed off into the trees.

Bandark followed close behind.

As Bandark's shield disappeared and the guards attacked, Thack held his ground, deflecting one of their strikes with his axe. Dryn shot an arrow at one the guards, catching him in the neck. The guard went down to one knee, grabbing at the arrow's shaft. The last guard rushed for Caswen as she held up her amulet. Magom thrust his hand out toward him and used his spell to send the guard flying back in the air, away from them. Thack cut through the guard he was fighting and went to finish the one with the arrow in his neck.

Litagus sent a barrage of negative energy bolts toward the diversionary group. Caswen conjured her golden shield before they hit. Magom let loose the three spells he had prepared: fire storm, ice shards, and acid bolts. As the spells reached the high priest, he brought up a green shield wall that stopped them all.

Magom shook his head. "This is not going to work. You all need to get away." He knew well that if Litagus held powers like Bandark's, nothing he could throw his way would likely reach the high priest.

"We need to give them more time," Caswen said, looking toward Rathen, Bulo, and Bandark, her face already strained with fatigue.

"I cannot defeat him quickly... I can only keep him busy," Magom said as he continued his spell attack. "He cannot attack us if his shield is up."

After Magom's next spell dissipated, Litagus quickly lowered his shield and sent another barrage of negative energy bolts. Caswen once again created her shield and strained as the bolts hit without penetrating. She collapsed to her knees, and as she did, the shield vanished.

Magom looked at Caswen. Still so young, he thought, so much potential. All wasted if she were to die right here, right now. He cast more spells to force Litagus to raise his shield again. "Caswen, run."

She looked up from where she knelt. He could not see the pain he knew must be etched in her eyes, but he felt her determination. "Marduke would never run away, neither shall I," she said, slowly shaking her head. "I'm not afraid… to die here."

Simple words, yet they triggered long-buried emotions. Magom's mind flashed to his long-lost love, Arina, and to his buried resentment of his father, who had kept him from her.

Today, I am human.

Magom allowed his rage to build like an inferno, fueling the energy swirling around him. The windy mass crackled and hummed with such ferocity it forced Dryn and Thack to back away.

He turned his glowing red eyes to the kneeling healer. "Today, you live. You have helped me find my own redemption, but there are still others who need you… Healer Caswen. Now go."

"I will not," Caswen yelled above the swirling winds.

Magom shot a handful of spells toward the high priest, forcing him to raise his shield once more. "Thack, Dryn, remove her from here."

They both nodded and lifted the healer to her feet, carrying her away.

"No!" Caswen screamed. "Let me go!" But they held her firmly by each arm, and her weakened form could offer up no fight. Magom could see Litagus turn his body, his eyes tracked the three as they ran toward the trees. No guards remained to give the trio chase, so he focused on the high priest.

Magom pulled on his remaining reserve energy, causing the violent swirl to lift him off the ground and hover within the storm. He cast several spells that forced Litagus to stop and shield himself. During the heat of the casting, Magom purposely aimed several acid bolts straight up and shot them high into the air.

Litagus lowered his shield and cast a barrage of negative energy bolts at the lich. The bolts hit the swirling winds and scattered; a few hit Magom without effect.

"Your negative energy will not harm me, priest."

Litagus admired the spell storm the lich had created around himself. Magom waited in silence. The acid bolts finally came down around the high priest, one striking him in the shoulder. Litagus recoiled from the pain as the acid ate its way through his robes through sizzling holes. He threw off his burning robes onto the ground, revealing a skeletal body bound tightly in cloth with blackened holes where the acid had hit. Magom smiled as he understood. This priest could be hurt. Defeated.

"Ah," said Magom. "So you are transforming into a lich…"

Litagus laughed, his hand still over his injured shoulder. "I'm so much more… far beyond even your comprehension."

Unimpressed, Magom remained silent, still suspended in the swirling air.

"You could join me. Help me rule the world as one of my generals," Litagus said. "I will become a god, and this world will be ours."

Magom took a breath and hissed it back out. "There was a time when I might have taken you up on that offer, but no longer. I have seen the good in mankind… and I wish to return to it. Today begins my redemption."

Litagus looked disappointed. "So be it. We shall see who's the superior spellcaster." He turned and walked back to his initial casting distance.

Magom took the opportunity to cast his spells of fire barrage, ice storm, and earthquake, attacking the high priest from all sides. Litagus spun around, raised his shield, and blocked the fire spell but struggled to block both the ice from above and the rumbling ground at his feet. Losing his balance, he fell, ice shards piercing his leg.

All the spell energy had drained Magom's swirling winds, slowly lowering him to the ground.

Litagus stood, blood seeping from under the wrappings around both his right leg and his left arm. Magom knew the priest had been severely injured from the attack. It would likely only take a few more good spells to kill this priest everyone had come to fear.

Litagus struggled to remain standing as he stared intently at the lich. He moved his hands and cast an inferno storm spell that rained fire down from the sky, encasing the lich in a swirling ball of fire. The flames were so intense that Magom couldn't see beyond them. However, his wind energy kept the flames from burning his bones. When the intensity grew too strong, he hurled his wind shield off, casting the fire away with it.

Litagus stood motionless, his eyes focused on the lich.

Magom had freed himself from the fire but at the cost of his shield. The next spell the high priest cast would have to be immediately countered by his own. He waited, but Litagus stood in silence. Suspecting an attack from behind, Magom turned around but saw nothing. He looked up just in time to see a large, solid wall of ice hurtling toward his head.

Well played, Priest, Magom thought just before everything went black.

Chapter 19

Rathen ran as fast as he could until his lungs ached and his head reeled. He slowed to a stop and stooped over, breathing hard, but Bulo came up beside him, swung him over his shoulder, and kept going, following Bandark along the path Rendrak had cut through the brambles. Thorns tore at the skin on their legs and arms, but Bulo never slowed.

The brambles soon gave way to a path, and they could see Rendrak up ahead, squatting over the body of the guard who had followed him, his chest sliced open. Bulo set Rathen on his feet, keeping one arm under his shoulder, and Rathen saw the Book of Ziz in Rendrak's hand. They had done it.

"Rendrak!" Rathen called out.

Rendrak responded with a nod as he stood up and sheathed his two glass swords.

A loud noise, like the crackling of thunder, pierced through the trees from where their comrades had been fighting Litagus.

"We need to leave," Bandark said.

"Right," said Rathen, dropping his head. What fate

would befall the members left behind? Yet the book must be taken to safety. And in his condition, he would be more hindrance than fighter.

They continued down the trail with Bandark in the lead, clutching the book under his robes. Bulo, one arm still around Rathen, helped him along, struggling a few times when Rathen's feet threatened to give out at their quick pace. Rendrak stepped to Rathen's other side and helped carry his weight. Rathen hated feeling helpless, but he couldn't do anything about it at the moment, not while they were running for their lives.

The howling of wolves surrounded them, but no tribesmen ever appeared.

Finally reaching the southern trails, Rendrak had to recut the trail they had made on their way in, since without the druid, they could no longer part the vegetation. Rathen kept looking behind them, hoping to see Magom, Caswen, Thack, and Dryn running to catch up. But they never showed.

Once secluded a ways down the cut path and out of the forest, the four men paused to catch their breath.

"Let's wait for them back at the camp?" Rathen said, wanting to put more distance between them and Litagus.

"We will ready the horses and leave immediately upon everyone's return," Bandark said. He continuously scanned the area, his eyes narrowed, brow creased.

"Let's push on then," Rathen said, sensing his urgency. He flashed a nod at Bulo to help him, since his strength had yet to return.

The half-day trek felt more like weeks to Rathen, his shoulder still throbbing. He was eager to saddle up and let his horse do the walking for him while he recovered. Just as the sun grazed the horizon, they approached the camp and saw it was just as they had left it. Remric sat by a low fire, preparing his dinner. When he caught sight of them, he jumped to his feet and ran over.

Remric glanced past Rathen, his eyes scanning the faces. "My father?"

Rathen placed a hand on the boy's shoulder, looking him in the eye. "I am sorry." Remric's eyes welled with tears, and he backed away from Rathen, shaking his head.

"Your father was a brave man. He died fighting by our side," Rathen said, stretching the truth a little. He knew that a considerate lie would serve the young man better.

Rathen reached into the small pouch tied to his belt and pulled out Apaca's owl carving. He held it out to Remric. "Apaca was working on this during the journey. I think he meant it for you."

Remric reached forward hesitantly and took the owl from his fingers. He stared at the figurine for a moment before clutching it to his chest. The boy sank to his knees and began to sob. Rathen nodded toward the others, and they walked toward the horses, leaving Remric to his grief.

Rathen walked over to pat his horse and take stock of everything he had left in his saddlebags for the journey home. The others followed suit except for Rendrak, who stood on the edge of camp, keeping watch.

"How much time should we give them?" Rathen asked, glancing over to Bandark, who continued to stare toward the forest.

"Not long," Bandark said. "If they have been defeated and Litagus is in pursuit, we should not linger this close with the book."

Rathen knew Bandark was right but shuddered at the thought of leaving Thack and the others behind. "I hope they will return shortly."

"As do I. But even if they do not, their sacrifices will not be in vain." Bandark patted the Book of Ziz inside his robes. "This book will help change the direction of the continuing war."

"Hopefully it will end it," Bulo commented as he finished his own preparations.

Bandark glanced toward Rathen and Bulo. "It will help, yes, but…" He cocked his head. "…what will you do now?" Bandark nodded at the two men as Bulo sat down next to Rathen.

"Take a long rest," Rathen said with a laugh.

Bulo laughed too, but Bandark's face remained stoic. "You can help us."

"I'm not sure I'd be much use to you anymore. Maybe I should be slowing down into a life of leisure," Rathen said half-jokingly.

"We have many men in need of a leader. You could be that leader," Bandark said, pointing his finger at him.

"I'm not sure I have it in me anymore," Rathen said bluntly.

Bandark nodded, looking as if he were about to speak, but he suddenly lowered his head and walked away.

Rathen glanced over to Bulo sitting beside him. "What about you?"

"I'll get back into the tavern and think about making improvements over a heaping plate of good food and a frothy ale. Thought about even building Thack his own tavern with the proceeds we've kept back. Somewhere in

Blackmane, maybe." Bulo paused. Shaking his head, he continued, "I was fixing to do the same for you… if you're interested."

Rathen smiled warmly. "A kind offer, but I'm not sure. Magom had me thinking about my legacy. I've been wondering if I shouldn't settle down, start a family."

Bulo looked at Rathen in disbelief. "You have someone in mind?"

Rathen knew that Bulo was asking about Davale. "No, of course not her. But that reminds me." Rathen tried to stand but gave up. "Bandark," he called out.

Bandark rushed back over to the campfire. "What?"

"I need to tell you that I saw Davale with Garrick's dagger when she killed Vargas."

Bulo did a double take. "What? I thought you killed Vargas."

"No, I cut off his hand that held the amulet, and he surrendered to me, so I let him live. As soon as I turned around, I heard him scream out and saw Davale behind him with Garrick's dagger."

"Good for you," Bulo said, slapping Rathen on the shoulder.

Rathen tried to hide the pain.

"Davale?" Bandark said, confused.

"Evah," said Rathen, understanding. "She told us her name was Evah, but she was actually Davale, the woman Garrick mentioned who worked for Litagus."

He looked up to see Bandark's face hard and cold. "Bandark?" His silence worried Rathen.

Bandark curled his hands into fists, "She never left our sight for more than a few moments in camp. She must have killed Garrick before finding us." Bandark was silent for a moment. "And to think she got so close to us."

Rathen lowered his head. "She deceived us—I should have been more careful."

"We all should have been more careful," Bandark said, raising his voice. "Garrick sacrificed everything on our behalf."

"At least she helped us get the book," Bulo spoke. He glanced over to Rathen.

"Do not defend her! The only reason we needed her to get us into the compound at all was because she killed Garrick before he could find us a way in himself." Bankdark stood rigid, his eyes focused on Bulo.

"No, no. I'm sorry." Bulo backed up, his hands held out.

"This is my fault. My responsibility," Rathen spoke. He knew he couldn't tell Bankdark about his indiscretion and hated himself for it. And Bulo wasn't helping trying to defend him.

"Just be grateful you are spared from informing Garrick's sister of his death." Bandark said, scanning the area again.

"Garrick was a brave warrior and will be remembered as such," Rathen spoke.

Bankdark stared into the distance. "That… abhorrent woman better pray that our paths never cross again."

"We should be leaving," Rendrak placed his hand on Bandark's shoulder.

Bandark relaxed his shoulders and nodded.

The four prepared their horses and were about to say their goodbyes to Remric when Rendrak called out, "They're back!"

Rathen strained his eyes to see three figures emerging

from the forest in the distance. Three. Not four. Soon, he could see Dryn and Thack holding Caswen in much the same way Rathen himself had been carried. *The lich. He didn't make it?* Out of all the members, he thought Magom would be the one to walk away from this.

Bandark mounted his horse and rode out to meet them. Rathen watched from a distance as he and Thack talked for a bit before Bandark dismounted and walked his horse beside the three back to camp. Rendrak and Bulo worked to get their horses saddled up and ready.

"Magom?" Rathen asked the three.

"He stayed behind. To give us time," Dryn said.

"Are you being pursued?" Rathen asked.

"We can't be sure," said Dryn.

"Then we ride now," Bandark said. "We must leave this area."

"Yukim glidfout narktom?" Rendrak asked.

Bandark shook his head. "No, we dare not open a portal in this area."

Rathen didn't know what was asked, but assumed the request involved them going home. Yes, they all wanted to go home.

As the other three quickly saddled up, Rathen pulled Remric aside.

"Do you need us to take you somewhere, lad?" he asked the boy.

Remric's face was solemn, his eyes staring blankly at a point just beyond Rathen's face. "That's kind of you, but no. I should return home to my mother."

"Alone?" said Rathen. "I could dispatch one of my men to go with you."

"That's alright," the boy said. "I know the way."

Rathen remembered that the druids were a very secretive people and doubted that any of his men would be let into their territory anyway. "But you have everything you need? Food, supplies? Has Bandark completed your payment?"

"My father…" The boy swallowed. "My father told me he was paid in full before we left. Our home is only a day or two's ride from here. No need to worry yourself."

Rathen nodded. "Best of luck to you, Remric. Your father did us, and our world, a great service, and he will not be soon forgotten. Please convey my condolences to your mother."

The two shook hands, Remric finally looking Rathen in the eye. "Thank you," he mumbled, releasing his grasp.

Inclining his head to the boy, Rathen looked up to see everyone on their horses, ready to depart. With a final goodbye to Remric, Rathen mounted, and the group set out onto the road. After a few feet, Rathen turned to look back and saw Remric on his own horse, disappearing into the trees. He wished the boy an easy journey

As they moved further along, Rathen peered into the shaded clearing where he and Magom had hidden the undead horse. The creature was now only a corpse, a decaying lump of flesh sprawled across the mossy forest floor. There were no signs that it had once been brought back from the dead. The sight of it troubled him. If the horse was no longer animated, then that must mean Magom's power had truly been lost—that he had been lost. Rathen hung his head, recalling his long talks with the lich during the journey. He had been a wealth of sage advice for one who had started out as an enemy. Rathen did not want to admit that he would miss the lich and his wisdom. Traveling would be much easier, as they would not have to avoid towns or keep him hidden, but Rathen regretted that Magom could not join the journey home.

Once they were beyond the trees and had returned to the open road, Rathen directed the group back to Andar, placing Thack behind them to make certain they were not being followed. Rathen longed to return to Tobermoar and the tavern, but first he had to return Caswen and Dryn to their home. Marduke's death would likely come as a shock to the temple, but at least they would be getting their healer back on schedule.

As they rode, there was very little conversation while everyone tried to recuperate from the day's events. Rathen fought to regain his strength, and he could see that Caswen attempted to do the same—although, as he watched her cast forlorn glances toward the back of the company, he suspected it was not just her exhaustion that kept her silent.

They rode for several days, only stopping a few hours each night to rest. By the time they reached Andar, Rathen's fatigue had hardly been eased; if anything, he slumped more, his muscles numbed. Caswen, however, seemed to have recovered much of her strength. He watched her as she rode beside Thack, hoping she was not distracting him from his watch, but he was not cruel enough to separate them on their last day together.

As the band of riders entered Andar, they were met with bird and insect sounds reminiscent of abandoned farm fields instead of the usual hustle and bustle of a small town. Only about three weeks had passed since their departure, but the town yawned in its emptiness, even more desolate than before.

Caswen could see the temple coming into view, but it did little to give her a sense of relief. She'd struggled to be noticed among her peers as the youngest and only female in the order; often she had felt weak and powerless beside those who did not take her seriously. But now, she felt different… she was different. However, soon she would find herself back in the same place, being passed over and underestimated. A sense of sadness and defeat washed over her already weakened body. She didn't want to go back to the way it was before. She couldn't.

Caswen tried to distract herself by looking at Thack, who rode beside her, but the sight of his strong jawline, his kind eyes, weakened her further. They both knew that what they had couldn't last forever with such different life paths before them, but Caswen had not expected time to pass this quickly. Thack glanced at her and smiled sadly. She knew they would soon have to say goodbye.

Turning away, Caswen eyed Rathen and knew his shoulder needed healing, but her powers barely held her upright. A healer unable to even heal herself sufficiently. She glanced instead at Bandark and Rendrak ahead of her, who had both seemed worried since the start of their return. She had learned a lot from the tall mage regarding other worlds and even her own, but ironically, she had learned the most from the lich. His wisdom and insight on life—and death— had imprinted his memory in her mind and in her heart. In the end, when she was willing to give her life, he had stepped forward and saved them all. Even if his heart had dried up and rotted away years ago, his soul still shined brightly. She would be forever grateful for the good deeds of a being she had once despised as a monster.

The group rode through the temple gates and dismounted, Dryn helping Caswen from her horse. Caswen thanked her sister with a smile and suggested she take care of the horses before coming in. This would give Caswen some time to confront the high priest alone.

Caswen stood to the side as Rathen entered the temple first, followed by the other fighters. Thack held back and stepped in beside Caswen, giving her hand a quick squeeze. As Caswen entered the temple, she looked up at the vaulted ceiling and took a deep breath. She thanked Thandrall for his strength and protection to see her safely home.

Piltan, the temple's assistant, greeted them at the door. He smiled widely as he saw Caswen arrive.

"We have come to return your healer," said Rathen. "Is the head priest around?"

"You mean the high—" Piltan started.

"Just fetch him," Rathen said, irritated.

When Piltan returned with Lazlo, dressed in splendid robes of gold and silver, only Bandark and Rendrak bowed to him. Caswen realized she would have taken offense at this when they'd shown up weeks ago. Now, although she admired the high priest for his dedication, what made anyone worthy of another's supplication? Lives had been lost in service to a higher good by those without any religious conviction. The impact humbled her. Not even priests had all the answers.

"Caswen, my child. We are relieved to see you safe,"

Lazlo said, wrinkling his nose. His eyes looked over her filthy robes, now such a dark brown it was hard to believe they had ever been white. Caswen stood tall in her messy garb. She had faced death many times over the last few weeks. Staying alive had been far more important than keeping her robes clean.

"Are you injured?" Lazlo asked her.

"I'll be fine," she said.

"Where is Marduke?" Lazlo asked, looking over the group.

"Marduke fell in battle," said Rathen. "We weren't able to recover his body."

Lazlo glanced up sharply. "That is unfortunate. He will be greatly missed."

Caswen prickled at the casualness of his words.

"He gave his life protecting others," Rendrak said. "He was a good man."

"Yes, he was," Lazlo said. "And what of Dryn? Is she dead as well?"

"She is out taking care of the horses," Caswen said bluntly, taking Lazlo by surprise. The high priest's coldness was setting her on edge.

"That's great," Lazlo said with a smile.

"We'll be off now," Rathen said. He walked over to Caswen, looking her in the eyes. She couldn't help but notice the sadness she saw staring back at her. "I thank you for your efforts in keeping me and my men alive. You will be remembered for your bravery, your strength, and your skill. You have my deepest gratitude." Rathen bowed his head in respect.

All the others followed suit, thanking her and bowing their heads before her as they would for a high priest.

Caswen did her best to hold back tears. She had never felt so much respect and admiration aimed at her.

"You're welcome. You're all so very welcome," she said, a few tears escaping her control. She turned away to hide her face, embarrassed, and the men began filing out of the room, calling goodbyes back to her. She turned back and waved, smiling through her tears. Thack was the last to leave, a few of his own sliding down his face. With a final nod in her direction, he disappeared out the door.

Lazlo started to say something to her, but Caswen wasn't listening. She couldn't let Thack leave like that without a proper goodbye, not after all they'd been through. Leaving Lazlo calling after her, she ran back outside the temple to catch the group as they said goodbye to Dryn. She stopped on the temple steps.

"You and your sister have come a long way," Rathen was saying. "I know Marduke would be proud of you. It was our honor and privilege to serve with such a skilled archer." Rathen shook Dryn's hand firmly, and the young warrior smiled.

"I'll try not to let it go to my head," Dryn said.

All the other men lined up to shake Dryn's hand, and Caswen could see that her sister felt it too. Finally being recognized for one's skill was among the greatest gifts one could receive.

When the last man, Bulo, had finally shaken Dryn's hand and returned to his horse, Caswen saw her opportunity. Running down the front steps of the temple, she spotted Thack toward the back of the group, his head hung low.

"Thack!" Caswen shouted, chasing down the horses. "Thack, wait!"

Thack stopped, pulling up on his reins and turning around. A few of the other riders turned to look back and, seeing Caswen, smirked to each other, but continued riding on.

Thack rode back toward Caswen, stopping the horse just before he collided into her. Scrambling down from his saddle, he strode over to her, put his arm around her waist, and lifted her into a kiss. She threw her arms around his neck and kissed him back, her heart pounding as it always did near Thack.

After a moment, they broke apart, Thack setting Caswen back onto her feet. She felt dizzy and held onto his arm to steady herself.

"I couldn't let you leave without saying goodbye," she said.

"I left quickly so that I couldn't tell you I love you," said Thack with a sheepish grin.

Caswen laughed. "Thanks for not telling me. It would have been really hard to let you ride away if I had known that. And then I would have had to tell you that I feel the same way, and where would that leave us?"

They both grew quiet, staring down at each other.

"It would never work," Thack said, wearing the same sad smile he had worn all day. "I'm a business owner; you're a soon-to-be high priest."

"We're from different worlds," Caswen agreed. "But maybe in another life, in a different world where we can make our own rules, maybe then we could build our own temple."

"A tavern temple." Thack smiled. "And we could host guests and serve great food and ale."

"And we could heal any weary travelers who came through our doors."

"And we could help people doing what we love—"

"With the person we love—"

"And we could raise our children in a happy home—"

"Surrounded by love and everything we had built—"

"At each other's sides for the rest of our days."

They stood together, staring into each other's eyes, their current world a distant thought as they imagined the life they could have had together. They allowed themselves to live the fantasy together for a few minutes that felt like a lifetime.

Finally, Thack said, "I'd better catch up to the others."

Caswen nodded. "You have all my best wishes for your happiness."

"And you, mine." With a final kiss on Caswen's forehead, Thack mounted his horse and rode away, leaving Caswen standing alone outside the temple. *Thandrall, protect him,* she prayed.

Returning to the temple, Caswen walked across the hall and up the flight of steps to her chambers. Opening her door, she entered the room to find everything as she had left it. Her saddlebags had been deposited in the center of the floor, but she would unpack them later. For now, she sat on her bed, taking in the smell and sight of her room.

Caswen had forgotten what a proper bed felt like. Suddenly overcome with exhaustion, she collapsed onto her pillow, hoping that a good night's rest might clear her thoughts.

It was morning when Caswen finally awoke, doubt still nagging at her thoughts. She sat up, realizing that she had fallen asleep in her filthy robes, but for some reason, she did not care. She sat in bed, looking around her room, still not feeling as though she had really returned. She stood and began to pace back and forth across the floor, trying to sort out her mind.

She thought of Marduke. She knew these halls would never be the same without him. She no longer needed his protection, but her need for him ached in her heart all the same. Despite that, Caswen knew her place in the temple would be as it always had been, and she could only continue to attempt to appease the high priest in hopes of gaining favor. The thought pained her. Lazlo had always encouraged her study and had told her she could become high priest one day, but what had he really done to help her? He had discouraged her from taking missions for two years after she had completed her training, refusing to recommend her for trips outside the temple, and the only reason she had been chosen to go with Rathen was because she had been the only healer left to send. Caswen could not face another two years or more cooped up in this tiny room, reciting meditations while lesser, male, healers were sent on missions. If that was all she had to look forward to, what was the point of letting Thack go?

Thandrall, give me the strength to continue. In frustration, Caswen kicked her pack where it still rested on the floor, and it tipped over, spilling its contents. Three large rubies all the size of her thumb rolled out of the bag and across the floor. Caswen looked at them in disbelief, stepping across the room to where the gems had come to rest against the opposite wall. Where had these come from? Caswen thought, picking up the gems to examine them closer. Each one looked extremely valuable. *Thandrall shall provide,* the memory of Marduke's voice whispered in her ear.

A new determination gripped her heart as Caswen noticed her meditation robes had been laid out at the foot of her bed the night before. She grabbed them, running out into the hall and down to the baths. There she discarded her filthy robes and jumped into one of the hot pools. She completely lost track of time sitting in the water, scrubbing herself clean in the relaxing warmth for the first time in weeks. With each stroke of the sponge, layers of doubt and weakness drifted away. The warmth of the water soaked resolve and strength into her pores. She felt the healing light of Thandrall flowing through her limbs. Finally, she sat back in the stone tub, holding up one of the red gems to the light of the morning sun streaming in through the windows.

Stepping out of the water, Caswen dried off, brushing her long hair and tying it back in a braid. She dressed in her simple meditation robes and left her filthy healer robes in the corner. She carefully cleaned her amulet, never taking it off, and went back to her room to pick up her bag. A morning meal of whole grain rolls, hard cheese, and fruit had been left by her door. She quickly stowed the food into her pack, not waiting even to eat, gave her room one last look, and, with a contented sigh, she left it behind for the last time.

Stepping into the main hall, Caswen saw Lazlo talking with Dryn. Dryn looked tired, her eyes still caked with sleep. She must have been talking to the high priest since she had awoken.

"Caswen, good morning. Are you feeling better?" Lazlo asked.

"I'm leaving." Caswen spoke with confidence, eager to get this over with and be on her way.

Lazlo eyes opened wide. "What? Why?"

"I am off to create a new order, which I will lead."

Dryn smiled brightly.

Lazlo looked her over and frowned. "My child, you are not ready to be your own high priest. There is still so much you need to be taught."

"I disagree," Caswen said. "This is something I must do."

"You're not strong enough, my dear."

"I'm not your child or your dear," Caswen snapped. "And it is obvious all but a few of the townspeople have moved away in my absence. With your indifference to the loss we endured, I know you are anxious to move from this town as well."

"You will come with us. Our order has outgrown this town, and it is time for us to move on."

"Well, I've outgrown you. I've learned all you have to teach me. Now, it's my turn to do some good in the world."

Lazlo looked confused.

"She summoned both the Shield and the Hammer of Thandrall on this journey, Lazlo," Dryn said. "I saw it myself."

"Is… is that true?" Lazlo looked at Caswen in amazement.

"It's true," said Caswen. "And in feeling the full strength of Thandrall's power, I have learned that healing and protection are one and the same. I will create an order of Thandrall where healers are also protectors, and its teachings will focus on the power of redemption to save others who have lost their way. In my order, we will not be called high priests or apprentices or even servants. And we will not wear gold or silver. We will be the humble servants of Thandrall, equally sharing his good with those who need us."

Dryn smiled proudly.

"Come now, child. You can do good within our order in Ryefall," Lazlo said, losing his patience.

"Thank you for all you have taught me and provided for me. I wish you well." Caswen bowed and walked to the door, ignoring Lazlo's pleas to return. As she reached the door, Dryn ran up to her, catching her by the arm. "You can't talk me out of this," she said.

Dryn smiled. "Doesn't your order need new members? Besides, I'm seeking my own redemption by making good on the second chance I was given."

"We both are," she said, smiling.

The two sisters hugged, then walked out of the temple doors together, arm in arm, for the last time.

Once outside, Dryn turned to her sister, her smile never faltering. "Where shall we go, Cas?"

"I hadn't really thought about it," Caswen said as they saddled up their horses, the noon sun shining down on them.

"It's your temple," said Dryn as she gathered her weapons and fresh leather armor from the livery's supplies, stowing them on her horse's pack. She carefully wrapped Marduke's sword and secured it on the side of her mount. "We can go anywhere you want."

My temple, Caswen thought. *My rules.* Creating a new order meant she could live as she wanted as long as she helped others in Thandrall's name.

As the sisters rode out of Andar, Caswen set their course south, toward a small village where a certain half-orc lived.

Chapter 20

Within the tavern of the small town of Andar, Rathen sat with Bulo, Thack, Rendrak, and Bandark. It had only been a few hours since they had left Caswen and Dryn back at the temple and checked into the inn for the night. The five men relaxed, speaking openly and eating greedily as the only patrons at the inn that night. They drained their mugs of bitter ale and shoved as much meat stew and bread in their mouths as would fit. The warm food helped Rathen recover some of his strength, although his shoulder still pained him.

"Are you two leaving tonight?" Bulo asked, breaking a long silence before scooping up another mouthful.

"No," Bandark said, gulping down his food. "Tobermoar is just a short ride from here, so we will see this through and depart from there."

Rathen nodded.

"Are you coming with us?" Rendrak asked Rathen. A certain look in his eyes caught Rathen's attention.

"What?" Rathen asked, confused.

Bandark placed his hand on Rendrak's shoulder. "He has not yet made his decision."

Rendrak sighed as his face fell to stare at the table.

"Were you serious before?" Rathen asked, recalling Bandark's previous offer.

Bandark looked up, adjusting the Book of Ziz that rested on his lap even throughout their meal. "Yes. Our armies need a leader."

"Rendrak is a fine man and a fine warrior. Can't he lead?" Rathen said. Beside him, Bulo and Thack both agreed with a grunt between spoonfuls of stew.

"I had thought so," Rendrak said. "Before I came to this world, I planned to request that the kingdom allow me to take over the forces." His eyes flashed to Bandark before returning to focus on Rathen. "During our quest, I have seen what it takes to lead men. And I know I do not have it. I am a fighter, proud of my abilities… but now I know my limits too."

Rathen nodded. He understood well. Skills as a fighter did not easily translate into leading other fighters. Besides, the burden of leadership fell heavy on anyone's shoulders. Battle injuries healed in time, but the pain of losing so many good men would always remain.

"I have seen your skill and sacrifice in battle and have come to know your capabilities as a leader," Rendrak continued. "I was skeptical at first when I was told of your deeds. But I believe you have what it takes to help us win this war."

Bandark nodded as Rendrak spoke.

Rathen recalled a few times in the beginning when Rendrak had ignored his orders. But he had changed as the quest went on.

"I would follow you back into battle any day," Rendrak

said, raising his mug in a salute.

Bulo and Thack likewise lifted their mugs, with a "Truly said," from Bulo, and the three downed their ale.

Bulo motioned to the innkeeper for refills, adding, "But not till after the next round, eh?"

Rathen smiled, but thoughts tumbled as the men returned to their meal. This last quest had invigorated his urge to lead again, but in a different world? With a different kind of men to lead in a war against the dark forces of Gothoar? Magom had encouraged him to chase a legacy, but this? Rathen had thought about a family, children, a legacy of that sort. His only barrier had been the revenge he'd sought on Vargas. With Vargas's death, Rathen felt ready to move on from the past and to pursue any future he wanted. What *did* he truly want? A cottage with little feet scurrying about, a warm hearth, and each day the same peaceful routine? How long would he be satisfied in that placid scene, especially knowing the danger Gothoar's forces posed to the world?

"So, I'd be captain again?" Rathen said with a forced smile.

Bandark shook his head. "You would be general, replacing our General Carlack lost in battle. You would be taking orders from the king himself. My father."

"Your father is the king?" Rathen had wondered how Bandark was able to pay for the druid's services, not to mention his expensive Merianite weapons. "And the man whom I took the sword from outside Ghrakus?"

"Rodimar. My brother."

Rathen sat up straight. "Why didn't you tell me? You should be carrying your brother's sword, not me."

"That is why I stayed silent," said Bandark. "I did not want you to question your possession of the sword. It is rightfully yours."

Rathen didn't know what to say to that, but Thack spoke up to offer his condolences for Bandark's loss.

Bandark held out his hand as if trying to calm the situation. "What is done is done. He was the youngest of us four brothers. Rodimar was the first to seek out the book in this world. When he failed to return, I followed."

"I see," Rathen said, looking over to Bulo and Thack and hoping either of them would discourage this foolhardy concept of leading in a war in a distant land. To his disappointment, they only smiled. "Give me some time to think about it."

Both Bandark and Rendrak nodded and went back to eating.

Rathen's mind drifted back to his days as a captain, and he recalled his aspirations of one day making general. Even his father had held that hope for him. *Ah, my father.* Rathen knew he had to make amends for leaving for Khorell without any word to his parents. There was much still to do.

The five men finished their meals and headed to their rooms, their footfalls and eyelids heavy, to enjoy a few hours of sleep in real beds.

In the early morning, just as the sun started to rise, the five still-drowsy men started for Tobermoar. They rode their horses from the stables at a slow pace so as not to awaken the citizens.

After a few moments, Thack pulled up on his reins, bringing his horse to a stop. The other four men followed suit, looking at the half-orc curiously. "Listen," he said.

Rathen had regained some strength, and his shoulder no longer hurt as much as it had, but he had to concentrate to force himself fully awake. Only silence greeted his attention. At first, this did not alarm him—then he realized what the complete lack of animal sounds meant: danger. He sighed. This wasn't over yet.

"Were we followed?" Bulo asked, looking about.

"Can't be certain," Thack answered.

"Then to Tobermoar, with haste," Bandark said, urging his horse faster down the empty streets.

They pushed the horses until they cleared the town and then settled into a normal stride. During the next few hours, nothing alerted them again, and they were able to take the shorter route through the towns since the lich no longer rode with them.

They pushed on, breaking only to tend to the horses and to pull a quick meal from their saddlebags. As night fell, they decided to continue riding since they knew the roads in the area well and did not want to waste time to sleep.

Well into the night, the town fires lit within Tobermoar came into view. Rathen shook the sleep from his eyes, anxious to get back to familiar surroundings. Smoke curled from chimneys and made the image of a warm home and a family all the more appealing. He carefully studied the area around them, listening to the croaks of frogs, the buzz of flitting insects. *Welcome home.*

Torches flickered outside the Traveler's Rest when they approached.

Thack took the horses from Rathen and Bulo, and Bandark and Rendrak offered theirs. Thack took their reins with a look of confusion. He glanced at Rathen, who gave him a nod. The men likely wished some rest before continuing on their way.

Bulo opened the doors and stepped in with a big sigh of relief. Rathen followed, and Bandark and Rendrak stepped in behind him.

The inn was empty, but Rathen assumed some patrons might be sleeping upstairs. From the kitchen, a red-headed young man sprang out. "You're back!"

"Fala, good to see you. Anything happen?" Bulo asked.

"The days have been busy, and we are nearly out of supplies, but I've ordered more," Fala said, his eyes wide, no doubt eager to hear about their adventure.

"Well done. Drinks?" Bulo asked, turning to Bandark and Rendrak.

"No, we must get the book to safety," Bandark said. He turned to Rathen. "We will take the book back to our world and start the preparations. It will likely take a few months, but when we are done, I will return for your answer."

"Understood. I wish you well."

Bandark nodded and walked toward the back door. Rendrak smiled at Rathen and saluted, placing his arms across his chest before walking after Bandark.

"Where are you going?" Bulo asked.

"Come and see," Bandark said, unbarring the back door and walking out into the night.

Bandark looked around the area. He approached a space beside some empty crates and barrels piled alongside the external walls that blocked the view from the street. He walked to the center of the space and bent down, running his hand over the dried dirt ground. He stood and took a handful of silvery dust from his pouch, sprinkling it into the air and letting it fall in a small circle in the dirt. He started to chant, and a shimmering door opened up where the dust had fallen.

Rathen looked at the door in amazement. Through the shimmering portal, he could roughly make out what looked like a castle in the distance. As the shimmering settled, he could see small buildings and a red sky in the background.

"We will return," Bandark said, walking through the doorway with the book in his hands. Rendrak gave a nod as he too stepped through after the mage. Rathen, Bulo, and Fala stood with their mouths open, gazing through the magical doorway with wonder. The door began to shorten and finally shrank away, disappearing completely.

The three looked at each other in silence and walked back into the tavern, Fala the last to enter. Rathen and Bulo headed for a table. "Fala, fetch some ale and cook up some eats for us," Bulo said. Fala stood still, his mouth remained agape. "Fala." Bulo shooed the boy with his hand.

"Ah, yes. Yes, ale. And food." The boy nodded as if grateful to return to realities he understood.

Bulo looked over at Rathen, still in shock himself. "They were serious about being from another world."

"Indeed," Rathen said, taking a chair that faced the front doors.

"So… are you really considering their offer?" Bulo asked, kicking his feet up onto the chair next to him.

Rathen sighed and waited for Fala to set down the ale before answering. Taking a long pull, he replied, "What do you think about it?"

"Well, I think it's great… but the whole other world thing makes me uncomfortable. I mean, a foreign land, well, that is one thing. But truly, another *world*?"

"So, no chance of you making the journey with me? I'm sure they serve drinks over there, too." Rathen chuckled.

Bulo looked up at the ceiling. "No, I'm fine here in Blackmane. While I like the occasional adventure or two, I actually enjoy the tavern life. I spent my youth fighting for my life. It's kind of nice to sit back and enjoy what I have. I feel I have earned it. Besides, I'm not as young as I used to be."

Rathen understood Bulo's thoughts but felt it would be a shame if they had to part ways. "I've got time to think about it."

The front doors slammed open from a kick. Bulo almost fell over trying to take his feet off the chair next to him. Rathen stood with his hand on his sword, still hanging from his belt, shrugging off the pain in his shoulder.

To their relief, Thack walked in, carting their saddlebags over his shoulder with his one hand. He paused when he saw their reactions. "It's just me."

"Well, go ahead and bar that door. There still may be something out there following us," Bulo said.

Thack dumped the bags and placed the bar over the door. He headed for the stairs. "I'm finally going to sleep in my own bed tonight," he said as he walked up. Despite his light-heartedness, a sadness clung to Thack's tone. Rathen and Bulo glanced at each other. There was little Rathen could do for him.

"Yes. A well-deserved rest," Bulo added.

Rathen smiled but knew sleep would do little to ease the pain of a broken heart.

Rathen and Bulo talked over a few more drinks and a

plate of sweetmeats about the mission and what was next for their lives. They even discussed what Bandark's world might be like and the obvious difference of their languages and the challenge it would be to communicate.

An hour or so had passed when a creaking floorboard in the back room caught Rathen's attention. He sat up straight, looking around.

"Did you bar the back door?"

"Not sure. Fala was last in," Bulo said with a look of concern. "Fala?" he called out.

As Rathen started to stand, three demon men rushed into the room from the kitchen. Each held black swords, their mouths agape as if in silent screams.

Rathen pulled his sword in time to deflect a swing from a black blade. The other two attackers rushed to Bulo, who stood weaponless.

The demon man before Rathen fought with superhuman strength, his exposed, red, elongated face shining in the firelight. Panic rose in his gut. He swung to attack, but the demon man easily pushed him aside. Rathen's shoulder lit up in pain, still not fully healed from his fight with Vargas.

He heard a crash from where Bulo stood. Rathen glanced over to see that the big man had smashed a wooden chair into one of the two attackers. Rathen turned back around and his attacker slammed into him, sending him to the floor. The fall jostled his sword from his hand, and the impact forced the air from his lungs. Rathen struggled to breathe. The demon man landed on top of him, raising his glistening blade with both hands and aiming the tip at Rathen's heart.

"Thack!" Rathen desperately called out as he grappled for his sword just out of reach.

Just before the creature thrust its sword into him, a metallic clang rang out from behind him. The demon man fell hard on Rathen's chest, his sword falling to the side. Fala stood over them with a large frying pan, his eyes wide and frenzied. He lowered the pan, its bottom bent from the impact to the demon man's head.

The sound of footsteps on the stairs gave Rathen some relief as he continued to fight for his breath, the creature still lying over him. He saw Thack, axe in hand, rush to Bulo's assistance out of sight. Unable to move from where he lay, Rathen could only hear the fight. Metal on metal clanged, and the crack of wood resounded, likely another chair crashed to bits. Finally only the heaving breaths of his two friends remained. Catching his own breath, Rathen looked up at Fala, who stood in place, wide-eyed and with the frying pan still poised for battle.

"Get him off me," Rathen called up to Fala.

The young man jumped, the frying pan clattered as it fell from Fala's hands, and the boy bent down to help push the demon man off of Rathen.

More footsteps sounded on the stairs as the sleeping patrons woke to investigate the commotion. They stood at the foot of the stairs, huddled in nightclothes, whispering and pointing at the demons on the floor.

Rathen and Fala fought to remove the body that crushed Rathen when it was suddenly lifted. With a grunt, Bulo threw the unconscious attacker aside, onto the floor. Rathen could see large cuts on both his friend's arms.

"You alright?" Bulo called out.

"I'm fine. Thanks to Fala," Rathen said, sitting up and bracing his shoulder with his hand. Blood spattered the area where the fight had taken place. The two demon men lay dead on the floor as Thack stepped over them toward Rathen.

"Well, these things lived up to their reputation," Bulo said, looking over his cuts.

"I'll fetch some bandages," Fala said.

Bulo nodded, looking over the bent frying pan on the floor. "Fala, I'll make a warrior out of you yet."

The sleepy patrons continued to look on as Thack dragged the bodies from the tavern.

"Go back to bed; it's all over now," Bulo said, ushering them away with a wave of his hand.

With a few mumbles, they all walked back upstairs.

Rathen's shoulder still pained him, but it was his pride that hurt the most. In his own town? His own tavern? And it took a boy cook to save him?

"Too bad we can't mount their heads on the wall. They would make for some great conversation," Bulo said.

Rathen smiled. He sheathed his sword and bent down to inspect one of the attackers' black swords. He held it up to the firelight. The metal reflected no light, unlike his own sword that shimmered. A unique metal, as was his, though different and unlike anything he'd seen. The few scratches in the blades etched through no coating or paint; the metal was simply black.

"There you go," Bulo said, grinning. "I'll mount those swords to the wall instead."

With a laugh, Rathen handed the sword to Bulo, who had Fala at his side, rolling a bandage onto his arm.

"That was a brave thing you did," Rathen said to Fala.

Fala nodded and looked away, smiling as if too shy to look at him.

Thack walked back into the tavern from the back, his face grim as he approached Rathen and stood beside him. He leaned over and whispered, "I've killed the one that was unconscious. I thought it... safer."

Rathen looked up at him and whispered back, "You did right. They cannot be allowed to go for help." He placed his hand on Thack's back. He knew the half-orc felt ashamed for taking a defenseless life. But it had to be done.

"I'm sorry... I should've known those things were tracking us," Thack said, his eyes lowered.

Rathen shook his head. "Not your fault. There're not normal men. Besides, we all knew something was out there."

Thack raised his gaze to him.

"I expected whatever was out there would lose interest when the book left this world," Rathen said, offering a smile. "What's done is done."

Thack returned the smile and walked away to start the cleanup.

They briefly unbarred the front door to chuck out the broken furniture. The twitter of birds filtered through the doorway, signaling the start of the day. Fala and Thack silently cleaned the remaining debris and blood from the area. Bulo held one of the black swords as he looked over the walls of the tavern. Apparently, he was serious about mounting the weapons.

With the threat gone and his shoulder aching again, Rathen wanted to rest. "Bar that back door too so I can get some sleep," he said.

"Already done," Fala called out as he soaked up blood with a rag.

Rathen walked upstairs, his steps plodding. He had

brought the demon men into his town, into his very home. Would others like them seek him out? How safe was Tobermoar now, the townsfolk he'd encouraged to move here? How safe was the world at large with the likes of Gothoar and his evil plans?

He fell into his bed, fully clothed, and rolled from side to side until his shoulder nestled into a less painful position. *Less painful.* Maybe that was what all legacies were about: finding your rightful place in the world. Not a place without trouble and pain. Just less painful. What place was that for him?

Chapter 21

Weeks after the fight in the tavern, Rathen set out on the long ride to Hullbeck. His shoulder had healed, but his mind ached with the guilt of having stayed so long from his homeland. How much had it changed in the decade since he'd laid eyes on it? As his horse walked along the streets and out of town, he thought back to his youth and his father. The old man hadn't been around often since his work had him living within the castle. The time he did spend with Rathen while he was home mostly involved weapons training out in the empty fields and hunting outside the kingdom's forests. Even from a young age, Rathen saw his father as a hardened man, shaped by his years of training and dedication to the kingdom's forces. After retiring as captain, he had helped Rathen's mother plow and sow and harvest the neighboring fields to support themselves. Rathen admired both of them for their strength and diligence.

Rathen spent the next week on the road, sleeping only in inns and always making certain to bar the door. He knew Davale was still out there somewhere, perhaps lurking in the shadows waiting for her opportunity to strike when his guard was down. He also suspected Litagus would come looking for the book sooner or later.

Finally, just before dusk, the familiar hillsides and evergreen stands of his youth emerged from the twilight, and he saw Hullbeck in the distance. The little town now stretched twice as far as it had when he last visited. More houses spread across the valley, more fields as well, and what looked to be a tavern stood in the town's center. How convenient that would have been when he was younger. He could remember when he and his friends used to sit in a local barn, drinking and sharing stories until morning's light.

He grew nervous as his family's house came into view. His mind flashed to all the memories he had of playing and running around the modest stone home, to which the years had not been kind. Grass grew wildly around it, several cracks were visible on the walls, and a few broken windows had been replaced by wooden planks.

Dismounting, Rathen tethered his horse to a broken rail just outside the house. From a broken window, he could smell the aroma of sweet bread, another memory from his childhood. He readied himself and knocked on the door.

"Yes?" an elderly woman's voice asked from within.

Rathen took a deep breath. "It's Rathen."

He heard someone fumbling with the bar on the door, and then the wood was flung open, its hinges creaking loudly. His mother appeared in the doorway, wearing a cooking apron. Her hair had grown all gray, and her skin had turned tough and wrinkled from her years in the fields. Despite her age, Rathen could see the same kind eyes and gentle smile of the woman he had known as a child.

"Oh my," she said, her eyes welling with tears. "Son."

"I'm home," he said, giving her a hug. It had been almost ten years since he had seen her last, but her embrace made him feel like a child again.

His mother pulled back and looked him over, placing her face close to his, trying to read every line and scar. "What happened to you?"

"It's a long story," said Rathen. "Is Father around?"

Her face darkened, and she looked away. "He's home, but he's not the same as he was when you saw him last."

Rathen's voice caught in his throat. "What happened?"

"Three years ago, he was working in the fields and just collapsed. His body healed, but he doesn't talk anymore."

"Can I see him?" Rathen asked, choking down his regret at waiting so long to return home.

"Yes, come in," she said, walking into the house. "I'll have some food for you here shortly."

"Thanks," said Rathen. "Where is he?"

"He's in the back."

Rathen walked through the home, the rooms smaller now, the ceiling lower, as if it had shrunk to only half the size that he remembered. Most of the furnishings bore scars of neglect, and the interior walls allowed wind to invade through whistling cracks.

As he entered the back room, Rathen saw his father sitting in a large wooden chair, looking out the back window, half of which was boarded up. Rathen's gut hit the floor. His father had aged beyond a decade. His hair had turned thin and gray, his frail body hunched over, and his arms resting on the chair looked to be mostly skin and bone.

"Father?"

His father didn't react. Rathen wasn't sure he had heard

him. He leaned down in front of him, calling out again. Rathen teared up to see a face so absent of expression, so devoid of life, like a statue of the man he'd once known, a statue whittled down by illness and weathered by time. His father's eyes, now a pale blue, seemed distant as they continued to gaze out the window. Rathen knelt in front of him. "Can you hear me?"

There came no response.

Rathen hung his head. He was too late. Gone was the chance to speak with his father about what had happened in Delvant's kingdom, what had forced him to leave. Gone was the chance to tell him of his triumphs and miseries over the past ten years. But something in him wanted him to try anyway.

Rathen sat down on the floor in front of his father's chair. He explained in slow speech what had happened as if his father could understand. He apologized for leaving them alone for so long and explained why he moved to Khorell to escape the world. Rathen spent some time talking about his companions and the quest to Castle Ghrakus, as well as the quest he had just completed. He finished the story by telling him of Bandark's offer of becoming the general of his armies in another world.

Rathen stopped and looked up at his father, whose face seemed sad and drawn. He wondered if any of his words could reach him. Then, he noticed his father's eyes turn watery, and a tear ran down his wrinkled face. Rathen reached out and took hold of his father's hand, talking with him until his mother called him for dinner.

Rathen and his mother ate in the kitchen while his father continued to sit in the back.

"Have you had a healer look at Father?" Rathen asked, enjoying the home-cooked meal of sweet bread, green vegetables, and a small assortment of fruit.

"We don't have such things out here, son," his mother said, taking a bite of her food.

Rathen wished he still had access to Caswen and her amazing capabilities. "I'll pay. I have some gold for you and Father."

"You don't have to do that," his mother said, scooping some more greens onto his plate.

"I insist. Let me help around the place before I leave."

"You've got the time? You're here to stay for a bit?" She looked up at him hopefully.

"Yes, I have a few days."

She smiled and nodded, the excitement clear on her face.

The next day, Rathen went into town and asked about healers. Word was sent to the local temple a day's ride away, and Rathen made the payment in advance to have his father looked at.

When he returned to the house, Rathen cleared the overgrown vegetation from the area, cleaned up around the house, and made a list of what needed to be replaced. He made another trip into town to buy wood, new windows, chinking to fill in the cracks in the walls, some new furniture, and heavy, lined drapes. He spent the night sitting with his father again, telling more stories of his friends and their adventures. This time he spoke about Bulo and his gladiator days and about Thack's character and unique background.

In the late afternoon on the next day, the healer arrived at the house. He was a young man, dressed in white robes and a red sash. His face was cleanly shaven, and he had a sophisticated demeanor. "My name is Pendle, from the Darion temple. You're expecting me?" the man asked.

"Yes, come in." Rathen examined the healer's silver amulet, bearing a symbol of a circle within a circle. "I know your temple and its powerful healers."

The man seemed intrigued. "Oh, how's that?"

"I knew a man named Zeller who wore the same symbol. A great healer. Out of Burem, I believe."

"Well, the name sounds familiar," the man said. "It is nice to hear that knowledge of our work is spreading."

Rathen nodded. "Well, come right this way. It's my father," Rathen said, relieved that a temple he knew had answered his call.

Rathen showed Pendle where his father sat, and then he and his mother waited in the kitchen as the healer examined him. Rathen pulled a pouch of gold pieces from his waist and sat it on the table. "Take this," he said to his mother. "It should be enough to get you through several seasons."

His mother looked up. "Oh, you need it more than we do," she protested.

"I can get more," Rathen assured her. "Take it."

"Well, thank you," she said, her eyes watering.

Rathen returned her smile.

It was evening by the time Pendle came back into the kitchen. Both Rathen and his mother eagerly awaited his diagnosis.

"He's weak. He suffered an injury inside his head that has grown worse over time. I've done all I can, but I could only heal so much," Pendle said. "Let him rest and see how he is in the morning."

Rathen nodded and thanked the healer. "We will."

Rathen's last day was spent talking with his mother about the last ten years, as well as how he got the scars on his face.

"Haven't you some young`uns? No family?" his mother asked.

"Not yet."

His mother looked up, her face serious and sad. "You don't have as much time as you think, son. Things don't get any easier. And the years don't stop for anything."

Rathen nodded. "I understand."

They continued to talk well into the night.

The next morning, Rathen reluctantly gathered his gear and loaded his horse. As he cinched the strap on his horse's belly, his mother called out to him from the doorway. "Rathen, come quickly!"

He followed her into the back room. Rathen rushed to his father's side, kneeling beside the chair. "Father?"

"Son, good to... see you..." His father struggled to speak.

"You can talk!" Rathen's face filled with joy. He had feared he would never hear his father's voice again.

"Thanks... to the healer." His father smiled.

"I was about to leave, but maybe I should stay..." Rathen said, never wanting his father's voice to stop.

"I understand... you have to go. I've... heard your stories... and I have to say... I would like to meet... that Thack one day. He sounds... like an interesting... young man," his father rasped.

Rathen smiled. "He is indeed."

"Congratulations... on becoming general... son." He moved his arm in a salute, his face contorted with the strain.

"In this world… or another… it is an… honorable rank."

Rathen returned the salute. "Thank you, Father."

Now, go… and… make me proud… son," his father said.

"I will, Father. I will."

After Rathen said his goodbyes and promised to return, he walked his horse from the house. Stopping at the end of the road, he looked back and smiled at the mended fence and clear windows and tidied yard. A wisp of chimney smoke wavered in the air like a fond farewell. *I hope they are more comfortable.* Rathen mounted his horse and headed out on the long journey back to Tobermoar.

Chapter 22

A month after returning from Hullbeck, Rathen sat alone at a table in the Traveler's Rest, his hands cupping a mug that had been drained dry a while ago. His eyes stared down at the table as his mind wandered in deep thought. He had spent the last few months considering his future and his legacy. With Vargas's death and the return of the book, his thoughts were clearer, but the decision still didn't come any easier. And just as Magom had said, Rathen knew there were always more men to lead.

He looked at his empty mug and then around the room. The hour was late, and all the patrons had either left or retired to their rented rooms for the night. Fala and the other service staff had left earlier. Rathen stood and walked over to an open barrel to fill his mug again. He glanced around the room and smiled, recalling how fun it had been to build with Thack and Bulo. *How could I leave this place?*

"Is this a private celebration, or can anyone join?" Bulo asked, walking down the stairs.

Rathen smiled and reached for a second mug.

"Have you decided?" Bulo asked, stretching his arms above his head.

They both sat down on two of the newly made wooden chairs at the table where Rathen had been sitting, and Rathen eyed Bulo briefly before answering. "Are you certain you won't join me if I leave?"

"Nah, I've already made plans with Thack on that second tavern. Ever since Caswen and Dryn showed up with their idea to start a new temple, I haven't been able to get him to shut up about the new tavern. The three of them are still out now, scouting a new area to build a tavern and temple within walking distance of each other."

Rathen laughed, remembering the exuberant joy on Thack's gray-tinged face when Caswen had arrived at their door. He had scooped her up in his arm and spun her about to the shouts and cheers of everyone present. He had no doubts they would be happy together.

Pulling Rathen out of his thoughts, Bulo continued, "I've had my fill of adventure for a while. Dealing with a whole new world would be too much for me anyway." He laughed, taking a swig of his ale.

"Yes… and Thack has Caswen and his new tavern to work with. So it would only be me going," Rathen said, staring down at the table.

Bulo shrugged. "New position… new power. I don't know. Sounds to me like a grand opportunity."

Rathen nodded. His thoughts grew more serious. "Garrick's death still troubles me and I feel the need to make amends."

"That wasn't your fault. His death happened before we ever met that woman."

Rathen shook his head. "I kept Davale's true identity from the group so I could get to Vargas. That's not fitting for a leader."

"Ah, you're only human. We all slip up from time to time. We just have to forgive ourselves and push forward," Bulo said, leaning back in his chair.

Rathen paused looking across the table at his friend. "You're right. Maybe helping Bandark will allow me to make amends with myself… and in a way Bandark as well."

A loud knock on the back door caused both men to bolt upright in their chairs. They looked at each other.

"Attackers?" Bulo asked standing.

"I don't think they would be knocking if they planned to attack."

"Well, it's not a delivery at this late hour."

Rathen pulled his sword and carefully approached the back door. Bulo snatched one of the demon men's swords that decorated the tavern's walls and followed.

"Who is it?" Rathen called.

"It is Bandark," a deep voice boomed through the door.

Rathen sheathed his sword and opened the door. Bandark and Rendrak stood in the doorway. "Come in," Rathen said, clasping their hands in welcome.

"Drinks?" Bulo asked, as they walked into the light of the tavern.

Neither Bandark nor Rendrak replied.

Their silence concerned Rathen. He looked up at Bandark's face to find it thinner and gaunt. The areas under his eyes were dark and swollen. "What's happened?"

Bandark paused. "The book is secure, but the war does not fare well. We expect an attack on our city of Soront within weeks. Have you made your decision?"

"I have," Rathen said without hesitating.

"Well?" Rendrak asked in anticipation.

"Just let me get my belongings."

The tense look on both men's faces relaxed. "Very well," Bandark said.

Rathen ran upstairs and quickly packed his gear. He rushed back down and followed the men out the back door. Bandark began sprinkling a glittery dust on the ground to open another portal. *This is it. No turning back now.*

Rathen walked over to Bulo and placed a hand on his shoulder. "I'll see you again soon."

Bulo nodded, returning the gesture. "Indeed, my friend."

Rathen turned to see the portal open. The same castle outline could be seen in the distance against a red sky.

Bandark cleared his throat to get Rathen's attention. Rathen took one last look at the tavern and approached to the two men. "I'm ready."

Bandark nodded and stepped through the door. Rathen waited for Rendrak, but Rendrak motioned him through first.

"After you… General," Rendrak said as he crossed his arm against his chest in a salute.

With a smile, Rathen stepped through the portal, anxious to see his new home for the first time.

Months later, in a desolate area of the world and under the cover of night, Davale trudged up the side of a mountain. Her daggers hung at her side, but instead of her leather tunic, a woolspun dress clung over her swollen belly. Approaching the bottom of a cliff, she took some time to catch her breath. She dusted off her clothes and straightened her dress. Taking a deep breath, she knocked hard on the cliff wall five times in rapid succession.

The sound of stone grinding came from the wall, and an opening appeared. A middle-aged woman wearing black robes cautiously peered out, her black hair hanging down around her shoulders over her pale white skin. She glanced down at Davale's belly and then met her gaze with narrowed eyes.

"Lord Vizilan calls," Davale whispered.

Upon hearing her words, the woman ushered Davale into the door. The woman peered into the darkness and shut the door. Davale walked into a large hall where a group of men and women wearing the same black robes stood in a circle. Davale continued to the center and stood. Soon, a robed figure from the other side walked up to her. He pulled his cowl from his head, revealing his pale white skin and solid black eyes.

"And we receive," he replied. His lips parted in a grin lined with pointed teeth. He opened his arms to embrace her.

The End

Other Books by Grant Elliot Smith

The Rathen Series:
Book 1: The Legend of Ghrakus Castle
Book 2: Into Bramblewood Forest

Coming soon:
Book 3: The Battle for Korganis

About the Authors

GRANT ELLIOT SMITH

Originally from Pendleton, Indiana, Grant loved to read from an early age. Saving up his allowance, he would spend it all at the local bookstore buying up as much as he could from the fantasy section. Writing had always been a passion of his. His first interest was poetry, which he wrote voraciously. Some of his early work from as far back as the 1980's can be found in various poetry anthologies.

Completing four university degrees, including a Masters in Sociology from the University of Essex in Colchester, England, Grant has lived and worked around the world, spending a number of those years in Japan. The sights and sounds from the various cultures he has seen help to fuel his imagination for writing. In his free time, he loves to escape into the world of fantasy and the paranormal.

Follow at:

https://www.grantelliotsmith.com
https://www.facebook.com/grantelliotsmith/
https://www.facebook.com/TheRathenSeries/

STEVEN H. STOHLER

Steve hails from the same hometown of Pendleton, Indiana and from his youth Steve had always been adventurous. At the age of twenty on a whim, he once hitchhiked to Florida from Indiana and ended up living there for seven years before returning.

From the age of twelve, Steve wrote various short stories and always held the dream of being a writer. Long-term friends of Grant Elliot Smith, the two teamed up to brainstorm the characters and events for the Rathen Series allowing Steve to live out his boyhood dream of becoming a writer. Steve even made a personal appearance in Book 1, *The Legend of Ghrakus Castle* in the form of the character Evets Relhots, which is his name spelled backwards.

Follow at:

https://www.facebook.com/mow.man.5